THREE
TO BE
READ

Books by PHILIP WYLIE

HEAVY LADEN

BABES AND SUCKLINGS

GLADIATOR

FOOTPRINT OF CINDERELLA

THE SAVAGE GENTLEMAN

FINNLEY WREN: HIS NOTIONS AND OPINIONS

AS THEY REVELED

AN APRIL AFTERNOON

THE BIG ONES GET AWAY

SALT WATER DAFFY

THE OTHER HORSEMAN

GENERATION OF VIPERS

CORPSES AT INDIAN STONES

FISH AND TIN FISH

NIGHT UNTO NIGHT

AN ESSAY ON MORALS

TOO MUCH OF EVERYTHING

CRUNCH AND DES: STORIES OF FLORIDA FISHING

OPUS 21

THE DISAPPEARANCE

THREE TO BE READ

THREE
TO BE
READ

Containing

THE SMUGGLED ATOM BOMB

SPORTING BLOOD and

EXPERIMENT IN CRIME

by

Philip Wylie

Rinehart & Co., Inc.   NEW YORK   TORONTO

PUBLISHED SIMULTANEOUSLY IN CANADA
BY CLARKE, IRWIN & COMPANY, LTD., TORONTO

LIBRARY OF CONGRESS CATALOG CARD NUMBER: 52-7156

CONTENTS

THE
SMUGGLED
ATOM
BOMB

THE SMUGGLED ATOM BOMB

A LANGUOROUS ocean breeze set sail from the Bahama Islands for the coast of Florida. It crossed the Gulf Stream and came ashore where autumn tourists sprawled on the allegedly golden but actually pale brown sands of Miami Beach. A breath of it, after crossing Miami, following a road lined with fluffy evergreens, swung finally into a stand of much larger trees: mahoganies, tamarinds, poincianas, gumbo limbos and live oaks. These it stirred audibly before it moved over a sun-brilliant lawn, entered the screened window of a dilapidated, two-story frame house and touched bright blond hair on the brow of a pretty, middle-aged woman who sat in a bed. She glanced up with the pleasant thought that the still heat of day was ended. She saw the clock. Three-twenty. She faced the screen, then, and called in a contralto that was penetrating without being harsh, "Charlee-ee!"

Her mind pictured her dark-haired, merry-eyed son, age twelve. The picture did not materialize and she remembered he was going to try to get a newspaper route after school. She conjured up the brunette glow and giggly adolescence of her younger daughter. "Marian! Marian!"

Again there was no answer and again she remembered. Marian had said she would be delayed. Eleanor, her eldest, wasn't due until four-thirty because she had a regular lab period that day at the university. Mrs. Yates, invalided eight years before in the accident that had taken her husband's life, leaned back on her pillows, still smiling, and wished she hadn't called. For she knew what would happen.

Feet strode on the crushed coral of the driveway. A foot tripped on the threshold of the back door. And a young man appeared, grinning, at the entrance of her downstairs room—a man

3

of less than twenty-five, a tall man and thin, a stooped young man with polelike arms and legs, eyes of a faded blue, unkempt hair the hue of new rope, and a determination of mouth and chin that did not fit his over-all diffidence.

"Duff," she said apologetically, "I didn't mean to bring you in from the barn! What in the world were you doing, though? You've still got on your good gabardine slacks!"

The young man chuckled, looked down as if to check the statement, started to answer and was obliged to deal with a slight impediment of speech before saying, "Oh! Oh—sure! Decided not to change. Not doing anything messy—labeling a lot of cans with small hardware in 'em."

She laughed. "Of course! You said you were going to. I'm so scattered! Well—I'm sorry I disturbed you."

"Not a bit. Nearly finished. Did you want something? Iced tea, maybe? Eleanor left things ready."

"Later, perhaps. No, Duff. Don't want anything. I'd forgotten the kids were going to be late. It's their afternoon to sweep and dust and scour."

His grin widened. "I'll do it. Give me an excuse to put off mowing the lawn till a cooler day. Besides, I'm a talented house cleaner."

She laughed again. Duff Bogan—Allan Diffenduffer Bogan—had been a boarder at the Yates home for more than a year. The luckiest boarder, she thought, that any invalid woman with three children ever had—though Eleanor couldn't possibly be called a child any more. "You go back and finish." Seeing he wouldn't, she added, "Or at least put on an apron."

He executed a comic salute and soon she heard a broom working upstairs. Not long after, came a bizarre din from the bathroom, and she lay on her pillows, chuckling.

He was, she thought, such a dear. A graduate student of physics at the University of Miami. He'd come over at the start of the first semester, the year before, when the Yateses had had a vacancy in the two-boarder schedule which augmented their slender finances. Who'd brought him? One of Eleanor's numberless admirers.

She thought back. It was that fullback, she believed, the one with that absurd nickname—Avalanche. Avalanche Billings.

"We have to have," she remembered saying to Duff, "somebody who can help around the place, take care of the yard and the station wagon—which is vintage and requires plenty of care. Somebody who can tend the trees and shrubs, won't mind doing dishes at times, and so on. The rate is low on account of the help I need."

Duff had regarded her amiably, even warmly, and replied, "Mrs. Yates, I was brought up in the family of an underpaid Indiana preacher. Housework, its simplification and efficient management, became one of my hobbies. I have other hobbies that might prove helpful."

She had taken him, on trial. After a week, she had come to feel Duff was indispensable. Now, he was like a son—except, of course, where Eleanor was concerned. He was too shy, too self-effacing to be like a brother to Eleanor, which somewhat interfered with his status as "son." Mrs. Yates sighed. Eleanor didn't give him much encouragement. Much? Not any. Which wasn't surprising in a girl elected Miss Freshman in her first year, the Belle of the Junior Prom, and who now, as a senior, was Queen-elect of the Orange Bowl festivities.

Upstairs in the bathroom, Duff Bogan had gone to work with equipment of his own devising—a "gun" for spraying insecticides and a second "gun" for dusting. First he dampened all porcelain, metal and tile surfaces with a water spray. Then he dusted with a scouring powder. Thereafter, a damp cloth in each hand, he polished furiously—which caused the din Mrs. Yates had heard. In fifteen minutes the bathroom glittered.

Perspiring in the damp warmth of the day, he called down the stairway, "What about Harry's room?"

"That, too," she responded. "He never locks it."

So Duff entered the quarters of the other boarder, Harry Ellings. A light dust mopping only was needed there. For Harry, who had been with the Yateses ever since the father's death, made his own bed and kept his own premises picked up. It wasn't, Duff

thought, much of a home for a fifty-year-old bachelor like Harry.
A living-sitting room in somebody else's house—a day bed and a
desk, a shelf of books, bridge lamps, old chair, a worn rug, a radio,
a few photographs, a calendar hung on the knob of the closet door.
That was Harry's residence.

He had a job as a mechanic with a trucking concern; before
that he'd been a letter carrier. He had quit during his early years
with the Yateses because of varicose veins, and had gone to school
to learn his present trade.

Church on Sundays, a Friday bridge game, his Wednesday
evenings practicing casting, a lot of porch sitting and radio listening, occasional fishing trips, few visitors, little mail—that summed
up all Duff knew of the other boarder.

Maybe, from Harry's viewpoint, it was a good life, whole and
satisfying. The thought depressed Duff. He finished dusting, helped
himself to one of Harry's cigarettes and stared out at the sunshine,
wondering, as young men do, what he would do when his degree
had been awarded and the uncertain world said wordlessly, "Okay,
Bogan; beat me if you can!"

He picked up the mop and noticed then, behind the calendar
that hung from the knob, a lock on the closet door, a lock newer
than the hardware of the Yates house, which he constantly repaired and replaced.

If he had not observed the lock, it is possible, although unlikely, that Duff Bogan's life might have been, relatively speaking,
as colorless as his estimate of Harry Ellings'. But Duff did notice
the lock and wonder about it, and nothing was ever the same for
him afterward.

Wondering about locks was not, in Duff's case, an idle exercise
in bafflement. Early in life he had been discarded by his school-
mates as a possible pitcher, fielder, end or basketball center. Com-
petitive sports revealed him as something of an Ichabod Crane
and, since his middle name was Diffenduffer, after his mother's
father, he had been called Duffer from the age of ten. He was
Duff only to the kindly Yateses. But though a duffer at games

and sports, he excelled in hobbies. Among them was a know-how concerning locks.

At eleven, Duff had sent ten cents for a booklet called The Boy Locksmith. Finding that people were either charmed by or aghast at his proficiency with skeleton keys, he had advanced to more elaborate literature on the subject. Before he reached high-school age he was much in demand where keys were lost or where trunks, barns, cabinets and the like refused to open. In high school, while other boys mowed lawns for extra change, Duff had repaired luggage and started cars that lacked keys.

To look at Harry Ellings' lock-fitted closet door, then, was to know how to get the door open rather quickly. Since it was unthinkable that the drab, good-natured star boarder had anything important or secret locked away, Duff felt no curiosity. But it would be fun, he thought, to open the door, set something alien in the closet—and wait for results.

Grinning, Duff ran down the back stairs, came back with selected tools, and took steps three at a time while Mrs. Yates gripped the binding of her magazine tightly—sometimes, when he rushed that way, Duff fell.

His hands, however, were not clumsy. They worked rapidly over the lock and soon the door swung open. Inside, Harry's suits hung neatly. On the shelf were suitcases, old and dusty. On the floor was a cubical hatbox of cardboard. Duff procured a metal wastebasket and set it on top of the hatbox.

He thought his joke would be more noticeable if he put the hatbox on the basket. Only he couldn't lift the hatbox. He took another hold and tried again. The cardboard threatened to tear, but the box didn't budge. So Duff untied the tape and raised the lid. Inside, was a hardwood box, well made, waxed, with an inset handle and a lock of a kind Duff had never before seen. He stared at this and then tipped over the box and its hatbox disguise—which could be done only with effort. The whole thing weighed about a hundred pounds.

He went downstairs then and interrupted Mrs. Yates' reading. "The doggonedest thing," he said—and told her. "What could he have—what could anybody have?—in a fifteen-inch box, weighing that much? Gold?"

"Harry?" She chuckled. "Heavens! I know what Harry does with every cent! Better put it back, Duff."

He went upstairs. It was about four-thirty. Harry wouldn't be home for more than an hour. Duff had opened the closet without curiosity; the box and its peculiar lock left him with no feeling but curiosity. He struggled with his conscience—and tried certain tools. When the lock clicked, he found it hard to raise the lid because of its weight. The underside was metal-lined. Lead. Whatever was in the box was packed in cotton. He raised the cotton and saw a very odd object of grayish-silver metal, machined and polished. It looked like a segment of a big egg, saw-toothed on one face, as a cog or gear would be. When he hefted it, he judged it weighed about five pounds. Maybe more.

He tried, as a graduate student of physics and a man with mechanical hobbies, to imagine what the object was. He couldn't, at first. When, presently, he had a single idea, he pushed it from his mind: too crazy. Nevertheless, after some very worried thought, he went downstairs again.

"Sweeping the kids' rooms," he called untruthfully to Mrs. Yates. "Bring you your iced tea before long."

He worked fast after that. With fine emery paper he removed a trace of the metal; with scouring powder he polished away the scratches made by the emery. He wore gloves and took extreme care. Having obtained a microscopic sample, he restored everything to the exact state in which he had found it. He left the cigarette in Harry's ash tray after thought which told him Harry could easily notice his room had been dusted that day.

He then hid the emery-paper sample in the barn, washed his hands repeatedly and did a quick sweeping job on Charles' and Marian's rooms. He was making iced tea in the kitchen when Eleanor drove up in the family station wagon.

"Let me do that," she said. "You've spilled on the drainboard and got ice on the floor!" She put a load of books on the table and turned her back to him. "Unbutton."

Duff smiled and undid little buttons between her shoulder blades where she couldn't reach easily. The dress was one of two cotton prints she'd found at a sale—yellow like her curly hair, light brown like her topaz eyes. She hurried from the room, called to her mother, and was soon back in the kitchen wearing an old dress and moccasins, instead of her high-heeled shoes.

A match struck; the burners of the kerosene stove slowly took fire. "I wish we had gas or electricity! Kerosene's so slow!"

She bent over a bin Duff had made from lumber scraps, and came up with an armful of potatoes. "Peel!" She emptied out a sack of green peas and started shelling. "What's new?"

"We had a burglar."

Her eyes glowed. "No! I bet he didn't steal anything! I bet, if he really looked the place over, and if he was a nice burglar, he left something for us when he went out! Five dollars, maybe, on the hall table!"

"I was the burglar."

"Oh!" Her eyes looked up and laughed. "What'd you rob? The kids' banks?"

"Harry's room. His closet. The locked closet."

"Harry hasn't got a locked anything! That poor, sweet guy is the world's openest book!"

Duff rinsed a white-peeled potato, cut it up, started another. "I'd have agreed, two hours ago. He's still probably innocent. Just keeping something that some pal asked him to put under lock and key."

"What are you talking about, Duff Bogan?"

He told her. "First, you see, it was going to be a gag. Then I got curious. The lock on that box was a new one to me. And then, the gadget inside—"

"Sounds like some sort of trophy."

"Trophy?"

"Sure," Eleanor said. "You know. Golfers get silver golf

balls. Anglers get gold-plated fish. Probably Harry won the Never-Missed-a-Working-Day-in-Five-Years prize at his company. Being a mechanic, it was probably a cogwheel, only silver or something."

"Oh." Duff thought about that. "It wasn't silver. It wasn't a cog. It wasn't engraved."

"Then," she said, snatching at a pea that popped out of its pod and rolled, "what was it?"

"It barely might be—uranium."

She was about to answer derisively. His seriousness sank in. "What?"

"The only thing I could imagine it looked like was a carefully machined part of something which, with other parts like it, would fit together to make a sphere. A sphere weighing maybe twenty pounds, more or less. It might have been any of a half dozen metals or a thousand alloys. Still, there's only one thing I know of, made of parts which fit perfectly into what is probably a sphere around that size. The pieces that come together to form a critical mass and go off with a hell of a bang."

"You mean an atomic bomb?"

"Maybe it's only a mock-up. A model, I mean. That's why I took a sample. To test and see what the metal is. I could be wrong, but I think Harry, whether he knows it or not, either has a piece of the heart of an A-bomb up there or else a metal model of one."

Eleanor began to laugh. "Harry—a spy?" When he didn't join her laughter, she looked at him for a long moment. "You think somebody's stealing more of our A-bomb secrets and Harry's being used to keep the thing—until time to move it on out of the country? Let's ask Harry where he got the box!"

Duff wished for a moment he hadn't told Eleanor anything. "Ye gods!" he answered. "Not really! I just—have to know what the metal was, now that I've seen the gadget. Chances are a million to one my idea is totally nuts. But if it did happen to be that millionth chance, then asking Harry anything would be a terrible blunder!"

"You're right about that," she said contritely. Then, hearing

a car in the drive, she murmured, "There Harry is now. Go clean
up, and I'll finish supper. At the least, get that repulsive apron off.
You look like a cross between Mother Hubbard and the Scarecrow in the Oz books!"

His smile was sheepish. "Okay."

Before he left the kitchen she asked hastily and in a low tone,
"Can you tell, from such a tiny sample?"

"I'm no microchemist. But I should be able to, yes."

"I hope you're crazy," she said earnestly.

Duff's room was not much different from Harry's save that
it was less neat and contained more books. In order to save time,
he had availed himself of an old-fashioned pitcher and wash bowl
which he'd found in the attic. He began shaving while Harry took
his daily shower. Charles Yates came whizzing home, bike siren
loud, his voice shrill as he shouted through his mother's window,
"I got the old paper route!"

Duff grinned, grinned again when Marian, panting after running three blocks from the bus stop, dramatically announced she
would be Titania in the play. He felt at home with the Yateses;
there had been a troop of young Bogans.

Gazing into the mirror, still wearing the apron over his
work-stained T-shirt, Duff thought about Eleanor's description of
his looks. Mother Hubbard and the Oz-book Scarecrow. His grin
faded somewhat, but a glimmer remained. He certainly was on the
bean-pole side. No girl like Eleanor would ever think of any guy
like himself in romantic terms. She was already Orange Bowl
Queen. Why, if she just wanted to, she could be in the movies!
Perhaps she'd do something like that when she graduated—to com-
pensate for being so poor, for endless cooking, washing, mending,
cleaning and bargain hunting. And for the constant care of her
mother.

In his small and rather dappled mirror, Duff saw that his eyes
were shiny. "Nuts," he said, and attacked his face with such energy that he cut himself.

Dinner was early. Eleanor had to leave at seven. On Mondays,

Wednesdays and Thursdays, from eight to eleven, she did filing in the offices of the Florida Electric Company. It was a job she'd got through a friend of her mother's, which netted a welcome eight dollars and ten cents a week.

Duff wheeled Mrs. Yates up to the table. The Yates youngsters, both dark-haired and dark-eyed, like their father, were so excited over their respective successes that Harry Ellings didn't notice the special looks directed toward him by Eleanor and Duff.

After dinner, after Eleanor had driven away in a station wagon as weatherbeaten as the house, Duff went to his room and made plans. He'd want one of the chemistry labs on a day when it wasn't full of freshmen doing Chemistry 101-A. He could do the physics all right—that was in his department. He'd need advice about the microanalysis. . . .

It took a week. But one week later—with shaky hands, because he had never done anything of the sort—he looked in the beat-up phone book beside a drugstore booth for the Federal Bureau of Investigation, dialed and closed the door.

A man answered. "I'd like to talk to somebody," Duff said, "about making an appointment."

"Just a minute." It was quite a long minute. Duff got ready another nickel.

"Yes? Hello? Higgins speaking."

"Oh," Duff said. "Well—look, sir. My name is Allan D. Bogan. I'm a graduate student at the university. I want to talk to somebody down there. I've run across something odd."

A slight pause. "Could you give me any idea of the nature of what you've encountered? We're pretty busy here—"

"I—I—I know that. Over the phone—" Duff hesitated. "Suppose I told you that I'm a graduate student in physics. The science that led to the atomic bomb—"

Mr. Higgins' voice, businesslike to begin with, cut him off sharply, "Would three-fifteen this afternoon do?"

"P-p-perfectly."

"Ask for me. Higgins. Slater Higgins."

The office of the FBI looked like any office. No fancy equipment visible, no gun racks, no alarm or communication devices. And Mr. Slater Higgins, in his own small cubicle, with its swivel chair and desk, its one large window, looked like any junior executive.

They shook hands. Mr. Higgins pointed to a chair with his pipe stem and said, smiling faintly, "What's on your mind, Duff?"

The younger man stared. "You know—"

"Checked, sure. After your call. Registrar. Got everything from your nickname to your lack of an athletic record. Tell you so you can skip it."

Duff sat silent, flushing a little. "Well, it begins with where I board. Did you check that?"

Higgins laughed. "Address is all. Shoot!"

Duff was embarrassed about the start of his story, since it involved curiosity and his unethical behavior. So he decided to give weight to his words immediately. "I have found a stolen part of what is plainly an atomic bomb."

Mr. Higgins did look at him sharply. But that was all. No exclamation. No excitement. "Okay. Start where it starts. Take your time."

The G-man was a good listener—putting in questions only when the narrative confused him or left a gap.

"I had to wait," Duff wound up, "until yesterday, to get a good chance to run the tests. They checked, all right. It was uranium. Uranium 235, I am sure. High neutron emission—"

"You can skip the technical part. That isn't for me. I'm a lawyer. An accountant. You sure?"

Duff hesitated. The sample had been extremely small. The tests had been difficult. The apparatus in the physics lab hadn't worked as well as he could have hoped. "I'm—sure enough," he finally said, "to come in here."

"Can you give us some of the stuff to test?"

"That's another thing. I did have a trace left when I got through. But—I'm cow-clumsy. When I finished the last test I started doing a dumb-headed dance—I was excited. I batted a bottle of sulphuric off a shelf—had to wash it and the last of my sample down the drain, but quick. The place was fuming up."

"Too bad." Mr. Higgins locked his hands behind his head, looked at Duff and thought for a while. "You could be mistaken about your experiment?"

"I don't believe so. It's possible."

"Stick around a few minutes." Higgins walked from the room. He was gone for quite a while. When he came back, his face was unreadable. He sat in his chair again.

"We'd like a look at that cached stuff, Bogan. I take it there's always somebody at home. Mrs. Yates."

"Not always. On sunny Sundays we wheel her to the car and lift her in and take her wheel chair along. Church. Harry Ellings never misses church."

"Good. You see, we'd also like to look at that thing without anybody knowing. If it does happen to be uranium, we want to know more than just that Ellings has it."

"Naturally." Duff felt better. "You'd want him to keep right on doing whatever he may be doing. He's probably innocent. The Yates family knows him mighty well. He doubtless thinks he's keeping something for a friend."

"Could be."

"And by watching him, you'd be led to some group that's stealing not just atomic secrets but actual bombs."

"The trouble is," Higgins answered slowly, "that, except for a trace stolen during the war, and a bit some character took home for a collection, we've never lost any uranium, Bogan. Nothing remotely approaching the quantity that would make the lump you described."

Duff's pale blue eyes were surprised. "No! Are they sure? Couldn't they make a mistake?"

Higgins chuckled without mirth. "Brother, can't you conceive the guarding and checking and cross-checking that goes into protecting something worth maybe half a hundred thousand bucks a pound? Something that we've spent billions to be able to make? They can tell you where every thousandth of an ounce is, every day, every minute!"

Duff's reaction was one of humiliation. "Then I must have pulled a boner at the lab! Maybe—having got that cockeyed notion—I saw what I wanted to see, in my tests."

The G-man's eyes were unsympathetic. "Probably. But you came in here and told us. We're used to that. Stories and rumors of A-bomb spies come in here as thick as reports of flying saucers. And we waste our lives on 'em all. Thanks, however. Provisionally."

Duff stood. "If you're going to investigate, I could leave a plan of the house. And some notes on the lock on the box. How to open it, I mean. And my door key."

Higgins grinned. "Right. Would help."

The following Sunday when they came home from church, Duff tried to find evidence that the FBI had entered and examined the house. There wasn't any such evidence.

On Monday, however, Duff was called from a class to talk to a Mr. Higgins who "insisted," according to a girl from the front office, "that the call was important and you should be disturbed."

"In a few days," Higgins said, when he had identified Duff, "we will call on your friend at your place. Ostensibly, we'll be checking another matter. Actually, we'll make ourselves an opportunity to take a look at the matter we've discussed. You aren't to give away the fact that we may have seen it previously. On some pretext, we'll call you up. We want you to see it again and tell us, if you can, whether it's what you originally—sampled."

"Did you see—the matter?" Duff asked breathlessly.

"Yeah. And don't act astonished when you learn what it is!" Mr. Higgins hesitated. "You might tip off the rest of the family, since you've discussed it with them."

It was curt, perfunctory, unsatisfying. He told Eleanor and her mother exactly what he had done, precisely what he had been advised to do. A few more days passed. There was no change in the behavior of Harry Ellings. The graying, inconspicuous boarder played bridge with his postman pals, went out to practice with his casting rod on an illuminated target range, did his work, and said nothing unusual until the end of the week.

Then, one night during supper, he changed the subject, which was a popular and interminable one: the kidding of Eleanor about her various dates by her younger brother and sister, who were particularly diverted by the salmon-pink convertible of a Mr. Prescott Smythe, of Omega fraternity.

"Don't be surprised," Harry interrupted abruptly, "if the Gestapo calls on me."

Duff felt the beginning of a start, and repressed it. He wondered quickly, too, if any man who had reason to fear the FBI would refer to the bureau in so insulting a term. It was evidence that Harry had no reason for worry.

Mrs. Yates was saying, "Gestapo?"

Eleanor said calmly, "He means the FBI. You been kidnaping people, or something, Harry?"

The star boarder grinned and then frowned. "Everybody at the plant"—it was his word for the trucking company that employed him—"is being processed. Supposed to keep it to themselves. But you know how fellows talk."

"Processed?" The term was unfamiliar to Mrs. Yates.

Harry stirred his coffee. "Checked. Questioned. There's been some fancy counterfeiting going on. A few guys on the lam. Unlawful flight, the Gestapo men call it. And they're looking for counterfeiting plates that have eased out of the state they were used in. A big trucking company, like Miami-Dade, is always being suspected of doing something against the law."

In the person of Mr. Higgins and an assistant, the "Gestapo" called that night. Although he had a chance to wink or mutter a word when Duff answered the doorbell, Higgins behaved as if Duff were a stranger. He asked for Mr. Harry Ellings and was conducted upstairs. Charles Yates said loudly as the two men climbed, "Real G-men! Golly! Maybe I'll be one!"

Nearly an hour passed. Eleanor and Duff washed and dried

the dishes. Marian and Charles pretended to do homework and actually discussed the visit of the FBI, speculating horrendously on its possible causes.

Then Higgins came to the head of the stairs. "Oh, Miss Yates?" When Eleanor appeared, he added, "You are Miss Yates? Will you come up a moment? And that other young boarder, too, if he will."

They went up. The box was open, in the middle of the room. Harry was sitting in his easy chair, looking angry. Higgins pointed to the object in the box. "Either of you ever seen that before?"

They had been instructed. They looked at the object. Duff squatted down by the box and scrutinized the curious piece of machined metal.

"No," he said positively.

Eleanor shook her bright head. "Not even the box!"

"I told you!" Harry said crossly. "I brought it in when they were on a picnic. Ye gods! Government snoops! Government snoops! I'm well within my rights—"

"What is it?" Duff asked.

Higgins smiled tightly and looked at Harry.

Harry raised his eyes to Duff and shrugged. "It's my life savings, that's what it is! Since way back when Roosevelt threw us off the gold standard and I had to turn in the gold I kept, I bought platinum. Finally made one piece of it. Harder to swipe. Made that box, in the end, and melted down old pieces of solder to wall it in lead. Too heavy now for any housebreaker to snitch. Then I got bad legs and had to have a lot of medical care. An operation. After that, a year in machinist's school—with board, room and tuition to pay! So I began cutting out wedges of the stuff and selling it. That's what's left! It's perfectly legal to own it and I'll be damned if I see what right the G-men have to make me haul it out and explain it. My secret—the only one I ever had—and no harm in it."

Duff looked at Higgins. Higgins said, "Ellings isn't kidding. He has a right to stash platinum away, and I did snoop. No search warrant—just noticed he kept his closet locked and asked for a

Prescott Smythe, or Scotty, ignored the reference. He rose. He crossed the porch to a large concrete urn in which was growing a huge vine with dark green, lacily slit leaves. He peered intently at the vine.

"There is nothing for breaking hearts," said a thin brother, "like a convertible. That's what the word means. It converts 'em."

Scotty Smythe finally spoke. "You know," he said in elegant tones, "when I stole this vine it was hardly two feet tall. I've had to swipe four pots for it, through the years. In graduated sizes. Now, look at it! Magnificent foliage. A *monstera deliciosa*, the botany boys tell me. Should bear fruit. Edible fruit. Never had so much as a cucumber on it!"

The brothers ignored the countermeasure. "Sad thing about Smythe," said the football player. "Stealing flowerpots. Now he's trying to swipe the Orange Bowl. The Queen, anyhow. As soon as a man recognizes a cutest college type, he's through."

Scotty grinned. "Okay! So, okay! I got it bad."

"What will your family say?" the thin brother asked in a somber tone. "Imagine the scene. You take la Yates to Manhattan, ride up in a marble elevator to your familial penthouse, whip out your golden latchkey, open the door and say, 'Mother, here's the girl I'm going to marry! This po' cracker chile.' Your mother can see the babe is a looker who would bring a blush of envy to the proud features—all the proud features—of Betty Grable. And has topaz eyes, besides. But your mother isn't fooled by mere externals. Not like you, Smythe! Raising a jewel-encrusted lorgnette, she frigidly asks the girl, 'Where are your Junior League papers? Even your first papers?'"

"Where does Eleanor's family come from?" a brother asked. "Anybody know?"

"Olean," said Scotty.

"I thought olean was something you spread on bread."

Scotty smirked. "Look, you jealous weevils! Olean is a town in New York State. It has history, paved streets, electric lights—and Eleanor Yates' birthplace!"

"We are worrying ourselves unduly," said a plump, shrewd-eyed brother who had apparently been reading a magazine. "I know, out of what we lawyers call our own knowledge, that she necked with Avalanche Billings last week. Kissed him, anyhow. I also know she gets orchids from a guy in the Miami Junior Chamber of Commerce. He raises 'em in his yard—which shows a good business head. And there are eight thousand other guys!"

The main object of the ribbing, evidently accustomed to it, again discussed his vine. "They graft things on trees down here," Scotty murmured. "Maybe a graft could be managed. If it won't bear its own fruit, perhaps a few limes would do. A mango or two, now and then. Even a bunch of broccoli." He turned. "Listen, oafs! What you see in these nice gray eyes is pure loathing! My sister belongs to the Junior League, true. Mother's farsighted and sometimes uses a lorgnette—I guess the first time most of you swamp Willies ever saw one was when she came to the Open House last year. I say, phooey to you gentlemen and I say faugh! I am going on a hayride tonight with Eleanor, so if anybody wants to borrow my car—"

He was overwhelmed by the onslaught.

Duff Bogan was standing in the Yates back yard, studying the sky. Several broken limbs needed to be removed from the live oaks, but that meant borrowing an extension ladder from a distant neighbor, and Eleanor had the car. Tree pruning, except near the house, was hopeless anyhow. There were broken branches all through the jungle. A whole tree had fallen across the water-filled sinkhole in the woods west of the house. He examined passing clouds. There was no prospect of showers that he could discern. He decided to begin a long-postponed operation: painting the sun-faded house. With the stepladder he could reach nearly half of it. He started, some while later, on the east wall. He heard but did not see Eleanor drive in.

But presently, from the back yard, a sharp whacking commenced. A cloud of dust eddied around the house and settled grittily on the fresh paint. He came down the ladder. Barelegged, in shorts and a blouse, with an old silk scarf around her hair, Eleanor was beating rugs. She stood with her back to him, and Duff, as often, admired the line of her chin, eye and forehead. She had high cheekbones and rather deep-set, slightly slanted eyes so his view, which he thought of as a one-quarter profile, gave a special outline of the anatomy of her beauty. The act of beating rugs in such a costume exhibited her body at its muscular best. He watched her for quite a while before he said, "Hey!"

She turned. "Oh, hello!" Gold tendrils had escaped the scarf and curled like shavings on a damp brow.

"One of us has got to quit—or at least move. I started painting the house a while back."

"Duff! I'm sorry! I didn't know!"

He grinned. "Would you mind if I transferred your carpets to the line behind the barn?"

Once there, she asked abruptly, "Duff, has anything happened?"

He shook his head. "Everything's stopped happening. I saw Higgins a while ago. The FBI checked Harry's story about platinum. So I guess I made one really sour bunch of mistakes." He told her the situation.

She dropped the carpet beater. "Only—you don't believe you did. Do you?"

"No."

Her look was thoughtful, measuring. "But you aren't absolutely positive?"

"I don't know. I've been chivvied around so much that I don't know. The tests I ran seem okay, on review. I thought that hunk of platinum didn't look exactly like the thing I sandpapered the first time. After all, though, it would be crazy. Us. Harry. A house like this. Mixed up in anything of that kind."

"Maybe not too crazy. Look at the facts that have come out of the samples swiped. The espionage. And no doubt there are plenty of other stories that haven't come out! That won't come out—until we get in another war and win it. Until we find a way to disarm the world and make it peaceful. Every government has things like that locked away. Hushed up. Some forever. It wasn't the craziness that made me think you were mistaken."

"Then what was it?" he asked morosely.

"Nothing, Duff. I never thought so. But I don't really believe Harry is a party to anything—sinister. I still thought there was some sort of hanky-panky. Did you ever consider it backwards?"

"What do you mean—backwards?" Suddenly his mild eyes flew wide open and his cigarette fell from limp fingers. He said, "Holy whirling cyclotrons!" He picked up the cigarette. "You mean, that was a hunk of U235 coming into the U.S.A.!"

She nodded. "If it was uranium and if platinum was substituted, it means there's a mighty ingenious gang, doesn't it?"

He whistled. Eleanor went on, "They—whoever they might be—would have careful plans to bring in atomic bombs piece by piece. Plans even to substitute something plausible, that resembled the real thing, if they got caught up with. And maybe to use innocent people as their agents. Harry could no doubt, for instance, get one of his truck-driver pals to take a box like that, or several, to some city up north."

Duff's Adam's apple made a round trip as he gulped. "A lot of the top men in physics have mentioned that very possibility!" He named names familiar in the news since Hiroshima. "They've said atom bombs could be brought into harbors in tramp steamers. Or smuggled into the country in sections and assembled in secret and planted—like mines, like infernal machines—to be set off in the centers of cities—perhaps by radio, at some zero hour!"

"That's what I mean," she said quietly.

Duff leaned backward and looked cautiously around the corner of the barn toward the Yates house. He leaned back and shook his head. "No. Every time I get on the idea, really think about it, it sounds too unlikely. This place. Us."

"Wouldn't a beat-up place like this, nobodies like us, be ideal? Couldn't things have been in Harry's room, passing through, for years, without us knowing? Don't you think you should call the FBI again?"

The cold water his imagination had needed was supplied by that suggestion. He started to speak, stammered, fell silent for a moment and then said, "Heck! The FBI probably thought of that angle ten seconds after they realized what I was talking about!"

"But they didn't mention it, Duff!"

His smile was faint, rueful. "They have a way of not mentioning all they're thinking about. Nix, Eleanor, but nix! I am not going to expose myself to another reprimand for taking up their time over nothing."

Her expression was disappointed, then angry—as if she were going to argue—and finally, unemotional. She knew about arguing with Duff when his mind was made up; it was like trying to talk a hole in a rock.

"At least," she said, after a while, "we might sort of keep watching Harry—or his room, anyhow. Then, if anything did happen—"

He nodded. "I was thinking that."

She picked up the carpet beater and turned her back. He saw the "one-quarter profile" again and heard himself say, "There's a dandy movie tonight at the Coconut Grove Theater, if you'd like—"

"I'm hay riding with Scotty Smythe," she answered. "That lamb!" She attacked a carpet Duff had hung for her.

Several evenings later, Harry Ellings, sitting on the front porch as usual, smoking a cigar, listening as usual to the radio, announced he was going to take a moonlight stroll. He announced it loudly through an open window. Upstairs, poring over a textbook, Duff vaguely heard and at first dismissed the words. Harry didn't go for many strolls, owing to his bad legs, but occasionally he took a preslumber ramble, and this evening, warm, moon-white, was an invitation.

Duff had finished a two-page equation before it occurred to

him that a "moonlight stroll" was the sort of thing which he had agreed with Eleanor ought to be watched. He turned his heavy book face down on his desk. He stepped into the dark hall and looked out the window. Through the trees, on the coral-white road, he could see Ellings walking slowly, apparently aimlessly, toward the west. Duff hurried down the back stairs, saying nothing of his departure, and started along the drive. The coral crackled, so he stepped on the grass, reflecting that he was poorly equipped by nature for any act, such as stealthy pursuit, that required a lack of clumsiness.

By walking along the roadside in the shadow of trees, Duff managed, however, to gain enough on Ellings to get him in view. And Duff was surprised—or was he, he asked himself—to find that the star boarder stopped now and again, looked back and seemed to listen, as if he worried over the possibility of pursuit.

The road was crossed by another about a half mile from the house. Harry turned. After walking some distance, he came to a region where there were no houses at all—an area of pines, palmettos and cabbage palms which was cross-hatched with weedy streets and sidewalks and provided here and there with the ghostly remnants of lampposts. This area, a quarter of a century ago, had been laid out as a real-estate subdivison. Then the boom had burst, and since that time the vegetation of South Florida had worked its way—vegetation aided by storms, heat and the rain. Harry walked with accelerated speed in this moonlit, ruin-like place, following the cracked and broken line of a sidewalk. Duff took off his shoes and stayed behind in the shadows.

Harry was certainly headed somewhere. Beyond the ruined development was a rock pit with a moonlit pond in its bottom, used now as a trash dump. Duff thought Harry might be on his way there, but he stopped short of it. He stood still. His cigar shone brighter, twice. He turned clear around, looking. Then he whistled.

From the undergrowth almost beside him, a figure rose. Duff thought its rise would never stop—thought it was a shadow, an optical illusion. For the man, who must have been squatting there, was one of the tallest Duff had ever seen—almost a freak, all but a circus giant.

The cigar, perhaps having served its purpose, was stamped out. The two men began to talk. Duff couldn't hear and did not dare go closer.

When the conference ended, Duff took a short cut home. He reached his room before Harry returned. He was sitting there, appalled by Harry's companion, and sure now that a direct and dreadful suspicion of the boarder was justified, when he heard voices in the driveway and the slam of a car door, followed by Eleanor's running feet and her voice, "Mother! You still up? Guess what? Scotty Smythe, that rich boy in Omega, proposed to me!"

Duff couldn't miss the thrill in her tone.

II

In a classroom on the "old campus" of the University of Miami, four young men were engaged in a discussion of the Uncertainty Principle with Dr. Oliver Slocum, a full professor of mathematics and a large man with twinkling eyes, no hair on his head, and a goatee.

"A common mistake," said the doctor, "made by many philosophers, has been to assume that the 'uncertainty' is neither logical nor empirical, and not even physical, but that it derives from a subjective interposition of the purely human observer, whereas—"

At about "whereas," Duff Bogan, one of the four graduate students present for the seminar, lost track of the thought. Since he already knew that the interposition of a machine had the same effect as the interposition of a person, and had known it since his mathematically precocious high-school days, he missed nothing essential.

Duff looked out the windows. He watched a huge truckload of dead branches proceed down the street past several pretty houses. He reflected that there were still hurricane-detached branches hanging serely in the Yates trees. His mind passed to greater worries.

There was the matter of the proposal of marriage to Eleanor Yates by Scotty Smythe, of the New York-Bar Harbor-Palm Beach Smythes. Duff had nothing against Smythe. He was a good-looking, intelligent, witty young man. Eleanor deserved the best. Plainly, she liked Smythe. The question was: Did Smythe represent the best? A lightweight, Duff felt. No character. Too smooth. Too social. Too much given to girl-chasing. It was Duff's belief, during the reverie, that he was thinking in abstract, detached and big-brotherly terms. Any suggestion that jealousy motivated him would have been met by a haughty, almost amused stare of his china-blue eyes.

By coincidence, yet not surprisingly—since Doctor Slocum greatly enjoyed discussing his part in the work of the Manhattan District; within the limits of secrecy, of course—Duff's wandering attention came back abruptly to a relevant speech: "Some of our early calculations on the subsidiary effects of nuclear reactions to bomb-released particles were rendered difficult by—"

Duff listened, hoping to be able to frame a question that might start a new line of discussion which would not advance the class in any way, but which might help him with another worry. Luckily for Duff, when the professor finished a sentence as long and as neatly balanced as a complex equation, Iron-Brain Bates, the grind of the group, took an ideal tack.

"Doctor," he said, "to deviate for a moment. How many bombs do you think Russia has?"

The mathematician frowned momentarily, as if he were not to be budged from the path of instruction. Then he grinned. "If our present political misadventuring continues, we will probably find out how many in the most pragmatic fashion. They will be dropped on us!"

The four graduate students laughed. Duff said, "Let's hope most of them will miss." And he went on idly, "Of course, any nation that had only a few atomic bombs could easily smuggle them into this country and distribute them at ideal sites, to be exploded at the time chosen by that nation."

"Easier said than done!"

"Why?" Duff asked. "Look at prohibition. Hundreds of tons of stuff brought across every border every week. Florida, here, was a center for it. Million bays, channels, waterways, lagoons, empty wastes of Everglades—"

"An atom bomb, Mr. Bogan, is pretty big. Very heavy."

"It could be built in small pieces. Imported, so to speak, in sections."

Hank Garvey, who intended to be a math teacher, said, "There's radioactivity. How do you smuggle radioactive stuff?"

The professor scowled at Hank. "You really ought to know, Mr. Garvey, that neither plutonium nor the disintegrative isotope of uranium is radioactive enough to be detected readily. Oppenheimer pointed out that you'd need a screwdriver to find a bomb on a ship—have to open every case aboard. Until you assemble a critical mass—enough of the stuff in one spot to set up a chain reaction—your plutonium or uranium would be comparatively easy to handle."

"Then," said Duff, "what's to hinder a nation from mining our cities?"

"Unpleasant notion," the professor smiled. "Mr. Bogan, you have always inclined toward the fantastic."

"What's fantastic about it? If you were a nation with only a few dozen atom bombs, and if you intended to attack, wouldn't you be smart to plant all the bombs you could exactly where they'd wreck the most vital industries or kill the most people, rather than risk them in bombers that might be shot down or might miss the targets?"

"There, gentlemen, we have an example of the very sort of pseudo-logic I discussed a week ago yesterday!" Professor Slocum's delight brought chagrin to Duff even before he went on, "Any nation with a few atomic bombs, only a few, would like to plant them in any enemy nation. True, gentlemen. Such bombs could be fabricated in sections, assembled later, armed and made ready for firing. They could be rigged for detonation by radio. The borders of the United States are comparatively unguarded; large objects and quantities of objects have been smuggled into this nation. So far, we see nothing to limit or to prevent the reality of Mr. Bogan's shocking implication that one cold winter night or one day—one busy working day—atomic bombs might be exploded without warning in a dozen cities or more. It is logical— to a point. To what point, gentlemen?"

Duff's three seminar mates contemplated the problem. They seemed unable to find in it any major syllogistic flaw.

Professor Slocum chuckled. "What defenses have we?"

"Well," said Iron-Brain, "there's the FBI—"

"Correct! The Federal Bureau of Investigation! Also a little-discussed but active body known as Central Intelligence. Also the various branches of Military Intelligence. The Immigration men. The Treasury men. Finally, an alert police force, sheriffs and the like. In other words, an invisible net protects our people. Many nets, I ought to say. A hole in one layer is matched by a fresh fine mesh behind the hole. In addition, in the camp of any enemy, in their secret societies, their so-called undergrounds, their cells and so on, this nation has undercover agents. Malevolent plotters are marked men. It would be impossible to set up an organization large enough to bring in, assemble, rig and conceal atomic bombs."

Down the hall a bell rang.

Two of the four students looked gratefully at Duff. He had succeeded in side-tracking old Slocum on his favorite theme for long enough to use up the period. Professor Slocum hastily assigned a double day's work for the next seminar and, smiling and nodding, skittered down the rather dim hall.

Duff walked into the sunshine feeling neither warmed nor illuminated. Logic was well enough. There was also such a thing as complacency. The world had been complacent about the Kaiser, about Hitler, Mussolini and Hirohito. A lot of the world had been wrecked owing to such complacency. Possibly old bald-headed Slocum was on the beam. But possibly there was a radioactive beam in the making, right in Miami.

As Duff walked toward his next class he gazed rather doubtfully down the palm-lined, flower-bright streets of Coral Gables. Far in the distance he could see the tops of buildings in the center of Miami—white towers above the flat green land. He tried to imagine a sudden and unexpected brilliance flaring down there, hurting the eyes, setting ten thousand fires, launching a terrible spray of gamma rays and sending forth a steely wall of blast across the city.

Somebody clapped his back. "Shut your mouth, Bogan! Flies'll enter!"

He grinned weakly. "Hi, Scotty."

"Must have been some dream!"

Duff nodded and walked along with young Smythe, who continued, "What dazed you, baby?"

"Just—fantasy. I'd been to a seminar in quantum math. Old Slocum got talking about atom bombs. I was imagining one going off in Miami."

He expected Scotty to laugh. But the somewhat younger man merely shook his head. "That old goat will never forget his dear old Manhattan District days!"

"You know him?"

"Slightly—in a painful way. He's head of the department where I keep flunking. Trig this year. Duff," it was said earnestly, "do you think there is any way for the feeble-minded—meaning me—to ever catch onto the mere meaning of trigonometry?"

"Why you studying it?"

"Had to have the credit. In science. To graduate."

"Why don't you come and talk about it to me? I bet I could straighten you out. Trig's a cinch. Trouble is, they teach it hard."

"Brother! You have poured the tea! Would you run over the topic with me some night? I'd appreciate it!"

"Glad to."

"What about day after tomorrow? It's one of Eleanor's working nights, so I won't be distracted. Be able to concentrate. At least till she comes home."

"Okay," Duff said.

He continued toward his class alone, watching the retreat of the elegantly dressed Mr. Smythe. Duff didn't need to glance down at his own faded jeans and frayed shirt cuffs to visualize the comparison or to think how odious it would seem to a young lady soon to serve as Orange Bowl Queen.

He threw off the thought and replaced it with another; in the process, no doubt, merely exchanging hostilities. Professor Slocum could be overconfident about American vigilance. He, Duff Bogan, could have been right about his tests. People—suspicion-proof people like Harry Ellings—could be busy on a project calculated to go far in overthrowing the freedom of the world. Somebody would have to investigate further, even if it was only an over-tall, underweight, overworked, badly dressed graduate student named Allan Diffenduffer Bogan.

"I don't know what to do, exactly," Duff said later in the day to Mrs. Yates, who had listened patiently to his story. "I can keep following Harry, of course. If he has a secret date with that big guy again—that darn-near giant—I can try to follow the big man when he leaves cover. I'm a lousy follower, though." He grinned. "One of my many hobbies wasn't being a boy detective. Or even trailing animals in the woods. I never did make a good Boy Scout."

Mrs. Yates smiled maternally. "I can imagine. Poor Duff."

"Oh," he hurriedly protested the pitying sound. "I had my compensations, remember. Best stamp collection in town. I could send Morse Code, as I taught the kids and Eleanor.   Pick locks and do escape tricks. I was the best slingshot marksman in the county."

She nodded and sighed. Her eyes rested on him wonderingly. He was twenty-four now, she thought. An age when lots of men had homes, jobs, families. But Duff was a sort of split personality. Half of him was stuck in his childhood and his innumerable boyish interests. The other half, abstract, precocious, was far ahead of most of the college boys brought home by Eleanor.

"Why don't you," she suggested, "go see that Mr. Higgins and tell him about Harry's meeting? He seemed very shrewd, from the glimpse I had."

Duff's long head shook slowly. "Not me! Not again! Not until and unless I can tell him something that'll really convince him."

"You afraid, Duff? False pride? Or what?"

His grin reassured her about false pride. "Mrs. Yates, I'm a small-town boy from the Middle West. I hope someday to get a Ph.D. in physics and maybe even to make a small contribution in some branch of the big field of ideas. All I'll probably ever really do is teach high-school kids about gravity and friction and Ohm's law. I don't think the stars wrote me down for a big melodrama like catching spies—or for a hero part, like saving my country."

"Yet you said—"

"Sure. I said! Got more mouth than sense! If what I really suspect is true, it's so crazy I don't believe it."

Mrs. Yates was a sentimental woman, though not a sentimentalist. During his recital of his hopes she had felt a mist in her eyes and turned her head away. Now, however, she looked back at him sharply.

"You say you don't know what to do. Well, you did one thing. You followed Harry and found his walks weren't entirely innocent moon-gazing. You can go on doing that. If I had legs to walk on, and if I were a man, and if I thought it was useless to talk to the FBI again right now, I'd look over that trucking company where Harry works. Maybe that great, tall man works there, too. Anyway, you could find out what cities the trucks serve. You could perhaps get a line on their customers. If Harry was using trucks to move—what you think—up north, then where the trucks went to would be something to learn."

Duff nodded. "That's not a bad idea!" He lighted a cigarette. "I could maybe apply for a job there. Look the people over. At night when Harry wouldn't be there to notice me around."

It seemed a useful project. Actually, if it had any immediate value, the effort served to give some occupation to Duff at a time when the conflict between his suspicions and his feeling that what he suspected was absurd kept him in a state of nervous anxiety. It also served to show him how inept he was at any sort of investigation.

The Miami-Dade Terminal Trucking Company consisted of a half-dozen large buildings in a light-industry section of the city on its northwest fringe. The buildings were low and very large. Some were warehouses, and these were provided with huge doors and long loading platforms; one was the repair garage in which Harry Ellings worked by day; in another, idle trucks of the company fleet were merely parked; the smallest building contained the business offices of the concern, which operated around the clock. At night there was a loneliness about the place in spite of the occasional arrival or departure of a huge trailer truck or of a smaller vehicle bringing merchandise from the South Florida area for reshipment.

Duff studied the scene. Colored loading crews worked here and there under flaring lights. A watchman made his rounds occasionally, throwing the round finger of a flashlight at the vast blanks of closed doors. Across the wide and intermittently rumbling street was a diner which boasted, with painted, illuminated signs, that TRUCK DRIVERS EAT HERE and WE NEVER CLOSE.

Duff walked around the establishment twice and then entered the front office, where a half dozen men worked at desks, smoked, roamed about with invoices in their hands and marked crates and cases and bundles.

"What do you want?" one of the men yelled at him from a desk.

Duff grinned. "Looking for work."

"What kind?"

"Any."

"We haven't got any kind. Just three kinds right now. Driving trucks—and you gotta be expert. Timekeeper. And paper work."

"No experience on those big rigs."

"You work a night shift?"

"Sure."

"Then come around in the daytime. That's when they hire the night force and the day force." The man seemed to think it was pretty funny that they hired the night shift in the daytime, so he laughed.

Duff laughed. "This company go to all cities?"

The man rocked his chair back. "You looking for work? Or transportation?"

"Work."

"Florida's full of guys that came down and couldn't find a job and want a free ride somewhere else."

Duff stood in front of a railing that crossed the wide, dingy room. "Look. Suppose I could bring a friend's business here? Would that help me get a job?"

"Wouldn't hurt none. What kind of business?"

Duff invented a business. "Making a modernistic line of furniture out of bamboo. Getting popular up north. He ships by rail right now."

"Fool to, I'd say."

"He's got a pretty good deal. Still, if your trucks go to all the big cities—regularly, I mean—"

"New York, Chicago, Boston, Philadelphia, Washington,

Baltimore, Pittsburgh, Detroit, Buffalo, Cleveland and Toledo, regularly. And points between. And unscheduled trips about once a month to ten-fifteen more cities. Would that suit your friend?"

"Sounds good," Duff said, and left.

He went over to the diner. Four big-shouldered truck drivers leaned on the counter drinking coffee, dunking doughnuts, listening to radio dance music. Duff ordered the same. The men were alert, fresh—waiting, obviously, for trucks to be loaded and their runs to begin. By morning they wouldn't be so tidy, so cleanly shaven, and they'd look tired.

"Miami-Dade a good company to work for?"

They looked at Duff closely. "Why?" one asked.

"Going to apply for a job."

The men shrugged. "Good as any."

"Where do they truck to, mainly?"

"All over," one man said, "this side of the Mississippi River."

"Some guy," Duff said, "that I ran across in an eating joint told me Miami-Dade was a place where a guy could settle down to a life job. Good management."

"It's all right," one of the drivers answered.

"This guy," Duff went on, "didn't give me his name, but you might know him." He looked at them and they waited. "Because he was the biggest guy I ever saw. Maybe near seven feet tall, and broad. A powerhouse."

Heads shook. "Never saw no giants around the joint. . . . You, Bizzmo?"

"Nope."

Duff paid and went out into the night to begin a long walk to the nearest bus stop. . . .

When, on the following afternoon, Eleanor took up the attempt to persuade Duff to see the FBI, he told her of his efforts. It was her afternoon to iron and his day to air and turn the mattresses. So their talk was conducted at intervals when he passed through the kitchen with his loads and while she continued to press clothes she had washed, with Marian's help, on the day before. It made for a rather incoherent discussion.

"In other words," she finally summed up, "either you don't think much of my idea or else you're too stuck-up to take a chance on annoying the G-men?"

He had three sun-warm pillows in each hand. He flung them up the back stairway. "I need something more before I bother the FBI."

"Wasn't seeing Harry meet that big man enough?"

"It'll have to be enough," he answered, "if it turns out to be all I can get."

"What in the world did you think you'd find at Miami-Dade that you couldn't find out just by idly asking Harry?"

He laughed—at himself. "Dunno. Whether there was a big guy working there, for one thing. Wasn't."

"Which means practically nothing."

"I know. Then I thought maybe I could find out the main, regular customers. Crazy idea, that one. You can't just walk into a firm and say, 'Who do you do business with?' and be handed a list."

"Harry'd tell you that too."

"Sure. And wonder why the deuce I asked. He's probably wondered already why the G-men were interested enough in his locked closet to ask him to open it and why that box intrigued them enough to make him open that. In fact, if what we think is going on is real, and if by any chance Harry knows what it is, which I doubt, then Harry is plenty worried by what has already happened. Worried enough, anyhow, so he'd never again have anything in that box in his closet except his precious platinum. I wonder how much it's worth?"

"Probably two or three thousand dollars," she said. "Awful funny way to keep your life savings."

He nodded. "Certainly is! Hard to melt. Hard to make that ingot of it. Be like Harry, in a way, though."

Eleanor licked her finger and absently tested her iron. "If

you really want to know where that company hauls its stuff, I could find out."

"You could? How?"

She resumed ironing, spreading out one of Charles' shirts on the board. "Well, I naturally know quite a lot of girls who work downtown—secretaries, file clerks like me, and so on. And the stuff they ship—"

"Cargo."

"The cargo is no doubt insured. It would be easy to learn what company insures it. Not hard to find who files for them. Possible to meet that girl or one of the girls. And you might—I might—get the dope from her."

"Would you?"

Her eyes rested on him. "Try? Sure, Duff! Why not? I'm more worried than you seem to be. I think your experiments were right. I think my idea that the stuff is being brought into this country is true. I'm scared!"

What reply Duff might have made was prevented by a distant roar, a whispering gush. It was a familiar South Florida effect: the approach of rain. Duff's arms and legs made wide, loose-jointed motions as he flung himself from the kitchen chair to the back door and out into the yard. A moment later a mattress thudded on the kitchen floor, then another and a third.

When the squall dinned on the shingle roof of the old house, Duff returned. "Narrow squeak," he said.

Harry came in behind him. They hadn't heard his car in the rain.

The next few days were uneventful for Duff—classes, laboratory work, hard study at home and, of course, more domestic duties than he could perform adequately. In Florida, grass grows all year around and must be mowed and trimmed unrelentingly; shrubs and vines and trees also need frequent trimming. In Florida, the blazing sun and salty air make painting as constant a requirement as on shipboard. In Florida, too, fish breed year-round, a fact which was to lead Duff to a new and painful experience. For some time, however, life went on in its usual pattern.

Harry Ellings even volunteered one day to help Duff. "Son," he said, "I generally wake around six. Leave the clippers out and I'll get after those hibiscus bushes."

"That'd be a help."

The older man shook his head sympathetically. "Having money is a wonderful thing. Not having it means day and night slaving. Work, work, work! Dunno how those Yateses keep their spirits so high sometimes. Look at that girl! Orange Bowl Queen, come Christmas! Going to college on a scholarship, she is. Has to get good marks to earn her tuition. Runs home to wash and iron and cook. Drives downtown three nights a week to earn a measly few bucks. Then goes dancing on her free nights, or posing for pictures, or fitting a costume, or attending some college party or meeting! The young sure have energy!"

Duff nodded. "She sure has, anyhow."

Harry Ellings went on, "Got it from her mother. Look at Sarah Yates. Lies there day and night—can't move her legs. So what? Does she gripe and whine? No. Knits. Sews. Makes all the clothes the kids wear. By golly, son, that's pluck!"

"Yeah."

"So leave the shears out. I'll pitch in, mornings. Money! Doggone! A person could use a barrel of gold!"

Duff didn't reply. He merely thought, for the thousandth time, that a simple, gentle, goodhearted, mousy guy like Ellings could never be associated with anything un-American. Anything dangerous, deadly, murderous. It didn't make sense.

Harry continued to talk, which was unusual. He gave a self-depreciating laugh and said, "Nearest I ever got to any money was that melted-down platinum. Guess it was kind of dumb."

He hadn't mentioned the cache before, except to grunt impolite syllables concerning its discovery by the G-men.

Duff felt himself stiffen internally. But he said, "Man has a right—"

"Oh, sure. Person like me gets crazy ideas, though. I sure did hate it when the country went off the gold standard. Figured I'd stay on a standard of some sort with my savings. Seems foolish now. I sold that metal and put the money in the bank." As he spoke, he took a small deposit book from a hip pocket. "All I got to show now is this here ink balance. Hope we don't get worse inflation."

From then on, Harry put in an hour or so at gardening every morning. Duff was grateful.

The days that were humdrum for him were filled with excitements for Eleanor Yates. Not the least of these was associated with her queenship and consisted of parade plans, the selection of maids of honor, newspaper interviews and appearances at lunches and other public affairs. Another source of excitement was the fond courtship paid to her by the amusing, cheerful Scotty Smythe in his salmon-pink convertible. He seemed to regard her tentative replies to his now-frequent proposals as proof of an arbitrary state of mind which would change in the long run. And he appeared to be unimpressed by the large numbers of other young males in the university and in the city who pursued her.

Some further part of her complicated life was made anxious, if not precisely exciting, by a decision to take into her own hands the matter of Duff's refusal to make any further immediate contact with the FBI. She had thought over the situation and decided it was her duty to do something, whether Duff felt that way or not. So she phoned the bureau, asked for Mr. Higgins and made an appointment.

The G-man welcomed the girl in his office one evening after dinner and before she was due at work. He told her that the newspaper photographs—even the colored ones—didn't do her justice. He asked her what was on her mind and she made the suggestion that had so startled Duff, "Did it ever occur to you that if nobody has stolen any of our bombs, somebody could be bringing parts into the country?"

She could see instantly that the idea had not occurred to the

G-man. And he, realizing she could discern his surprise, made no effort to camouflage it. "No. Not to me, anyhow. McIntosh may have thought of it."

"McIntosh?"

"Head of this office." He looked at her thoughtfully for a moment. "Interesting—highly unpleasant idea."

"There's this." She told him about the night Harry Ellings had gone for a stroll, about Duff's secret pursuit and about the furtive meeting with the man seven feet tall.

He doodled while she talked. "That's odd," he said. "But, again, we've got everybody who might be involved in any such a thing pretty well tagged. And there's no superman in the bunch. I know that. It's my business to know."

"Harry Ellings isn't tagged."

"No."

"Isn't it possible, somehow, that there could be a whole group you aren't on to?"

His eyes flickered. "Hardly. I won't say it couldn't be. We've had one or two nasty surprises along that line. Like some of the scientists the high-ups cleared, who turned out later to be plain spies."

"That's what I mean."

He pondered again. "Look here, Miss Yates. I'll talk to Mac. We did a pretty good work-up on your boarder. There are a thousand reasons why a man could meet a pal in an empty lot at night. Some legal, some not, but none necessarily what you're thinking about. I doubt, for instance, if the kind of organization you imagine would ever use a guy so big he'd be identified half a mile away. Ever think of that?"

Eleanor shook her head. "No."

"Your other boarder, Bogan, probably never did either."

"I guess not."

"Well, I'll talk to Mac. We may see Bogan again. We may want to talk to you again. There's a lot we might do. Of course, if anything else should come up—anything of the sort that young

Bogan's waiting for—inform us at once. And don't let anybody else know you've noticed any such happening. You or Bogan."

Eleanor flushed. "He doesn't know I came here. He wouldn't come. He was too much afraid he'd merely be starting another wild-goose chase."

Higgins chuckled. "He should see our files! That's our commonest form of chase! Well, thanks."

It wasn't particularly satisfactory. Mr. Higgins had been polite, but not much worried. He had thanked her. Yet she felt that if she had been Duff, instead of a pretty girl, Mr. Higgins might have delivered a scolding for suspecting fire where there was hardly even smoke. She kept the visit to herself.

In the matter of learning the regular large customers of the Miami-Dade Terminal Trucking Company, Eleanor was more effective. She had no trouble finding the name of the insurance company that did the underwriting for Miami-Dade. She knew two girls who worked for the firm. She found out where they had lunch. She cut two classes to be at the right drugstore at the proper time. Both girls were flattered to eat lunch with what they called a "celebrity." When they learned Eleanor had "a friend" who was thinking of using the Miami-Dade concern for shipping, but who was trying to find out exactly where the truck fleet went regularly —so as not to pay special or excessive rates—the girls were amused by Eleanor's "friend's" astuteness and readily agreed to supply her with a list of regular drop points.

Two days later Eleanor had the list: firm names, street addresses and cities. "Miami-Dade," one of the girls had scrawled, "hits all these joints at least once per wk."

Eleanor proudly gave the typewritten pages to Duff that evening.

He was pleased. "Marvelous! Marvelous!"

"Elementary," she answered, in Sherlock Holmes' conventional words. "Elementary, my dear Watson."

"What about a movie tonight?" he asked.

Her head shook. "Gotta work tonight. Overtime."

"Doggone! It's Saturday. I forgot!" He laughed. "Can't go, myself. I've got a date with your boy friend again."

"Which boy friend?"

He made a face at her. "Guess, gal."

"You mean Scotty's coming? For some more math tutoring?"

Duff chuckled. "Yep. And you know what? I'm getting paid! Three bucks for an hour of the old sines and cosines." Suddenly he was embarrassed. "Is that all right? I did it for free the first time. He got by his next exam after that. But then he insisted on coughing up. Said he'd pay any other tutor. And he can afford it."

Eleanor's eyes were shadowy. She sighed. "Of course, it's all right, Duff. It's just too bad, somehow that you have to tutor my—"

He pushed the tip of her nose with his forefinger fraternally, fondly. "Tutor your suitor? Glad to. Three bucks a week comes in right handy."

She looked away. "And Scotty can sure afford it. Goodness, he's rich!"

"Pretty nice guy," Duff nodded. "The dough doesn't seem to dizzy him any. And he's a bright lad, besides. It's only that he and trig aren't soul mates. Still he's coming along. I taught him what trig was for. That interested him. Once Scotty got onto the fact that there's a practical angle, he did real well."

Eleanor smiled. "He's a practical sort of boy, Duff, in spite of the gay-blade exterior."

"Yeah." Duff felt suddenly very much outside Eleanor—her life, her friends and the places where her life would undoubtedly lead her. "Yeah. He's nice."

That was when she kissed him. She kissed him hurriedly, almost in confusion, certainly impulsively, and she missed his cheek, getting his chin instead. But when she did it her eyes were shiny. And she said, "Duff, you're a love!"

Then she ran out to the barn and drove away. Duff heard Scotty's car hoot as they passed each other; the pink convertible came crackling up the drive. But during that time Duff stood where he was, beside the front door, even when he heard Scotty Smythe's feet on the worn porch boards. *She kissed me,* Duff thought. And he thought, *She kissed me because she feels sorry for me.* It was the kind of idea that made a man want to kick walls down, even in sandals, such as he had on. Nobody wants to be felt sorry for by a girl. By anyone.

But when Scotty reached the door, Duff had recovered. His smile was hospitable; he took in Scotty's new, herringbone-Angora sports jacket, and said, "Hello, Pythagoras."

Scotty replied in the gravest tone, "Good evening, Euclid."

After Scotty had paid gay respects to Mrs. Yates and briefly teased the younger children, who were studying, they went up to Duff's room and settled down to work.

Duff possessed the second most important faculty of a true teacher, as well as the first—which is to present new knowledge lucidly. The second is the ability to perceive the mental gaps and blocks in a student—the points at which, for individual reasons, he fails to grasp the subject. Often it is not stupidity, but a particular shape of a special personality or a bad background in previous teaching which causes a student to appear unintelligent. In Scotty's case it was both; no previous teacher had ever given him the feel, the sense and excitement of mathematics. Under Duff's tutelage, Scotty's attitude changed; he learned to appreciate the reasons behind the symbols.

Their hour went quickly and was extended to a second hour. Finally, however, Scotty broke up the session, "Getting late, pal. And we're already a week ahead of my class. Wouldn't my old man be startled if I got good marks in trig!"

"You will."

"Darned if I don't believe you're right!" Scotty went down the stairs, looked into Mrs. Yates' room to say good night, and opened the front door. "Tell Eleanor I couldn't wait for her. Omega meeting in the A.M. Tell her"—his eyes lighted up—"that any time she wants to shop for jewelry suits me."

Two red taillights swept down the drive. Duff stayed on the porch. An old moon had risen; it threw shadows across the silver nebula of lawn. An automatic smile on Duff's long, earnest face slowly faded. He imagined the excitement with which Eleanor might "shop" with Scotty, or some other boy, for a diamond ring. He would have been less than human if he had not also reflected that any diamond he could buy would be almost invisible. Yet no purposeful thought of himself and Eleanor and an engagement ring entered his head.

He sighed into the moonglow and noticed the glint of it on the lily pool he'd built the year before—partly in pursuance of a hobby and partly to embellish the Yates' lawn, which, at the time of his arrival, had been unkempt.

Years before, in Indiana, Duff had become interested in aquariums. He'd built several of wood and window glass, stocked them from local brooks, and sold a few. In Florida he had soon observed that pools could be dug in the underlying limestone; they needed only a little cement to waterproof them, and frost never heaved the ground. He had also found that tropical fish could be raised outdoors, that some species were native, and that colored water lilies of many varieties could be obtained at no cost when the university was separating its plants. So he had built a pool some twenty feet long and fifteen feet wide, trapped mollies in a nearby canal and bought a pair of wagtails.

Having noticed, some days before, that a new crop of mollies was due—and not feeling in a mood to sleep—Duff now went back to the house, procured a flashlight and walked down to the pond.

Sure enough, half a hundred tiny minnows swam in the open places and among the water plants and hid under the lily pads. Four of his crimson, night-blooming lilies were out, each one as big as a dinner plate. His torch moved about, touching the flowers, penetrating the clear water to search out snails and to follow the upward dive and downward lunge of water beetles. A small branch had dropped on one of the day-blooming lilies, and Duff walked over to a cabbage palm where he kept a dip net for retrieving such objects.

The branch lay among the lily pads at a place where they intermingled—reddish leaves floating alongside green. The surface was covered densely in an area as big as the top of a dining-room table. But, in dipping out the branch with one arm while with the other hand he aimed the flashlight, Duff opened up a space between the pads. It wasn't a wide gap, but it was wide enough to allow the light beam to penetrate the water to what should have been the bottom of the pond—and wasn't. A board was revealed.

Duff tossed out the small branch and pulled the lily pads farther apart. He presumed the board had fallen into the pond during the October hurricane, and wondered why it hadn't floated. He thought it might be a section of one of the boxes in which the lilies were planted, a section come loose, but held under water by a nail.

With the idea of "box" on his mind, Duff gasped audibly. He pushed hard at the leaves. It was not a side of a lily box and it was not a board. Leaning, holding his light closer, he could now see the top, the grain of hardwood, the glimmer of varnish or wax, and a glint of brass screw heads around the sides. Probing again with the net and changing his position, he thought he made out handles at both ends of the box.

He switched out his light. He let the lily pads float together, covering a hiding place that wasn't as ideal as Harry's closet, since, from time to time, Duff cleaned out excess algae in the pond and scrubbed its sides, wading hip-deep. But it was a good-enough hiding place now, because he performed those chores at long intervals and had finished them just after the blow in October.

Those thoughts had taken seconds only. He leaned the net against a tree and walked along the east side of the house. Harry's lights were on. After a moment, he saw Harry as he passed the window—Harry in pajamas.

Duff went back quietly to the pool. The thing to do, he reflected, was to wade in, get the box and hide it somewhere else.

Or, better, put it in the station wagon as soon as Eleanor returned from work and drive straight to the FBI. This one, Duff thought, would probably contain uranium—pure uranium—shaped for a certain use.

Duff sat down on the grassy edge of his pool. He took off his shoes and socks. He was excited, exultant, and also afraid. He did not know just what he feared, just why he was afraid. Then, abruptly, he did know. It was the disturbance of a leaf behind him or the tiny sound of a pine needle snapping underfoot. A very near sound, too near to give him time to escape or even to whirl around for attack. For he was sitting and there was something, somebody, in the dark right behind him.

For a second or two he was unable to think at all. Then, when he thought he heard the whisper of a swung weapon of some kind, he tried to lunge as far forward as he could. Fear was a sickness in him as he plunged, and fear was his final recollection. There was a ringing sound, a bursting in his head that he sensed at the instant and never afterward remembered. . . .

In the house, Harry turned out his light and went to his window. He looked at the moonglow. From the sinkhole west of the house came a murmurous croaking of bullfrogs. At last he walked to his bed and lay down to sleep.

Mrs. Yates, weary and warm under her reading light, pulled toward herself the pivoted bedside table that Duff had built. With a pencil, she wrote a good-night note to her daughter. She pinned the note to her wheel chair and gave it a push which rolled it through the door and into the living room where Eleanor would see it.

Marian Yates slept peacefully; damp curls of her dark hair overspread her pillow. Charles Yates, having finished the last installment of The Queen of the Planet Brandri, tossed Fabulous Science Magazine onto the floor and switched out his light. There was silence, deep and tropical.

After a while, car headlights swept into the Yates' driveway. Eleanor parked in the barn, came in by the back door, read her mother's note, smiled a little, and switched out the living-room light. The porch was in the shadow, but moonlight poured on the lawn. She stepped out to look at it and saw, as her eyes accommodated themselves, that one of the big branches torn off by the hurricane and stuck in the trees had come loose and fallen into the lily pool. She also saw something that glinted beside the water. Even so, she would have gone to bed; she was very tired. But, as she turned, she heard a sound. A low, bubbling mutter. A horrible sound. She rushed for the flashlight, but it was not in its place. She knew instantly that what she had seen glinting on the lawn was the light.

"Duff," she whispered frantically, and she ran out the front door.

She picked up the light. Worked the switch. Aimed at the mass of dead leaves, twigs and thigh-thick branch in the pond. With flinching nerves she saw that the water was stained red. And then she saw Duff—Duff's head. The scalp was open. His eyes were shut. He didn't seem conscious. But his hands, on the pond edge, were grasping feebly and he had his mouth out of water. He was trying to say something.

"Duff!" she cried.

He muttered.

"Duff! I'll get help! Can you hang on?"

His blood-streaked face looked up. His eyes showed now as slits. His teeth bared. His lips worked. "Scream," he finally enunciated. "And look behind you."

She swung around—and saw no one. But she screamed.

III

Emery McIntosh, chief of the Miami office of the FBI, listened to Higgins without interrupting. He was a medium-sized man of about fifty with a bald spot on the top of his head, nattily dressed in tropical-worsted suit, silk socks, black, highly polished shoes and a white shirt with a stiff collar. When he did speak, there was little in his accent to suggest his Scotch descent. But the ways and even the looks of his ancestors might have been read into the crisp mustache which matched his sandy hair, the blue glint of his eyes, the extraordinary firmness of his mouth and the deep, rather melancholy timbre of his voice. McIntosh looked, Higgins reflected, like a Presbyterian deacon dressed for taking up a Sunday collection—which he was and had been about to do when the younger agent had telephoned.

"And the lad's coming along all right?" McIntosh finally asked.

Higgins nodded. "Hardly a lad. Twenty-four."

"But still in college," the G-man sighed. "That keeps 'em young. One minute they can act like wise old professors. The next, fall apart like adolescents."

Higgins' grin was quick. "Well, Bogan is different. And he's all right. They had him in a hospital soon after midnight. Eleven stitches."

"Any tree bark in the wound?"

"Several bits, the surgeon said."

"I see."

"I'm not sure you do," Higgins answered stubbornly. "The poor guy was clunked more than once. He could have been blackjacked. And then that limb could have been hauled down from the tree. And after that he could have been pounded a couple with it. I think they thought he was dead."

"If there was a human agent—any 'they' at all! A big 'if.'"

Higgins shrugged in a swift, shadowy way. "All right. I couldn't find tracks on the lawn or in the shrubbery. Hasn't rained lately, so why should I? Nobody in the family heard or saw anybody. He must have made a big splash, going in, but the house is fairly distant. Ellings' room's on the other side. The mother and the girl were asleep. The boy's room is on the back."

"Ground wet around the pool? That box—if it existed—would have come out dripping."

"The ground was wet, all right. But it would have been soaked by the splash of the man and the limb anyhow. There might once have been an impress of the box on the grass—it would have been heavy. But the police were there first and they had it fairly well trampled."

McIntosh sank lower in his swivel chair. "Tree?"

"I gave it a going-over. You could see where the limb had been jammed. Rubbed the bark of a sound branch. You could see that it hadn't been attached by much. A few slivers of wood and bark. It weighed around a hundred and fifty pounds. It could, so far as signs show, simply have come loose while he crouched there, and dropped on him and conked him, turned as it hit the pool, and swatted him again. It could, for all I can surely prove."

McIntosh looked at his watch. On its chain was a Phi Beta Kappa key. "You say the lilies were in wooden boxes. Could one of them have changed position so he mistook it, at night, in a flashlight beam, for what he imagined was related to his other—discovery?"

"How can anybody answer that except Bogan himself? He said he saw the box plainly. Said he saw brass screw heads. No screws in his lily boxes. And it's hardly anything he'd dream up. Besides, the lily boxes have no tops. They're filled with compost, and that's covered with white sand."

"One might turn turtle."

"Yes. Except that it would haul under water a conspicuous bouquet of lily pads and buds and flowers."

"You believe there was a box and Bogan got slugged and the box was taken away while he was unconscious?"

"Yes."

"And you believe"—McIntosh took time to make himself say it—"that there was uranium in the box?"

"Or some other part of an A-bomb."

"I don't."

Higgins started to say something argumentative, changed his mind, and smiled. "I don't blame you."

"Not one tangible piece of evidence! Bogan once had what he called a sample, a few particles he filed off, and he claims he analyzed them—which is difficult even for a specialist, and he wasn't that. But he lost what was left of his sample before we could work on it. Ellings did have a hunk of platinum on hand, and that's peculiar, but it's not uranium. Ellings met a man we're supposed to believe was seven feet tall. Phooey! Ellings doubtless met a man. He may even be busy with some deal—a little smuggling or the passing of stolen goods. But do you realize what you're saying when you talk about A-bombs?"

"Yes."

"I doubt it. You're saying, man, that whole cities are being prepared for slaughter without warning! And you're saying this is being done by people we have no whisper of, line on, word about—not a notion of, a smell, scent, track, trail or even hunch about!"

"Exactly."

"Frankly, I think that's impossible."

"You can't say it's impossible, Mac."

The Scotsman shrugged. "Very well. As unlikely as flying saucers. Put it that way. On the other hand, grant, for a second, it's true. What then?"

"That's what I'd really like to discuss."

McIntosh put away his key and folded his hands across his chest. "All right. We'll discuss it. I will. In the first place, any such an underground outfit actually doing any such thing wouldn't hesitate for a second to murder this Bogan lad, or the whole Yates family, or any hundred other people."

"Obviously."

"Second, such an outfit actually might use the Yates house. It's off the beaten track. No other houses near. Rundown. Surrounded by big trees. Not conspicuous. And protected. Those Yateses would be about the last persons anyone would suspect.

of doing anything criminal or harboring criminals. Mother a cripple. Beautiful young daughter—Orange Bowl Queen. Normal Americans. Two boarders. And a man like Ellings, if he were an enemy agent, would be ideal because he's got such a long, hardworking, churchgoing, commonplace history."

"Check."

"Third, the whole routine you're trying to sell me would therefore have worked—except this Bogan lad had a lot of cockeyed hobbies. Like picking locks. Like housework. And he's a physics graduate student, so when he sees metal, he's curious. He has, besides, a hobby of raising tropical fish and water lilies. When he can't get a satisfactory answer from us, he takes on another hobby."

"Yeah," said Higgins dryly. "The hobby of danger!"

McIntosh sniffed. "Nosing! He gets nosy. He gets the girl nosing, even. And he gets bopped on the bean by a branch—and lucky his brains weren't knocked out." McIntosh unlocked his hands and flattened them on his desk. "Not a sign that anything happened but a branch fell! Ellings, the logical one to hit Bogan if all this wonder dust is real, was in bed. Mrs. Yates saw him come downstairs. So who hit him? Presumably, somebody coming for or standing guard over the alleged box in the lily pool. So now what? Four-five days, Bogan's out of the hospital. Ready to nose some more!"

"We could tell him to quit. Tell him the bureau was taking over from here on in."

The Scotsman scowled. "Which is exactly what we don't want anybody to know!"

There was quiet elation and relief in Higgins' voice. "Meaning, we are taking over?"

McIntosh frowned harder and then smiled. "If it weren't Sunday, I believe I'd swear. Of course, we're taking over! However, we won't accomplish anything unless all and sundry really believe we've missed our cues by deciding the injury was an accident, the box a myth. You can see that?"

"Sure. The Yates place is hot. It will be as long as we're interested. Or the cops. Anybody. Maybe it always will be, from now on, and maybe—if Ellings was merely being used—we have only one hope: finding out who used him. But there's one difficulty about telling Bogan and the Yates family that we don't feel anything was going on around there. It's Bogan himself. He really believes what he reported. I believe it. And if we give him the brush, he's undoubtedly going to push right on with—"

"His hobby of danger?" McIntosh smiled bleakly. "I suppose he is. But—still just being hypothetical—if there is such an outfit as you take on faith, will they be badly alarmed by a physics student's attempt to catch up with them? I think not."

"They near killed him."

The bureau head was silent for a long time. Finally he said, "See here, Hig. If this operation is real, maybe several million people might get killed all of a sudden. Good Americans. Risking the life of one or two or even a family isn't important. If it's not real—which is my opinion—there's no risk."

Higgins gestured as if to protest that logic. Then he said, "Yeah."

McIntosh consulted his watch again. "You go back to the hospital. Tell Bogan that we did have a watch on the place ever since he started bringing tales to us. Tell him no stranger or anybody else was even near the hammock trees that night. Tell him we're calling off our men. Let him feel we're sick and tired of a lot of to-do that pans out as nothing. Give him the notion that his accident, and his 'theory' that it was something different, is the last straw. He's already sore at us for apparently doing little. If you say we did a job of watching he knew nothing about, and are quitting now because this time we know he was mistaken— well, it'll leave him high and dry."

"Sure will," Higgins said. "And I hate to do it to him. He's a nice guy, Mac. Got brains. Sense of humor. Guts."

"Can you think of a better way to handle it?" McIntosh rose and set his Panama carefully on his head. "If I hurry, I can just

about hit the middle of the sermon. My wife'll be annoyed." He
put his arm over Higgins' shoulder and propelled him toward the
single elevator in service on that Sunday morning. "You haven't
really got this thing focused yet, Hig. Remember what I said. If
it's all a pipe dream, no harm done. If it's not, we have to run
the risk of one man being in danger in order to have any chance
at all, ourselves, of stopping something"—as the elevator came,
he hesitated—"that we'd gladly sacrifice every man in the bureau
to stop."

Higgins, with those words, felt the full impact of his chief's
fear. He walked around the building and got in his car and started
toward the hospital again. He could tell Bogan that a man under
great strain often mistranslates what he sees and hears, and Duff
Bogan had certainly been under strain.

Thinking about it alone in bed, after Higgins had gone, Duff
agreed that Higgins might be right. After all, they had watched
the house. They had acted, when he'd assumed they were ignoring
his story. It could have been a lily box, bright insect eggs, a falling branch. Or could it? In his mind's eye, going over and over
the scene, he could see the slots in the screw heads. Insect eggs
didn't have slots. He could tell them that. But they wouldn't believe it. He could hardly believe it himself. Maybe it wasn't true.
The FBI didn't believe it, and the FBI wasn't dumb, so why
should he?

With the last shreds of consciousness—of consciousness free
of head-splitting pain—Duff answered himself: It was real and
awful and growing worse because nobody would do anything
about it. So he would have to do what he could, as soon as he was
able to leave the hospital. He'd have to work alone.

It was only afterward, long afterward, that Duff could col-
late and define the moods and incidents that followed. At the time
they seemed unrelated and inexplicable.

His head mended rapidly. The doctors were pleased. Duff
explained to them with simulated hauteur that physicists had
tough brains. He missed Thanksgiving at the Yates home, but not

the meal, as Eleanor borrowed from a restaurant a portable food-warmer and brought turkey with trimmings to the hospital. Three days later he was released, bandaged, but whole again.

Immediately upon his return, he noticed a difference in the temper of the household. Mrs. Yates seemed nervous and worried. The two younger children were cross and strained. And Harry Ellings had been suffering from what he described as "attacks"; he stayed away from work twice. Eleaner showed the change most sharply if more subtly.

She was, if anything, lovelier than ever and seemed more aware of her attractiveness. Miami's best beauty parlors had vied for a chance to give her wavy, tawny hair its prettiest cut; they had taught her new uses of make-up. Stores in Miami and Miami Beach had supplied her, for the first time in her life, with a luxurious wardrobe. These gifts were, of course, donated for publicity—the traditional due of a Bowl Queen.

She was edgy, Duff thought. No doubt she was overtired. The mere fact that he had lain for a week in the hospital had meant a large addition to her work. And now that Charley Yates spent every afternoon carrying newspapers, she was short another helper. Her own job, the demands made on a Queen-elect and the burden of housework were more than enough for any girl. But, in addition to that, she had arranged several dates with other young men than Scotty: Avalanche Billings, the fullback, for one; and Tony Bradley, a Miami businessman, for another.

She seemed glad to have Duff back at home one minute, and the next, annoyed at everything. "Christmas is coming," she kept saying, "and we're so broke and there's so much to do."

When he tried to reassure her, she turned away.

Finally, they quarreled over the subject of most quarrels: practically nothing. He had worked late in the laboratory on a difficult problem. When he reached home, Eleanor was in the kitchen, and he went immediately to help.

She said petulantly, "Where in heaven's name have you been?"

"Over on the campus. Working."

"Fine thing! I needed you here! The pipe's plugged under the sink!" She picked up a pan of hot vegetables and drained them over a larger vessel." See?"

"I'll fix it right after dinner."

"You'll have to or wash dishes in the yard! The kids are going to the movies tonight."

She lifted the lid on a skillet of sizzling meat. He noticed that she was wearing no apron and hadn't changed from a particularly pretty dress—gray and scarlet—in her new wardrobe. Her mood communicated to him.

"You'll get spattered," he said. "Let me turn the chops. You've no apron on."

"You set the table," she said. "It isn't yet. . . . I don't know why Marian's late!"

"But that meat's spitting all over the place."

She muttered something that sounded like, "Mind your own business," seized a fork, and immediately was splashed so that the fresh dress was turned into something for the dry cleaner.

She said, "Damn!"

"I told you so."

She whirled from the stove. "You tell me nothing, Duffer Bogan! All the aprons were dirty and I was too darn tired to change!"

"I'm sorry."

"Sure, you're sorry! So am I sorry! I'm sorry my kid sister is probably giggling with some pimply boy in a schoolyard somewhere! I'm sorry you had to work late and Harry's feeling rotten! I'm sorry we can't afford a cook, or to eat out once in a while, or even own enough aprons to keep neat! I'm sorry we're so mousepoor, and right now I'm even sorry I've got what people think are good looks—except that maybe I can use 'em, somehow, to get this family out of a lousy mess that goes on forever!"

It wasn't like Eleanor. It was nothing like her, Duff thought glumly. She had even called him by the derogatory form of his nickname. He felt pity, but he thought it was no time to show it. Perhaps, too, he felt in a deep recess of his personality, where his aware mind couldn't look, the blaze of resentment.

"All you have to do," he said stonily, "is to say 'yes' to Scotty Smythe. I'm sure he'd manage things fine for everybody. You wouldn't need boarders, so I'd be delighted to hunt up some other place—" It was childish.

He had never heard her shout in anger. She did now. She raised her fork and stabbed it in his direction and yelled, "Get out of this kitchen!"

As he went through the living room, Mrs. Yates called nervously, "What's wrong, Duff?"

He answered, "Nothing," and began to set the table. She didn't offer to make up, so he didn't.

The day after that, Harry Ellings announced he was going to take a week of his annual two weeks' vacation to go up to Baltimore to see some doctors about his condition. When Duff learned that, he wanted, once again, to let the FBI know. But Higgins, the G-man, had been very final in his last talk at the hospital. The FBI wouldn't be interested in Harry's trip, and though Duff ached with anxiety over the potential danger of it, he felt he could do nothing.

When Harry returned, he didn't seem improved. His color had become a grayish yellow. His appetite was bad. His hands shook constantly. His neatly parted gray hair seemed to be getting thinner almost day by day. He talked little and spent most of his time, when he wasn't at work, lying on his bed.

Nobody gave him much attention—the Yates family was demoralized. Dinners were hurriedly prepared. Every night, afterward, Eleanor either drove to Miami to her job or went to a meeting or had a date, leaving the dishes and most of the housework to Marian, Charles and Duff. With Eleanor absent, and while he worked with the youngsters, Duff could revive the old feeling of cheerfulness, but when Eleanor was at home a jittery gloom prevailed.

In early December there was a cold spell. It was the sort that Florida chambers of commerce would like to keep hushed up. Frost crept over the Everglades. The power company put every generator in service to meet the load of electric heaters glowing in tens of thousands of homes. People with fireplaces stoked them, so that all Dade County was spiced with pine-wood smoke.

During the night, millions of dollars' worth of winter vegetables stiffened, took on frosty carapaces and perished ignominiously. Duff chopped wood and the younger Yateses did their homework around a fire while a kerosene heater burned odoriferously in their mother's room. In the morning, which was sunny, but, to natives, shockingly cold, public schools stayed closed and many business firms failed to open, owing to the absence of employees who had no overcoats to wear to their jobs. Duff went to his classes, however.

He was chilled through by midafternoon and stopped in the Student Club cafeteria for a cup of coffee before taking the bus. There he spotted Scotty Smythe, sitting alone, looking morose. Duff carried his cup over to Scotty's table.

"Coming for your lesson tomorrow, Sir Isaac?"

Smythe looked up. "Hi, Einstein! Guess so."

"Haven't seen you around lately. What gives?"

Scotty stared thoughtfully at Duff. His lips drew out in a somber line. But his eyes flickered. "You observe here," he presently replied, "a young man, five foot ten and a quarter, one hundred and fifty-eight pounds. Hair, muddy black; eyes, putty gray; occupation, college senior. He is carrying the torch."

"Fight?"

Scotty contemplated the question. "No. Brush."

"Meaning what?"

"You notice any change in Eleanor lately?"

"She's tired. Nervous. On edge."

The younger man turned over those words in his mind. "Minimally," he said in the end. "She is also suddenly interested in a laddy-boy named Tony who owns half the hardware stores in

Florida, or will, when his pappy kicks off or retires. This chump is pretty to look at; he went to Princeton, and he has a convertible too. Chartreuse."

"I've seen it. And him."

Scotty went on musingly, "Now, Eleanor never did okay my proposition exactly. But I felt she was interested in me. Seems not. No time for Smythes these days. She's also taken to going places with that large charge of human barge knows as Avalanche Billings."

"A wholesome boy," Duff said, not enthusiastically.

"In a nutshell, man, you've said it all! It's not enough that his pappy is a brewer. His boy had to be an athlete too. Nearly All-American, you may have noticed. Avalanche is a clown—makes the girls laugh. Outside of rugged good looks—destined to become bloated as the years pass—"

"Very little," Duff agreed.

"A cipher. A zero. A zed. What she sees in him—"

"Not even a convertible," Duff murmured.

"*Touché*, pal!" Scotty chuckled dolefully. "You don't sound so doggoned elated yourself."

"Things are melancholy," Duff agreed.

Scotty was silent. He finished his coffee. He eyed Duff for a while. "Speaking of beer and such," he said, "and I was, by inference, a while back, are you a drinking man?"

"No," Duff replied. "Not a matter of scruples. Purse. And lack of experience."

"I was sitting here," Scotty continued, "considering the poor condition of my soul. I was thinking of ringing up a babe and buying same a drink or two. Only a lack of companionship prevented me from recourse to the anodyne. But it runs through my mind, now, that if you'd consent to the measure, I might ring up two babes."

Duff grinned. "You forget my devoirs, chores, duties."

"On the contrary. I know your routine. I know the kids could manage things one evening without you. You could meet me at the Palm Paradise Café at eight o'clock, and I would bring the ladies. It would be my party. Celebration for an *A* in a math test."

"You know," Duff answered after a moment, "I think I will! I feel in a mood to do darned near anything!"

"I'll pick a dame accordingly," Scotty grinned.

When Duff had gone, Prescott Smythe took from a pocket a small black notebook and began earnestly to con its pages. Listed in them were the names and phone numbers of several scores of young ladies who would gladly consent to help lift any shadow from the Smythe soul. The problem was to find one who would serve Duff in the same way. Duff was not, Scotty reflected, the kind of collegian, or post-collegian, who impressed young women. His small talk was unreliable. He had said once that he didn't dance much. As far as Scotty knew, he had never been seen to take a cocktail or even a beer. He had dated no coeds, so there was no grapevine information available on him.

Scotty turned pages all the way to the *S*'s before he halted for any length of time. His finger rested on the name of Indigo Stacey. "Indigo Stacey," the entry read, "99-7663." And under that "bru —vgl—s—tt—cw—wfi." That, in Scotty's code, meant, "Brunette, very good-looking, sexy, too tall, college widow, worth further investigation." He remembered. Peculiar dame, but handsome. Graduated two years before. Lived with another gal in a bungalow near the campus. Liked older guys, even as a student; very tall and helpfully man-crazy.

The trouble with old Duff, Scotty reflected fondly, was that you had to get to know him to appreciate him. He gave the first impression of an absent-minded Leaning Tower of Pisa, and it took time to find out that he was as human as anybody and far brighter than most.

When the object of such meditations reached the Yates home, his feet were cold both literally and figuratively. He called to Mrs. Yates and then backed away from telling her. He dallied in his room and heard Eleanor come home, and finally went downstairs, where he found the two women together. In a kind of panic, he considered trying to tell Scotty by phone that he couldn't make it, but, instead, he blurted, "Won't be here for supper. Sorry, folks."

Both women stared. It was true that he was occasionally absent, but always after giving long notice.

Eleaner said, rather crossly, "You might have told us!"

"Date," he answered uncomfortably. "Just made it."

"A date"—Eleanor was sarcastic—"with some little group, I bet, that does calculus for party games!"

"Dame," he said coldly.

"Who?"

"That would be telling." He was rather pleased by the half-angry, half-startled look on Eleanor's face, but mystified by the smile Mrs. Yates gave him behind Eleanor's back.

Duff dressed. He put on his topcoat. He caught a bus at seven-fifteen. He got out nervously a half block from the Palm Paradise, and walked uneasily toward its glittering, one-story-high electric sign. He went in.

What happened after that, he never clearly understood. Scotty was sitting at a ringside table, under revolving rainbow-hued lights, with two young ladies, one a girl with brown bangs who satisfied every detail of the "cute-college-type" description, and the other a stately, almost regal brunette with black hair, a heavy chignon at the nape of her neck, dazzling dark eyes and a smile, as Duff was introduced, which shocked him by its warmth and intimacy. He sat down, and there were cocktails. Scotty and his girl danced, but the tall brunette expressed herself as delighted not to do so, and she listened to Duff's words, which flowed with increasing ease—as if every one were a jewel of remarkable brightness.

There was dinner, a very gay meal with a bottle of red wine. There was coffee with brandy in it. There was a floor show. Duff was further startled and pleased when Scotty, in a moment during which their ladies were absent, said, "You know, old-timer, when I called Indigo, she'd heard of you and seen you around, and said she was dying to meet you and already planning how to do it."

"Wonderful girl," Duff said. "Why me?"

"She goes for serious types, I guess," Scotty answered. "Only girl I ever heard of named Indigo."

"Suits her, though."

"Deep purple? You bet! Well. Have fun, Archimedes."

"I'm having a wonderful time."

He was. The wonderful time continued. There was a long drive in the convertible, windows wound up against the chill, and Indigo Stacey snuggled close as a further thermal measure. A Miami Beach night club and another floor show. A still longer ride back to Coral Gables—a ride on which Indigo said, "You can start kissing me good night about here, Duff."

"Here" was some miles from her bungalow.

When the two young ladies had been deposited at their homes, Scotty suggested a nightcap.

And it was in a small bar not far from the campus where Duff, far removed from normal reticence and warmed by the fellowship of Scotty Smythe, shared his problem.

"You know, Duff," Scotty had said, turning his nightcap highball in his fingers and not tasting it, "I can't figure you out. On a party, you're tops. You have fun. At school the work doesn't seem to bother you—you breeze through it. And yet you act like a man carrying a mountain on his back all the time. Why?"

"Because I happen to be one," Duff answered. And suddenly, without planning it, he told his story, beginning with the day, which now seemed long ago, when an old hobby had led him to pick the fairly new lock of a closet door.

Excepting for an occasional quiet expletive, Scotty listened to the account without interruption. At its end, his expletives were many and vehement. But they wound up mildly. "Ye gods," he murmured. "I'll say you carry a mountain around. But you've got to do something."

Duff shrugged miserably. "What can I do?"

Scotty drummed on the table, his drink forgotten. "Not much,

here. Ellings—and whoever else is involved—that super-jerk you
saw, no doubt—will certainly be careful not to act suspiciously
for a while. But I bet they are using that truck company to ship
the parts! What I'd do, if I were you, is take that list of customers and go north for the Christmas holidays! I'd look into as
many places those trucks serve regularly as I could. Because if
you found even one that was a drop—"

"What," Duff asked disconsolately, "would you use for
money?"

Scotty smiled sympathetically and thought a moment. "I was
going to fly up home for the holidays," he said. "Come back after,
with the family, as far as Palm Beach. But I could drive. We
could. We could stop off at the various cities."

The Yates family was surprised and disappointed by Duff's
sudden announcement that he was going home for the holidays.
It was a very hard thing to do, and he almost hated himself for
his decision. Eleanor took the news especially badly. She accused
him of deserting. She reminded him that he wouldn't see her as
Orange Bowl Queen. And she burst into tears. But he stuck to his
story that he was going to Indiana to visit his family.

Even Indigo Stacey, at whose home he spent an evening playing
bridge—the one game in which he was expert—expressed disappointment. She told him that she had developed a "large passion"
for him and that the approaching holidays would be the "longest
and dullest in years" without him.

He felt, therefore, very much like a fugitive when, carrying a
big, beat-up cheap suitcase, he took the bus, ostensibly to the
train. Actually, at the station, he was picked up furtively by Scotty
Smythe.

In Washington they put up at a second-class hotel, donned
old clothes and began "job hunting" at the regular delivery
places of the Miami-Dade Terminal Trucking Company. These
were stores, markets, wholesale houses and other trucking firms.
There seemed to be nothing suspicious about any.

"Trouble is," Scotty said at supper that night, "we don't know what we're looking for. We do know it wouldn't be anything conspicuous. To locate a receiver of the freight we believe is moving, evidently might take fifty guys a month. And I've got to show up at home pretty soon. I got one idea."

"What?" Duff was leg-weary, insult-weary, discouraged.

"General Baines. Three stars. Friend of my old man. Has something to do with Military Intelligence. Maybe the FBI didn't see your tale as anything but hallucination. The Army boys might be different."

"We could try," Duff agreed.

They tried the next morning. The general was located by phone in his office in the Pentagon Building. He told Scotty that he was "right busy." He agreed, however, that, since the matter "involved national security," he could spare a few minutes.

So Duff and Scotty wound their way through the Pentagon labyrinths, found the outer office, waited half an hour, and at length stood face to face with a uniformed, silver-haired, paternal-looking officer who worked in an atmosphere of maps, papers, flags and autographed portraits of great men. He was cordial and quiet.

The general's reaction to the narrative was familiar to Duff; it angered Scotty. When the interview was ended, when the two young men were out in the winding, sloping corridors again, Scotty said enragedly, "He thought it was a gag! Tried to be polite! Tried to shoo us out, like a couple of flies at a picnic! Got positively humiliated when we kept talking! Annoyed too."

Duff shrugged. "That's how the G-men felt about it!"

"What a country! Easy pickings for an enemy!"

Neither Duff nor Scotty had any way of knowing that, the moment after they had left General Baines' office, he had picked up his phone, switched to a special line, and said, "Chief of Staff. It's an emergency call."

The two self-appointed investigators reached Manhattan in an aggrieved mood.

Ordinarily, the elegance of the modernistic, duplex Smythe

penthouse would have awed Duff. The warmth with which he was
received by Scotty's white-haired, aristocratic-looking mother
would only partially have put him at ease. The amiability of
Scotty's father would have helped. On the other hand, the cool
though well-mannered greeting of Scotty's sisters—Adelaide, home
from Sweet Briar, and Melinda, back from Vassar—would have
frightened him. As things were, however, he was so downcast about
the journey that the skyline view from the picture window had no
impact for him. Even the palatial surroundings, the silver and
damask at dinner, the dressed and dated, orchid-wearing sisters
scratched only the surface of his mind. Inner suffering enabled
him to appear more poised than he would otherwise have been.

Duff spent a night at the Smythe residence, and then put up at
a small, midtown hotel. Scotty had wanted him to remain in his
home, but Duff had been too embarrassed for that, too aware that
he lacked the clothes, even the temperament, and above all the
funds for the round of entertainment on the Smythe holiday
schedule. His hotel bill was to be paid by money which Scotty
wanted to "give to the cause" and which Duff insisted he would
only borrow.

The three days remaining before Christmas Duff devoted to a
survey of Miami-Dade delivery points in and near Manhattan.
It was an exhausting and fruitless effort. He posed, according to
the nature of each firm, as a potential buyer, shipper, customer or
job seeker. He learned nothing and spent the lowest Christmas in
his life—alone at his hotel, unable to engage even in his vain re-
searches because every place in the city was closed. He thought
of the Yateses all day and of the work his foolish venture had added
to their slim yuletide.

Then, on the day after Christmas, his patient checking of the
list Eleanor had contrived to get for him led to a warehouse located
in the downtown area of Manhattan, three blocks from Broadway,
near Wall Street. There was nothing remarkable about the warehouse. In fact, it was the least provocative of any of the places

he had visited, inasmuch as he was able to see, by peering through a very dirty window in the early twilight, that the mammoth interior was absolutely empty. Duff would have gone back to his hotel, then and there, tired, defeated, shamed by his absurd efforts, if he had not heard, while he was still peering, the sound of a door closing somewhere. An empty building is unsuspicious; an empty building with someone moving about inside it is different.

Duff crossed the street and fixed his eye on the vast brick structure overtowered on both sides by taller buildings which were as grimy. He buttoned his coat under his chin. He crouched in a doorway.

It began to rain. The rain brought quick darkness, shiny streets, spattering traffic and a glitter of light on the cobblestone pavement. At last a little door cut in the truck entrance of the warehouse opened slowly. A man came out. One of the tallest men Duff had ever seen in his life—a man proportionately broad.

The misery, the despair, the frustrations of past weeks disappeared in the first sharp breath Duff drew. For this huge specter against the night was like an abrupt light in a long and dreadful darkness. The man looked up the street, down the street and across the street. He flipped up his coat collar and strode toward Broadway.

With surging excitement, Duff followed. He was sure it would be simple to do. The man towered above the other pedestrians; he would stand out a block away, even at night. People, furthermore, looked up at him in sudden astonishment and made extra way for him, which added to the ease of pursuit. On a city street, furthermore, Duff felt that his own clumsiness would be no handicap; there was noise and confusion everywhere.

But what Duff hadn't thought of soon happened. The huge man stopped walking abruptly. Duff dived into a doorway. The man again looked up the street, down the street and across it, as he stood at the curb. He had that habit; evidently, he seemed to suspect or fear he might be followed. Quite suddenly, then, he took keys from his coat pocket, bent, opened the door of a parked car, climbed in, switched on its lights and drove into the traffic stream.

Duff searched so wildly for a cab in which to follow that he neglected to notice the license number of the car. There wasn't an empty cab in sight. When Duff thought of the number, the big man's car had disappeared.

He was ashamed of his error. But now he was no longer without resources. He would have to find a hardware store that was still open, and make certain purchases. He would have to learn, after that, the timing of the watchman's rounds, if the empty warehouse was watched at all.

It took him an hour to locate a store. He gave half an hour to watching the warehouse. No man seemed on duty there. He crossed the street in a hard, icy rain—a rain now welcome—and applied himself to the lock on the small warehouse door. It was difficult and he was forced, whenever a pedestrian passed, to exhibit a bunch of keys and pretend he was having trouble finding the right one. Nobody stopped him or questioned him, and eventually the door opened. He went in, turning on a flashlight as he did so.

He hurried through an office that showed, by closed roll-top desks and gritty furnishings, long disuse. Another door led to the main floor of the place. A ramp in the rear sloped up through cavernous emptiness to a floor above. Another like the first rose to the top floor.

Afraid that there might be a partitioned room-within-a-room on the two upper floors, Duff climbed both ramps with his flashlight switched off. He found that in the whole building there was nothing—nothing but over-all grime and rubbish in the corners, nothing but spiderwebs and a scuttle of rats somewhere in the walls, nothing but gleaming specks on the ground floor of rock particles such as constitute the underlying base of Manhattan and stick to wheels of vehicles—nothing but hollow silence, the dusty odor of desertion and the dim-heard rumble of the great city outside.

The very emptiness of the building had at first seemed meaningful. The meaning now appeared only to be that it was waiting for some new and perhaps different cargo. It had been a storage garage; more recently a warehouse. Now, perhaps, it had changed hands and was being prepared for other uses by the towering and somehow terrifying figure of the man whose face Duff had not yet clearly seen. The giant. Duff thought of him in that term.

He left the building cautiously and hurried for the subway. No use to call Scotty now; Scotty would be at a post-Christmas party.

And no use, Duff thought, to get in touch with the New York FBI office. What would be added to his story by the report of a menacing figure lost in the night and an empty building?

He was hungry, wet and weary as he went up the steps of his nondescript hotel.

The desk clerk stopped him. "Mr. Bogan! A Mr. Smythe has been trying to get in touch with you. Been here twice and phoned every fifteen minutes since!"

Puzzled, Duff went into a phone booth and dialed. The ring was answered instantly by Scotty, "Duff! Thank the Lord! Look! Eleanor phoned at half past four this afternoon—"

"Eleanor!"

"Asked for you. Talked to me. I've talked again to her since."

"How'd she know where I was?"

"Called your family in Indiana, first! You evidently wrote 'em you were spending Christmas with me—gave 'em my name—something."

"Oh. Yes, I did! You mean Eleanor phoned clear to Indiana?"

"Listen, chump!" It was then that Duff got the overtones in Scotty's voice. "Harry Ellings is dead."

"Dead?"

"Died in bed. The family thought he'd been up early working

in the yard and got a ride to Miami. So they didn't find him till afternoon. Charley." Scotty said the name grimly. "Tough on the kid to find the body. Could have been heart failure—probably was, the doctor thought. But that's not all. Eleanor said she'd found something. Can you imagine what? She said she wasn't able to move it."

"A box!" Duff all but shouted.

"I presume so. Look, pal! We gotta get back, and fast! I've been frantic for you to call! My old man's working on the air lines —they're loaded. If he can't chivvy space for us, I have a pal in Mineola with a sweet, fast job, War surplus plane he bought. I told Eleanor to phone Higgins or Mr. McIntosh at once."

"I'll be over in fifteen minutes!" Duff said. "Whatever is happening, this time it looks as if we were going to prove something they'll believe!"

IV

The commercial air lines were sold out to the last seat for the holiday season. Scotty's father was unable to get reservations. So it was in the plane of Scotty's friend that they left an ice-coated airfield, shortly before midnight. The plane, as Scotty had promised, was fast. They made one stop for fuel, in Savannah, and swept south over the Everglades at dawn.

A red sky at morning, Duff reflected, wasn't a "sailor's warning" in Miami. Just a custom of the country. And he reflected— thinking of whatever came to mind in order to wear away the interminable hours of flight—that it was an advantage to be rich, like the Smythes. To have friends with planes, who'd make an emergency hop from New York to Miami just for fun. To be able to have a convertible you were too rushed to drive put aboard a freight car by the family chauffeur. Money meant things like that. But it didn't necessarily "corrupt character," as Duff's preacher father firmly believed and as Duff himself had vaguely assumed. There was nothing corrupt about Scotty Smythe's character.

Duff was dozing when the plane bounced, braked, turned and taxied. Its pilot looked back. "All out!"

Scotty said, "Thanks a million, Al! Go on over to my place—"

"Nope. Gotta get back. Check in here, and out."

"Wonderful thing of you to do."

"Rather fly than eat. Well—"

There was the slant of morning sunshine, the Florida smell of flowers and mold and warmth, the sleepy look of people around an airport at daybreak. They carried their own bags to a taxi and started for the Yates home.

When they reached the house no one appeared to be awake. Duff unlocked the front door. Scotty tiptoed in behind him.

From across the living room came the murmur of Mrs. Yates, "Who's there?"

Duff was smiling. "Me and Scotty Smythe. A pal of his flew us down."

A hand-knit bed jacket, blue as her eyes, covered her shoulders. Her golden hair was disheveled and as she sat up she reached for a comb. "I'm a sight! I'd dropped off—"

"I'll get you some coffee. Eleanor and the children asleep?" He waited for her nod and went to the kitchen.

When, after a few minutes, he came back with three cups of coffee on a tray, Mrs. Yates had fixed herself up. She smiled tiredly at him. "It's like you two boys to rush down here—"

"We were badly worried!"

"You needn't have been. Not to this extent! I was telling Scotty about it. When Charles found Harry Ellings, we were upset, naturally. He's been a member of the family for so long! He was so quiet—so nice! I don't suppose we'll ever find a boarder who will replace him." She sighed. "He'd been ill, of course. His heart just stopped. His funeral is arranged. Eleanor has been trying to get his friends together. There aren't many."

Duff couldn't hold back the question any longer, "What about the thing Eleanor said she found? Was it another box?"

Mrs. Yates' head shook. "The same one. That Mr. Higgins came last night. Poor Harry! He must have been a little off balance about money! He told you he'd sold his platinum, didn't he? Well, he hadn't. He did open a small savings account, but apparently he couldn't bear to part with that—metal. He just moved the box."

Duff tried to hide an enormous disappointment. "Oh."

Her smile was wistful. "So perhaps it was in your lily pond, Duff. Perhaps he fetched it out between the time you were taken to the hospital and the time the police and all the others searched. He'd put it up in the tree house."

"Tree house?"

"Didn't you ever notice it? In the woods, toward the house from that pit with water in it? Eleanor's father built it when she was little and it's stood all these years."

Duff remembered the weathered platform.

"It was a very sad Christmas for us," Mrs. Yates said. "And poor Eleanor was exhausted, anyhow."

Duff finished his coffee and signaled to Scotty. They went out on the lawn.

"It looks," Scotty said ruefully, "as if we've been hurrying ourselves and friends around without any need."

"I'm glad I'm here, though. They can stand help." Duff thought a moment. "Do you believe it's possible that all the rumpus could come from Ellings' merely moving that box around?"

"What about seeing the big man in New York?"

"Sure. That. I've got to tell the FBI that—and take a razz, probably. But if all the rest of it isn't coincidence—if it was just Ellings' platinum hoard—then two extra-tall men could be coincidence."

"Could be," Scotty agreed with grim sympathy.

"Only—" Duff shrugged and began again. "Only I had a feeling that there was something about that empty warehouse that

meant something. I got one of those spooky impressions. Whatever it was, I can't bring it up to view in my mind. Tried, off and
on, all the way down here."

Scotty removed his jacket; New York clothes were too warm
even for the early sunshine. He sat down on the grass. "You can be
certain, if what you suspected had been going on, that it would
take a big organization. Brains. Imagination. Planning. Either there
is a mob engaged in a very elaborate routine or else nothing was
happening. Harry was a hoarder whose heart failed, and a branch
hit you, period. The thing that gets me is, if any such thing
is going on, why hasn't anybody, anywhere, got onto any of it, so
the FBI or General Baines—would have some notion?"

"Maybe I've wasted a lot of your time, Scotty. And more than
a hundred borrowed bucks."

"Forget it!" Scotty grinned and got up; he stretched and
walked down the drive to the place where the sleeping cabdriver
had parked in the shade.

At ten, Duff presented himself in the office of the FBI.

Higgins listened, somewhat dazedly, to Duff's account of the
trip to New York. When Duff finished, the first thing he said was,
"Haven't you got any sense at all?"

The younger man flushed and stammered. What he finally got
out was, "Apparently not!"

Higgins summed up his view of the affair, "To start with, you
go on a wildgoose chase. If any customer of Miami-Dade was the
sort of drop you thought of, you had no chance of finding it out
just by making a call. Take a hundred men, working weeks—
short of some lucky break. So your scheme is dumb. The next
thing you do, just because you can pick locks, is break into what
you call a suspicious building. That was plain crazy! If you'd
run into what you suspected, you'd be lying on the bottom of the
Hudson now in a barrel of cement. Fortunately, the joint's
empty. But you saw a man—a whopping big man—come out.
You'd also once seen Ellings talking to some flagpole-sized guy.
There are many big men, Bogan, and unless a man stands beside

somebody whose height you know, how can you tell how big he is exactly?"

"If you'd seen him! Here in Florida. There on Broadway—"

"So, all right! He gets in a car. Drives off. You never notice its license! So there's no way on earth of tracing him. Even the FBI can't find a man in New York by merely knowing he's outsize."

Duff's face was a deep scarlet. "I know. I'm sorry. I'm at last beginning to think I was souped up over nothing."

For perhaps a minute, Higgins merely looked at Duff. When he spoke again, his brisk manner had left him. His tone was level and there was nothing sarcastic in it. "Look here, son. We've checked you from hell to breakfast. You're a solid citizen, from a solid family. Can you keep your mouth shut?"

The long series of disappointments and embarrassments suddenly, incredibly vanished. Duff said, "Yes."

Higgins rocked back in his chair. "I wouldn't tell you this if General Baines hadn't been brought into it by you lads. He thought you ought to know. One more crazy thing you did! A three-thousand-mile, cockeyed chase! And you go interview the Chief of Intelligence—through Smythe's pull! Okay! Look. There is something going on in the country, Bogan, that involves a group of agents we've only just got wind of. It could be—what you came in here claiming a while back. Getting A-bombs stashed here. It could be. It could be something less spectacular—some other sabotage system. Like making arrangements to start diseases, epidemics. We don't know. We haven't connected your boarder— your late boarder—to any of it. But something's happening!"

Duff said, in a near-whisper, "I see."

"One more thing. The head of this outfit may be just such a big guy as you keep describing. Six-ten, possibly even seven feet tall—and heavy, besides. He's been seen. He apparently carries orders or gives orders. The men he sees are apt to move on afterward. To turn up missing."

"Who is the guy?" Duff asked.

"You tell me!" Higgins was angry for an instant. "Three or four times, in various cities, our men have spotted him making a contact of some sort with somebody. Always at night—probably because he was so big. Conspicuous. So far, he's eluded us. The people he's spoken to have been checked. Nothing on any of them—just like Ellings. Loyal Americans. We don't care to pick up any of them at this stage of the game. No single one probably knows enough to mean much. Or to point to many others. So we wait. Watch. And, I don't mind telling you, we worry!"

Duff repeated, "I see."

The G-man rocked forward abruptly and resumed his ordinary crisp manner, "What I just said, you never heard. The Yates place may have been a freight station. It may have been a mere blind. Tell nobody what I told you. I presume, with Ellings dead, the Yates house is safe enough. It's now under FBI surveillance, in any case, and that's also under your hat. Go about your business perfectly normally. Keep your eyes open. If you notice anything, phone here at once. I'll give you a list of people to talk to, in case I'm out. But don't—absolutely don't—try to do anything! If you phone us, be sure you aren't being listened to. That's all." He wrote busily for a moment and handed a list of names to Duff. "Memorize it on your way home and then burn it. We don't want anybody to know that the FBI is interested in you or the Yateses! Understand?"

"I certainly do!"

Higgins rose lithely and held out his hand. "Fine! I might add this: We weren't such chumps as you've probably imagined. We didn't quite believe your tale, but lately we have been watching. Nothing and nobody suspicious has been near the Yates house since you left town. And look. If anything does come out of this, we'll be grateful. Tips from people like you have helped us before. The tips you gave—that we seemed to brush off—may be a big help now. See?"

Duff saw.

When he went out on the street, his steps had new confidence. A great deal of his life was unsatisfactory: the Yates family was sad and Eleanor was pretty sore at him, or had been, before his trip to New York; he was broke and in debt to Scotty. But he hadn't been such an utter fool as he had believed. Even though, he suddenly reflected, he couldn't tell Scotty about that. Not yet, anyway.

Eleanor had just risen when he returned. She was wearing a light green, very sheer negligee that was part of her new wardrobe. He thought she was pale and thinner.

"Deal old Duff! I'm so glad you're home!" She was suddenly embarrassed. "Oh, doggone it! When I called down, mother said you were out. I'm a fright! You can kiss me if you can stand it."

"I just can." He grinned and kissed her cheek.

She stepped back and surveyed him. "Come in the kitchen!" When they were there and the swinging door had shut, she went on, "Duff, what happened? Mother told me you'd gone right off to see Mr. Higgins."

He nodded.

"Where's Scotty?"

"Went back to his place. Tired. We flew down in a private plane. Didn't sleep any too well."

"Tell me all about it! Your trip! Why on earth didn't you tell us what you were doing?"

Duff walked over to the stove and poured coffee for himself. He felt as if he needed a dozen cups. He refilled her cup and added the two teaspoons of sugar she liked. "Look, Eleanor. What Scotty and I were doing was checking the trucking places. We didn't find anything important. And from now on the FBI is taking over— whatever there is to take over. I'm out of it. And I promised to quit talking about it to a living soul. And I'm dead tired."

She said, "Well, I'm half dead! This Queen business is exhausting." She sighed and then laughed. "All right. I won't ask. Positively eaten with curiosity, but a lady to the end. Anyway, I'm dreadfully glad you're back again!"

The phone rang. She ran to answer.

Outdoors, Charles and Marian came in view. They were carrying pails of warm water, mops, cloths and a box of soap powder.

Without ado, they began to wash the outside of a kitchen window, their dark heads bobbing in busy unison. Presently Charles called to Duff to lower the top section of the window, which he did. Duff remembered that Mrs. Yates had held a family council at which a list of necessary vacation chores had been drawn up. Charles and Marian were evidently working their way through the list. It wasn't much of a holiday, Duff thought, but they didn't appear to mind.

Eleanor stopped talking, started back, and the phone rang again. Her voice took up a new conversation with a pleasure he knew to be simulated.

Meanwhile, through the now-open window, Marian and Charles began to discuss their sister, somewhat for Duff's benefit.

"Phone again!" Charles said disgustedly. "Rings all day! You answer, it's for Eleanor. Your pals try to phone you. The line's busy!"

"A pain!" Marian agreed. "The doorbell rings, it's flowers for the Queen. Or it's a telegram for the Queen. Or clothes in big, fancy boxes. You walk out on the porch, some character is waiting for the Queen—maybe even with a mustache and in striped pants. Every time she skids past you, she's got on something new. Gifts from the local couturiers." She made deliberate hash of the French word. "You pick up a newspaper and what do you see? The Queen, wearing her million-dollar, photogenic smirk!"

Duff chuckled; he was back "at home" all right. And very glad to be.

The phone rang a third time and Eleanor came through the door. "You, Duff."

Through the window, Charles leered. "Amazing!"

"A gal," Eleanor went on, her eyes a little curious. "With a voice like a torch song."

From that, Duff knew who it was before he reached the phone. He wondered how Indigo had learned of his return. Probably she'd run into Scotty Smythe. He also wondered what she wanted—and found out. In fact, after elaborate refusals and protests, he eventually found that he was going to have dinner with her. When he hung up, he saw Eleanor in the doorway; she'd been listening; her expression was indignant, and not even humorously so.

" 'Indigo,' " she mimicked. "She's notorious!"

Duff was surprised, embarrassed, and slightly annoyed. "Is she? She's also darn good-looking!" He shrugged. "I can get the kids' dinner—and then go out—"

"The kids can get their own!" She seemed unduly disturbed. "But, no fooling, she isn't your type, Duff."

Her attitude somehow pleased him and yet made him feel obliged to seem resentful. "Brunette, you mean?"

"She's actually Russian. Her parents were."

"Wha-a-a-t?" He drew the word out skeptically. "Never met a more American dame in my life."

"How did you meet, by the way?"

"Scotty dug her up. She lives in the Gables."

"I know where she lives!" Eleanor retorted hotly. "Scotty would!"

"He told me," Duff responded with heat, "that she wanted to meet me. What do you mean, she's Russian?"

"She wants to meet any person in pants! Being tall, she likes tall ones, if available. White Russian, she was. Family came here to Miami during the revolution. Ask mother."

Mrs. Yates, whose door was open, could not avoid overhearing. She called, "Children! Quit squabbling! . . . Eleanor, Duff has a perfect right to go out with Miss Stacey if he wants." They heard the catch in her breath that indicated she was turning her wheel chair, and then she appeared in the doorway, smiling. "Stacey wasn't the real name, Duff. It was, originally, Stanoblovsky. They changed it to Stacey. Back in the old days, before Walter and I came to Florida. And I guess the local people were fairly proud of having them. They were nobility, till the Bolsheviks threw them out. Maybe in 1917 or around that time. They made money here in lots of different businesses, mostly in selling cars. Mr. Stacey, Indigo's father, had a big agency. Her uncle's still—"

"Indigo!" Eleanor repeated scathingly.

"I always thought it was a very attractive name. The girl's mother chose it because she claimed it was the prettiest word in English."

"That's what some broken-down Russian noble would think!" Eleanor turned angrily to Duff. "Go ahead! Fall for that towering twerp! Have a marvelous time with her! Everybody does!"

"Eleanor!" said Mrs. Yates reproachfully.

The phone rang again at that point. Eleanor seized it, and instantly her voice became honey-sweet. "Of course," she smiled. "I'll manage, somehow! I've got to appear at the Watercade at four. And then there's a cocktail party for me on the beach. And the ball. But I could spare a few minutes, maybe, between eight and nine."

Charles came through the swinging door. "Is anybody getting lunch? Or do we just starve to death quietly?"

After lunch, Duff appointed himself a task that the Yateses had avoided. Harry Ellings' room had been examined by the police, but his possessions had not been packed and the room had not, of course, been prepared for a new boarder. Nobody had even spoken about a new boarder. But the Yates budget meant that one would have to be found, and very soon.

Duff first packed Harry's clothes in his suitcases. Then he put Harry's letters, papers, pictures, books and personal knickknacks in cartons. These he moved to the barn and stored in its loft until they should learn what to do with them. The men who had gone through his effects and read every word of his correspondence had found no will. Mrs. Yates knew of none. He'd had, apparently, no relatives with whom he had kept in touch.

When all of Harry's belongings had been removed from the room, Duff commenced to clean. There was dust beneath the bed which showed that the police, though they might have looked there, had not moved it. Duff presumed, however, that they had probed every square inch of the mattress, and when he stripped it off he thought he could see, here and there, tiny openings that long pins might have made. He carried the mattress outdoors. He went back and commenced, with the Dutch-wife neatness on which his mother had insisted, to dust the bed frame.

It was on the inner edge of a steel angle iron that he found the capsule. He presumed it to be one of the large, pliant kind in which liquid vitamins and other medicines are commonly administered. Something Harry had used long ago, dropped and lost track of. It must have fallen between the mattress and the wall and rolled onto the bed frame. But the capsule wasn't dusty. And wetness showed at the ruptured edge. Also, Duff could see dents where teeth had recently come down on it to bite it open.

It was brown and egg-shaped. He sniffed. Its odor was medicinal, not identifiable. He decided that it was something Harry must have taken just before his death, something the police hadn't noticed the day before because they were looking for nothing of that sort. He went to his room to get an envelope and tipped in the capsule without touching it. He finished cleaning the room thoroughly, and then, for the sake of the family and their memories, he rearranged the furniture.

After that, with the envelope in his breast pocket, Duff went outdoors. He knew now that the Yates place was being watched and he thought he could locate the agent on duty. He walked clear around the large rectangle of roads by which the property was bounded.

At the back of the property three Negroes were busy in a languid, hot-afternoon fashion, clearing the overgrown edges of the paved street. There was no one else. He then decided the watcher was hidden in the woods, and entered them. The undergrowth was thick and he went cautiously, as he was very sensitive to poisonwood, which abounded in the hammock around the house. He passed the platform where Eleanor had found the box again. The G-men had it now. Platinum. He thought of that and shrugged.

He came, finally, to the sinkhole. It was about twenty feet one way and thirty the other, overhung by big trees, with a big tree blown across it, and deep enough to contain water. Such sinkholes, common in Dade County, were caused by the eating out of soft limestone by underground water. When a pocket was thus formed its roof eventually collapsed. Most such "glades" were dry, but some, like this one, had been deeply eroded and held pools of dark water.

Duff looked in. The water, gleaming in the shade, reached back out of sight beneath great, thirsty roots and an overhang of limestone encrusted with fossil shells. Around its rim were faint signs of visitation. Kids came there occasionally—though forbidden by their parents—to catch minnows in traps or just to throw stones for the sake of the splash. The water was too shallow for drowning, but a person could have a nasty fall into it.

Looking down, Duff remembered the night he'd seen one of the mysterious boxes—if there had ever been "one" among many—in his own homemade lily pool. That thought led to another: the sinkhole reached back out of sight around its rim, and he was wearing old clothes. He could go back to the house for a rope or use a tree. He decided on a tree and found a suitable one nearby, a small palm uprooted by the October blow. He scrambled down it and landed thigh-deep, in warm water.

The bottom was mucky. Overhead was an oval of blue sky. Around him, the sides of the hole curved back and the water glinted in gloom. Sometimes, he recalled, there were alligators in these sinks. He saw none. He walked around the edges, peering into the recesses, stirring up mud.

Presently he came to an area, hidden from above by the overhang, which had been visited by somebody else. Perhaps by several people. And perhaps often. It was a kind of roofed room, open toward the pit; its muddy floor emerged as a soft bank. The bank showed many signs of feet—old markings and some probably not very old. There were flat marks, too, where boards had evidently sunk down into the mucky sediment. One or two boards were visible now, and he located another with his foot, then others. They'd settled beneath the surface of the ooze.

The footprints weren't plain, except for one, which he studied.

It was the mark of the side of a man's shoe. The man evidently had fallen on the tarlike stuff. But his leg, curiously enough, had left no print. Duff decided that the man must have turned his ankle to make such a mark.

He wondered if the FBI had investigated the sinkhole. Doubtless they had; probably the footprints and boards were signs of FBI scrutiny, though there were other possibilities. The little fish in the pool were sought by kids and also by men; they made excellent bait. Some angler might have set minnow traps there from time to time, using boards to stand on. Tramps might have found shelter in the half cave. High-school boys might have used it as a place for a gang meeting or an initiation. It was hidden and pretty far from the Yates house.

Wet to the waist, he shinnied up the tree again. He hadn't yet found the watching G-man that Higgins had said would always be near. He finished a search of the hammock without luck, returned to the house, took the capsule from his pocket, washed himself outdoors with a hose, and afterward changed his clothes.

Then he went up to the bus line, rode into the Gables and phoned Higgins from a booth in a drugstore. The G-man didn't seem much interested in the capsule, but he told Duff to leave it with the druggist to be picked up. Duff went home to help with supper for the kids.

Indigo came for him in her car after dark. When they drove down Flagler Street together, on the way to Miami Beach, the crowds, the lights, the Christmas decorations seemed out of key with his life and his mood and his fatigue.

"It's beautiful!" Indigo kept pointing to everything. And she said, "I'm so glad you're back! I was lonesome for you."

He watched her drive, looked at her sleek, dark desirableness, breathed the perfume she wore and felt sure it was called Damnation or something of the sort.

He grinned. "Glad to be back! I was going kind of stale. I'm tired, besides."

"For being tired, the extra cocktail is recommended."

"Probably go straight to my head."

"The very effect I had in mind."

Duff laughed. "Why, Indigo? How come?"

Her lucent, dark eyes flashed briefly. "Why? Who can say why? I saw you on the campus one day. And again at a football game one night. I asked people who you were. Why?" She shrugged as she turned the car. "When you get a certain kind of feeling you shouldn't ask why."

They dined and sat afterward in a moonlit patio on the edge of the sea. At midnight they drove back to her house and kissed good night. Duff, for a reason he couldn't quite name, refused to go in to have a nightcap, and went home by bus because his refusal angered her. They quarreled on the doorstep, and she went in, finally, slamming the door in his face.

During that space of time the capsule left in a drugstore made a journey to the FBI in Miami and thence to a laboratory. About two o'clock in the morning, when Duff was in bed, but unable to sleep, owing to alternate waves of self-approval and self-castigation over his rather alarmed flight from Miss Indigo Stacey, Higgins, who was sound asleep at home, reached from his bed to snatch up a ringing phone.

"Yeah?"

"This is Ed Waite, at the lab. Sorry to wake you."

"Okay. What?"

"That capsule. Anybody take the stuff?"

"Probably." The G-man was wide awake, then.

"Person that did is dead, if so."

Higgins evaded the implied question. "What was it?"

"Aconitine. Enough to kill a few horses."

"How would the person die?"

"Like heart failure," Ed said. "And you couldn't find the stuff by autops. It combines chemically with substances in the body and disappears."

"I see. Thanks." Higgins was about to hang up.

"One other thing, Hig. I don't think that dose was made in U.S.A."

"No? Why?"

"Because I never heard of anything like it. Aconitine isn't used to put animals out of misery—nothing like that. And the capsule wasn't any kind—chemically speaking—manufactured here. Different base. The gelatin part, I mean. Another thing: It isn't a little item anybody would whip up to poison somebody else."

"No?" Higgins sounded skeptical. "Why?"

"You couldn't feed it secretly to anybody. Too big. They'd see it or else feel it and not swallow it. And you wouldn't want to try to bust it over somebody's soup. Skin's tough. It would splash and spurt all around."

"I see. Well, that's good work, Ed."

"Only thing it could be, Hig, I figure, is something I've only read about."

"What's that?"

"Well, if you were a foreign agent in somebody else's country, for instance, and you thought you might be nabbed at any point and you wanted to be sure you'd never talk, you'd carry around something about like that. Taped to you someplace. In a crisis, you could pop it in your mouth, bite, swallow—and quick curtains."

Higgins said, "Thanks, Ed. Keep it to yourself."

"Right."

When Duff wakened, it was after ten. He leaped guiltily out of bed and took a shower. Then he tiptoed downstairs and learned from Mrs. Yates that the precaution hadn't been wasted: Eleanor was still sleeping.

"A whole bunch of people drove her home last night around three," she said. "This being Queen is bad for girls, Duff. I thought I'd brought up Eleanor so nothing in the world could turn her head. But with everybody in the city at her feet—with dates every second and things to do and all the clothes and the photographs! I'd hate it if—"

"If what, Mrs. Yates?"

"Oh, if she got glamour-struck. Thought she could get in movies. Anything like that. Eleanor's actually serious—and a simple person. A homebody. If she got yearning to be rich and famous and all that, she could make a wrong marriage! Even if she didn't try Hollywood."

"I wouldn't worry too much. She's levelheaded. And I don't believe it hurts a girl to be Cinderella once in a lifetime. Something to remember."

"If she doesn't develop a prince complex! Yes."

The doorbell rang and Duff answered it.

Higgins was standing there, smiling. "Hi, Bogan."

Duff opened the screen door. "Come out in the kitchen, will you? I just got up."

In the kitchen, Mr. Higgins told Duff briefly about the capsule.

"You see," he concluded, "how we can all go haywire. My men went through his things with the police. Never looked under the bed—which is the first thing an old maid would do. Never looked, I mean, beyond seeing nothing big was there. Thought I'd have a squint, myself."

Duff bit toast he had made. He shook his head. "Too late. I cleaned the place yesterday. You think, then, that Harry—"

Higgins exhaled slowly. "Knocked himself off. Sure. They do. The heat was on him. His people"—Higgins cursed softly—"whoever they may be, were probably sore at him because you started uncovering Harry's business. I think when Harry went to Baltimore he was trying to contact somebody. We had men on him the whole time."

"You did!"

Higgins' eyes smiled, but not his lips. "This isn't any amateur outfit, Bogan! Yes. But he never made a contact—not that our men saw, anyhow. He did consult doctors. He said he was sick —and I guess he was. Sick from fear. The doctors couldn't treat that. So he came back here and maybe got the word. Or knew his number was up because they didn't get to him in Baltimore. So he took that thing—and probably coughed the skin of it out as he died."

"That means," Duff said gravely, "Harry knew what he was doing the whole time."

Again the G-man swore. "It means that, whatever the hell they are trying to do! By now, I'd give a leg to know. A life, I guess! I'll take a fast gander at the room, even though you did clean it up."

Duff nodded. "Okay. Incidentally, I tried to find your agents around here yesterday. They must have been taking a day off."

Higgins stared. Then he laughed. "You thought you could deliver the capsule to my men, hunh? They were here, just the same, son. As I said they'd be."

"But there wasn't a soul! Except some colored road workers!" Duff, seeing the G-man's look, broke off and blushed. "Oh!" He joined ruefully in Higgins' chuckle. "I did find one thing, though. There's a sinkhole"—he pointed out the window—"beyond the banyan and those gumbo-limbo trees."

Higgins said he'd have it looked over. Perhaps it had been; Duff couldn't tell from the G-man's response. Higgins went upstairs and returned to the kitchen shortly. He said to Duff, who was eating a home-grown banana and drinking coffee, "Brother, you sure would make some girl a wonderful wife! When you clean, you clean!"

Duff walked down the drive with him. "Thought you didn't want any—people to know you were still interested in this place?"

Higgins nodded. "I checked with my road crew before this call. If anybody peculiar had showed up, I'd have got a signal and you'd have had to sneak me out."

"There's another item. Harry's funeral. That's tomorrow. Since we know now what Harry was, perhaps the family—"

The G-man shook his head. "No. They're going?"

"They intend to. Even Eleanor plans to cut some of her schedule."

"Lovely girl," Higgins said absently. "No, Bogan. Things have to keep seeming normal around here. We'll have a man at the services, of course. There won't be many people. Some of his old letter-carrier pals. A few from the garage. Some of the cronies he used to fish and spot-cast with. You and the kids and the missus, you go. Don't tell 'em Harry was a spy."

The word, even then, shocked Duff. "A funny person to be one."

Higgins said grimly, "That's the worst thing about it! About those—those— Hell! No word for 'em. They reach the insides of patient, peaceful, law-abiding guys like Ellings! Rot out their hearts! And yet leave their outside just like always. You see some good-humored, industrious chap. Courteous, helpful, loves kids, sticks around home. Maybe, long ago, he was slighted or hurt or made to feel inferior. Something—something that switched him over to that crooked, rotten, enemy line! So he goes overboard. He keeps on looking like a good citizen. But in his head, night and day, he's scheming to kill or enslave every man and woman and kid in the country! You know, Bogan, it's the ability to do that to people that frightens me more than all the war and defeat and national uproar and trouble put together. It gets me!" He tried for a better phrase. "I hate it!"

Duff said, almost whispered, "Yeah. Me too."

Higgins doubled his fist, stared at it, unclenched it. "Shooting it out with gangs. That was easy! Tagging tax violators. That's just work! But finding out that people who do things you've been led to admire are just rotten, low, filthy enemies! Traitors! It makes a man sick! It scares a man!" He nodded curtly and walked away toward the road.

Duff went over to the campus that afternoon. He had left some notes in a laboratory locker, he explained to Mrs. Yates. He had decided to go over them during the holidays and to finish a thesis on certain aspects of electromagnetic fields and radiant particles. He smiled when she answered him by making a funny face; she didn't know what he meant.

Even to himself, Duff did not quite admit, until he walked up to the bungalow, that he was really going to Coral Gables to try to call on Indigo. He felt ashamed of running away from her. He also felt more than a little intrigued by her avowed passion for him; it was an unprecedented experience and Duff, after all, was a young man. He had always liked girls, but he'd never really had a girl of his own. Any other young man, undergraduate or graduate student, or any young instructor, for that matter, would almost surely have accepted Indigo's passion with enthusiasm; even with a certain smugness. The fact that he was wary of her made Duff wonder if, perhaps, when the right girl came along, he wouldn't know how to behave. In that case, he'd wind up a bachelor.

On account of such sensations and speculations, it seemed very necessary to Duff to make amends for refusing her offer, on the evening before, of a nightcap—a possible euphemism for something more personal and disturbing than alcohol, which had scared him away.

There was a car parked in front of Indigo's pretty, modernistic bungalow. Her own car was in the garage and the sedan of the girl with whom she lived was not there. Duff shied at the fact of a caller and then decided that it might be better, diplomatically, to see her first in the presence of others. So he stepped up to the front door and dropped the chrome knocker. Nobody answered. That surprised him because he had heard voices inside. He knocked again, loudly, but there was no response.

So she did have a visitor, but she didn't want to be disturbed. Duff reflected gloomily that a girl like Indigo could easily find a thousand admirers and doubtless would brush one off in a hurry for behaving as he had. He walked slowly away. *Great swain, I am,* he thought. *Casanova and Don Juan rolled into one.* He reminded himself never to tell anybody of his behavior and its swift rebuff.

He spent two desultory hours in the lab and went back to the Yates house with a crowd of bus riders who held a general discussion on the prospects of a University of Miami victory in the Orange Bowl game. It was only days away. *And thank the Lord for that,* he thought. Perhaps afterward Eleanor would return to normal.

It was dark when he reached home. Dark—and Mrs. Yates was fretting. "I wish this business was over, Duff. It's nearly six. And Eleanor's due at a banquet at seven. And she has to change, but she's not home yet. I know it's not her fault that she gets delayed—"

Charles was setting the table. Marian was cooking. Duff inspected the contents of pots and pans on the oil stove and told Marian—making her happy by doing so—that the guy who won her would have not a good cook, but a real chef.

He took his notes upstairs, looked through them and straightened up the room. He heard Charles calling numbers, asking for his sister and getting unsatisfactory replies, for he kept dialing. Duff lay down on his bed and read a chapter on nuclear engineering.

He was interrupted by the boy's voice, coming worriedly up the stairway, "Hey! Duff! Eleanor never did get to the Fashion Parade today! I just found out!"

He closed the book, tossed it on his table and clattered downstairs. Mrs. Yates had wheeled herself into the living room. Her anxiety had visibly increased. "Charley just reached someone who was there, Duff. They waited for Eleanor till half past four. They tried to call here, but the line was busy all the time. No wonder. The calls that come in. So they went ahead without her."

Duff said, "Probably got her dates mixed. Wouldn't be surprising! She had some shenanigan at Fort Lauderdale for tomorrow. Bet she went there by mistake. Probably come in, any minute."

"It isn't like her," Mrs. Yates insisted.

Duff grinned rather soberly. "She isn't herself, these days."

"She wandered off with somebody," Mrs. Yates went on. "I

didn't see who. I'd wheeled into the kitchen to block a sweater, and she'd changed to that gorgeous brown dress she was to wear at the Fashion Parade today. She didn't take the car and I don't know who was to call for her. Scotty came by and they talked a while, and then he drove away and I had a glimpse of her standing out by the banyan. After that, somebody must have picked her up."

Marian, who had gone into the stair hall, now called, "She certainly is getting absent-minded! She didn't even take along the hat that goes with the new brown rig!" Marian came, then, carrying a hat the color of Eleanor's eyes, with canary-yellow trimming.

It was not until then that Duff became alarmed. But alarm, when it appeared, was instant and formidable. She wouldn't go without the hat. She was orderly. She was responsible. She had a good memory. And lately, she'd been almost vain; so much attention would have made anybody conscious of beauty. It was hard to imagine that Eleanor would barge away when somebody arrived to pick her up—without a hat that, obviously, was a main part of a planned costume for a very important social event.

As he felt ice inside himself, Duff instantly dissembled. "Maybe Scotty knows about it."

He went to the phone and dialed. He got Scotty's roommate and, presently, Scotty himself.

"Hi, you phony Sherlock!" Scotty said.

Duff frowned at the greeting and then realized that, as far as Scotty knew, his idea about the boxes had been mistaken and their trip to New York a blunder. He grinned tensely and asked about Eleanor.

"No," young Smythe answered, "I didn't see the Queen depart. I had a little colloquy with her around three, and I blew. I left her among the Yates trees and shrubs."

Duff thanked him. He tried two members of the Orange Bowl Committee without success. He phoned the people who were sponsoring the banquet and asked if they had heard anything from Eleanor.

They hadn't. The family tried some of Eleanor's closest girl friends. Nobody knew anything about her.

"We're probably going bats for nothing," Duff said. "After all, she was terribly balled up with dates. Let's eat."

Eight o'clock.

No sign of Eleanor. Duff called a number Higgins had given him, and a sharp voice said, "Rolfe, here."

"My name is Allan Bogan. I live at the Yates house—"

"Right. Where you calling from?"

"There."

"Better use another phone."

"No. The thing is, Eleanor Yates has disappeared. I mean, she was due home over two hours ago—been missing since around four."

"Right. We'll check."

Duff hung up, wild-eyed.

"Who was that? The police?"

Duff nodded. "Sort of."

Mrs. Yates began to cry a little.

Duff nervously walked out on the porch. If they had seized her—if they had taken her away—who were "they"? Why had they done any such thing? Where had they taken her?

There could be a reason. Weeks before, unsatisfied by his effort to convince the FBI that something was happening, she had gone to see Higgins without telling him. Since his return from New York, Duff hadn't exchanged confidences with Eleanor or anyone else. Higgins had forbidden that. It was possible that Eleanor had found out something so final, so telling, that she'd been— What?

"They" wouldn't mind killing a girl. "They," perhaps, were working to kill millions of people. You couldn't even think, rationally, of what "they" might be planning.

Duff paced back and forth on the porch. It was a warm evening, but not so warm as to explain the sweat that burst on his brow, soaked his shirt. Only fear could explain that.

V

Four night-blooming-jasmine bushes which Duff had raised from cuttings blossomed along the edge of the veranda. Their perfume, so heady that some people cannot bear it, saturated the darkness and drifted downwind, exotic and sweet. When Duff noticed it, his attention came only in the form of a memory, a memory that Eleanor was very fond of jasmine. He tried to tell himself it was insane to imagine that, simply because she was missing, Eleanor had been kidnaped and perhaps killed by people whose very existence was shadowy.

He paced the porch, wondering what else might have happened to her, what less-horrifying thing. She had last been seen in the big yard, by Scotty and her mother, over near the banyan. He stood at the porch rail and looked at the black arcades beneath the trunks of the great tree. Had somebody been concealed there?

Suddenly, as if he had been told, Duff realized what had happened: Eleanor hadn't previously known anything that had made her freedom or her existence a danger to "them." What had happened was that she had heard something from the lawn, down near the banyan.

He raced through the house, startling Mrs. Yates and the two children. "Be right back! Ten—fifteen minutes!"

He picked up the flashlight. In the barn, he shouldered a ladder.

Charles yelled, "Need me?"

"No, Charley! Stay with your mother."

It was hard work moving through the jungle with the ladder. Time and again it hooked over trees and fouled up on boughs or vines so that he had to use his light, stop and maneuver. When, finally, he reached the sinkhole, he was panting heavily. He stood there, afraid to swing the beam of the electric torch. He shut his jaws and aimed the light down and around the edges. He didn't see what he feared he would: a body. A girl's body in a brown dress.

The ladder splashed in the water. It was, he noticed, abnormally muddy. Plenty of time to settle since he had roiled it. In the water, he plunged for balance as his feet settled uncertainly. His torch circled the recesses. All he saw was water, rock and innumerable roots. A big moth flew through the light beam. He pushed forward under the rocky roof of the edge.

There were fresh tracks. He was sure of that. He was surer still when he could no longer find the one print that had held his attention, the mark of the side of a shoe on a foot that seemed legless. "They" had been in the pit that afternoon, taking the boxes away. But how had they kept from being seen?

Eleanor, because she had gone over to the banyan, must have heard a sound in the woods and gone to look. In daylight he could probably find the marks of her heels. She had gone to look. And that was that.

Where was she now? Alive? A prisoner? He groaned and only the walls answered sepulchrally. His flashlight fell sharply on the stones and threw sharp shadows. The recess was deeper than he'd thought. He waded back. It seemed to turn at a projecting wall. Following the turn, Duff found a new feature of the sinkhole. An arch of limestone, shoulder-high, spanned some ten feet of water. He leaned and shone his light along its surface. The tunnel, half air and half water, led into the distance in a meandering line as far as he could see.

Some hundreds of yards away in that direction was the overgrown real-estate development where Harry Ellings had had his furtive rendezvous with the gigantic man. And beyond those cracked sidewalks, cabbage palms and broken lampposts was the old rock pit, now used as a dump.

Sinkholes, if they held water, were sometimes connected, underground, with others. This one could communicate with the water in the rock pit. In that case, the value of the Yates land to anyone wishing to store desperate cargo was self-evident. Such cargo could be unloaded at night in the old quarry and dragged through this tunnel to the place where he stood. It could then be buried in the soft ooze. And no one watching the house or its surrounding grove of jungle trees would see a sign of coming and going. Duff peered again. Surely the boxes went out here that afternoon. Perhaps Eleanor also—

He started into the opening and changed his mind. The tunnel might go to the quarry. It might be a blind pocket. It might have a hundred forks and turns; he could get lost underground. It was not sensible, not even sane, to explore alone. Taking gasps of air, he yelled "Eleanor!" repeatedly. Nothing came back but echoes.

He left the pit and raced toward the house. As he rounded the banyan tree he heard a distant siren.

Mrs. Yates saw him enter and paled. "You're wet!"

"I'm all right. I was looking in that rock pit in the woods. Nothing. Don't worry so, mother!"

He changed to dry clothes as rapidly as he could. When he came down, Higgins, with two men in business suits whom he'd never seen and two cops, had just come in. Duff jerked his head at the FBI man and they went to the kitchen, where he told Higgins about the sinkhole.

The men, soaking wet, yelling in the low, rocky passages, found a route to the quarry. They found ample signs that men had used it—often and for a long time. They found evidence that vehicles had driven up to the quarry at a point different from the one used by dump trucks. But no trace of Eleanor.

Near midnight Higgins sat with Duff in the kitchen. Both were muddy to the waist. But Higgins had been on the telephone for twenty minutes. He gulped coffee now and wiped a sticky forehead with a sodden handkerchief.

"Nothing!" he said to Duff. "No lead! Nothing new on the whole proposition. What we've got to do is go over it."

"Go over it!" Duff groaned. "What do you think I've been doing since it started?"

Higgins ignored that. "I've got every man we have looking into everything they can think of! Mac—my chief—will be here soon. Reports will come in here. Now! Let's go back to that day when you went upstairs to clean the rooms and you noticed Ellings' closet was locked and you decided to pick the lock. You talk. I'll ask questions. Start in!"

Duff stared at the other man, wondering if this was a useful effort or merely a kindly attempt to keep his mind from the final happening. It didn't matter. Either way, it was better than just being silent and frantic.

Higgins and he covered every detail. McIntosh came and stayed a while, talked on the phone, issued orders, tried to comfort Mrs. Yates and Marian and Charles, and left.

Higgins and Duff talked on, without effect. Sometime after three in the morning, Higgins stopped alternately sitting and pacing. "Bogan," he said, "I know you can't sleep. But I've got to. For me, it's a job."

"I understand that."

"So I'm starting home. If you hit on anything else, let me know. If we can think of another thing for you to do, we'll call you. This is rugged."

Marian was asleep in a chair in the living room. Charles was asleep on the cot in his mother's room. And Mrs. Yates didn't say a word when he looked in. He went upstairs. After a while he lay down. Through his mind rushed the events he had just so painstakingly discussed with the FBI man. Little by little, in the dark, they ran less swiftly. And after a time, Duff sat up, rubbing his hair, putting his feet on the floor. He had told himself, with a different mental tone, that no feverish attempt such as he was making could accomplish a thing. He reminded himself that he was a scientist, capable of concentration, attention, analysis.

What I ought to do, he thought, *is take it like mathematics. Check back. Look for discrepancies. Things not included. Things*

not explained. Mistakes. Also, I should extrapolate. Imagine. He
felt more detached, less frantic.

There were several elements not satisfactorily accounted for.
Little things. Why, for example, had the warehouse in New York
been empty? And what had there been about it that had impressed
him as meaningful, but that he had never called to consciousness?

He had the answer to that, abruptly. The floor of that vast
building had glittered faintly with the micalike brilliance of such
broken stone as is excavated in Manhattan. He'd thought of it
as coming in from the streets on truck wheels. Actually, it could
have come from excavating in the building. And they wouldn't
have wanted things stored there if they had wanted to dig. Before
this instant, Duff realized, he had conceived of an assembled
A-bomb as something in a huge case or a truck above ground.
Why not bury it? The warehouse wasn't far from Wall Street. An
A-bomb going off there, even underground, would destroy the
financial heart of New York City, of America.

That was one thing. He could tell Higgins to have them tear
up the floor of the place. Then, perhaps, they'd get tangible—and
terrifying—evidence. That idea, a fresh idea, one in which he had
confidence, excited him; his mind raced anew. But he saw the
error of that. He had to think, not feel.

The second idea he evolved had to do with Harry Ellings'
history. It was odd, in a way. He'd been a letter carrier. Developed
varicosis—he had said. He limped a little and complained of leg
pains. True. That could have been put on. Why? Because, Duff
reasoned, a bad leg might have been a first step in training for a
new job. If Harry had belonged for years to a secret underground,
the organization might have wanted him to be in a trucking company, where freight could be forwarded secretly.

It would be easier, Duff thought, and a great deal safer, to
retrain an established underground member than to try to persuade some unknown mechanic to turn to treason. So, perhaps,
Harry had feigned the bad leg, learned to be a mechanic and moved
into Miami-Dade Terminal Trucking Company as part of a plan.

That way Harry could retain his mask of ordinariness. The idea was strengthened, if not corroborated, by the existence of the quarry, the sinkhole and the connecting tunnel, and by Harry's meeting with the huge man near the quarry.

That pattern, while logical, seemed not to lead any further toward Eleanor. It took Duff more than an hour—an hour of slow, relaxed new thought. He had been turning over in his mind all he knew about the man seven feet tall. He had actually seen the man twice: one evening in New York, one night with Harry Ellings. The FBI also had reports on the man. Two different agents, on two different nights, had seen the man enter a place. But not come out. They'd lost him, both nights.

Why nights? Did he come out only at night, because of his great stature, as Higgins evidently believed? Or could it be that there was something about his immense size which wouldn't look natural in daylight? Could size be a kind of trick? Itself a ruse? The figure, menacing, looming, weird, had obviously perturbed even the sanguine G-men. Was that intentional?

Could a man, Duff asked himself, who was, say, Duff's own height—two and a half inches over six feet—add the balance? Special shoes, such as many very short men wore to increase their apparent height, would help. He might wear a wig, too, that increased the size of his head. But the man had been taller even than that, Duff thought. Stilts would do it—little stilts.

Duff remembered the imprint in the mud. A shoe, laced over a wooden form from which a steel bar rose to a second shoe, would do it. The steel bar wouldn't have to be very long, either. Nine or ten inches. And if a man so equipped fell over, as he might in a mucky place, the side of his shoe would be printed in the mud, and there would be no ankle for ten inches above it, but only a steel rod which mightn't touch the mud at all. Then there would be left exactly such a print as Duff had seen in the mudbank.

The possible meaning of that, in turn, was clear. He and the FBI had been searching for a giant. But the man they wanted, actually, was perhaps no taller than Duff. Size, and especially vast size, is the most conspicuous of all human characteristics. If a veritable giant was seen entering a building and then even a dozen merely tall men came out, no one would connect the first man with the others.

Almost, then, Duff phoned Higgins. But Higgins was sleeping, and Higgins needed sleep. In a couple more hours he would telephone the G-man. Meanwhile, he would go on thinking. There might be still more that could be dredged up and made to mean something other than what he had supposed, until then.

He tore open a new package of cigarettes, saw how his hand shook and forced himself to be calm again. By and by, it grew faintly light. He realized he had dozed a little when the thwack of the morning paper on the porch made him start. He went downstairs in stocking feet. It was light enough by then to read the headlines:

Orange Bowl Queen Vanishes

Police Search for Missing Eleanor
Yates
Kidnaping Feared
Crank Suspected

Duff couldn't wait any longer. He dialed Higgins' number, got a sleepy "Yeah?" and began to talk excitedly. Fifteen minutes later he hung up. He knew that he was close to tears, but only when he heard himself sniffle did he realize that fatigue, humiliation and a sense of incompetence had actually brought tears into his eyes.

About the particles on the warehouse floor, Higgins had said, "Hunh! Interesting! I'll pass it on to New York."

But about the idea that Harry Ellings' entire life had been planned, the G-man was brief and cutting, "Good Lord! We've assumed it was that way for weeks!"

A similar response greeted his theory about the huge man.

"Did that just occur to you? We've been on the lookout for any-body of any size for a hell of a while!"

Duff said wretchedly, "I shouldn't have phoned."

"Oh, sure. That warehouse hunch is solid. And my alarm will let go in less than an hour, anyhow."

Nevertheless, Duff felt disappointed; he felt as he had ever since the beginning, foolish. The FBI and the police knew. They could and did think and act. And he chimed in afterward with his half-baked hunches. Bitterly, he started toward the porch, but he heard Mrs. Yates crying softly, and he went in to try to comfort her.

Cars surrounded the Yates home, parked in the drive and on the lawns—police cars, press and radio cars, Orange Bowl officials' cars and the cars of friends, neighbors, curious strangers. They had accumulated all day.

Mrs. Yates and Duff were obliged to keep telling people that they had no idea where Eleanor might have gone, with whom or whether she could have been kidnaped. Because of the numbers of people, the shock and the confusion, they had sent Marian and Charles to stay with friends.

Some time after lunch Duff observed that Mrs. Yates was not strong enough to bear both her anxiety and the thronging people. He arranged with the police to get her moved to the home of the friend who had already taken in the youngsters. The police saw to it that neither the reporters nor the merely curious followed the Yates station wagon, and when Duff returned to the house, the crowd was thinning.

Toward late afternoon he was alone. As far as he knew, not even the police or the FBI were keeping watch. The Yates place had served its final purpose where Ellings' colleagues were con-cerned. And if Eleanor should happen to come back home some-how, he was there. He believed she was dead. So, he was sure, did the FBI. But Duff knew he would not give up hope until it was certain.

He went upstairs and lay down exhaustedly. By and by he

realized it was the afternoon of Harry's funeral. They had all forgotten. No matter. He slept because a time comes when no one,
whatever his anxiety, can stay awake longer. When he woke up,
the sun was setting. He realized he had been dreaming about the
events of the past weeks and remembered vaguely a jumble of faces,
including the face of Indigo Stacey. He lay thinking about her, and
it occurred to him that she represented another of the anomalies
he'd sought the night before. Scotty had once said that Indigo
had wanted to meet Duff even before their first date. Duff wondered
why, as he had wondered at other times. He wasn't the type for
whom glamour girls fell on sight. Still, Indigo wasn't an ordinary
glamour girl. A White Russian—or at least her parents were that.

He thought now about their history. Had Indigo's father and
her father's brother necessarily been loyal to the Czar? Necessarily fled the Bolshevik revolution? Was it possible that a con-
spiracy against America could have been forming back in the
days of Lenin and Trotsky? Could Indigo Stacey have had a special
reason, related to everything else, for wanting to meet him? Had
her "large passion" been an unsuccessful attempt to find out what
he knew? Who—and where—was her uncle? Apparently, according to Mrs. Yates, her now-deceased father and her uncle had become successful businessmen.

He phoned the house where the Yateses were staying. He said
there was no news, but that he would like to ask Mrs. Yates a
question. Her answers were tremulous.

"Uncle?" she repeated perplexedly. "Why, no, Duff. He didn't
like Stacey for a name. He's Stanton—a very important person in
Miami. On directorates and owns businesses. As a matter of fact,
he is a director of the trucking company Harry used to work
for."

The telephone directory listed an Ivan L. Stanton, 4300 River
Vista Drive, Miami Beach.

Duff walked about in the darkening house. He thought of
calling Higgins again and cast the thought aside. Stanton was too
well known to be made a sudden object of suspicion. A connection

between a young lady's interest in a graduate student and the possibility that a leading businessman was also a criminal syndicalist would probably make Higgins believe Duff had lost the last of his senses. Besides, Eleanor would hardly be anywhere near the Stanton place, even if Stanton was connected with her disappearance and even if she was still alive. An immense underground organization could take the girl to any of a hundred places.

And in that moment Duff had the last of his new ideas. He and the FBI had assumed they were dealing with many members of a secret society—scores, perhaps hundreds. That very assumption had made Higgins marvel that no trace of such a group had been uncovered.

Why, Duff abruptly asked himself, would it take many people? A few could accomplish all that Duff suspected had been done, if they had time enough. At least one would have to be an engineer. But the fewer they were, the better their chance of undiscovered activity. And if one of them owned part of a trucking concern—

Duff went to the barn garage. He backed out the Yates station wagon. There was nothing more he could do at the Yates house. The theory on which he was operating was tenuous, all but incredible, yet he had no other.

Before driving away, he had a protective impulse. He returned to the house and wrote a note which he left on the dining-room table.

Flagler Street was still Yuletide-gaudy in the twilight. Its red and green decorations made a gay tent. When he stopped for a traffic light, a newsboy intoned, "No trace of missing Bowl Queen! Read all about it!" He drove on. Down Biscayne Boulevard, across the Causeway.

The inland passage gleamed with lights from big houses and the lights of Christmas trees. Many homes were strung with colored lights and many palms wore crowns of lights. Boats were tied up at private wharves—speedboats, luxury fishing cruisers, houseboats, yachts. He passed No. 4300, a Spanish residence set back from the street, with a seagoing yacht of its own, brightly lighted trees in its yard and a wall all around.

Duff turned into a side street and went back on foot, furtively. There were no pedestrians. For a moment, as he peered around the ornamental coral entrance posts at the big house, Duff had a feeling of hopelessness. The estate looked civilized, secure, and so remote from what tormented him that Duff considered turning back. Then, in the first real confirmation of his frantic weeks, he saw it: a little square of whiteness, of almost luminous whiteness, in the shadow. He made as sure as he could that he was not seen, crossed the drive and picked up a woman's folded handkerchief, not dropped on the walk, but tossed, it seemed, toward the entrance post. His fingers shook as he saw the initials: E. Y.

He found a rubber tree that overhung the wall and, after a look in each direction, disappeared in its foliage. He dropped onto the lawn. Moving from bush to bush, he reached the big house.

The lawn lights intensified the shadows. As long as he didn't expose himself to the red, green, blue and yellow shimmer, they would dazzle anyone looking out of the windows. Duff moved along the wall behind thick crotons.

There were four men in the library, drinking cocktails. Dinner guests, Duff imagined. No women. There were three or four servants in the kitchen and pantries; they, also, were men. At the back of the house, a concrete driveway and a paving-stone walk led to the dock where the yacht was moored. Two decks, about eighty feet long. A motor was running somewhere aboard her; she showed lights.

Duff barely managed to hide himself in time when a rear door opened and a man carried a carton of supplies to the ship. The man wore a white coat and Duff heard him speak to someone on board.

"Last load?"

"Yeah."

The yacht—he couldn't see her name—was going to sail soon. He tiptoed into the darkness of overhanging vegetation; his eyes searched the nearby grass and shrubs and planks swiftly, not very expectantly, but with care. When he saw at the base of a tree a second square like the one now in his pocket, he smiled, slightly, grimly. Perhaps she had struggled to cover what she had done; perhaps she'd managed it secretively. But she'd left two tiny markers.

He didn't risk retrieving the second one; he was already on the pier, near the yacht. Instead, he walked along the sea wall a short distance, stepped over a short stretch of water and clambered aboard the boat near the bow. He could hear men talking in one of the cabins, aft; a smell of cooking came from the galley. He hid behind a lifeboat lashed to the triangle of deck at the bow.

The back door of the big house opened; men came down the walk. Duff had an instant in which he saw with horror a silent foot close beside him before there was a shocking flash and he lost consciousness. . . .

He was in pain; the moaning sound he heard was his own voice. He was tied and gagged. And he was on a moving ship. He thought for a while that he was blindfolded and then he realized the place where he lay was pitch-dark. There had been a woman in the room because he could smell perfume. Presently he thought it was the kind Eleanor used. The engines of the boat slowed. Duff heard voices outside.

"Hello, Coast Guard!"

Thinly, the answer came, "Making a check of outgoing boats, Mr. Stanton!"

"Come aboard! Taking a little party for a cruise!"

"No need to board you, Mr. Stanton! Go ahead!"

The water roughened. Duff knew they were outside the bay. At sea. He heard a murmur in the dark and thought it was Eleanor's voice. Excitement surged through him. If he could let her know he was there—that the groaning she must have heard had been his! He tried to make a clearer sound, but the gag stifled him.

He doubted his senses then. All this was hallucination, nightmare. But she continued to murmur, and presently he noticed her complaining had a single form. A long moan and two little moans afterward. He moved his mouth in what might have been a near-grin if he had not been gagged. Telegraphy had been a hobby of his, long ago. And he'd taught the Morse code to Charles, Marian and Eleanor. If she was using it, she was signaling his initial: D. He started a series of moans to spell out "Eleanor," but he'd gone only as far as the second *e* when she signaled back, "Duff."

So, for minutes, they alternately made sounds. In that time Eleanor stated, "Heard a noise at sinkhole. Looked. Was grabbed. Brought here. By whom?"

He prepared to reply in the dark, but to his dismay, a third voice spoke, "Very darn ingenious!" And all the lights went on.

It was a big cabin with two bunks and modernistic furnishings. On a tubular chair sat a man of about sixty—tall, gray-haired, wearing a white dinner jacket—one of the men Duff had seen in the house drinking cocktails. Beyond him on the other bunk Duff could see a female knee and the brown dress Eleanor wore.

"I'm Stanton," the man said.

Duff made a sound. Then, realizing Stanton had listened in on their conversation, Duff moaned in code, "Ungag us."

The man bent over Duff. His expression was cold. He had high cheekbones, rather pale gray eyes—features that spelled his Slavic ancestry—features vaguely familiar through newspaper photographs of important Miamians giving parties, heading charity drives.

Stanton stared at Duff a moment and then spoke, "I've been waiting for you to come around ever since we cleared the Coast Guard." He paused. "Your—visit—wasn't precisely expected. But we took no chances. You were seen coming over my wall." He turned to Eleanor. "I think you both know why you're here, in a general way. My yacht is heading for an island in the Bahamas. A small one, uninhabited and far from any others. We won't be spotted there, even from the air, because that island"—he smiled chillily—"has been arranged so that my yacht's hidden when she's in. It has been a transshipment point for cargo from—another country. Cargo brought here by me. Your interrogation won't begin till we reach that island, a while before daylight. I'm glad we have Miss Yates along. We'd intended to question her. But it will be more effective to use her as a means to get the truth out of you, Bogan."

Duff could feel his muscles freeze. "What truth?" he painfully signaled.

Stanton leaned over him for a moment, bracing himself on the far partition for support as the yacht rocked heavily. His face was passive. He might have been talking about the weather, which was warm, clear and breezy. "Through the unfortunate fact that you got onto Ellings' part in our work, Bogan, my value to my cause has suffered." He was silent as, apparently, he thought of his cause. He shrugged. "Ellings believed for some time that he had you—and the FBI—fooled by the device he'd had prepared for just such a meddlesome discovery as you made. But when we found his stratagem hadn't been entirely effective, we had Ellings destroy himself. And went on with our—assignment."

The ship heaved and he balanced again. "You and Miss Yates will also be destroyed. But it is necessary for us to learn, before your deaths, precisely how much information about my activities the FBI has. This will be painful—as painful as certain trained men on board can make it—for you both. We cannot judge whether our work is accomplished and will stand up or whether it must be done over by others, until we have made certain that neither one of you—and you especially, Bogan—has held anything back. Anything. That means the last hours will be—rugged—for you both."

He went out. Minutes later three men carried Duff to another stateroom. Its light was extinguished. Sweat-soaked, Duff lay in the darkness, trying to get his mind to work at all. Here and there in American cities the bombs had certainly been planted and were waiting for an unknown zero hour. The FBI, the Army, all intelligence services, surely knew that now. But not at what sites, in what cities.

After torturing and killing Eleanor and him, Stanton would be able to decide whether to flee the country or to go back to his palatial home, his business affairs, his social prominence and his underground activity. What he had to know was whether the FBI had connected him in any way with Ellings or with the gigantic man—evidently Stanton's own disguise—or with the sinister boxes.

Duff clamped his teeth on his gag. He writhed in the ropes that rawly confined him. He thought that the torture had already begun, not with the physical pain of lying there, but with the knowledge of what was to happen to the girl. For the rest of his life he was to dream occasionally about that long night of agony.

Toward morning the ship entered calm water, slowed, reversed and touched a dock. Men came for him, blindfolded him and heaved him onto a stretcher. He felt the open air on his face. His bearers walked on planks and then on sand for a little way, and finally down half a dozen steps. A door slammed. He was dumped out on a cement floor. Soon the door opened again and the men moved in once more. He heard Eleanor murmur as she was tipped onto the concrete, and he heard the heavy door shut again. He tried to communicate with her as he had before, and was frightened because he got no response. She had probably fainted.

Nearby, in an adjoining room or cell, he heard steps, grunts, thumpings, as men moved objects about. A sick stretch of time went by and then the door came open, clanged shut. Hands ripped his blindfold away. He saw plain chairs, bare tables, two kerosene lamps, four men including Stanton, Eleanor's form on the floor and four bare walls. An underground storage room on the island, probably camouflaged above, Duff thought.

"Start with the girl," Stanton said to his men. "She's out," he added, after shaking her. "Or pretending." He gave her a terrific slap—a slap that knotted Duff's nerves. "Out," he said. "Open up the case. Get the ammonia."

One of the men fiddled in a case that Duff could not see. He smelled ammonia. Eleanor muttered.

Someone took the gag from Duff's mouth. He worked his jaws and tried to lick his lips with a dry, numb tongue.

Stanton came to him, stood over him, suddenly kicked him. "All right. Start talking. From the beginning, and tell everything you know. The first run through it, we won't hurt you—unless you hold out."

Duff found that he could hardly speak at all. They poured a glass of water and gave it to him. Then a second. And he began to tell them the now-overfamiliar story, starting with the first instant of suspicion. He talked slowly, carefully, using time, yet without any real hope that delay would help. He told nearly all the truth because he knew that if they began to do to Eleanor such things as he had read they did, he would try to stop them with the truth anyway—or with lies or by any other method. If he had been alone, he would have held out to the end or as near the end as his sanity lasted.

There was nothing in anything Duff knew to suggest that Higgins had traced a connection to Stanton. And only one way Higgins might learn. That Stanton was a director of the trucking company would seem, to the FBI man, irrelevant. Some big shot had to own it—some man exactly like Stanton. That Harry Ellings and Stanton had been allied in evil would not occur to any reasonable person.

Duff finished.

"That's it?" Stanton asked. "All?"

"All."

Stanton turned to a corner of the room that Duff couldn't see. "Got that water boiling?"

Duff said, "I couldn't add anything if you tore us both apart inch by inch! You must know that! Why not simply—kill us both?"

Stanton smiled a little. "Just to be certain. And besides, I owe you something special. Because of you, they'll find the one in New York!"

Duff began to pray.

And the door opened. Daylight showed.

"Boss!" a scared voice called.

"Hold it!"

Stanton left. He did not return. Ten minutes later the door opened and a man shouted, "All out! Taking off! Leave 'em lay! A damn Coast Guard plane went over twice!"

Time passed. Duff thought he heard the ship's engines. Then silence.

A while after that the chamber was filled with reddish light, a thunderous blast. A pressure wave banged Duff against the floor. The concrete walls cracked. Sand gushed into the room. It turned furnace-hot. He thought he was dying and realized, seconds later, that he could see sunlight in the swirling, wrecked chamber.

He rolled across the floor. He got his arms up against a sharp edge of rent metal. It took fifteen or twenty choking minutes to free his hands, as long again to untie his legs. Then he crawled to Eleanor. She was half covered with sand and her nose bled.

They began digging feebly with bits of debris. Before long they had made a way out. The room where they had been was under the island sand. Around them now were barren dunes and coral escarpments, blue sea and blinding sun. In front, in the painful sunshine, they saw a tall stand of mangrove and the well-hidden mooring where the yacht had been tied. They looked out to sea and spotted the yacht, hull down.

The island was small—not a mile around—and except for the concealed pier, the now-smoking storage cellars, a few palms, patches of weed and water birds, there was nothing but tropical ocean. Eleanor stood with him for a moment and then collapsed.

Duff carried her away from the wreckage of the underground chambers. "More dynamite might go off." It was the first thing he had said.

He took her down the dunes to the beach and they washed in the limpid, warm salt water. Eleanor had a spell of shuddering and sobbing. He held her in his arms until she had mastered the spasm.

"What happened? Where is this?"

Duff shook his head. "Bahamas. It was their base. A Coast Guard plane came by twice. Might have been an accident. But probably Higgins is close to the answer. I left a note, anyhow! So they beat it. Blew up the works. But they'd built that cellar like a fort, luckily for us! The blast didn't bring the ceiling down —which they probably presumed it would. Just caved the walls some."

"Bury us?" she said in a sore-throat tone. "Alive?"

"Would they have cared which way?" The wind blew on them. The sun shone. "We'll have to figure out how to get along here till somebody comes for us or till we can signal a boat going by," he said.

"Let's find some shade. We'll sunburn."

They moved to the shade of three coconut palms. The yacht was gradually lost on the blue emptiness of the Gulf Stream. For a while they lay on the sand, silent, resting.

Then Eleanor cried, "Look, Duff! Look!"

He barely glanced toward the sea. Then he threw himself on top of her and forced her to lie face-down on the earth. She gasped, struggled.

"Lie still!" he ordered.

A wave of pressure eventually swept the island, bending the trees; it was accompanied by an immense rumble. Only after that did Duff sit up. Far out on the sea a cloud made unforgettable by the news pictures rose toward the blue zenith. A many-hued, mushroom-shaped cloud with fire flashes eddying enormously in its midst.

"Atom bomb," she whispered.

Duff spoke, too exhausted for emotion and yet unable to stop the working of his mind, "Maybe they destroyed themselves that way. Maybe they thought they—and it—would be captured. Maybe an accident. They could have got too many cases of uranium too close together—a last one, dropped down through a hatch. That might have done it."

For perhaps an hour they watched the cloud rise, change shape in the strong winds aloft, and start to dissipate.

"Somebody else," Duff had said, "should have seen it. Though there are darn few ships in these parts, I imagine." His eyes moved from the distant, separating clouds to the beach; they followed its curve to the Bahama Banks, a glittering, empty infinitude of shallow sea. "Anyhow, it'll show up on plenty of instruments and a slew of people will be down here, looking, pretty soon."

Eleanor said, "Was it close enough to—to hurt us?"

He stared at her, then smiled, and found a lump coming in his throat. "Lord," he murmured, "why didn't you ask that before? No. Too far away. The radiation here couldn't have amounted to anything."

The girl smiled back. "Glad I had a physicist along to tell me."

The first half of the Orange Bowl game ended in the usual pandemonium. Teams trotted from the field and were replaced by bands in red uniforms, in blue, in green, in gold and in the white of the University of Miami. Thousands of colored balloons rose in the sky. The combined bands began to play. Floats moved sedately from the corners of the stadium and paraded around the field. One of these—an immense replica of an orange—proceeded to the center of the field and opened magically. The Orange Bowl Queen stood inside it, and girls on the floats, pretty girls in bathing suits, began to throw real oranges to the crowd. The governors of three states marched forward with what the program called "a retinue of beauty" to crown the queen.

Standing in her robes, smiling, waving, Eleanor felt happy. She was very tired, but everything would soon be over.

In the Yates box, Duff grinned at the yelling of Marian and the shrill whistling of Charles. He handed a pair of borrowed field glasses to Mrs. Yates, who faced her wheel chair to see every detail of the coronation.

Duff gazed at Eleanor, standing straight and lovely, as he

mused on the recent, dramatic past. They had been discovered on the island by a Coast Guard plane which flew in to investigate. A second plane had taken them back to Miami, where they had landed secretly. Eleanor had given out the story that she had suffered a "loss of memory" due to "exhaustion and an accidental fall" and spent two nights with "a friend in Fort Lauderdale." Nothing about kidnaping, about enemy agents, about a mushroom cloud rising where a boat had vanished. That would not become public, Duff reflected, until it was all over.

He felt a hand on his shoulder and turned to see the grinning face of Scotty Smythe. "Duff, old boy, can you come over to our box for a few minutes? Dad and mother are there. And a couple of other people who want to see you."

Out on the sunlit field the coronation ended. Eleanor's float led a circling parade to the jubilant blaring of bands. Duff followed Scotty along an aisle of the jam-packed stadium. He greeted the Smythe family happily, and found himself, to his surprise, shaking hands with General Baines, and then with a physicist he had always wanted to meet, a Doctor Adamas who was a member of the Atomic Energy Commission.

The general presently murmured to Duff, "Adamas and I actually came down to see you."

"Me!"

"We both are flying back to Washington as soon as possible after this dandy game. If you could spare us a few minutes now, for a stroll outside—"

It was there, between the stadium walls and the parked cars, that Duff got the shock of his life. He walked along slowly with the general and the scientist.

The soldier did most of the talking. "No use, Bogan, of my telling you what the country owes you. We've dug out that bomb in New York. One in Philadelphia. Two in Washington. Soon have them all. The Stacey woman talked."

"I should have figured her out sooner," Duff said, with a self-depreciatory shake of his head. "And the country owes Scotty

Smythe far more than me. After all, if he hadn't driven over to the Yateses' to help me, and if he hadn't come in when nobody answered his knock, he'd never have found my note or phoned Higgins where I'd gone, and why. The search for the yacht wouldn't have started." Duff shuddered slightly. "They'd have got away with the whole thing!"

"There is nothing tangible we can do for young Smythe," the general replied, grinning at the disclaimer. "His father, my good friend, is amply endowed with worldly goods. In fact, Bogan, the father thinks your influence has made a serious man out of a rather featherbrained boy."

"Scotty was always a man," Duff answered defensively. "He just liked to look frivolous."

"The point is," Adamas said dryly, "you've done a very great, very brave and very brilliant service to your country, and one for which there cannot be, at this time, any public reward whatever."

Duff laughed. "Reward? Why should I get a reward? Anybody would have done what I did—and better. If I hadn't been so dumb—"

The general's mouth dropped open and snapped shut. The scientist coughed, cleared his throat and looked closely at the trunk of a nearby palm. And he spoke. "We've gone over your records, Bogan. The FBI has quite a dossier. Besides being a twenty-one-carat fool for danger, you're a good man in the field. My field. Our field. A certain nuclear project is being moved down here under old Slocum. We'd like you to work on it as you continue your studies. We've fixed it so the work itself will contribute toward a doctorate."

Duff had been trying to say he'd be glad to work on any project the Atomic Energy Commission thought he was worthy of. But the mention of an opportunity to get his final degree made him stand still. Tears came in his eyes.

"D-d-don't deserve anything of the sort," he stammered.

General Baines snorted, "Damn it, man! Stop the modesty! Surely you realize what you saved the country from!"

"A lot of people besides me—"

"Fiddlesticks! Rubbish! You can continue your studies here. Take your M.A. Then your Ph.D. And have a job meanwhile. It will pay you seven fifty a month, Bogan, and I have orders from the President of the United States—who wants to shake your hand someday, incidentally—that you're to accept."

A roar came from inside the stadium as the opposing teams returned to the field. The scientist, after a look at Duff, took the general's arm. "Let's watch the kickoff."

Duff couldn't speak. When he was able to control his emotions, he walked back into the frenzied stadium and joined the Yates family. He saw the game, and didn't see it. He was thinking that he was a rich man now. For a minute he had imagined that "seven fifty" a month had meant seven dollars and a half. Then he knew. He could rent Harry's room and they wouldn't need to find another boarder. He could put in some improvements, like an electric stove. By and by he'd be a doctor of philosophy, an atomic scientist. Miami made a touchdown and he was only dimly aware—

After the sun set and as the first unimportant-looking buds of the night-blooming jasmine commenced to explode their honey-sweet perfume into the twilight, Duff sat alone beside his lily pool. They'd just come home from the game. He hadn't told the Yateses, yet, about his reward; he was afraid, still, that he'd break up— maybe blubber.

Eleanor had been escorted home, minutes before. He expected she would leave again, soon, for another dinner party.

Charles kicked open the front screen. "Hey, Duff! Kitchen faucet's leaking!"

The homely need somehow bolstered Duff. He laughed. "Washer coming up!" He had shut off the water when Eleanor appeared—in a house dress.

"I thought—"

She read the thought. "I begged off, Duff. After all, I did say I'd been ill. I'm cooking tonight—thank heaven! No more Cinderella! The coach is a punkin again and the horses are mice. And am I happy about that!"

Duff nodded vaguely. He felt that women were impossible to understand. He tinkered with the faucet and she came close, watching him. There was a way her hair curved at the nape of her neck. There was a certain shape of her eyes and a special light in them, a topaz light. A warmth and a femininity about her. She had lovely lips. And he knew the girl very well—though not, perhaps, well enough to do what he did, which was to put down the wrench, take her in his arms and kiss her, hard. Alarmed afterward, he let go.

"I'm sorry! I couldn't help it! I'm still distraught—judgment's shot!"

Her eyes shone. "Sure is! You let go. Why?"

Duff turned away a little. "I've tried to be a brotherly kind of a guy, Eleanor. It's a beam I can't entirely stay on. But after all, your type of man is some really elegant person, like Scotty."

"Scotty is pretty elegant," she answered very softly. "He had a big crush on me. I had to kind of bust it up—pretend I was crazy about six other lads. He caught on. I mean, he caught on to who I really did care for. So he pitched in to help that guy. It's like Scotty."

Duff nodded and his blue eyes were never more vague, more forlorn. "Then there is somebody."

Her first words of love were, "What does a girl have to do in the case of scientists—hire a marriage broker? You dope! You oaf! You nitwit! You precious dumbbell!"

Marian, who had come quietly through the door, yelled, "Mother! Duff and El are having a quarrel!"

Her big sister ignored the interruption and went on talking to Duff in a strange voice, "Yes, there's somebody! Somebody who ought to find out—seeing I phone all over the country to get him when I'm in trouble! Seeing how jealous I am about his dating another girl! Somebody I've practically been married to for a year and a half! At least, I've had him around, like a husband.

And we've had all the trials and tribulations and domestic problems and discomforts and the scrimping and misery and work of marriage, together. Enough to know for sure we could make a swell team! And none of the joy, except a sort of—distant companionship."

"Mother," Marian bawled jubilantly, "I was wrong! They're necking!" She added in mock horror, "You better come out here and chaperon!"

Eleanor drew away a little and said, "I've loved you, you lug, since the day you came stammering in here, towering and shuffling, polite and uneasy, asking for a place to board that was 'reasonable'! Everything at the Yateses' is reasonable, Duff—even poor —and maybe we're crazy if we get married, the way it is. But we'll make out. I know it!"

"About that," he said, and gulped, "maybe I ought to tell you. I just got a job."

SPORTING BLOOD

SPORTING BLOOD

"CRUNCH," said the girl.

"Present," the skipper replied, without looking up from his work.

"*Hello!*"

He took a turn with a wrench. "Hello, Marylin."

There was a brief silence on the Gulf Stream Dock. The sun of early autumn shone fiercely on the city of Miami and its grey-green Bay. Sandals tapped. The *Poseidon* rocked minutely as the girl came aboard.

"Aren't you glad to see me?"

Crunch grinned in the relative gloom. "All I can see in here is machinery." Marylin Brush was one of his favorite female fishermen. But you couldn't let Marylin dominate a situation—quite. She had a tendency to try to do so.

"We just got back."

"That's great."

"Aren't you going to leap up and hug me, or anything?"

"You'd have to spend the weekend at a dry cleaner's."

"Oh." She came closer. A blonde who wore her locks in long natural waves. A tall girl, strong looking, dressed in what is called a play suit—a garment separated amidships by a sun-tanned stretch of no garment at all. It would have caused Marylin's grandmother (who had been presented by the American Ambassador to Queen Victoria) to fan the air with her kerchief and fall in a quick swoon.

Crunch spun the wrench. "How's the family?"

"Wonderful. As usual." She sounded lugubrious.

"Excepting you."

Her voice was startled. "How'd you know that?"

"Elementary, my dear—"

She interrupted. "Crunch! I'm in love! And it's *ghastly!*"

"What's happened between you and Roge?"

"It isn't Roger."

Crunch put down the wrench. He wiped his hands on some overused waste. He stood—bringing above the deck level a face, shoulders and chest clad in honest perspiration and much black grease. Marylin Brush and Roger Benton had been "one of those things" ever since he'd been the captain of his prep school football team and she'd been a swimming star at Miss Wainwright's Florida Academy for Girls. *Brush-Benton.* The nuptial headlines had waited only upon their graduation from the University of Miami. Then their two families would unite as naturally as the confluence of rivers and life among the elite would go on—reinforced in strength and impressiveness.

"Not Roger?" His eyes—bluer, clearer, for the dark streaks around them—took in the tall girl, from painted toenails to the matching bow on the top of her head. Everybody liked Marylin. He smiled. "Hello, again."

"I guess I hadn't better shake hands, at that. Crunch, you old such-and-such, I'm glad to see you! How's fishing?"

He swung himself on deck. "Good. Who's the unfortunate guy?"

"Everything's wrong with him," she answered dolefully, sitting on one of the daybeds. "For instance. His name's Ramsay. And not only that—but Ramsay Binney. Isn't that silly?"

"Is it?"

"The family thinks so. They keep referring to him as Rusty Penny and Dopey Benny and Rumsey Bunny and names like that —as if they couldn't remember. All my brothers—and Dad and Mother, too."

"What else?"

"His parents were medical missionaries."

"Hardy lot. The best."

"He grew up with them—they tutored him till he was ready to come to America for college."

"Very enterprising."

"I think so," she said, nodding. "But it was on Poaki."

"Poaki?"

"There!" She jumped to her feet, rummaged amongst some charts and spools of line, found a package of cigarettes, put one in Crunch's mouth and one in her own, and lighted both. "*You* don't know, either. And you're a ship's captain! Nobody—positively nobody—ever recognizes Poaki. That's where Ramsay came from—and it's simply unheard-of!"

"What's Poaki?"

"It's an island in the South Pacific. Copra and pearls and the natives were head-hunters when the Binneys landed there—"

"Had you heard of it before you met—uh—Ramsay?"

She sat again. "No. Not even me. But that's not all. He's a research epidemiologist."

"Certainly your folks can't complain about that. After all—with the Brush Foundation—"

"Can't they! That's where I met him—at our Foundation this summer. We went to Cincinnati to dedicate a new wing—and he made a little speech—and I met him afterward. I saw to it that I did. But you should hear my family! He's only interested in tropical epidemics. And they keep telling me if I marry him I'll spend my life in places like—well—Poaki. Catching things—eastern sprue and filariasis and so on. It's practically unbearable!"

"The guy in love with you?"

"How do I know?" she asked.

Crunch started to say, "Oh," and changed it to, "I see."

"When they noticed I was getting a crush on Ramsay, they yanked me places. The Adirondacks in July and Maine in August and I didn't catch up with him again till six weeks ago in New York. But he's coming down here soon." She said it with firm satisfaction. "He's going to do some work on Brill's disease. Isn't that marvelous?"

Crunch smoked.

The girl's lovingly shaped mouth became somewhat straight and possibly even hostile. "Don't say you're against me, too! Crunch. I'm going to marry Ramsay—and that's final."

"What about Roge?"

"He'll still have football—and polo, when he graduates." She gave Crunch no opportunity to comment upon games as a solace for her graceful, sun-tanned hand. "Which brings me to the worst thing of all. You know how athletic my family is."

Who didn't? Crunch thought.

Wherever there were amateur sports, there were Brushes. Wherever the Great Outdoors beckoned, Brushes—father and four sons—cousins and nephews—responded. When Olympic Games were held—the name of Brush was read off, usually in first place, in this event or that. The Brushes were rich—they had been for generations. And the Brushes were interested in science as well as the subsidy of science. But the Brushes were also interested in every known physical challenge—and they seemed to be born with a uniform aptitude for taking up any gage. High mountains, square with cliffs, had been first scaled by Brushes. Track records had repeatedly collapsed under Brush assault. College coaches yearned for the matriculation of Brushes. Princeton once had three enrolled at the same time. A great year for sports at Princeton. Two worlds records for deep-sea fishing bore the name of Marylin's father—and of these, one had been established on board the *Poseidon*.

The picture occupied the skipper's mind for a moment. "Yes," he said. "Your folks are sure athletic."

"Ramsay isn't."

Crunch allowed himself the, "Oh." He pronounced it flatly.

The girl ground out her cigarette. Her eyes flashed greenly —and in this case, the color was a signal of danger. "Is that all that matters in a man? Beef? Brawn? How far he can throw a discus? How high he can toss himself with a pole? How big a mountain goat he can shoot how far away? How hard he can swat a ball with a stick? Is that the only important thing?"

"You're a little bit athletic, yourself. And your family—"

"—eats and sleeps physical culture! So what! Ramsay grew up on a tropical island. He never saw a game—a sport—till he was eighteen. He doesn't like physical competition. He's serious minded—and very bright. He has an I.Q.—alone—of a hundred and sixty-seven! He has a B.S., an M.A., a Ph.D., and an M.D.— and some of my brothers had to beat their brains out to get merely a lousy A.B. Ramsay can talk seven languages, including Malay and Chinese, and my family can't even shop in Paris without being gypped. He likes me because he said so and he told me he wished he was good at something so the family would think better of him."

Crunch began to see light. "Is he—healthy? I mean—?"

"Of course he's healthy! He's no weight lifter, like Clayton. No Hercules, like Dodson. No born blacksmith, like Pierce and Davidson. But my brothers make me sick! They ought to organize a vaudeville act—tearing up telephone books and building human pyramids! Letting elephants walk on their stomachs . . . !"

"When's he coming down?"

"Next week."

"And you want me to make a big game angler out of him?"

The girl stared. "How on earth did you guess that?"

"People think," Crunch answered rather unsympathetically, "that fishing is mostly luck—and that the right skipper can bring the luck. You ought to know better. I might fish this boyfriend of yours all autumn—and he could still wind up a dub. If you're planning to make him a present of a charter—and expecting me to hang him onto something that will go over big with your brothers—"

"Present? Did I say that?" She had blushed a little. "Ramsay's uncle owned railroads. That's why his parents were missionaries and that's why he went into research: conscience toward humanity

—paying the debt back to society. I simply persuaded Ramsay that he ought to try fishing because he might like it—and he said he'd look you up. Beyond that—I haven't anything but a little hope. And if you could see the beating I'm taking at home about Ramsay, you'd know I have precious little hope, too! I love him—and I'm going to make him marry me—but I just wish—wish and wish— that he would do something that made him a little more popular with everybody else I care for in this world!"

Two tears slid down Marylin's cheeks. She wiped at them with the back of her hand and walked to the cockpit. "If you can help me, all right! If you won't, that's all right! It's my mess." She leaped lightly back onto the dock. Near-by skippers and mates looked at her with appreciation.

The sight of a Brush in tears—even a female Brush—profoundly shocked Crunch. He started after her, calling, "Marylin! I didn't mean to upset you . . . !"

But she went, without looking back.

Ramsay Binney made a very poor initial impression. Before Crunch knew who he was, he caught Binney stealing, and stealing from a child, at that.

It happened some days later.

The *Poseidon* had come in from a successful day in the Gulf Stream. Her customers had departed, leaving three sailfish, tagged for the taxidermist, on a fish rack which thus became the cynosure for small boys, mothers, fathers, pretty girls, girls not pretty, less lucky anglers, and others. Des, the mate, had gone to make a phone call. Crunch was relaxing on the stern of his cruiser in the warm, pre-sunset glow. His eye fell upon a man—a stranger—sitting on one of the dock benches.

The stranger held his head tilted back and sidewise—staring up into the roof which covered a part of the dock. Not staring, Crunch presently decided, but deliberately posing a profile that might have interested a film producer. Hawklike nose, firm chin, full lips, lofty brow, and a tangle of chestnut hair that looked—in the skipper's disdainful opinion—like the feathers of an enraged partridge. Not far from the stranger were three attractive girls and it was Crunch's opinion that the man had assumed the Byronic attitude for their benefit. The guy was well built—maybe twenty-eight years old—and the women were covertly aware of him. Dopes, Crunch felt.

Now, however, the man moved his head. He searched in the crowd—apparently looking for something or somebody previously observed. He rose and moved toward a boy who was ardently viewing the sailfish. He took some object—surreptitiously—from the boy's back pocket. He hurried along the dock railing, then, to the open locker of the *Clara*. He glanced about warily and reached into the locker.

By that time, Crunch was on his feet. A pickpocket, evidently. A sneak thief of some sort. But the man went back to the bench —so Crunch waited for developments. In a minute, the gent brought up a slingshot—which was evidently what he had swiped from the boy—and fired at the rafters a metal bolt or nut or screw—which must have been what he took from the *Clara's* locker. The man was not satisfied by his shot—so he tried again—and then again. The third time, something besides ammunition fell to the dock. The man leaped forward and apparently assaulted it. Then, rather to the skipper's amazement, he carefully collected the bolts and nuts, slipped them back into the locker, advanced upon the boy stealthily, and returned the slingshot. The boy gazed unknowing at the fish.

Crunch wondered what had dropped. He hopped ashore and sauntered along the dock. Where the man had rushed was a large, squashed scorpion. Crunch turned. The man was watching him.

"Good hunting," Crunch said.

The man flushed slightly. "I was afraid if I went clear to the dockhouse for a pole—it would get away. Scrabbling around up there—it could drop any time on some one, and they sting. I'd noticed that kid had a shooter—"

"They sure do sting. My name's Adams."

"I know," the man said. "I watched you dock. Nice catch. I'm Ramsay Binney."

Crunch concealed a marked surprise. They shook hands. "Come aboard."

Ramsay Binney started aboard, failed to notice the fishbox in the stern, caught his heel, and went into the cockpit like a cavalryman dismounting without command. He sprawled, that is —whacking knees, elbows, forehead and shoulder. Crunch helped Binney to his feet.

"You hurt?"

Certainly he was hurting. And his trousers were torn.

"Hurt? Tut-tut! I hope I haven't damaged the boat."

"The *boat?* Man—we throw live marlin into this cockpit! You're sure you're all right?"

Ramsey tested himself, smiling embarrassedly. "I'm used to falls. Born clumsy. Father was clumsy, too, and his father before him. It's hereditary."

"Well—sit." Crunch indicated the fighting chair. Ramsay Binney looked at it for some time, shook his head perplexedly, and sat in it cautiously. Crunch lounged against the fishbox. "Cigarette?"

"Don't smoke, thanks."

Crunch struck a match—and inhaled. He gave Ramsay Binney a chance to start a conversation—which was disregarded; his attention seemed concentrated—rather apprehensively—on the equipment of the *Poseidon.* Finally the skipper said, "Marylin Brush told us to be on the lookout for you."

"Oh, yes."

"Said you might be interested in doing a little fishing."

"H'm'm'm'm."

"She"—Crunch tried another tack—"thinks a lot of you."

The young doctor flushed. Even his ears turned red. But he said nothing.

"Des and I—Des is my mate and he'll be along soon—have done a good deal of fishing with her."

"So she told me."

"And, of course, her father and brothers."

The flush, up until then, had deepened on the face of the doctor. At the word "brothers," however, it left like a switched-off light. A whiteness replaced it—the whiteness of an indoor man, further paled by emotion.

Crunch felt a reaction that was part sympathy and part amusement. Dr. Binney's stratagem with the swiped slingshot and bolts had changed the skipper's initial feeling of wrath. But the Brush boys were the best. Furthermore, there was no real excuse for a man with Binney's build to be completely a bookworm and student. Crunch didn't insist that all men should be anglers—although it seemed a sensible idea to him; but he did feel that a man in good health should have some facility at some sport or game. That's what muscles were for, in a modern world.

Since Binney said nothing, Crunch went on, deliberately, "The boys have hauled in a lot of big fish, doctor. Their old man has two world's records. One, for mako on medium tackle, made on this spot." He thumped the gunwale.

Ramsay Binney stood up—tripping a little on the footrest. He was exceedingly pale, now. "See here," he said.

Crunch waited. Nothing followed. "Yes?"

"See here, captain. Can any thumb-fingered galoot learn fishing?"

"Anyone can try. Des and I are good coaches. Whether he learns or not is in the lap of himself—and Providence."

"If just once—just one time—in *anything*—I could—!" He had spoken under great stress. He broke off.

"Could what?"

"Clayton! Dodson! Pierce! Davidson!" He said the four names fiercely. "Egad!" His large eyes were a studious brown, but they flashed now. "I'd trade anything but my medical education to beat any one of the Brush boys at anything! *Anything*, captain. Even table tennis. Yes. Even croquet! They knocked me off the lawn so many times I tore my pants"—he glanced down—

"worse than this, going back and forth through the rosebushes!"

"Marylin said—" Crunch began peaceably, but he was interrupted by pure indignation.

"What in Sam Hill has this to do with Marylin? It's far past that! I suppose I did fall in love with Marylin. It does happen, evidently. She wanted me to 'take up' something—for her family's sake. I tried golf. *Egad!* Sickened me! Grown man—chasing a pill. Dodson's a champ—the idiot! I cracked my ankle with a seven iron. Fishing, she said. Anybody can do it. Women under a hundred pounds catch monstrous tunas, she said. Deuce take what she said! I don't even know how I feel about her, any more. Spoiled. She'd have to be handled firmly, in any case. It's those four boys—!" He strangled.

Crunch thought, for a moment, that Binney was going to burst into tears. Rage was shaking him. He smote the arm of the fighting chair such a blow that Crunch had to tighten it, later.

"Inferiority complex," Dr. Binney went on. "Everything in the United States gives me an inferiority complex! Never saw an automobile till I arrived here at eighteen. Don't drive. Don't skate. Don't dance. Don't bowl. Can't play bridge. Never on a baseball team—or track, football, hockey. I've got the biggest inferiority complex on the eastern seaboard! Never would have known it, if I hadn't met that girl. Had it covered over with books. Buried myself in studies. Then—I encountered her—and these four Olympian brothers! I wonder how they'd stand up on Poaki? I'd like to get them—and their dratted games—on a head-hunt!"

"Huh?" Crunch said. "Head-hunt?"

Dr. Ramsay Binney's burst came to an end. He blushed again. "Forget I ever mentioned it. Dad never knew. It was outlawed —long ago. The natives took me along on one—that's all."

"What happened?"

He sat back in the fighting chair. "Nothing. For a minute, we threw spears at each other—then everybody ran—and I cut my foot."

Crunch was disappointed. "Oh."

The doctor nodded. "Island life's not very exciting. Nothing glamorous. I've told Marylin that—over and over." He sighed. "I'll mosey along, now, I guess."

"What about the fishing?"

He rubbed his face with his hands. "Futile, don't you think?"

"Never find out on shore."

"I've got about three weeks before Dr. Jarvis arrives to start work here. Still . . ."

"Why not try it—tomorrow? Just the day?"

Ramsay pondered. "Why not?" He sounded listless. He rose listlessly. "Crack of dawn?"

"Any time you like. Seven? Eight?"

"Seven's fine. I'll be here." He went—without falling.

Des arrived.

"Who was that bird? The one just stepped ashore?"

"Marylin's boyfriend."

Des thought that over. "Looked upset."

"Yeah. Funny guy. Last word in research. But about a generation behind in the language. When he's excited, he says 'egad' —and means it. He also says 'galoot' and 'mosey along' and 'dratted.' "

"No kidding!"

"Guess that's what missionaries say when they're riled clear through. Nine years of college and medical school haven't changed him any."

"Marylin will, though—in a lot less time."

"I'm not so sure she will."

"Meaning what?" Des asked.

"Search me. He's a new type on our logbook."

"Stand by for our passenger," Crunch said in a low tone, "and get ready not to laugh."

Des peered and murmured, "Wahooo!"

Dr. Binney was striding down the dock. As he passed each of

the moored charterboats, silence fell—an awed, incredulous silence.

It was a hot morning, but it was not a hot morning on a remote, Pacific island which had felt the influence of Spain, Holland, England and France. It was a hot morning in the American city of Miami, Florida.

The *Poseidon's* customer carried, on one arm, a huge wicker hamper. This, presumably, was lunch: Marylin had undoubtedly explained that the customer brings lunch for all. In his right hand, the doctor carried a large, red silk parasol, open, and casting upon his person a pale, crimson light. About his loins, he wore knee-covering, British shorts. Above these was a shirt of native design and material which looked, one of the captains later said, as if it had been made from old battle flags. The belt supporting the shorts was of reptile skin and, hitched to it, on the left hip, was a large Boy Scout knife in a leather sheath. The man's legs were bare. He wore native sandals, woven of straw. His head covering, however, was the most conspicuous item in his costume—a sola topee, freshly clayed to whiteness, fixed by a strap that crossed the upper lip and stuffed with small green leaves which, as the doctor walked, kept falling on his shoulders in a verdant shower.

"No lei," Des croaked and dived down the ladder to hide his mirth from the doctor.

Crunch went gravely to the stern.

"Top of the morning to you!" Binney cried.

"Wonderful day," Crunch replied without showing any other sentiment than amiability. "Come aboard." He braced himself for any emergency. Binney leaped, tottered, and made it.

"This is about what we wear," he said, as if he realized his haberdashery might need clarification, "on Poaki."

"Looks comfortable."

There was some sort of sound below. "My mate," Crunch went on imperturbably. "Sneezing. Hay fever. This is—allergy of some sort. Oh, Des! We're all set. Come and meet Dr. Binney."

The *Poseidon* fled the dock. She churned through the Gov-

ernment Cut and past the buoys. Des lowered the outriggers while
Crunch began to explain the rudiments of big game fishing. There
was a mild easterly breeze and, in consequence, a slight chop. Binney listened to the lecture and experimented with rod-tip, reel
brake, and gimbal. He quickly understood the workings of the
outriggers—intellectually, at least. And Crunch noticed, as the
Poseidon took the motion of the waves, that his passenger showed
none of the misgivings which indicate easy liability to seasickness.
He kept his balance readily, unconsciously. It was evident that
he had been on the water before.

The baits went out. A big mullet on the starboard outrigger,
a whole balao on the port—and a strip bait on the center line.
Twenty-four-thread line on both sides—nine-thread in the middle.

"All you do," Crunch said, "is keep your eyes on the baits.
If you feel a fish—hit it. If you see one following—with a fin up
or a bill out—it looks like a stick—holler for one of us and we'll
coach you. Just watch the baits."

Dr. Binney watched the baits. Crunch had never seen anybody watch baits as Binny did. He sat in one position—moving
gently with the boat. His eyes were glued to the sea. He did not
wiggle, twist, ask a question, say a word, or move an unnecessary
muscle. His parasol had been folded and discarded but he still
wore knife and helmet. After an hour, Crunch asked him if he'd
like some beer or water.

"Neither, thanks, old boy. Fun, isn't it?"

He sounded, Crunch decided, as if he meant it. Not a thing
had happened. Not a rise, a swirl or a strike—not a fin sighted or
even a turtle seen. But the doctor was—for some reason—getting
a kick out of it.

So another hour passed.

Crunch hated to mar a proper attitude, but he began to feel
that his advice was being taken a little too earnestly. "Look," he
said. "When I told you to watch the baits, I didn't mean you had
to concentrate like a man—" Crunch was going to say, "watching
the clock on his execution day." But he broke off, instead, "After

all, Des, up on the canopy, is helping you look. And I am—most of the time."

Binney seemed disappointed, almost hurt. "But I enjoy it! Used to spear crabs when I was a boy. Sharpen a stick—raise it—and wait for hours for one of the nippers to get in range."

"Well—if it doesn't tire you . . ."

They had lunch. Other boats were flying sailfish flags. Crunch saw the *Clara* take a big dolphin and he saw Jake Westover, on the *Tulu*, miss gaffing a big 'cuda. But the *Poseidon* was finding nothing whatever. Dr. Binney, eating sandwiches, drinking a Coke, consuming four bananas, did not budge from the chair or bend his eyes from the baits. It was inhuman. And the lack of fish was abnormal. And yet—it happened.

Every day, with some exceptions, at least one boat came in skunked. And occasionally—although less often than in the case of most—the *Poseidon* was the unlucky vessel. This was such a day.

Des yielded the controls to his skipper. Crunch tried trolling past likely weed "edges." He tried the inshore water. He took a long cruise into the deep indigo of the Gulf Stream. He even circled around the *Pirate Hussy* when she hung three sailfish at the same time, hoping to hit a school. No luck. He trolled slowly —and he trolled fast. When the sun slanted low, he gave up. Des reeled in the lines and Dr. Binney at last rose and stretched himself.

Crunch was crestfallen when they reached the dock. "No explanation—no alibi," he said. "I suppose you won't be interested in giving us another chance. But—"

The doctor was beaming. "Why—it was magnificent! Haven't had so much fun for years! Enjoyed every second—and I'll be at the dock at eight tomorrow—if you're free."

When he had gone, Des said, "Whaddaya think of that?"

Crunch didn't know quite what he thought. "Seems patient."

"Patient! One of his ancestors must have been a statue!"

"Good sailor."

"I kind of think he's been at sea before. We'll ask him, to-morrow."

When they asked him, he laughed a little and shrugged. "Well—never in a ship of this sort. Outrigger canoes in Poaki is all. With the natives. You can imagine how it is out there. What they did, I did."

He had left the red parasol at his hotel on the second day—but he still wore the helmet. The second day, moreover, was different from the first. In fact, the *Poseidon* had hardly rounded the turning buoy at the edge of deep water, where ocean-going vessels sail, when Des yelled from the canopy, "There's about a nine-foot hammerhead off to starboard. Shall we try for it?"

The doctor spun around. His eyes glittered. "Egad," he said. "Shark."

A hammerhead shark, Crunch thought, would be ideal. A strong and lunging beast which, however, lacks great speed and does not jump. Perfect for the novice. He waved his mate to advance upon the shark. He took down one outrigger line and wound it in. He advised the doctor to reel in the strip bait. He handed to the doctor the rod which carried the whole mullet and seated the butt in the gimbal. "If he rises, we'll see him. If he takes the bait, the line will fall from the outrigger. When it comes tight, hit him."

Presently, behind the mullet, which danced whitely in the azure sea, a yellowish-brown shape showed vaguely.

"He's coming," Crunch said. "He smells it!"

Dr. Binney braced himself quiveringly. There was a large splash in the vicinity of the mullet and it vanished. The line sifted down from the outrigger, lay on the sparkling chop, and slowly straightened out. "Now," Crunch said quietly.

Binney struck. He struck hard enough, Des later said, to set a hook in concrete. And he kept on striking.

Crunch thought the rod would snap—or the line would break. Neither disaster occurred. The shark began to run, hard and steadily. The reel buzzed. Binney was in a nervous transport.

"He's getting away from me, captain!"

"Sit tight. When the run stops, you can get him back."

The run finally did stop, and the skipper showed his passenger how to heave back slowly and reel quickly thereafter, as he lowered the rod. This procedure, known as "horsing," is standard. Binney worked the shark to within thirty yards of the boat. Then it went away again—at a tangent. He fumbled anxiously with the star-drag—turning it the wrong way. The shark, thus relieved of tension, ran much faster.

"Something's gone wrong!" Binney shouted.

Crunch explained. The angler flushed, and tightened the drag. Again, he stopped his quarry and heaved him back toward the boat. The struggle continued in this fashion for some half hour, at the end of which Binney brought his fish so close that they had a good look at it—snaggle of teeth, gruesome eyes on the ends of long stalks, floundering tail. This spectacle so stimulated Binney that, before Crunch could take measures, he stood up, carried the rod to the stern, threw it on deck, seized the line in one hand, whipped his knife out, put it in his teeth, and began pulling on the line. "Egad!" he bellowed through knife and clenched teeth.

The hammerhead had by no means abandoned the battle. Perhaps the sight of Binney had upon the shark as electrical an effect as it had on the fisherman. At any rate, the shark lunged around and away, splashing mightily. Line sizzled hotly through Binney's hands. He hung on—while Crunch grabbed the rod and tried to make him take it.

"Never used anything but handline in Poaki!" Binney yelled. He took a turn of line around his arm. Inevitably, it snapped. "Never had on anything that big, either," Binney said quietly, as he sat down. "Sorry, skipper. Boner—wasn't it?"

"Well," Crunch said slowly, "it was only a shark. And your first fish. What the heck!"

Up on the canopy, Des was staring straight ahead, battling with an unborn chortle. "Egad!" he murmured to himself—and

suddenly bent double. Crunch caught sight of him even as he began attaching a new leader to the broken line. "Allergy's bothering
my mate again, poor chap."

Dr. Binney presently hung a big bonita on the center line.
Big—as bonitas go, Crunch thought. It bored straight down at a
tremendous rate, directly astern of the boat. Des speeded up to
give the doctor an angle on his fish. But Binney, who had already
mentioned his lack of co-ordination, now exhibited that lack. As
the fish sounded, his rod-tip fell lower and lower. He responded
to a series of jerks with a further lowering of the rod. Crunch
warned him—but he mistook the advice not to drop his rod as a
command to do so. When the tip, as a result, lay across the gunwale, it broke, and so did the line.

"Huh!" said the doctor. "Live and learn, eh? Put the rod
on my bill, skipper, and the next time, I'll hold it high."

Another man might have been enraged at his bad luck or—
if he had character—at his own stupidity. Binney took this last as
a matter of course. "Never was good at such things," he smiled.
And he began to whistle a hymn.

It was the sailfish which authenticated Binney as the problem
angler of all time. If they had not seen the performance, Crunch
and Des would have believed an account of it from very few persons. Sailfish were hitting well in spite of the previous day's ill
fortune. This one was a small specimen—a thirty-pounder, perhaps. As far as it was concerned, it did nothing unusual or un-
conventional.

Around four in the afternoon it swam up behind the starboard bait, followed a while, and hit. Binney saw it first—he was
fishing, still, with endless concentration—and called out. Des was
at the topside controls. Crunch had gone below to obtain cokes.
There was a breeze blowing. The outrigger line dropped and the
breeze wafted its lazy slack toward the cockpit. Des bellowed,
"Don't get tangled in that line!" Crunch heard, and dropped the
bottle opener to rush on deck. He was too late.

The line had fallen across the doctor's sola topee. In trying to brush it away, he had managed to wrap it around the hat. It came tight. The leather strap caught on it. The hat was jerked ferociously from the doctor's head and hurtled overboard, casting its contents of small, green leaves on the deck, the gunwale, and the sea—into which it vanished, drawn by the rushing fish. The entrance of the hat into the sea added pressure on the fish, for the topee was firmly entangled in the line. It became a sort of sea anchor. The fish leaped. It leaped several times.

Staring with excitement and awe, murmuring, "Golly! My lord!" Binney thoughtlessly eased his rod-butt up out of its gimbal. The sailfish now ran—and the rod turned round in his hands. This circumstance drew Binney's attention and he struggled gamely. He seemed to need three hands to get the rod—now under great strain—turned around again. He tried to make up the deficit by contorting himself oddly in the fighting chair and using his foot to help support the rod. Meanwhile, the sailfish raged around toward the port side of the boat. This brought the rod—already upside down—around sidewise. Binney's toe slid between the line and the rod. His sandal was whisked away. The racing line burned against his foot. He stood up and pulled on the rod. It came up along his leg and he lifted until, in a split second, he had the thing above his knee. His khaki shorts now protected him from further line-burn. The line raced along one side of his leg and the rod bent upon the other and he scrabbled about, trying to reach behind himself to get hold of the reel handle.

Crunch grabbed him at approximately that point, sat him down, and removed the busy rod from his abraded limb. He reset the rod in its socket and bade Binney to continue fishing.

That should have been all there was to it. The sailfish was obviously firmly hooked. The sola topee had acted as a drag when Binney's gyrations had prevented him from applying suitable tension. The sail jumped a few more times, fought stubbornly for some twenty-five minutes, and Crunch boated it. He socked it on the head, disengaged the hook, and stretched it on the stern for Binney to admire. Binney spread its huge, polka-dotted dorsal and tested its rough bill. In so doing, he knocked it overboard. It eddied bluely in the foaming wake—and sank.

Crunch looked up wildly. No Des was in sight. For a terrible instant, Crunch thought his mate had fallen overboard in some paroxysm. He jumped up on the gunwale. Des was lying flat on the canopy. His abdomen heaved. Tears ran down his cheeks. No sound came from him.

Crunch went back to the side of his passenger. "Well—" he said, "we darned near got one, anyhow. Technically, we did."

Binney seemed slightly stunned. He rubbed the various chafings on his leg. "I'm sorry."

"Forget it, doc. We'll try to find another."

The doctor seemed to meditate. Presently he chuckled. "That was about the most ludicrous thing I've ever done yet."

"You're unfamiliar with the gear, after all . . ."

"Hopping around," Binney amused, "with my leg trapped between rod and line—fumbling for the reel . . ."

He began to laugh. At first, he just laughed a little. Then more. Soon, his mirth—hearty and unrestrained—sounded across the Gulf Stream. And Crunch laughed, also. When he saw that his customer didn't mind, he gave full expression to feelings he had contained all day long. Des, getting up on his knees, was astonished to observe the two men rocking with laughter and slapping each other on the back. Des joined them. He felt that, for years to come, in any truly somber hour, he would be able to relieve his depression by recalling the spectacle of the dancing Binney. Egg Jones's *Golden Loon* passed near-by—her lines trailing in the sea. All hands turned to watch the *Poseidon* and listen to the hilarious din which rose from her canopy and cockpit.

"Any guy," Crunch said to Des that evening, "who can laugh so hard at himself is okay."

"Don't start me in again. My sides hurt."

"I'm serious. He may be eccentric. The fact that he looks like a movie actor is odd. But I like him."

"How you going to teach him to fish?"

Crunch snorted—and checked himself. "We started him in too big a league. Tomorrow, we'll take him out bottom-fishing. He says he's done some handline fishing in outrigger canoes. He'll be okay at that. We'll work up gradually—from handline to rod and reel on grunts. Then groupers. Then amberjack. Then we'll risk sailfishing again."

Des said soberly, "I'd just as soon sailfish with him, any day. Maybe he can dream up another."

They were laughing again when a female voice said, "Hey!"

"Marylin," Crunch called through the warm gloom. "Come aboard. We've been getting set for tomorrow again."

She came aboard. She was wearing something that hissed like silk—something dark and simple and expensive—along with a perfume that was charged with a mixture of heartache and what's good for it. Her arms gleamed and her gold hair glittered like Christmas tinsel in a half-dark room. "I'm looking for Ramsay. Thought he might be down here. He didn't come over this evening."

"We sent him home in good condition—more or less."

"Meaning what?" she asked quickly. "How did he do today? Is he going to turn into an angler?"

"It's a little early to tell—" Des ventured.

"—but," Crunch added, "he is certainly trying."

She sat down. They gave her a cigarette. "He would be. He's stubborn as a mule. He won't marry me."

"No?" Crunch said that.

"Not—yet." She sounded as if it were merely a matter of time.

"How do you know?"

"Because I asked him last night—point blank. We were in the garden—the little formal one—necking—"

"Ye gods!" Des exclaimed. "Does he neck?"

Perhaps her lips were smiling. They couldn't see in the murky cockpit. At any rate, her voice was light. "Neck? Oh, yes. Ram-

say necks. Maybe he learned at Harvard. I sort of think though—
from the way he does it—that it's one of those things he picked
up from the natives." She seemed to nod. "No Harvard man I ever
knew . . ." Her tone changed. "However. He said he absolutely
wouldn't marry me at this point. He said I wasn't docile." She
sounded annoyed. "Is that what a man wants in a woman? Do-
cility?"

"Maybe," Des suggested vaguely, "that's a native idea,
too."

She thought it over. "Phooie! Look. Has he caught anything?"

"In a sense," Crunch said.

"What do you mean—in a sense?"

They explained—in some detail.

Marylin listened grimly. She was not amused even by the
episode of the entangled sailfish and the sea-going sola topee.

"Why I have to be so crazy about a stumblebum . . . !" She
shrugged it off. "What charters have you two got in the next ten
days?"

"September," Des said, "things are slack. People don't plan
to fish. Afraid of hurricanes. Usually—the weather stays swell and
the wind fails to blow."

"Meaning none?"

"Meaning," Des replied, "that your Ramsay was a godsend.
The night he showed up, I was phoning a guy I know who runs a
brick yard to see if I could get a temporary job there. Lot of con-
struction going on—"

"Dad has got one of those merciless ideas of his."

"What?" Crunch asked.

"To charter two boats and take Dodson and Pierce and
Mother and a girl they know and Ramsay and me, of course—and
make a trip down to Key West. Fishing."

"Our Ramsay," Des said firmly, "isn't ready for it."

"That's just the point. They think if I'm cooped up with him
—where the boys will shine and he won't—I'll get over it."

"Did it ever occur to you that you might?" Crunch asked.

"No!" She said it sharply.

"Tell Ramsay not to go."

"He'd go," the girl answered. "That's the hell of it. He's getting to loathe my family. But he'd go just because he won't give up on anything—ever."

"Yeah." Crunch smoked. "Your Ramsay, Marylin, in his very peculiar way, is a whole lot of fellow."

To Crunch's surprise, he found himself kissed. "That," she said, "is the only nice word I've heard about him in months!" She sat down again. "You boys really like him, don't you?"

Des said, "Yeah. We like him. We like him enough to hate to see him take a beating. No kidding, Marylin. That guy ought to stay in his laboratory—or wherever he works. On a boat— he's—"

"Out of this world." She nodded and her hair twinkled. "Poor lamb. The whole idea of the trip makes me sick. I can just see Ramsay falling overboard and Dodson or Pierce diving in and saving him. Or Dodson catching a marlin—and Ramsay incessantly missing even snappers."

"We might put a few—difficulties—in the way of your brothers," Des suggested.

"No, sir!" She said that with firmness. "My brothers are all right. I love my brothers. It's just—how to get them to see that Ramsay's all right, too. They're every bit as serious minded as Ramsay. Dad's trained them all to run the business and to run the Foundation. So they're going to have to work hard all their lives, too. It's just that Ramsay never had their opportunities— and he has no aptitude, the way they do . . ."

"Very little," Des agreed.

"Go on," she said, "be funny."

Crunch snapped a cigarette, watched it ride its red trajectory to the water, heard it hiss, and heard, after that, the swirl of a fish that was sure to find paper and tobacco a great disappointment. "Listen, Marylin," he said. "Get up the trip. Ask your guy. We'll do something to help him out, if we have to train a sailfish to jump aboard."

"Maybe," Des suggested, "he could learn to catch flying fish in that hat."

Marylin spoke hotly. "Try isolating viruses, someday, Des. That, Ramsay can do—extremely well."

He answered contritely, "I'm sorry. But—no kidding—even though I admire him, I can't help remembering. I never saw anybody get his foot caught in his tackle before."

After a while, she rose and bade them good night. She sounded uncertain and unhappy. "It'll be an ordeal—from start to finish," she said. "But please—please help me! Us."

"We'll do what we can," Crunch assured her, assisting her ashore.

"But don't expect miracles," Des called.

Skipper and mate sat a while in silence. "Think he's stuck on her?" the latter asked eventually.

"Yeah. Plenty. The way he flushed. Little things he said."

"I do, too."

"Poor *galoot*," Crunch murmured. "I'd hate to be in his shoes."

"Sandals," Des reminded his captain.

II

Marylin had said the fishing trip to Key West would be an ordeal. It was the business of Crunch and Des to see that, come high wind, high water and hades itself, no fishing trip was an ordeal for anybody. Sometimes they failed. But, as a rule, they brought back to the dock contented customers and when they said the time-honored, "Hurry back," the *Poseidon's* guests usually did return, if not this year, then next. The reputation of fishing guides depends upon the matter of "hurrying back." It is not an easy business—and far more men, good men, have lost out in it than have ever, like Crunch and Des, made a sound living at it.

Crunch had a delicate cargo and a tough assignment. He thought over the situation as he stood in the morning sun and steered south from the jetties off Miami—south and a little east till he reached the Gulf Stream. Then west a bit. On board the *Poseidon*, besides himself and Des, were Marylin, Ramsay Binney, Marylin's brother Dodson, and a friend of his—one Olivia Brarely, an Atlanta girl.

Des put out baits. The two couples drew matches and took places accordingly—Dodson on the center rod, Marylin port, and Olivia starboard. Ramsay Binney sat on the fishbox astern and talked, not to Marylin, but to Olivia. She seemed interested.

A girl with long, black hair, flame-blue eyes, red cheeks and Dixie in her voice—a petite young woman, very well shaped and very much aware of that. Marylin affected to be just slightly amused that Ramsay was talking to Olivia—and it took only a fraction of Crunch's discernment to measure the falsity of that pose. Crunch, himself, was slightly surprised by Ramsay's attention to the southern girl, which had begun with their meeting and ripened, in half an hour to the present stage—the stage of anecdotes about life at Harvard, snatches of which Crunch could hear above the engine pulse.

Dodson, who had invited the girl, did not care much about the monologue, either. That was to be expected, however. As far as Dodson was concerned, Ramsay Binney had two strikes on him and a glass bat.

Things, for the first half hour of a doubtful trip, were not shaping up well, Crunch thought.

Astern, and out to sea aways, was the *Sea Pike*—with Ronney Boles at the controls, Skid Wilkins as mate, and Mr. and Mrs. Brush together with Pierce, another son, as passengers. Presently the *Sea Pike* found something. Crunch saw her lose weigh, and turn a little; he made out a bent rod in the capable hands of Mrs. Brush. He shut down lightly on the gas levers and put the *Poseidon* in a

very wide turn. When it was completed, he saw Skid lean over the
Sea Pike's side and gaff a nice dolphin. Both boats started down
the Keys again in their original, relative positions.

"Come over and sit by me a while, Ramsay," Marylin said.

She said it pretty sharply, Crunch thought. She was tired
of the monologue to Olivia.

"I'm okay right here." Ramsay said it pleasantly, and returned to a story he was telling about ritual dances on Poaki.

Marylin didn't push the invitation. She slid lower in her
chair, however, and sat very still. Dodson stared at Ramsay icily.
And only Crunch saw that, a moment later, Ramsay almost did
rise to go to Marylin's side. He glanced at her—glanced again—
and his jaw hardened. He sat back on the stern and started another
island yarn for Miss Brarely's benefit.

Crunch wished something would break this up. He began
to have visions of some first magnitude sulking—or even of scenes
—on board his usually happy ship. His wish was answered. There
was a change in the shimmer of the wake where Dodson's bait
bobbed and surged in the bubbles. Crunch opened his mouth to
call. But Dodson was just as quick. He looked—looked again—
and shifted his right hand to his reel.

A fin came out—then a bill. The bill lunged foreward. Dodson
slipped off the drag and let the line drop back. When the sailfish
picked up the bait and ran with it, Dodson felt the slight accelera-
tion and knew it was time to hit. He snapped on the drag, stood
and struck. He then took a folded handkerchief from his pocket
and put it between the rod butt and his abdomen, for padding. He
struck again. The sailfish now hove itself into the air and every
one saw it. Dodson waited until the fish reached the top of its
leap—then he whipped back his rod slightly and spilled it on the
sea-surface with a calculated and dazing smack. The sail jumped
five or six times in succession—and Dodson threw it off balance
every time. Then, when the fish ran wildly, he held his rod in one
hand, propped against himself, and stuck the other in his pocket
—insolently.

It was perfect fishing, Crunch thought. In something less than
twenty seconds, Dodson Brush had felt the tap, dropped back,
hooked his fish, jarred it on every jump, and set himself for the
ensuing run. The skipper looked at Ramsay Binney and found
that the young doctor was watching—not the fish—but the angler.
Watching with almost desperate concentration. And now, as Dodson began to reel smoothly and rapidly, Ramsay, unnoticed by anyone but Crunch, imitated over and over the movements he had
seen Dodson make.

Marylin was standing. "It's big, Dod," she said excitedly.
"See how fast you can bring it in." She looked at her watch.
"Nine-eighteen."

Olivia said, "Yeaaaah, boy!" loudly. Then she added, "Kill
it, Dod!"

Dodson didn't "kill it"—but he made short work of it, especially for light tackle. When the fish ran, he tightened the drag
to the last possible ounce of tension. Any more would have snapped
the line. When the fish came toward the boat, he gathered line
with amazing speed. When it sounded he stepped close to the
stern and put on pressure again—turning it back up toward the
surface in two or three minutes. When it "tail-walked" he spilled
it once more. In ten or twelve minutes, it was making mere half-
jumps that did not clear the water, and Dodson was getting it
nearer to the boat with each one.

Not long after that, Des reached for the leader. "Want it?"

Dodson smiled and shook his head. "Put him back to grow
bigger."

Des nodded, leaned, grabbed the bill in a gloved hand, wiped
his eyes clear of spray from the threshing tail, backed the hook
out of the gristle in the jaw, and let go. The sailfish lay still for
a second, receded astern, shook itself, and swam lazily away.

"Eighteen minutes and ten seconds," Marylin said. "Pretty
good."

Dodson grinned and motioned Ramsay to his chair. "You're
up, pal." He reached for the monkey rail and swung himself

lithely up on the canopy. Olivia watched him go up and blew him
a kiss.

"Fun," Dodson said to Crunch.

"Very neat fishing," Crunch answered. "Never saw better."
He noted that Dodson was not panting and there was no sign of
perspiration on his face. A large, frank face with copper freckles
set beneath reddish blond hair and above a pair of shoulders that
might have belonged—and did belong—to a fullback.

The two boats trolled uneventfully for a while.

Crunch felt better. The taking of the sail had relieved a bad
mood. Marylin began singing "Nature Boy"—and Olivia har-
monized. She was good at it.

"How do you like the professor?" Dodson quietly asked
Crunch.

Crunch turned from the long vista of horizon and low keys
to the cockpit. He stiffened. "Hey, doc," he called.

Ramsey wheeled and gazed up enquiringly.

Crunch gestured with his fingers and shook his head.

Ramsay regarded his own fingers, then, and realized he had
wound his line around them several times. A strike would have
broken the line and probably cut his fingers. He flushed and ex-
tricated his hand.

"Nervous guy," Dodson said to Crunch. "Isn't he?"

"I like him." The skipper eyed his passenger directly and
candidly. "A lot, Dod."

"The clown prince of twerps."

"Use some imagination, Dod. Suppose you'd had his background?"

Dod was bitter about it. "All right. Suppose I'd had. So what?
I'd have learned *something* on that damned island! After all—it
was surrounded by water. You should see the oaf in a swimming
pool! We had him in ours—and he uses some kind of native breast
stroke that looks like a bowlegged platypus swimming in maple
syrup."

"I never saw him swim, I admit."

"You may. He's the type that falls off boats. If I'd been raised on his island, Crunch, I'd have learned to climb trees. But he's high-shy. Or shoot. Or throw rocks. Or use a bow and arrow. Or weave sisal. Or some damned thing. So far as I can find out—he just studied at home and taught the natives hymns. And then what? He's been in America nine years. Nine years, Crunch! But he still talks like something out of the nineteen-tens—at least when he's upset. And he hasn't even learned to drive a car!"

"He's worked hard."

"To be a brain—he's worked hard. To be a person—he hasn't lifted a finger. Take a gander at the hair-comb on him! Looks like what you shake out of a vacuum cleaner."

Crunch chuckled. He couldn't help it.

Dodson shook his head sadly. "Marylin—that moron! We've only got one sister—Clay and Pierce and Dave and I—and we swore we'd make sure she married something A-number-one. This isn't it. One part intellectual giant, one part matinee idol, and one part jellyfish. It won't do, Crunch. What'll be left for her when the honeymoon ends? How will she explain it, all the rest of her life? Ye Gods! Look at what's coming up!"

Crunch had been facing the bow, steering his course, during the homily. With a feeling of apprehension, he turned again. There was a sailfish behind Ramsay's bait—and Ramsay had seen it. But Ramsay, having fiddled nervously with his line and having been warned against that, had transferred his fiddling to the ring that held his reel in its seat.

The sailfish struck. Ramsay snapped off the drag. His reel slewed back and forth a few times and fell to the deck. With agonized eyes, Ramsay glanced up at Crunch, but Crunch had no solution for that one. It was up to Des—and luck. Unfortunately, Des was cutting a bait.

Ramsay knew there had to be tension on the line to set the hook. So he grabbed the reelless rod and the line in both hands and struck. The line sizzled—but he hung on. And now the reel began to leap about the deck. Des made a pass at it and it bounced

ten feet from his hand. Marylin nearly caught it as it hopped up
and hit her chair. It ricocheted from the gunwale and struck
Olivia, who cried, "Ouch!" Then the line on the reel backlashed,
stopping the crazy revolutions of the spindle. The hooked sailfish,
however, was still going away at something like thirty miles an
hour. So the reel lifted itself from the deck, flung like a bullet at
the rod, smacked Ramsay's hands, and thus broke the line. Having done that, the reel dropped to the deck again.

"Very pretty," Dodson murmured to Crunch. "*Ve*-ry pretty!"

Marylin began to giggle.

Olivia wailed, "Darn it, I'm going to have a black and blue
spot!"

Des picked up the reel and studied it. "Humh," he said.

Ramsay Binney looked shamefacedly from Marylin to Olivia
to Des and then up, to Dodson and to Crunch.

"If anybody has any suggestions to make," he said, grinning,
"I don't want to know what they are. Olivia, let me see your injury. I'm a doctor, you know." And then, after a glance at the
trifling bruise on the girl's shin, he sat down quietly in his chair.
"Bait her up again, Des," he requested. "Hope we have plenty
of tackle aboard."

For one moment, Crunch noticed a flicker of admiration in
Dodson's eyes. But it died. "That chump," he muttered. "That nitwit!"

Key West is one of the most glamorous towns in America.
But many people have gone there, looked, listened, and left with
the impression that they have taken unnecessary lengths to visit
a village of no great interest. Those are people without imagination, without sense, without the spirit of adventure—people to
whom travel means invidious comparisons and nothing else.

Key West is on an island, which, in itself, is romantic. The
island is set in a spot where the Gulf of Mexico meets the Carib-
bean and both these meet the Atlantic. The Gulf Stream runs
around it like a purple sickle. Many of the town's clapboard houses

are made of solid mahogany—the original, Keys mahogany. It is maritime. Once the center of the sponge fisheries—Key West is still the chief port for green turtles and the steaks and the soup that are made from them. It has a beach and a ruined fort; coral grows under the sea in a gigantic garden all around Key West. At night, the United States Navy promenades its streets and drinks beer in its murky bistros. Spanish is spoken on its thoroughfares —black, Cuban hair gleams in its neon lights and black eyes flash in the glitter of its traffic.

It looks like Salem, Massachusetts, or any other eighteenth century town with a sea-going tradition. Something like Salem. But the shade trees are different—cork oaks and sapodillas, monstrous, corrugated ficuses, gumbo limbos, palms, palmettos, mangoes spreading like maples, and great, mysterious branching mammoths that were brought by sailors from Madagascar and Ceylon and Java and the natives have forgotten the names of. Frangipanis bloom in Key West, cereus and jasmine by night, and orchids in people's backyards—the kind that florists breed and the kind that spring up on stumps in the Everglades to the north. Here is to be found the southernmost house in the United States; and ninety miles away lies the tropical isle of Cuba.

There is no frost.

They sell electric refrigerators in Key West, automobiles, chewing gum, mixing machines—and the drugstore is any American drugstore, except that it is air conditioned—even in winter. The visitor can dine on a "turtleburger" as easily as on hamburger— or on Cuban bread and black bean soup, *arroz con pollo*, local limes and bananas, conch salad, Morro crabs; he can have local tortoise shell carved according to his fancy or buy a sponge, direct, from the man who harvested it. He can buy a seashell collection, too—or pick up his own, on the beaches.

At night, the moon rises in one ocean and sets in another. Spicy pine from the upper keys burns on cooking fires and the aroma, mingled with the exotic honeys of the myriad flowers, floats through the streets and the treetops, pervades the old, gabled

houses attached to the ground by steel hawser against the day of
a blow, and drifts in high, hotel corridors. This scent—sweet,
pungent and sea tinged—is the island's spirit, its ester, and the
sensitive visitor acknowledges it subtly. He—or she—is still in
North America, still in the United States, to be sure; but the
mood here is different from the rest of the land—more impas-
sioned and yet languid, more primitive, and yet savored with old,
unfamiliar cultures of hot countries.

The Brushes, their guest Olivia, and Dr. Binney, had taken
rooms in the Hotel Tropic of Cancer. Crunch and Des slept on
board the *Poseidon* as did Ronney Boles and Skid Wilkins on the
Sea Pike. By day, they fished on the reef and in the Stream. In
the evenings, they dined together at the picturesque eating places
of Cayo Huesco—which is what the Cubans called the town.
Friends usually joined them—friends from the mahogany houses
and friends from other fishing boats and houseboats, who had
ignored the hurricane season. For the Brushes—mére, pére, fille
and fils—were the sort of people who had friends everywhere on
the earth, in every walk of life. Let an airplane containing a Brush
be forced to land in Timbuktu or Patagonia and soon that Brush
would be lunching with an acquaintance he or she had made years
before in Alaska, or Tibet, or London.

On the fifth night of the expedition, the Brush party was dining at a large table in the Pearl of the Caribbees Restaurant. At
the head of the table sat Jerome, the senior Brush, a tall and
powerful man—grey haired, grey moustached, and grey eyed, with
a deep voice given to laughter. His attention wandered now and
then, in spite of himself, to his daughter and thence to Ramsay
Binney. Each time, he frowned all but invisibly. Mrs. Brush—
handsome, ungreyed, poised perfectly—concealed her own inner
anxiety. She affected to be pleased with Dr. Binney and took almost
as much interest as Olivia in all that he said. Crunch and Des,
of those at dinner who did not belong to the family, were aware of
constant tension. And Binney himself, of course, was keenly conscious of it. But Mr. and Mrs. Weber and their two pretty daugh-

ters, from the yacht *Beryl*, had no idea they were present at anything but a delightful, informal dinner party.

The room contained several dozen tables, a long bar, a dance floor and a band stand. Its walls were covered with trellises and upon these grew paper vines bearing implausible red flowers. Behind this mural bower, rosy lights glowed. There were many other diners—and waiters who spoke better Spanish than English.

With the conch chowder, Pierce Brush rose and raised his wine glass. Pierce was the dark brother—the tallest and also the thinnest—the one who held the pole-vaulting records, the hurdler, the brother who was interested in the technical work at the Brush Foundation more than the executive opportunities it offered.

"A toast," he said, "to Ramsay."

"A toast!" one of the Weber girls cried, and lifted her glass.

Others followed suit.

Pierce looked into the wine thoughtfully. The table quieted. "To Dr. Ramsay Binney who, after misadventures and vicissitudes too numerous for mention, has, in the past few days, actually succeeded, alone and unaided, and virtually without incident, in bringing to boat several members of the genus Lutianus, locally known as snappers, as well as various mackerels and small members of the bass family—to wit, groupers. I suggest we rise in appreciation of this virtuosity, this intrepidity, this formidable exhibition of strength, skill and endurance, and confer—"

"Cut it out," Marylin said sharply.

"—confer upon the eminent-to-be scientist the honorary degree——"

"Stop it," the girl said.

"—of Master of Meager Fishes, Honoris Causa. Dr. Binney. Well done!"

Ramsay had accepted the start of this ribbing with his usual, rather meek grin. Marylin's interference made him blush. Crunch, watching him with the others, thought that—for an instant—he was angry. There are limits beyond which no human patience will bear up. However, after the toast was drunk, Ramsay stood up, smiling again, and said, "I wish to thank one and all, and Pierce in particular, for this undeserved recognition. His prowess in the piscatorial field, along with his prodigious feats in other fields of sport, make this honor unique for me. I only wish there were fields in which Pierce and I might compete on more even terms. Unfortunately, my forte lies in the realm of intelligence."

It was a biting riposte and everybody laughed—excepting Pierce who was, probably, the most intellectual of the Brush brothers. His knuckles went white around his glass and he glared at the doctor.

Olivia said quickly, "Why doesn't somebody toast me? I caught a sailfish, after all."

Mrs. Brush took that up.

Dodson framed the toast for Olivia.

But as the meal continued, even the Webers realized that there were strained relations amongst their hosts. Crunch signaled approval to Binney when he got the chance: the doctor could dish it out, when he felt like it, as well as he could take it. But he appeared to be discomfited by his speech. He ate uneasily.

All that could be expected to follow the rather insulting toast and its still more insulting rejoinder was a heightening of antagonisms. Pierce was now personally peeved at Binney. Marylin was sore at Pierce. Mr. Brush senior was annoyed. His wife became unnaturally gay and chatty. Dr. Binney held his embarrassed flush. Dodson attacked a turtle steak with violence. The waiters poured more wine.

"I wish I had never let Ramsay go on this trip," Marylin whispered to Crunch. "I wish I'd never urged him to try to learn to fish."

"Too late." Crunch glanced at the doctor. "He's determined to learn, now—and when he gets determined—well . . ."

"I know," she said. "Stubborn people are wonderful when they're helping you out. When they're not . . . !"

These were expectable circumstances. But, wherever Ramsay Binney went, something unexpected was likely to happen.

The band filed in as the dinner guests were served coconut ice cream. It was a rumba band and a good one. As it began to play, a blissful expression came over Dodson's freckled face. He looked at Olivia and inclined his head. She nodded. They danced. Crunch asked Marylin to dance. Mr. and Mrs. Brush danced. Pierce took one of the Weber girls, and Des the other. Patrons— among them some Cubans who were expert—filled the floor.

Ramsay watched them, for some time. His eyes were interested and yet, Crunch thought, after a glance or two, a little sad. Here was another Brush accomplishment that left him out.

Crunch liked to rumba. He and his wife, Sari, had won several amateur contests in that dance and Marylin was a skillful partner. *Lot of professional lessons*, Crunch thought. He went into a fast spot turn, reversed it, walked his girl around, and closed again. The tempo changed. The music stopped, presently, and they switched partners.

Crunch was dancing with one of the Miss Webers—and not in a place where he could see the band—when the music itself became somewhat different. It was the bongos, Crunch thought—the small, double drums. Somebody else was playing them and the whole band was following. Whoever it was had terrific rhythm and a beat Crunch had never heard, in spite of his familiarity with the rumba bands of Miami. The new player made the drums roar with hands that flew like sticks on a snare drum. He made a loud, sharp, exclamation for the long beat. He played briefly in that cadence and shifted to contra-tempo—roaring all four beats, rattling them, hesitating minutely before the last—and drumming them squarely and lightly when the song grew softer. Then he changed to a kind of syncopation—loud and soft and loud—that sounded less like the civilized and sophisticated rumba music of modern bands and far more like the African bush music from which rumba, like jazz, has been derived.

Crunch knew, then. He danced around the side of the floor and up to the band. Already, some of the Cuban couples had stopped dancing to admire. Ramsay had taken off his coat. He had tucked in his necktie. He held the two little drums between his knees, like a professional. But he played them like a native—a native of far-away Poaki, who had recognized the kinship of Afro-Cuban rhythm with his own, elemental drumming. Ramsay had learned something on Poaki, after all; he had learned to drum barehanded so well that the present band leader conducted with enchant-ment and every man in the orchestra played with a kind of rever-ence.

Dodson danced up with his mother—and stopped. He looked. "Ye gods!" he said. "El professor!"

Crunch saw Marylin—standing with Ronney. She was smiling a little, not surprised, her eyes slightly shut, looking as if she had always known, always understood Ramsay to be capable of such bizarre virtuosity. His hair flew. His eyes closed. He seemed not to realize anybody was watching. The walls quivered. The build-ing throbbed. The night and the very ground seemed to beat. And that, Marylin obviously felt, was all right in the man she was crazy about. It was, too, Crunch thought.

The piece came to a sudden, crashing climax. People yelled and whistled. The orchestra leader asked Ramsay, in Spanish, if he would like to suggest something. Ramsay was still only vaguely conscious of his audience in spite of the noise it had made. He nodded and shut his eyes again.

The leader let Ramsay drum alone for a moment. Then he brought in maraccas, a violin, and a big drum. The pianist and trumpeters stayed out of it. Nobody knew what Ramsay was play-ing. It began slowly. It accelerated. It created feelings—dim, primor-dial sensations of fear and loneliness and rising excitement—which civilized people brush out of their minds in childhood. The beat was, still, the same as the rumba beat. It could have been danced. Crunch—and perhaps others—could imagine that it undoubtedly was danced—by men wearing feathers, clay daubed, barefooted—and women with grass skirts. It reached a speed and violence almost beyond tolerability—and then, swiftly, whispered to silence.

Again there were cheers. From the night outside, people began sifting into the Pearl of the Caribbees to listen—many of them dark-visaged Cubans. The music continued.

Marylin moved through the standing listeners. "Isn't he wonderful?"

Crunch said, "Yeah," and meant it. He thought that—on familiar grounds—Ramsay had ample co-ordination.

But Pierce heard her and said, "Damned cannibal jam session! I want to dance."

"It's interestin'," Olivia agreed, and she looked at Dodson. "But I much prefer to dance, myself."

That was enough for Pierce. He walked up to Ramsay and waited for him to finish his next *tour de force*. "Look, pal. The ladies would like to dance—and your concerto has stopped the fun."

Ramsay shook himself slightly. He saw the room again, and Pierce. His rapt expression faded away and his amiable smile took its place. "Why—sure," he said. "I didn't mean to hold up the show. I just saw those drums—and they're like the kind we had in—"

"Poaki. I know."

Ramsay stepped down.

There was immediate, bilingual protest. Pierce had not calculated the effect of the drumming on its Key West audience and, particularly, on the Cuban faction of that audience. A thin, excited gentleman with dark sideburns took Pierce by the arm and turned him a little. His Spanish was incomprehensible in detail but easily enough understood in purport: he was furious at the interruption. Pierce yanked away from the man—who seized him again. Two more came to his verbal aid. People were yelling, "More!" and "Encore!" and "Bravo!"

Mr. Brush senior sought out the proprietor and told him that the floor should be cleared, the regular music should be played, and he and his guests should be permitted to take their coffee—and to dance without further hubbub. The proprietor, who had himself been enchanted by the bongos, somewhat loftily suggested that if Mr. Brush wished this to be done, Mr. Brush should undertake it himself.

Whereupon Mr. Brush, who had once enjoyed exactly such problems, turned to the clamorous dance floor, narrowed his eyes, and said, "The way I feel this evening, I have half a mind to."

"Half a mind to what?" Dodson asked, who had seen his father in altercation and pushed up to his side.

"Throw these monkeys out and finish dinner decently."

Dodson studied the scene. "Not a bad idea."

People were trying to push Ramsay back to the bandstand. He was now visibly horrified by the pandemonium he had so innocently caused. He kept shaking his head and refusing to play any more. When the shouting and the pressure reached a level that, for him, was intolerable, he pulled himself free of the press of people, jumped awkwardly behind a pillar in the Pearl of the Caribbees, and stepped quickly through a side door. He felt that his playing had been another *faux pas*—another foolish spectacle—and, as a man will under such circumstance, he stepped rather savagely into the deep, pungent night, and stayed there.

Meanwhile a burly citizen of Key West—not Cuban, but an enthusiast of the rumba—had overheard Dodson's statement that throwing a few people out of the restaurant would not be a bad idea. He was a little drunk and he presented himself. "My name," he said, "is Coxley. Will Coxley. I never saw you around Key West before. It's our town, though, and we like good musicians down here. We don't like strangers threatening to throw us out of our own eating joints. If you insist on trying—suppose you begin with me."

This startled the usually good-natured Dodson. "Oh—hell," he said. "I'm sorry."

Mr. Coxley poked Dodson with a thick forefinger. "You should be sorry. Good and sorry. You might get hurt, otherwise."

This caused Dodson to slant his head. "Really?"

Mr. Brush senior said, "Come away, son. This is absurd."

Mr. Coxley now turned to the father. "Stay out of it, you hippopotamus."

People were gathering, now, around this new nucleus of trouble. Dodson eyed Coxley and tried to walk through the crowd. "Throw *him* out," somebody said.

And somebody tried.

"Throw out the whole bunch!" another voice shouted, as the scuffling began.

Crunch, from old experience in such situations, knew that there were enough people who were drunk enough, and enough Cubans who were sufficiently excitable, to make a very quick shambles of the Pearl of the Caribbees. Fists were already smacking and shouts were rising in the knot of men around Dodson. Mr. Brush, senior, was taking off his coat, calmly—and Pierce was already hammering his way in toward his brother. Crunch took charge, then, of the Weber ladies, of Mrs. Brush, of Marylin and Olivia. Aided by Des, he conducted them rapidly to, and through, the side door. Other ladies were leaving, frenziedly, by the same route. Some were screaming for the police and some were just screaming. The ladies from the *Poseidon* and the *Sea Pike*, however, retired in an orderly, if indignant, manner.

Crunch and Des, joined then by Ronney and Skid, moved thereafter toward the fray. "Don't hit anybody if you can help it," Crunch ordered. "Just haul them off."

It was strenuous. Crunch began peeling away the outer rim around Pierce, Dodson and their father. One of the vine-covered bowers was smashed and fell upon the combatants. A guitar was raised and shattered on Pierce—without effect. Somebody commenced throwing electric light bulbs—which burst loudly and accomplished nothing. Des saw a man take a knife surreptitiously from beneath his trouser leg and look at it. He took the knife away from the man and, on second thought, knocked the man beyond any further contemplation along such lines.

The four charter boatmen reached the center of the mill at about the same time. "Come on—Dod—Pierce!" Crunch yelled.

They began struggling and fighting their way toward the door. Mr. Weber, on the outside of the crowd, opened the door. And so, presently, they were ejected into the street—partly by design and partly with the violent co-operation of various customers of the Pearl of the Caribbees.

They stood there, panting, under a wan electric light. "Anybody hurt?" Mr. Brush asked calmly.

Nobody was hurt—beyond bruises, a few small cuts, and large damage to habiliments.

"When things calm down," Mr. Brush went on, "I'll come back and pay up. Too bad to ruin a nice dinner party. On the other hand —I rather enjoyed it. That lug who called me a hippopotamus will hold his tongue another time, I believe."

"I wonder what happened to Binney?" Pierce asked, between breaths.

A voice came from the gloom near-by. "I'm right here. I was watching through the window."

"Watching!" Pierce sounded aghast. "And you didn't come in?"

"Why should I? I can't box. I'd probably have been a liability."

"Have you ever thought of *trying* to box and wrestle—when your own gang was in trouble?" Pierce's voice was bitter.

"No. I was brought up to believe that sort of thing shameful." Ramsay felt that the statement satisfied nobody, including himself. "I would have gone for the police, but you all seemed to be protecting yourselves well enough."

"What a pal!"

"You mean," Dodson asked incredulously, "you won't get in a fight, even when you're responsible for it?"

His father stopped that. "Be fair, son. He didn't start it. You did. If you and Pierce had let him go on playing, we'd have been life buddies of every rumba fiend in the joint." He started walking toward the hotel.

The others followed.

"My folks," Ramsay tried to explain, "were peaceable. Part of their creed. And I, personally, detest to hurt people. If I'd known my playing would make so much trouble, I'd never have dreamed of starting it."

In the bright, air-conditioned lobby of the Hotel Tropic of Cancer the ladies waited nervously. When, one by one, the men filed through the revolving door, each woman made her own census, and reacted with her own brand of relief. Each, save Marylin. She was the first to notice that Ramsay Binney, though missing his jacket, was untouched—while all the others bore the bruises and scratches, the incipient black eyes, the torn pockets and rent shirts which are the stigmata of minor brawling.

"What didn't happen to you?" she asked, ignoring the interest of forward-pressing strangers.

"He stayed outside," Pierce answered, "and watched through the window."

Marylin didn't say a thing. A strange expression came on her face. It wasn't contempt or anger, Crunch decided. It was a kind of humiliation, coupled with a faraway look that went beyond Ramsay into distant time. Crunch realized that she was thinking —not that he was a coward, which her family had obviously concluded, but that she was going to have to suffer a good deal with Ramsay Binney as a husband. And something about Marylin's sudden set of her jaw, her indignant glance at her family, gave Crunch a deep feeling of sympathy for the girl. Sympathy —and understanding of just how much she liked the doctor. It came, perhaps, from the fact that Crunch's own wife, in marrying him, had taken a man for whom her background hadn't exactly suited her.

And it had worked out mighty well, Crunch thought. He

winked encouragingly at Marylin—and at Binney—when he got
the chance.

The *Poseidon* was softly creaking her hawsers as Ramsay
came aboard. It was pretty dark, but Crunch could see, in the feeble
rays of a lamp on a near-by street, that the doctor's cheeks glittered. He'd been crying. At least, he'd shed tears. Walking around
town, probably.

"Hate to disturb you fellows," he said in a low tone. "But I
left a suitcase on board . . ."

Crunch got up. Des followed. They came out into the cockpit,
in pajamas.

"Suitcase?" Crunch repeated.

"Yeah." Ramsay sat down. "I thought I'd take the night bus
back to Miami. Slip out. They'll have a better time without me."

"Marylin won't," Crunch said.

"I talked with her earlier. Mind if I sit down? I'm kind of
—I guess, exhausted."

Crunch sat and so did Ramsay. Des lighted a cigarette and
leaned against the cabin.

"Marylin," Ramsay went on, after a while, "did her best to
persuade me to stick it out. She has an all-time high crush on me.
And, being sort of spoiled, she won't give it up. 'She's right and
the world is wrong.' That sort of viewpoint. But the truth is—I'm
an ass."

There was silence. Lapping water broke it—and stilled itself.
"How do you feel about her?" Crunch finally asked.

Ramsay started as if greatly surprised. "I'm here. I've done
the things she told me—or tried to. Doesn't that explain how I feel?"

"Not necessarily."

"I will love that girl," he said stiffly, almost primly, "till my
dying day. And if it were a question of just the two of us—I could
manage. I may seem unsophisticated to people like you. But I
know something about women. She has the makings of one of the

best. But it isn't a question of just two of us. It's a question of a big family—those bright, athletic brothers—big houses in a half dozen places—a hundred times as much money as I have—and more. It's a question of being the hereditary donors and managers of a great Foundation. Of taking it for granted that they are dedicated—and their wealth is—to human service. And then, on top of that, of becoming spectacular sportsmen just for fun. Just because they're nice people and full of beans. It's a question of a way of life perhaps different from what mine can ever be— an attitude—society—people—a million things. I could marry her —sure I could. Tonight—and in the face of her family. We all know that. But—no matter what I did in my work—even if I ever do something valuable—I'll always be the freaky brother-in-law —the dope—the dithering one who gets helpless when things are exciting. I'll always trump Marylin's ace, as they say."

It was Des who spoke, then—in a kindly voice. "You're doing better every day, Ram. No fooling."

"Ram." The doctor savored that. He laughed a little. "Maybe so, Des. But I'm so jittery, the way things are, that I haven't any confidence about anything I do. And that's not all. I'm proud of my folks. Medical missionaries—in a hell-hole. It was tough— the first dozen years—mighty tough for them. They stuck. They're old-fashioned—and they made me that way—but I'm proud of them and proud of Poaki. It's quite a place. The Brushes will never understand that."

Silence again. The somber silence of assent—or something near it.

"So I'm leaving."

Then Crunch said, "You love the girl, don't you?"

"Of course."

"Stick around, then."

His head shook.

"Ram. You don't quit easy, do you?"

"I think not."

"Well don't, now. I pretty nearly gave up my gal—several

times. We've been married a lot of years, now. Got a boy—a real one. And a gal—brand new. Nice house. A piece of a fishing camp in the Keys. This boat and a good business in her. Came from not quitting."

"I'll just make some new flub, if I stay . . ."

"So what?"

Ramsay thought for a long time. Finally he seemed to smile. "As you say—so what. Thanks fellows. I'll leave the suitcase on board."

They went back to their bunks. As they started toward sleep Crunch said, "Des—watch him like a hawk tomorrow, will you? Somehow, we've got to keep him out of trouble."

It was a bright day, the next one. Bright, hot and calm— with a steamy haze in the distances over the sea. A white sun. The *Poseidon* went out across the reefs and her passengers—Marylin and' Ramsay, Dodson and Olivia—leaned over the gunwales and looked down through the crystal fathoms at the coral formations, the big fish, the flashing schools of small fish, the weird gardens. Even when Des put out baits—where the water was sixty or seventy feet deep—every detail of the bottom could be seen under the hull of the *Poseidon*. On the sandy stretches, sharks lay motionless. Rays flattened themselves out—diamonds with tails. Amberjacks turned in the clear water, swimming up and then down over roller-coaster currents.

"I'd rather watch, almost, than fish," Olivia said.

And Ramsay, at her side, agreed heartily.

Crunch understood that relationship, now. Ramsay was too nervous to talk naturally with Marylin in the presence of her brother. So he had chattered nervously with Olivia through the days. It was not even an unsubtle effort to create jealousy in Marylin; just a defense. Olivia was friendly and talkative. She made it easy for him.

Poor devil, Crunch thought.

And not long after that—not long after the bottom faded out of view—becoming indistinct at a hundred feet, a blur of light

and dark after that, and invisible where the Gulf Stream rolled
—Dodson hung the mako shark.

It was the biggest mako Crunch had ever seen. And Dodson
hooked it on twenty-four-thread rig.

An epic battle began.

III

The mako made a pass at the bait on Ramsay's side. Its dorsal
was like a scythe. Its tail broke water. Its round, black, bulging eyes
seemed to glare at the *Poseidon* and at the people on board. Crunch
thought it was between eighteen and twenty feet long.

Marylin gulped, "Look, everybody!"

The pale belly of the terrible shark turned up as it veered
away, apparently in reaction to the sight of the boat.

Crunch, on the canopy, found himself grateful that it hadn't
taken the bait. Not Ramsay's bait, anyway.

It was gone from view.

"What on earth was that?" Olivia shouted.

"It was the grandfather of the makos," Crunch answered.
Then he saw it again—deep—a torpedo, a small submarine—shimmering darkly behind Dodson's outrigger line. "Dod! You better
be set! He's looking you over!"

"Looking over twenty-four-thread? I'm laughing."

"In a minute—you may not be!"

The blue blur rose, defined itself, thrust a sharp nose—a prow
—above the slick sea, then opened its cavern of teeth—teeth as big
as axheads. It engulfed the bait.

The line slanted down—slowly at first—and then stretched
tight in the air so that it hit the surface with a small, running slap.

Dodson stood and struck. His reel went crazy. Olivia leaped
from the center fighting chair. Dodson shot into it and slammed his

rod-butt home in the gimbal. His rod took a heavy bend and the reel continued to scream like something broken loose in fast machinery.

Crunch, thin lipped, shoved both throttles to their extremes. The *Poseidon's* motors tried to drown out the reel. Everybody was staggered by the forward thrust. The boat went around, skidding a little, and set out in pursuit of the mako. But even full speed did not seem to diminish the rate at which line melted from the reel spool.

"How many yards?" Dodson yelled.

"Nine hundred," Crunch yelled back.

"He's got six or seven—already!"

"We're doing our best! Hang on!"

"Till it breaks," Dodson answered grimly.

They leaned forward—not closely enough to interfere with Dod, but enough to watch that melting of line. Soon, the remaining quantity was but an inch in diameter. Desperately, Dodson tightened the drag. It accomplished nothing. The inch shrank, shrank—and then there glinted under the last few turns of line the brass axis of the reel. It was all over. Marylin swore to herself. Dodson glanced down and shook his head.

But it wasn't all over.

The great shark made a mistake. Having felt the hook—having bulleted through the sea for half a mile—and having accomplished nothing by that measure—it leaped.

Crunch had been praying for that.

It leaped—high—huge—cobalt blue—and so far away that it seemed to Ramsay and Olivia, who had never seen a fish take so much line—that it could not possibly still be attached to the *Poseidon*.

But Dodson knew. He whispered, "Oh, boy!" and leaned on the rod.

The mako turned in the air and splashed back, headed toward the boat. It swam as it landed—and now the rush of the *Poseidon* at the rushing fish put slack in the line which Dodson recovered at his best speed. The mako jumped again. Dodson kept winding.

"Roll it, Dod!" Marylin chanted. "Wind it in, baby! If you boat that fish you'll hang up a record nobody'll touch for a century!"

He got in a hundred yards—two—three—four. Then the mako changed direction and the chase was on again. But, this time, the shark swam no faster than the top speed of the *Poseidon* and the angler neither lost nor gained much line, while they covered—in a huge arc—a good two miles of open sea.

A mako is a mackerel shark and unlike the other sharks. The mako's tail is built like the mackerel's and it swims with the speed of a marlin and the energy of a tuna. It leaps—and other sharks sometimes leap when hooked, but none so high, so violently, or so often. It is not grey, or greenish, or yellow-brown. It is blue. It has round and bulging eyes. It does not have rows of slicing teeth, like many sharks, but a mouthful of immense, sharp, hard teeth meant to grasp and rend. It is a game fish and some who have caught makos regard it as the toughest of them all, tougher than broadbill, than blue marlin, or the black demons of the Pacific, or the white, or the tuna, or the majestic broadbill. As a rule, a big mako will play havoc with the heaviest tackle—tackle more than twice as strong as that used by Dodson.

But with skill, Crunch kept thinking—with such an angler— with plenty of time—and with luck, especially—it could be . . .

He did not dare bring that thought to a conclusion.

Dodson hung the mako at ten-fifteen. At noon, they were many miles above Key West, out in the Stream a mile or more, and the fish was running just as hard as ever—a few hundred yards at a clip. It had quit leaping, for the time being.

Shortly before one o'clock, the mako sounded. It started from a point about two hundred yards astern of the *Poseidon* and went down in swift lunges, twenty or more yards at a time. The reel wheezed and was still, wheezed and was still. The rod-tip bowed down and down. At five hundred yards, the shark stopped. The line now descended tautly and almost vertically over the stern.

And the mako, somewhere in the darkness of the abyss, moved along—surging this way and that.

When, exerting himself strongly but cautiously, Dodson tried to heave the fish up—even a few inches—the mako responded by sullenly shaking its head and yanking a few more feet of line from the reel.

"Let him stay there," Dodson finally said. "The pressure won't do him much good. And I can't budge him with this gear. Couldn't—with a winch—I bet. What do you say we eat?"

They hadn't talked much. They had just watched—breathless—concentrated—clenching things when the mako leaped or raced—bending a fraction of an inch in sympathy with Dodson's even, heavy labor. Crunch had cut down the motors to match the dogged speed of the fish. They moved along slowly and calmly, like a ferryboat.

Des said, "I think I'll stay behind the chair here—in case we have to make any quick maneuvers. Marylin, you set up the bridge table."

"I'll help," Ramsay offered.

They opened out the legs of the bridge table between the day beds. They brought, from the galley, potato salad and hard-boiled eggs, cold cuts, open cans of ice cold fruit, and iced coffee. They handed a plate and a glass up to Crunch. They served Des—who ate standing. Marylin, Olivia and Ramsay ate at the table, hardly looking at the food but watching Dodson instead. Afterward, Marylin fed her brother.

"How's it going?"

He grinned. "Dandy."

"Tired?"

"Hell, no." He laughed. "Neither is the mako."

She filled a pail with water, dipped a sponge, and wiped the perspiration from his face and chest. He had long since taken off his shirt.

The mako sulked until half past two. Then, suddenly, Dodson felt the pressure stop. "Broke off," he called.

"Broke off hell!" Crunch yelled back. "He's coming up!" He threw forward the throttles to get the *Poseidon* clear of the spot where the fish might emerge and to give the angler a chance to wind slack without fouling the propellors.

At the peak of his upward swim, not far from the boat, the mako burst into the air—once—twice—and again. They could clearly see the now-twisted leader and see that it entered the mouth of the giant fish. Hooked deep. Crunch wondered if the teeth would ultimately cut through the stainless steel wire leader. Another risk.

Little waves spread from where the three jumps had been made and lapped the *Poseidon*. The rod bent and straightened and bent again as the shark tore away a few feet under the surface, zigzagging, circling on itself, circling the boat. For an hour, this furious race continued and then, after a long, straight run, the shark began to bulldog against the fisherman—keeping his distance—yanking out a foot or two of line—yielding it—yanking again.

It was after four o'clock.

Ramsay found himself near Marylin. "What a tremendous fight!" he said in a low, admiring voice.

Her eyes answered. She squeezed his arm.

"What stamina!"

"Dod's good."

"Very good."

"He's gaining now, do you notice?"

Inches—feet—inches again—Dod began heaving the great shark toward the boat. Its forked tail broke water. Its dorsal showed. It turned away, sculled, struggled, and was turned back.

But Dodson was tired, too. He showed it in pallor—in excessive sweating, and in the nervous way he occasionally let go his rod with one hand and tried to wipe the pouring perspiration from his eyes. He had been on the fish for six hours by that time. The boat was some twenty miles from the point where they had hooked the mako. In the whole time and distance Dodson had not relented once, for a moment. It was not surprising that even he was wearying. However, he had his fish coming toward him, and that fact gave him new strength. His hands whitened. The rod creaked. His great back muscles showed like ropes.

And Ramsay, to help out, took a large, clean handkerchief from his pocket. He folded it catercorner, twisted the two ends, and went up to Dodson.

"If you like, Dod, I'll tie this around your forehead. Keep the sweat out of your eyes."

"Sure, pal. Good idea. Wish I'd had it right along."

It was, probably, the word "pal" that threw Ramsay off. His hands began to perspire. They made the first knot clumsily. Dodson had to move his head to give a heave on his incoming fish. He brought his rod up again and held still. But now, with a heavy flurry, the mako turned about and lunged away once more. At the same moment, from sheer exaggerated effort, Ramsay lost his hold on the handkerchief. Dodson's head swept it forward and it fell onto the racing line. The line whipped it into the first guide, where it jammed. Dodson made a frantic grab at the handkerchief, but it was too late. With the line held fast, the lunging mako broke it instantly—and was gone.

Nobody said anything for a long time.

Then Dodson put on an exhibition of the sportsmanship for which he was justly famous. He grinned at Ramsay. "Wasn't your fault, old man. The big ones usually get away. We'd have lost him—nine chances out of ten—when we tried to get a flying gaff in him. Ask Crunch."

But Ramsay knew that Crunch had been hoping. So had everybody. All day. And—which was more—he knew that only a fumbling idiot would have lost his hold of both ends of a mere handkerchief.

Olivia burst into tears.

Marylin went below.

Dodson stretched his mighty frame and looked up at the expressionless skipper. "Hell of a fine fight, anyhow."

Crunch said, "Yeah, Dod. Yeah."

Des leaned over the gunwale as if the sea was something he had never seen before—something he wanted to inspect closely, for a long while.

The *Poseidon* came around and started the long trek back to Key West. They were going to be late getting in.

The next evening, the Webers gave a dinner for the Brush party —not at the Pearl of the Caribbees, but in the large dining room of the Hotel Tropic of Cancer. Morale among the Brushes and their guests was not high. Only Marylin and Ramsay had fished that day—with indifferent success, owing partly to the fact that they had gone out late, come in early, and taken only a desultory interest in trolling. The Webers were, of course, ignorant of the loss of the mako. All four of them, led by Mr. Weber—who was rotund, bald and full of energy—were eagerly entertaining their guests when Ramsay arrived—late.

He walked through the dining room and up to the big, busy table, looking even more uncomfortable than was his want. His very appearance stopped conversation; it trailed away—died to nothing. Ramsay smiled with an effort and opened his mouth to apologize for being tardy.

Pierce Brush said loudly, "Hi, there, Drop-the-Handkerchief!"

The Webers looked at Pierce, wondering what he meant.

But Crunch watched Ramsay because Ramsay had stopped cold. His color, such as it had been, drained to whiteness. His hands clenched. For a moment, Crunch had an impression—weird and spine tingling—that Pierce was in tremendous danger. Crunch slid his legs under his chair to stop something sinister. It wasn't necessary.

Ramsay's lips began to move. He was counting, Crunch realized. Then he understood: Ramsay was counting ten. His color came back a little. The expression in his eyes—the tautness of his lips—disappeared. He smiled his humble smile.

" 'Evening, everybody." He said it rather proudly—for some reason. "Sorry to be late. I got reading . . ."

Conversation was resumed. Mrs. Brush found an opportunity to lean forward and whisper to Mr. Weber, "We're a little strained tonight. Some carelessness on the part of Dr. Binney caused Dod to lose a record mako the other day—just when he had it beaten."

Mr. Weber passed this item to his daughters. Cocktails were served. The meal proceeded with reasonable decorum.

It was toward the end of it that Mr. Weber made his suggestion.

"All you Brushes, I understand, are a little tired of fishing. I've got a proposal that might interest you. The boys, anyhow."

"What is it?" Dodson asked.

"Any of you ever dive—in a helmet?"

Both Brush boys—and their father—said, "Sure," at the same time.

"I've got a special rig—built according to my ideas—takes you down darn near seventy feet—if you want to go. Comfortable. Just a helmet that straps on—but covers only your head and shoulders. Fixed for escape from the straps—so there's no worry in it. Hand-operated compressor."

"I've always wanted to try it," Marylin said.

Mrs. Weber interrupted. "Dad is crazy about fooling around under water on the reefs."

"He *was*," said one of the Weber girls.

Mr. Weber laughed. "My physician in New York said I was over-age for diving. My wife and daughters agree. So it's unanimous—with me abstaining from the voting. But I've got the rig—the weather's flat—and I'd be delighted to lend it to you."

Pierce and Dod said, "Swell!" and, "Elegant," respectively.

"Furthermore, I've got a diving site for you."

"I don't think you ought—" Mrs. Weber began.

Her husband smiled at her. "Mother—I'm talking to a lot of husky men. Maybe it was too much for me." He turned to Crunch. "Know where Scuddy Cay is, Captain Adams?"

"Sure. About fifteen miles west—and a little north—from here."

"Check. Well—about a mile due west, in the Gulf, near a marvelous stretch of grouper reef, is a wreck."

"Of what?" Dodson asked.

Mr. Weber's eyes twinkled. "That's the question. It's a very old wreck. Last year—diving myself—I got two cannon off her. British-made, in 1750. I also got the remains of a Bible—French—published about 1725. But the wreck itself is so much caved in and so grown over with coral that I didn't have a chance to work out what sort of vessel she was. A Spaniard, I suspect."

"How'd you find her?" Des asked.

"Looking for new and better grouper holes in the *Beryl*. If you want some fun, though, you can go down to that wreck with crowbars and poke around. Might find something—might not."

Pierce said, "Great!"

"It would give me the pure willies even to watch," Olivia said.

"What about it, skipper?" Dod asked.

Crunch nodded. "We've run off diving parties before. It's simple. Rig the pump in the cockpit. I've got a ladder that fits the side . . ."

"Then it's set. Dad?"

Jerome Brush nodded. "Count me in."

"Me, too," Ramsay said.

They looked at him surprisedly—as if they'd forgotten his presence.

"If nobody minds," he said hastily.

Nobody spoke for a moment.

Then Jerome Brush said, "Sure, doctor. I take it you've used a diving helmet?"

Ramsay shook his head. "Never even saw one—except in movies."

Pierce groaned.

"The thing is," Dodson said diplomatically, "we'd worry about you, doctor."

Ramsay sighed softly. "I'll be content to be a spectator."

That relieved the Brushes. Jerome said, "Be a big party, Crunch."

"We'll manage."

The morning was hazy, flat calm, brilliant—like all the recent days. Hurricane weather with no hurricanes in view. Crunch had pointed out repeatedly to prospective customers that September was a good month for fishing—that the hurricanes came only at intervals of years—and that the weather, barring a blow, was usually perfect—especially for poor sailors. Muggy and glassy. He'd sold few September trips by that little lecture, however.

The *Poseidon* had loaded the diving gear from the *Beryl* early. The four Brushes and Ramsay came aboard. Olivia had decided to stay on shore with Mrs. Brush. Crunch cast off and Des headed for Scuddy Cay, a small, swampy-looking island almost out of sight of all other land.

They took careful bearings from the marks Mr. Weber had made on the ship's chart, but, even so, it was almost an hour after their arrival in the proper area before Marylin yelled from the harpoon pulpit, "Hey, Des—what's that yonder?"

It was a dark spot. It became a ship-shaped shadow as the *Poseidon* drew near. Des cut the motors.

They coasted, marring the immaculate surface. All hands peered over the side. Slowly, they came to the spot. Fifty feet down, in water as clear as any spring, they made out every detail of the wreck. She lay on sand. Probably she had been buried in sand for a century or two and laid bare again by the currents only recently—as time went. Even so, she was well shaken down and flattened out in most places and she supported a thick encrustation of corals, sea mats, fans, millepores and other marine growths. Long weeds trailed up from her, bending in the current. A sand shark lay along side of her and, behind the shark, was the big diamond of a dug-in sting ray. Filtering through the staghorn corals, the sea pens and fans, were thousands of fishes of every color. They could make out where some ribs ran and they could see that the forward timbers were still upright. It was as if the

Poseidon floated on air—as if they were in a balloon, close to such a landscape as imaginative painters invent to represent the flora and fauna of another planet.

"Golly!"

Des said that. And when Des said "golly" in such a tone, there was reason for wonderment.

"It's beautiful," Marylin murmured. "But I'm not sure I'd have the nerve to go down there, after all."

"Sting rays?" Dodson chuckled. "They scram when they see you. And that little shark wouldn't hurt a baby."

"It looks octopusy," she said.

"They never get big around here."

"Morays, then?"

Dodson laughed. "The thing in the case of morays is to leave them alone. You stick your hand in their hole, and those big eels can really bite. I ought to know. I got bitten twice diving off Turtle Rocks, in Bimini."

Pierce said sarcastically, "What's your opinion of it, doctor?"

Ramsay raised his face. "It's like heaven." That was all he said.

Crunch had been watching the motion of the deep seaweeds and also the slow drift of the *Poseidon*. "I think," he said, "if we take her north and a shade west and get the anchors holding good, we can drop her straight back, stay right here, and set you down beside her."

Des nodded.

Half an hour later, Dodson, who had matched with his father and brother and won, was in the helmet. Des helped him down the ladder to the water. Pierce began pumping.

Ramsay came up. "At least—I could do that?"

Pierce scowled. "Look, doc. I hate to be mean. But this is just what you can't do. Sure as hell—you'd bollix the thing up and old Dod would have to shake off his helmet and swim out of it. It's deep down there and he'd hurt his ears and bleed his nose and we'd lose the gear and it would be your fault."

Ramsay said nothing.

Crunch thought that it was bad tempered. He also understood Pierce's feeling about the importance of proper air operation. After all, there were plenty of men on board—reliable men—to keep the pump-handle stroking evenly.

Marylin picked up a four-foot, narrow, boxlike gadget, which had handles and a glass bottom, and put it over the side. The bubbles rising from Dodson's helmet were riffling the surface and making it hard to see. Through this device, however, as through a glass-bottomed bucket, she had a perfect view. She watched Dodson go down and down and down through the gin-limpid sea. It was a long trip.

But at last the rope which Crunch and Des were paying out went slack.

"That wreck stands a lot taller than it seems from here," she reported. "Dod looks like a pigmy." She handed the instrument to her father.

He peered into it. "Well—Dodson's walking up to the side. He's giving it a poke with the crowbar. He's knocked off a lot of coral and junk and stirred up some marl. Now he's coming out of that. Yoiks! Look at that old stingaree take off for other parts!"

Crunch took a turn. "He's apparently going all the way around. Yep. Des—hike up the lines a little. That's good. Hold it—or you'll lift him. Right! Now he's climbing aboard. It's quite a high climb. Now he's snooping along it. All I can see is the bubbles and his red trunks. He's in the clear, now. Walking up on what was the cabin or the poop or the forecastle, or something. Now—climbing down the side. Going up to the bows—if they are the bows. Hacking away. I guess he's trying to bat the coral off in the spot where he thinks her name might be."

"Didn't they have the names on the stern in those days?" Marylin asked.

"Search me. Guess they did. Anyhow—he's working on those forward timbers."

After a considerable period, Dodson signaled that he would

like to be brought up. He climbed the ladder slowly after he emerged and took off the gear—with help. His face was enthusiastic. "We ought to be able to find out a lot about her—if the light and the weather stay like this. She's been messed up and spilled around by the currents. They come in, down there, and give you a shove every now and then. I knocked a lot of guck off her forward part—and found this between two timbers."

He held out something flat and metallic. He picked up a bait knife and scratched it. It glittered.

"What is it?" Marylin asked.

Dodson shrugged. "I wouldn't swear—but doesn't that look like gold? And hasn't it got a bird shape—sort of? I think I've seen some Inca or Mayan gold ornaments like that at the American Museum."

"For heaven's sake!" Jerome Brush said then. "It does! Of course—"

Dodson nodded. "Could be merely a keepsake of one of the crew—or somebody—that got lodged there. But we ought to look. Your dive, Dad."

They watched Mr. Brush descend. He shooed away two large barracudas which slid in from nowhere and took a considerable interest—either in him, or his bubble stream. Then he attacked the timbers Dodson had worked on—breaking and prizing away the coral—peering at it as it fell, turning it on the sand with his shoe, and squinting through the cumbersome helmet at the revealed timbers. He worked a long while and came up with the report that he had found nothing—no more Aztec gold, or whatever it was, and not even the beginning of a name on the timbers.

"We have time," Crunch said, "for another dive. Then maybe we should knock off for lunch. After all—this weather will probably hold and we've got the afternoon. We can also come back tomorrow if we want."

Ramsay had gone up forward and was peering into the water from the harpoon pulpit when Pierce descended. Direct visibility there was not much blurred by the breaking bubbles. He watched

Pierce—feeling as helpless and, in a sense, as alone as he had ever felt in his life. They would not even let him man the pump. They had no confidence in him in any way. They detested him. And they were—excepting for the cracks Pierce made—being decent even about that. He was too wretched to stay near them, too burdened with self-reproach and feelings of inferiority to take a turn at what Marylin called the looking glass.

She was using it, now—reporting what she saw.

He could see it, too. Pierce went down and down as Crunch and Des payed out rope. He touched the sand, picked up the crowbar his father had left stuck in it, and advanced upon the coral-covered prow. This he assailed with tremendous energy. Soon, the muck he stirred up obscured him from view.

Ramsay rolled over on his back and let the sun burn down on his face. He was tan, now—as tan as any Brush. Any sporting, athletic, enormously energetic young Brush. He was in as good shape. He should and could have enjoyed the trip—if only it weren't taken as a game with tricky rules, and played every inch of the way competitively. Such competitiveness, he thought sadly, was for kids—or for men in a war—but not for the pleasure of grown people.

It was then that Marylin screamed.

He sat up instantly and leaned in order to see around the cabin. She still held the glass-bottomed box.

"Ohhhh!" she screamed. "The whole forward end fell over on him!"

Ramsay rolled and looked down. There was a vast cloud of murk. The current was clearing it except at one edge, where a struggle was going on.

He looked astern again. Des pulled on the lifeline—gingerly and then hard. It was dead—caught.

Jerome Brush had grabbed the box. His voice was awful. "I can begin to see, now! Pierce is there—lying there—flat! Pinned by timbers I think! My God—the helmet's slipped off him—or he's gotten himself free of it! Pull!" An instant later he yelled,

"Stop pulling! You're hauling him farther under! The line goes from him—beneath the beams—then up. He's trying to get his legs out!"

Des, paper pale, looked to Crunch for direction. Crunch seized the box and stared.

"What do you make of it?" the father asked imploringly.

Crunch was as white as Des. "Give a heave on the air line, Des. The helmet's pinned, too—and we gotta get it up because somebody's gotta go down there and dig him out. He'll never last long enough—"

Mr. Brush snatched the box away and stared. "Drowning!" he shouted. "Drowning before my eyes!"

"Shut up!" Crunch ordered. That stopped that.

Des was trying. Ramsay and Dodson were at his side. Crunch came in. All four hove on the air line. It broke.

Crunch said hoarsely, "Get out the dinghy anchor, Des. We'll make a grapple. He might still be able to hang on—if we can get it straight to him . . ."

"You'll never pull him from under those timbers!" the father said hoarsely. "And he'll be unconscious in a few more seconds . . ."

Dodson leaped on the gunwale to dive.

Crunch grabbed him. "Don't waste your strength." He pulled Dodson back. "It's sixty feet."

Des came with the anchor.

Ramsay took it and went over the side with a jump and a splash.

Nobody moved.

Nobody had noticed that he had been stripping off clothes and breathing and gulping air.

There were no bubbles, now.

They could see.

See everything. See Pierce digging crazily, in the sand beneath his pinned legs. See the line that went from his waist under the beams. See the helmet, smashed and held by timber and broken coral. The clearing of the remnants of forward structure had undermined them or weakened them and an eddy of current had done the rest.

Ramsay went down—slowly, it seemed, clinging to the anchor. He landed about fifteen feet from the doomed man. He walked forward, slowly, it still seemed, carrying the anchor. He apparently patted Pierce on the back. Pierce clawed at him and then lay over on his side. Ramsay took a stance and tried the beams. They moved a little—stirred up muck—but not enough. He picked up the anchor again and looked about. He saw the crowbar and recovered it after a struggle. He walked back, carrying the bar now, and set it under the beams. He bent his back and the beams moved farther. He hunted again, found a chunk of coral, and shoved it in with his knee as he levered the beams. Then he looked for more coral of the right size.

Pierce had stopped moving—after one small, last series of threshings and twistings.

"He's dead," the father groaned.

Crunch, lined with the rest along the rail, said, "He's got ten minutes sure—twenty, maybe—and possibly even more—if Ram can get him!"

Two of those minutes passed. No one at the rail moved.

Then Dodson stood. "I've got to try for it. Got to." He dove.

He swam down and down and down and then, when still far short, he turned and swam up. Des grabbed him at the ladder.

"No use," Dodson whispered. "No use at all. I can't make it." He shuddered.

Crunch hardly paid him heed. He saw, now, that Ramsay was looking up. Three minutes.

Ramsay kicked off.

Crunch left the gunwale. He got out another crowbar and went below. He came back with a shovel—kept in a locker to dig the *Poseidon* off mudbanks, when and if necessary.

Ramsay broke water. He swam—with his strange stroke—to the ladder. He was breathing hard. "Shovel."

"Right here," Crunch said.

" 'Nother anchor."

"Bar do?"

Ramsay nodded.

He came out, chest high, on the ladder. He belched and began to draw immense, whistling breaths. He showed signs of strain, but not of undue strain. In fact Crunch thought that, before he let go again, he half-grinned at Marylin.

He went down with the shovel in one hand and the heavy, second crowbar in the other. Down and down in the clear, bluish water. He landed a little nearer to the inert, pinioned body of Pierce Brush. He went back to work in the same, methodical-looking way. Actually, it was the weight of water that slowed his movements. They lined the gunwale again, watching. Marylin whimpered softly—and did not know it. Mr. Brush prayed gently, continuously. Crunch held his own breath as long as he could—and did not know it—and did not notice when he let it out.

"It's inhuman," Dodson finally whispered.

Crunch said, "No."

They looked.

Ramsay prized on the beams and shoved in his coral wedges—looked—repeated—looked—and levered again. Sand and marl swirled around him and around the unconscious, drowning man.

Now Ramsay took the shovel and began to dig. Two minutes. He kept digging. Two minutes and a half. He tried Pierce's shoulders and dug again. Then he set his hands under Pierce's armpits, leaned with the running current, and pulled, furrowing sand with his heels. The inert form slid forward, Ramsay took another hold. The figure moved again.

Three minutes.

He looked up but he tried one more time.

Pierce came free.

Ramsay started up with him.

Crunch nudged Dodson. "You can dive down and help now," he said. "That was a pretty long time."

right, pearl diving. . . . Ye gods, I never thought to ask him if
he got any pearls! He got Pierce—isn't that enough?"

Marylin led Ramsay toward the door. "Did you?"

"Did I what?" The door turned and the aromatic dark en-
veloped them.

"Ever get any pearls?"

"A few," Ramsay smiled. "Quite a few, in fact. You'll see,
if you ever happen to marry me."

The formal announcement of their engagement was made by
the Brushes at a lawn party, on a Junelike December afternoon.
Green acres, ornamented here with topiary art, there with a blue
swimming pool, and yonder with a maze and a tennis court,
stretched from the large house to the azure bay. They were now
populated with hundreds of persons. Among these were Crunch
and Des, dressed for the occasion, beaming, greeting many an old
friend and customer.

Crunch walked to a long table and took a cup of punch. He
handed a second to Des. They made each other a small, nearly
invisible toast.

"Marylin looks terrific," Des said.

"Nice gal. I think Ram can handle her, too."

"Easy!" Des said. "She'll graduate this year, though. And
he'll probably take her to some faraway spot. I'll miss 'em. Had
fun watching the guy finally learn to fish."

Crunch shook his head. "Ram told me yesterday he had a
lot of work to do here on Brill's disease—and several other things
have turned up. I'll bet they stick around for a while. Miami could
use a good research epidemiologist." He stared across the wide
lawn at Dr. Binney.

Ramsay was bathed in a sensation of bliss so deep and ex-
tensive that he almost knew—but not quite—it could not endure.
He, too, was sipping punch—and talking to a favorite Brush aunt
—Aunt Augusta—who had flown down from Seattle. A large

woman, characteristically, with a high pile of white hair, a fog-horn voice, and a gentle heart. She eyed Ramsay thoughtfully. "You're a strange choice for my niece, young man. But I think . . ."

Ramsay's attention wandered. There was an unobtrusive commotion amongst the guests. Pierce stepped up hurriedly to Crunch and Des. They set down their glasses—unfinished—and followed Pierce through a tall hedge.

Clayton—the weight-lifting brother—and Davidson—the boxer—soon went through the same hedge, quickly.

Ramsay said, "Excuse me," to Aunt Augusta. He departed.

Beyond the hedge was the maze and beyond the maze he heard voices. Voices raised in anger. He knew the maze—Marylin had taught it to him under romantic conditions—and when he came out on the other side he found the four Brush boys, Crunch and Des, and a tall, very husky stranger who was talking loudly.

"I say I'm going in—and I say you can't stop me."

Dodson saw the doctor. "Stay out of this one, will you, Ramsay?"

The young stranger thereupon broke past Dodson and Clayton and rushed up to Ramsay. "You're the person I wanted to see. Hello, wise guy!"

"Who are you?" Ramsay asked.

The man said nothing. He was somewhat taller than Ramsay and a good deal heavier. He came closer, glaring.

Pierce spoke flatly. "This is a bird named Roger. Marylin used to go around with him."

"For a lot of years," Roger said hotly.

"She told him about you, Ramsay," Pierce continued, "and broke it off, long since. This cluck is somewhat drunk—"

Roger took it up on his own. "—and so I came over here, Dr. Ramsay Binney—to bust you wide open!"

"You did?" Ramsay seemed to doubt it.

"Just one smack," Roger continued. "That's all. You took

my girl, but I don't give up easy. I'm going to fix it so you'll spend
your honeymoon picking teeth out of your throat."

The Brushes—as well as Crunch and Des—moved in slowly.

Ramsay glanced at them and shook his head.

Roger stepped nearer still. His hands closed.

Davidson spoke. "You better step back, Ramsay. The guy's
a fighter. A dirty one, too—I've boxed with him. One poke—and
you'll be in rotten shape for a party. Just back away—and we'll
close in—toss the monkey out of the grounds . . ."

Ramsay did not back away. He eyed Roger and murmured,
"I wouldn't want to hurt him."

Roger said, *"Whaaaat?"*

Ramsay said. "Marylin's mine—and that's that. It's tough,
but it happens. I'm sorry. I'd—I'd like to be your friend."

"What you are going to be, is my meat."

"I said—" Ramsay's voice dropped—"I don't want to hurt you.
And I might. So don't swing, I warn you."

Roger swung.

The muscles of six extraordinarily powerful men tensed. From
where they stood, they couldn't spare Ramsay the first haymaker.
But they could stop a second blow.

The first haymaker, however, went wide. Ramsay had moved
—with incredible swiftness. "I tell you, Roger," he repeated, almost mournfully, "quit that! I'm not sure but I might seriously
injure you."

Roger's eyes were blindly enraged. He gathered himself and
rushed in. The six men now waited: maybe the doctor wasn't
bluffing.

What followed was in no sense boxing. It was not wrestling,
as wrestling is known. It was not jui-jitsu. Ramsay was everywhere.
His hands, legs, arms, elbows, shoulders—flew like shadows. He
was on his knees for an instant. For another, he seemed to sail in
the air.

Roger was bent to one side, then the other, turned around,
struck in fifty places; his punches went wide, weakened, ceased.

Quite suddenly he shot into the air and fell with a heavy thud. Ramsay was on him again, but this time not attacking. While Crunch and the four brothers stared—breathing hard, a little shocked—Ramsay tested Roger's neck and then his shoulders.

"Nothing broken," he said with immense relief. "Egad! I was scared I'd really hurt him!" He felt the pulse in Roger's neck. "He'll come to—in about five minutes."

Silence.

Finally Pierce said, in a meek tone, "Ram, I thought you didn't fight?"

"I don't. This isn't fighting—as a sport."

"Just what *do* you call it? That oaf should have mangled you."

Ramsay frowned. He was not panting or perspiring—but he was looking rather unhappily at two small grass stains on his trouser knees. "Have to change, I guess. Maybe one of you will lend me something?" He bethought himself of the question. "What do I call it? *Oeenee-mao-paakii.* That would translate, approximately, as 'the way of the serpent.' It's also called, 'the ninety deaths.' "

"Poaki?" Dod asked, humbly.

Ramsay nodded. "I didn't really put the pressure on, you know. Took it very easy. Yeah. The head-hunters taught me. For a head-hunt, on our island, if you waste your spear, and have to come to grips, it's always your head or the other man's. Our tribe—before Mother and Father stopped them—had 'the way of the serpent'—and they hardly ever lost a head."

"I can imagine not," Dod said.

Clayton snorted.

"I'll get you some trousers," Pierce offered. "Come on, Ram. That guy'll be hard for you to meet again—ever."

The doctor looked at Roger once more. "He'll be stiff and pretty lame for a week or two, poor chap!" He shook his head sympathetically.

Crunch and Des walked back—skirting the maze judiciously.

They were seized upon by Aunt Augusta. "Aren't you two the celebrated fishermen? I'm so glad to meet you! I'm Aunt Augusta Towers—née Brush! What are you both grinning about? Canary-swallowing of some sort!"

Des looked the aunt over placidly and decided he liked her. "We've been watching Ramsay."

"Where *is* Ramsay? He left me—quite rudely, I thought—"

"He had a little business to tend to," Crunch replied. "Urgent. But trifling—for Ramsay—it turned out. He'll be back in a few minutes."

Augusta nodded. "I was just saying to him that I thought he was a rather—well—*curious* choice, for Marylin."

"He'll do," Crunch murmured.

"Oh, I'm sure. But—really—he's no athlete, like the others—"

"No," said Des. "No athlete."

"Wretched at games, I hear."

"He's learning. In time—with confidence—"

"Not," said Augusta, "an outdoor type, at all."

Crunch raised an eyebrow. "Wellll—in the usual sense possibly not."

"What I mean is," Augusta continued, "that you'd expect Marylin to pick for a husband somebody who was a *sportsman.*"

Crunch and Des looked at each other and then at Augusta.

Crunch said, "As to that—I think you can call Ram a sportsman, Aunt Augusta. I really do."

EXPERIMENT IN CRIME

EXPERIMENT
IN CRIME

A RINGING denunciation of crime was responsible for the entrance of Professor Martin Luther Burke into the demimonde. More accurately, the challenge of a lovely young lady precipitated the event. And the weather had something to do with it.

Men's lives are often—and fittingly—compared with the courses of rivers: one life is a noisy torrent, another is a lazy meander, and a third is a mere tributary. Some rivers flow inconspicuously for great distances only to encounter a geological fault that turns them abruptly into crashing falls and bellowing cataracts. So it was with Professor Burke.

For his first six years he had merely grown, an undersized and unnoteworthy lad in a New England village—a mere rill. For seventeen years, he had thereafter studied—a small stream growing with the volume of knowledge. He had been an instructor after that, teaching sociology and psychology. Full professorship was accorded him in his thirtieth year, after a wartime interlude in which his forte had been disregarded by the Army and his knowledge of languages had been exploited. He had censored endless thousands of letters written by homesick G.I.s in other tongues than English. His collected lectures had been published. Now, as a professor of socio-psychology at the University of Miami, his course in life, like the courses he taught, seemed certain to flow serenely—a river without dash, a river that neither floods nor dries up, that scarcely changes even when it freezes.

The trouble was the weather, to start with.

It was an unsuitable day for scholarship. A warm haze hung over the land and sunlight filtered through it, lying on the lush vegetation like melted butter. Birds sang alluringly. A clump of bushes, planted directly under the windows by a thoughtless landscape architect, sent into the lecture room an unsettling perfume. It was bad enough for the young lady students to wear commercial fragrances with names like Tumult and Triple-Dare; that nature should conspire in the fashion was all but intolerable.

Professor Burke paused in his lecture on Crime and Civic Corruption. "Greater Miami," he said, "unfortunately furnishes a cross section of the socio-psychological ailments under discussion." As usual, the mention of their own region instilled new interest among the students. "In this resort area the demand for what is called diversion reaches a nadir. The gambler, the bookmaker, the racketeer and the vice overlord line the pockets of the politician for illegal protection. I refer you here to *Studies in Antisocial Organisms* by Waite and Treachness, which contains a masterly chapter on South Florida . . ."

As he dissertated upon Waite and Treachness, his own eye wandered to the window and the green world beyond. MacFalkland was just passing—on a bicycle—golf bag jingling on his back and his hirsute chest showing through the open triangle of a rather loud sports shirt. MacFalkland had no four o'clock class. It was one bit of evidence—a chip in a large mosaic—which made Professor Burke sure that not he, but MacFalkland, was destined to be made Head of the Socio-Psychology Department, when there were funds enough for its establishment. Professor Burke found in a corner of his brain the unwelcome reflection that MacFalkland looked as if he still had several decades of teaching in him. He shook off the mordant idea.

"The criminal," he heard his voice assert, "is an intellectual defective. His crimes are evidence of the fact of his psychological inferiority. You might note down the phrase." They noted it down while he glanced at his own typed manuscript. Vacation would be along soon, and he, too, could wing golf balls into the sunshine for three weeks. He wished he had MacFalkland's shoulders. "The man guilty of corrupting the body politic is, essentially, lacking in imagination and logic. He saws off the limb which sustains him. Crime is identical with the lack of intelligence."

He glanced at his watch. He had one minute of lecture left—
and twelve minutes of class time. He wound up his ringing denunciation—and banished hope, among those who imagined they
might be dismissed early, by an old ruse:

"Any questions, ladies and gentlemen?"

A hand went up. The hand of Miss Marigold Macey. In spite
of her campus-belle appearance, in spite of the frame of curls
which seemed to escape her upswept brown locks by accident,
and in spite of the further fact of her good marks, Miss Macey
had a way of asking rather sharp questions.

"Yes, Miss Macey?"

She stood up politely. Standing, even in blouse, skirt, and
low-heeled shoes, she was still unstudentlike. A little older than
the other girls, for one thing. Her education had been interrupted
by work having to do with the Red Cross. Several of his male
students were as old as she, and even older—for a similar reason:
the War.

"I was wondering, Professor Burke, if you were acquainted
with any gamblers, racketeers, vice overlords, and so on?" Her
voice had a New England accent—although he understood her
parents had lived in Florida for more than a decade.

"I fail to see the relevance of the question," he said firmly.

She picked up her notebook and flipped pages. She sounded
apologetic. "Last October—in your lecture on the Techniques of
the Socio-Psychologist, you said this: 'The true student accepts no
theory *per se* and takes no hearsay evidence; he tests every asser-
tion against his own experience in society; he investigates for
himself.' " She closed the notebook. "That's what you said. I took
it down in shorthand. Naturally, I wondered how much testing and
investigating you had done—to lecture about crime."

Professor Burke flushed slightly. His class was amused. "At
the time," he said, "I was discussing public health, sanitation,
slums, and so on. I hardly feel that such advice may be construed
as urging association with criminals."

"I see," the girl said. She did not sit down.

"Was there another question?"

She nodded. "In November," she said, and he bridled a little at her accuracies, "you advised us to read a book called *Social Non-Norms,* by Ledbetter, Shrieben and Morissey. I read it—all eight hundred pages. And *they* say a criminal is sometimes a person of superior intellectual ability who cannot stand the restrictions imposed upon everybody for the sake of mediocrities. They say that *brains* may thus lead to crime—rather than stupidity . . ."

Professor Burke made a mental note never again to recommend any book which he, himself had found too dull, ponderous and turgid for thorough perusal. He had skipped that part, evidently. But he did not like mutiny in his classes. He cleared his throat. "In my opinion, Ledbetter, Shrieben and Morissey erred in their appraisal of that particular subject. They worked carelessly, from inadequate material and false premises—"

"Shrieben," Miss Macy interrupted, "spent two years in the Capone organization in Chicago . . ."

He had forgotten that, too. "A romantic," he said, "rather than a scientist. Shrieben mistook cunning for true intelligence. Every holder of an ordinary degree of Bachelor of Arts is the mental superior of any criminal."

Another hand went up—the hand of Wally Stratton, formerly of the Eighth Air Force and currently of the Football Squad. Obviously, he intended to go to the defense of the physically nubile but mentally thorny Miss Macey.

"Mr. Stratton?"

"Wouldn't it be an interesting idea to get some gangster in here to debate the matter?"

Professor Burke saw his opening. "Any gambler, or gangster, or other such person among your associates would be welcome here, Mr. Stratton." The class laughed.

Mr. Stratton sat down rather sheepishly. Professor Burke made his usual pre-vacation speech—wishing all of them a pleasant trip home, a safe return, and an interlude of Merry Christmas combined with Happy New Year. He repeated that he hoped none of them would use his course as an excuse for turning to crime: the faculty would disapprove, he ventured.

Several of them came forward to return his greetings and wishes. Among them was Miss Macey, who had to wait while Miss Orme extracted from the professor the titles of books to read over the vacation period. He glared at her ensnooded hair—which always reminded him of a beaver's tail—and gave her the toughest list he could think of. She would eat it up, he thought morosely.

Miss Macey shook his hand and said, "Merry Christmas! Stay out of pool halls and don't pitch pennies!"

He picked up his lecture, remembered he had forgotten his hat, and walked slowly from the long chamber.

II

Some moments later Mr. Stratton overtook Miss Macey on the palm-lined thoroughfares of Coral Gables.

"Sip, drip?" he asked.

"Sure, boor."

They turned in the direction of a drugstore. "That Burke," he said, "shoe-horned himself out of a hole with a crack at me. Cheap trick. You had him surrounded."

Her brown eyes performed a small minuet. "I was investigating. All fall, I've wondered how much of Martin Burke was theory—and how much was experience."

"Why didn't you ask me? I know the type. Pure brass before a class—and outside, pure mouse. When their mothers look in their mouths to see if, maybe, there's a silver spoon, they find a bookmark. I bet he never got five paces away from an encyclopedia in his life!"

"He's cute," she said demurely.

"Cute!" Mr. Stratton bridled. "That dodo cute?"

"If he's a dodo," she said, stopping to pick a blossom from a city-owned hibiscus, "the best years of your life are shot, too, Wally. He can't be more than thirty-four."

"He was born at least twenty-eight, which is my age. How a dame can see anything in such a oiseau . . . !"

She fixed the flower in her hair. It was reddish brown and salmon. It matched her skirt and did no harm to her skin and her eyes. "He's such a pleasant contrast to the average American male—like you—always leering down rudely from among the chandeliers. A small girl such as me resents the effect of modern nutrition. She feels as if she is dating stepladders all the time."

"Flooey," said Mr. Stratton, who was six-four. "When the moon comes pouring up from the Gulf Stream, do you think about some tame rabbit like Burke? Some one-watt theory-maker? Does he set the petite pulse bouncing?"

"That's what I've wondered all autumn."

"You'd be throwing yourself at a human hamster."

He pushed open the drugstore door. A blast of undergraduate clatter rushed out with the conditioned air. They entered the soda fountain of youth and he pointed to a vacant booth. "Park, lark."

"Delighted, benighted."

"And no more sighing over the professor. As soon as I tap a waitress, I am going to work on you, myself—"

"He gives me maternal feelings," she said, as he began waving his arm, "which mother wouldn't recognize as such. Sometimes I wish I were the local type—Southern, coy, extraverted. I would lead him astray—slightly . . ."

The object of this mild controversy made his way along Pondosa Boulevard and turned into Philomel Court. He turned again into West Cortez Circle. Some boys, playing baseball in a vacant lot, cracked out a hard hit which caromed off a lemon tree, whistled through a plumbego hedge, and rolled toward the sidewalk. Professor Burke ran forward automatically, fielded the ball adeptly, held it until the runner had made a well-earned circuit of the coconut bases, and threw it to the shouting pitcher. He walked on, grinning.

A man slightly under medium size, with a tendency to stoop. A man with eyes now blue and now grey—now steely or ironical and again soft, or vague. A man whose dark hair was worn in a wavy pompadour—an expedient arrangement that exposed all of a rather high forehead. A conventional dresser—in polished brogues, heather socks, gabardine slacks, a light-weight tweed coat, a dimly striped shirt and a conservative blue tie, fixed with a plain gold clip. The stem of a pipe showed in one pocket; from the other, his folded lecture protruded.

Nine strangers out of ten would have confidently guessed that he was a college professor. If they had seen him field the home run they would have added that he was a good egg—and at peace with the world.

Professor Burke was a good egg, insofar as scholastic tradition permitted him good-eggishness. He had New England virtues and a New England conscience. His character and life direction were well established, before he entered the First Grade, by the firm-minded Congregationalists who had been his parents. At thirty-three, he was exactly the way he expected to be at fifty, save that he hoped by then to be a Department Head. He had self-assurance, calm, and a near-fanatical courage of an occasional conviction. He was shy.

At the moment, however, he was not at peace.

He turned into the rather jungly lawn of the house where he had dwelt since his arrival in Miami, after the war. He stumbled on its front steps—which was unusual. He put the wrong key in the lock of the door to his upstairs apartment.

"Martin!" his landlady called. "What's wrong? I'm on the side porch having tea. Scones, too. Come aboard!"

Bedelia Ogilvy was the widow of a retired Naval officer who had quietly passed away in his bed before Pearl Harbor—an event which would certainly have brought him to a more violent demise. Occasionally, Bedelia used such terms as, "Come aboard."

She was said to be the homeliest woman in Coral Gables; she was
certainly the best cook in that flower-spangled suburb. She had
taken Professor Burke very dubiously, and on probation, as a
roomer-boarder. After three weeks, she had begun using his first
name. After three months, he had commenced unconsciously to
regard her as a sort of relative whose pleasure at feeding him
superbly was as normal as her constant cross-questioning, anent
his mail, his friends, his students, other professors, their wives,
and such further lore as might interest her.

He walked around to the side porch, opened the screen, and
ducked under the spiny arms of the bougainvillaea. Bedelia sat
like a resting camel, behind a rattan coffee table. Her august and
bony frame filled the settee. Her large, pale eyes, enlarged further
by spectacles, seemed worried. "What's the matter? You're skittish.
I can tell."

He knew she could. He did not even try to guess the criteria
by which she had detected his nervousness at the distance of thirty-
odd feet. "Hypocrisy," he said glumly.

"Hypocrisy? My dear man! The world's full of it! Take it in
your stride!"

"My own."

An alert look came into her eyes. "Yours, Martin?"

He told her. He told her his basic advice to his students and
of Miss Macey's probing. His eyes even glimmered with appreciation of his predicament. "There I stood—parroting a dozen authorities on criminology—and preaching direct experience—yet
I never so much as met a pickpocket face to face in my life! It's
absurd!"

"You are hardly expected to be everything you discuss."

"A point I tried to suggest. It fell rather flat. We were
not prepared, in Israel Putnam Teacher's College, for the present
postwar generation." He sighed and popped a scone into his
mouth.

"Break the next one in two," Bedelia said absently. "I've
heard you mention Miss Macey before. Attractive, isn't she? I

noticed her picture in the paper when she was elected a sorority president."

"Very attractive." He skipped hurriedly over the fact and railed at the modern student: "Married and with children! In business! Working at places like race tracks! One of our students is a hat check girl in a night club—not in my classes, I'm relieved to say. No, Bedelia. We were not prepared for leadership on campuses where the world—the nonacademic world—pushes in at every door. I felt extremely inadequate today. I questioned myself. What right have I—after all—to invite my students to sup at the wellsprings of experience—and to reject them for myself? It's snobbishness, in a way. I felt tempted . . ." he broke off.

"Tempted, Martin? How?" She seemed to relish the idea that he was tempted by anything.

"Well—I can hardly say how. Here we live—in the very midst of a world we never encounter. We read of it in the papers. We learn of it in sociological texts. But the University Campus is as far from the gay life of, say, Miami Beach, as if an ocean lay between—instead of a bay crossed by three causeways. I lecture on gambling. But I have never observed the fact. I was tempted to take precedent in my hands—and go and see."

"Why not?" she asked quickly.

His iced tea halted in mid-air, as if by an invisible brake. "I scarcely expected such a reaction from you!"

Bedelia balanced jam on the remnants of a scone. "Martin, did it ever occur to you that a man can become stuffy—by not resisting stuffiness?"

"Stuffy? A harsh term, Bedelia."

"Why don't you put on your dinner clothes, Martin, and drive over to the Beach and watch some genuine, illegal gambling. You might even see a gangster."

"Because," he answered, obviously wishing the subject had never reached that point. "I haven't the price of a costly meal in my pocket. I would hardly indulge in gambling. And I would hardly patronize such a place with no such intentions. Finally"—he smiled with satisfaction—"I wouldn't have the faintest idea of where to go!"

"The Club Egret," she said, "which is off Collins, at the north end of the Beach. Mrs. Witherspoon told me Wednesday that she lost a hundred and twenty dollars there, the night before. It was probably ten dollars. I have some cash—and you can give me a check. I've kept cash in the house ever since I first moved here. Went to the bank to get the money for a rail ticket and found it was Lee's Birthday! I drew out a hundred dollars the following morning—and I keep it on tap. No telling what obscure Southern heroes might close the banks, I thought—and how was I to remember the date of Lee's Birthday?"

"Really, Bedelia," he said uneasily, "it's most kind. But I wouldn't think of it."

Her face took on an expression of sympathetic contradiction.

III

He did not know whether he was elated or depressed. The long drive from Coral Gables across the luminous causeway to Miami Beach was exhilarating but not reassuring. He had previously been swimming at Miami Beach. He had played golf there on occasion. He had never visited it at night—and at night the homes seemed richer and more mysterious—the streets strange and a little confusing. The hotels were altogether startling: bathed in colored light—fretted and fringed from top to bottom in cascades of electric glitter. It was opulent and it was ominous.

He located the Club Egret—and drove past it. The Club Egret was boldly set amidst showy residences. It had no windows. Under its portico, attendants were serving the owners of vehicles which markedly outshone his prewar, hand-repainted coupé. Conscience urged him both ways. To enter was folly; not to enter, after

being committed, was weak. He drove around the block and under
the portico.

An obviously disenchanted attendant handed a parking check
to him. He gave the man a quarter and received audible thanks.
He walked up a flight of stairs.

He found himself in a foyer. There was a checkroom at his
left—and a curtained hall—guarded, apparently, by two men in
tuxedoes. Straight ahead was a bar—long and shimmering—low
lighted—with tables and people at the tables. Men in sports coats—
in plain suits—and a few, he saw with relief, in dinner jackets.
Overhead was a rosy, vaulted dome. To his right were steps going
down—into a tremendous dining room where people in twos and
sixes and twenties were busily consuming dinner. The dining room
had grey walls with chromium trimmings, a thick, grey carpet,
and glass stars in its ceiling; behind each star was a colored light.
A large orchestra played rhythmically on a podium. People were
dancing. The polychromatic stars twinkled in what seemed to be
orchestral tempo. It was dim in the room. The expanse of white
tablecloths, the gleaming dance floor, the lofty ceiling and stellar
lights, made the professor think of the snowcape under a Christmas tree, expanded magically, so that human beings could walk
into it.

The headwaiter came forward. "One?"

Professor Burke was escorted into the shimmering, theatrical
wonderland. He was seated along the wall.

"Something to drink?"

"A martini. Very dry."

Professor Burke was familiar with the best dining places of
Boston. One of these had a bar that turned like a merry-go-round.
He was familiar with night clubs through rare visits to the motion
pictures. A single cocktail was his limit. However, he knew a good
martini from a fair one. He was served a martini he regarded as
excellent.

He ordered dinner. He began to look, covertly but searchingly,
at the people around him. He thought of them in terms of the text-

books and newspaper articles. They were largely—he felt—gamblers, gangsters, corrupt politicians, labor czars squandering the dues of union members, ladies of the evening, and the like. It would have surprised him a good deal—and disappointed him even more—had he realized that nearly all the men and women were respectable citizens of, or visitors to Miami Beach enjoying an evening of dining and dancing—and not even planning to gamble.

When he cut an excellent filet mignon—for which he would pay a shocking seven dollars—he beckoned the headwaiter. "Where is the gaming room?"

The phrase was not the ordinary one. And it was not customary of newcomers to ask that information of the headwaiter. "You—oh—have not been here before, sir?"

"No, I haven't."

The headwaiter said, "Quite so," and walked away, leaving the professor deeply embarrassed.

The office of Mr. William Sanders was paneled in cypress. In these walls were slots from which the two principal chambers of the Club Egret could be discreetly surveyed. The room also contained a powerful wall safe, expensive, modernistic furniture, and Mr. Sanders himself—a very tall man, lanky, and pleasant. His smile was ready, almost constant; his voice quiet and amiable. One needed, as a rule, a second glance to note that his eyes had a quality like the blade of an adze—seen edge-on.

There was a knock on his door.

Mr. Sanders glanced up from his desk. He said nothing. The door opened and a man entered—a thick-shouldered man with black hair parted in the middle and black eyes of the sort called liquid. The term connotes fluidity and warmth. There was nothing warm about The Tip. If there ever had been, it had turned to ice years before, during The Tip's childhood on the streets of South Chicago.

Mr. Sanders still said nothing.

"There is a laddie-boy outside whose looks I dislike." The Tip touched the ruby-red bow above his soft evening shirt. "Table eighty-six. Are you sure, Double-O, that you have all the dope on tonight's operations?"

Perhaps six people in the world called Mr. Sanders "Bill." Possibly twenty people called him "Double-O" to his face. Thousands, however, used that name when he was not present—though they called him "Mr. Sanders" when they accosted him. Newspapers, also, referred to him on frequent occasion as "Double-O" or "Double-O Sanders."

He regarded The Tip with a smile. The Tip's words showed not the slightest trace of Chicago's streets or even its universal nasal register. The Tip spoke in pure American Park Avenue—an eastern accent which, itself an imitation, is readily copied by anyone who is willing to practice affectation. Smooth phoniness amused Double-O. He answered the question.

"Who's ever positive he has all the dope, in this town? Tonight's operations are set—sure. What's wrong with the guy?"

"Just—keeps looking the place over. The customers. Could be a new Fed income-tax snooping. He asked Rudolph where the 'gaming room' was. Sounds too sappy to be solid. If he is a Fed, he's outsmarting himself."

Double-O crossed to one of the discreet slots, his long legs moving like jointed crowbars. He peered. "I see what you mean," he said, after a while. "I'm willing to bet he's a husband with a wife at a hen convention—afraid somebody he knows will see him here. But tell Connie, anyhow."

Professor Burke ordered coffee and a cigar. He was pleased by the pulchritude of the cigarette girl—and startled by her costume. Hardly enough clothing, he thought, for a large doll. He tipped her a quarter and lighted the cigar. Like everything else in the establishment, it was of superlative quality. He blew smoke.

He was filled with a sentiment of self-satisfaction. The fact was that he liked the Club Egret. The fact also was that, even while he enjoyed the music and the lights and the spectacle of the people, he was contriving a few sentences to slip into his next year's lecture—sentences which would make it plain that he had personally investigated the dens of iniquity and found them a tinselly sham.

The house lights went down. A master of ceremony took possession of a microphone—in a cone of smoke-washed light. The professor recognized the first joke as almost identical with one which had been used by Plautus, a little more than two thousand years before.

A girl said, "Hello!"

He turned with surprise—and some discomfiture. The young lady, not identifiable in the dark, was standing at his side.

"May I sit down?" she asked in a warm, husky voice.

"Why, certainly. Of course!"

The professor hurried to assist her. She had long, blonde hair, done up beautifully. Her arms and shoulders were bare, as if she had swum part way out of her evening dress. The dress itself winked, and glistened. Her nose turned up slightly. That was all he could discern—excepting that she wore a perfume which had a stunning effect—as a spray has a stunning effect on an insect.

The professor felt slightly guilty, and the resultant course of his thoughts was to be expected. There are some men whom no women, however predatory, however young and inexperienced or old and desperate, will try to pick up. Instinct warns them that the attempt would be futile from every viewpoint. Professor Burke was the archetype of that species of man. And, since no such effort had been made in his case, he suspected none now. He assumed, instead, that the young lady was a former student of his, or a former undergraduate—and that, having recognized him, she had ingratiated herself out of the common, feminine love for scandal. It was, of course, scandalous for him to be dining at the Club Egret.

"My name," said the lady, "is Connie Maxson."

He failed to place it—which in no way surprised him. It usually took him a semester to learn the names of his students— and he seldom remembered them long.

"Would you like coffee? Or a drink?" he asked resignedly.

"Love one."

He beckoned. The lady ordered Scotch and water. After reflection, he said, "The same."

"Enjoying yourself?" she asked.

He raised his eyebrows and blew smoke in an ironical manner—hoping she would be able to read the gesture. "You would hardly expect a professor of socio-psychology to enjoy himself here. Say rather, I am enjoying the spectacle of a rich, moronic element indulging in pleasures which deprive the body politic of integrity."

The girl said, "Well!" After a moment she asked, "On a vacation?"

"I drove over from the Gables, naturally. Vacation doesn't start for several more days. This is in essence a research project. I'd even intended to watch the gambling for a while. Possibly to squander a few dollars as a sort of payment-in-kind for the experience. The headwaiter, however, was rather huffy about my inquiry."

The house lights went on suddenly.

The girl was extremely beautiful—and the professor was sure he had never seen her before in his life. He would have remembered the face, even if not the name. She was staring at him. She ignored the tango artistes who now appeared on the dance floor.

"Is that straight?" she asked.

"I'm afraid," he said, coloring a little, "that we don't know each other, after all. I assumed you'd been one of my students at the University of Miami."

The drinks came. She made a feint at a toast, sipped, and said, "No, professor. I'm a—sort of hostess—around here. I went to college in the north for one dismal year. Couldn't stand it. Came back here—and couldn't stand the family, either. Gin rummy on the even nights and backgammon on the odd. I—took a job."

"My name is Burke—Martin Burke."

"And you were just looking around?"

He explained in some detail. She was amused, surprised—
and, somehow, pleased.

"You're certainly right!" she said. "You shouldn't lecture
without background. Now, I tell you. When you're ready, I'll see
that you get into the gambling room. If you want, perhaps I can
fix it up for you to meet Double-O."

"You mean the notorious Double-O Sanders?"

"He's a lamb, really! Strictly a gambler. No rackets and no
other angles. Some of the most important people in the United
States come in, regularly." Miss Maxson finished her highball.
"I've got to leave you. Thanks for the drink. Ask for Al in the
foyer—and he'll show you to the"—she smiled—" 'gaming room.' "

IV

He thought—along Tennysonian lines—that she was a delightful creature. He found himself also repeating—along undergraduate
lines—that she was a warm swarm. He watched her move among
the tables until she was out of view.

Then he called for his check, paid it, tipped ten per cent, added
fifty cents, and beckoned to the girl in doll-clothing for another
cigar. A corridor led to the gambling room. Al held back the
velvet curtain and the professor sauntered through.

He found himself entering a most luxurious room—a room
with a lower ceiling and restrained decoration. There were three
roulette tables, a cashier's window, two tables surrounded by men,
troughlike affairs in which dice were bounding, and other games
with which he was unfamiliar. Large floor vases of beige roses
were set about. The air was cool and clear, in spite of the continual
smoking of its hundred or so occupants. It was like an elegant
drawing room—with this exception, he thought: the guests were
hypnotized.

They stood around the tables, light reflected up into their faces from the green baize, the polished mahogany. Some were obviously nervous—their hands toyed with chips or twisted handkerchiefs. Some were strenuously nonchalant. Some were stoical and without expression. The women, he thought, seemed more eager and anxious than the men—a natural result of their more emotional natures. There were women of sixty—even seventy— in fur wraps, wearing jewels. There were young women, with and without jewels. The most continuous sound was the soft talk of the croupiers. The loudest sound was the clatter of fortune set up by the dance of the ivory pellets around the rims of surging wheels.

For a long time, he watched. No one spoke to him—no one seemed to mind his surveillance. He presently realized that there were other onlookers. He studied the game. Roulette, he soon saw, was childishly simple. Hardly more complex than parcheesi.

He was not in the least tremulous when he went to the cashier's window and purchased twenty, two-dollar, or white, chips. His face was impassive when he returned to the table he had selected. He put two chips on Red. The wheel spun and the number was called. The croupier put two chips on his two. He left them where they were. After the next spin, he had eight.

He thought of a number. The number he thought of was nine. He put four chips on nine and four on black. Nine lost. He tried again. Nine came up. He was dumbfounded by the number of chips which were pushed into his possession.

It may be that the best system for winning at gambling is to play with the sincere purpose of losing—of losing a politely decent sum so that (for example) in future years one may warn one's classes, with a little personal anecdote as an illustration, against the folly of betting on the turning of a wheel. In any event, Professor Burke won. He soon noticed that some of his intent associates were waiting until he placed his bets—and following suit. He began to be embarrassed by the size of his pile of chips. He exchanged some for what he called "counters" of a higher denomination. He thought up numbers—and then deliberately bet on others, with the firm intention of defeating himself.

He did not know how long he stood there. An hour, perhaps. It might have been two. He felt a hand on his shoulder and turned shamefacedly. It was Miss Maxson again.

"You're doing peachy, Professor!"

"I'm mortified."

"Mortified? Why, for heaven's sake?"

"I can't seem to stop this winning streak."

"Can't *stop* it!"

"Naturally—it's out of the question for me to make a profit on a venture of this sort. In my position. You can see that."

Miss Maxson picked up some of his chips. "Give us blues," she said to the croupier. "For the whole thing."

The trade was made. "You'll help me—play them in?" He seemed relieved.

"Professor, I'm going to get the money. This is your night. And it's your time to quit."

"But the money isn't mine!"

"It's as much yours as any money in this room is anybody's." They were attracting attention. She moved closer to him and whispered. "No fooling, Professor! Cash in the chips while you've got a lead! It's smart. The Club won't miss the money. I'm terribly glad you won. Please!"

Groggily, he picked up the chips and walked to the window. He was paid eight hundred and eighty-six dollars. When he put the bills in his wallet, his hands shook: it was by far the largest sum of money his wallet had ever contained. It was equal to two month's salary. Gambling money, criminal money, illicit gain— and he was accepting it because Miss Maxson insisted! Because, perhaps, he was accustomed to carrying out the orders of the opposite sex to the letter. It always saved trouble—he had learned that, long ago.

He looked up at Miss Maxson and she smiled.

He looked back at the table and the place where he had stood had been closed up. They had forgotten him already—taken his departure, with his winnings, as a simple matter of course. He could not think what he was going to do. Keep the matter secret—obviously. His whole evening's escapade had boomeranged!

"Buy me another drink?" She was still smiling.

"Of course!"

"We'll go back to the bar."

They did not, however, go back to the bar. They started—and that was all.

A man in the uniform of a police officer came suddenly from the corridor. He was not holding a gun, but he was wearing a large gun. Behind him were what seemed to the professor a platoon, at least, of police.

The man shouted, "All right—everybody! Stop the wheels! Hold those dice! This is a raid!"

There was silence. Then funny noises began. Women escaped. Men swore. Voices quickly rose up the scale. The place roared.

The police officer held up his hands and gestured at the sounds—as if they were tangible and could be pushed. "Listen, everybody! *Lissssen!* All we're taking is the wheels! Before any dame faints, or any damn fool guy tries to start anything—*lisssen!* We're not hauling you in. We're not even taking names. Just keep out of our way while we get the wheels—and then you can go quietly. I don't want any arguments"—he stopped for a man who had hurried up to him—"and I don't give a hoot how important you are! This is a raid. The joint is closed!"

While this speech was being made, Professor Burke had been as aware of Miss Maxson as of the spectacular pandemonium. She had glanced—rather furtively—at her watch, when the police rushed in. It seemed an odd thing to do. Hysterical reflex, no doubt. She had grown rather pale, after that. He supposed, since she was a hostess, that she was going to be arrested. The idea annoyed him.

But now, keeping her eyes on the police—who were already pushing one of the tables toward the corridor—she said softly, "Stay here and wait for me, will you?"

"Certainly."

She tapped on an inconspicuous door and was let into the cashier's booth. From there, she vanished.

He turned with interest to the scene around him. One or two of the ladies lolled in chairs and their escorts fanned them. Half a dozen of the gentlemen were in states of apopleptic rage. Professor Burke felt this was uncalled for: the law was Right—ergo wrath was wrong. They were gambling; they had earned this their discomfiture.

At the same time, he felt intensely gratified that names were not to be taken. He could imagine the attitude of the Dean—the President—the entire Faculty—if the morning papers disclosed that he had been seized in a raid on a gambling establishment! The thought brought perspiration on his brow.

A passing policeman noted it. "Pull yourself together, Bud," he said amiably.

Miss Maxson, meantime, had entered the office of the owner. Double-O was sitting on, not behind, his desk. His eyes were like flint.

The Tip was there, too—looking frightened. Several other men—in tuxedos—stood about uneasily.

"They were an hour early," the girl said.

"Tell us something we don't know!" Chicago grated in The Tip's voice, this time.

Double-O Sanders looked toward her—his eyes seeming to see nothing. His lips moved. "It's a cross."

She swallowed.

His head turned slowly, so that his gaze was fixed on the safe. "They'll take all of us—and the operating dough—to Headquarters. I don't know who ordered this. But I do know they wanted to find the dough right here. They'll hold it for a cut. Maybe take it all." The faintest scorn sounded in his quiet words. "Legal confiscation."

The Tip said, "Let's split it and lam."

Double-O appeared not to have heard that. "All of us—except

you, Connie." He turned toward her again. "Those cops know you?"

"I don't know any policemen." She smiled faintly. "Except one traffic cop named McGuire."

He handed the envelopes to her. "Get going."

"If they don't see me coming out of here."

He walked to the safe, after a moment. He masked it with his body and spun its dials. The door opened. "Envelopes," he said. "Plain, white. Large. Top left drawer."

The Tip hurriedly procured them. Double-O took three. Into two of them he put unopened packages of bills—into the third, a partly exhausted package. The girl saw the denominations. She grew paler.

He handed the envelopes to her. "Get going."

She took two books from a case behind his desk. She put the envelopes between the books. She wrinkled her nose at him and the door closed behind her.

The Tip said, "No kidding, Double-O! A dame . . . !"

Mr. Sanders raised his adze-blade eyes.

The Tip looked away.

There was a knock on the door opposite the one Miss Maxson had used.

"Come in, boys," Double-O called. "Not locked."

Miss Maxson approached the professor—through the crowd. Most of the tables had been pushed out of the room now. Their leg-marks showed in the deep carpets.

The officer looked in. "All right! Get going! We've taken the Club personnel—so you'll have to find your own cars in the yard. I've got a couple of men out there to unscramble you—but drive easy, and you won't get scrambled!"

The girl drew him deeper into the crowd. She handed him three hefty envelopes. "Keep these for me, will you?"

He thrust them into his jacket pockets—two on one side, one on the other. They showed. She started to protest—and changed her mind. Maybe it was better that way.

She dropped the books on the nearest chair. "Would you take me home? I have no car."

"I'd be delighted!"

It seemed very warm out of doors. The Club Egret was near the sea and the night air smelled salty. They walked around to the parking yard. Cars were starting—motors accelerated as if in anger, headlights snapping on. It was confusing. He finally found his repainted coupé. She got in. He started the motor. A slow, gear-gnashing, bumper-banging defile moved indignantly toward the street. He drove to Collins and turned south.

"I'm sorry about the raid," she said.

He looked at her buoyantly. "On my account? I wouldn't have missed it for anything! Though I regret winning. However! It was a risk I chose to take. I'm most grateful to you!"

"You don't owe me—or the Club—anything!" She said it in a peculiar tone. *If he knew what was in his pockets . . . !* He would never know—she thought.

"Where do you live?"

"On Di Lido Island. That's one of the Venetian Islands . . ."

"I know."

"The raid," she said, "was just window dressing. We ought to be open again in a day or two."

He was surprised. The car swerved a little—and he braked. He looked in his mirror to be sure he was not endangering traffic. "You mean those weren't police?"

"Oh—they were police, all right. What I mean is, we have raids early in the season and late in the season—before the big money arrives in Miami and after it goes—to satisfy the reform element." She explained the technique of the South Florida gambling raid—a gesture greatly satisfying to right-thinking citizens and of little hardship to casino operators.

Professor Burke listened while he turned right on Forty-First Street, went over the high, picturesque bridge and turned left on Pine Tree Drive.

Then he said, "I don't know whether it means anything or

not, but there is a large sedan following us. It's been behind us
ever since we started down Collins." He looked away, then, from the
tunnel his headlights made between the Australian pines. She had
not replied.

Miss Maxson appeared to be sick. She glanced back. She drew
a couple of shaky breaths. She tried to light a cigarette—and used
three matches.

And at last she said, very earnestly, "Gee, Professor, I'm
sorry I got you in this one! Those are—hijackers."

V

Most men who found themselves in Professor Burke's situation would have been alarmed. Miami Beach, through the center
of which he was driving, advertises to the world its attractions and
its distractions. It is more quiet about its civic detractions. Not the
least of these is the boldness and the frequency of its robberies.
Holdups of bejeweled, home-bound revelers, burglaries, and daylight stick-ups of cash-carrying citizens are almost a part of the
local climate.

It was of this that Professor Burke somewhat anxiously
thought. "Don't be so perturbed," he said. "At the end of this
street is a fire station. Suppose I simply turn in there?"

"That would be the last thing to do! Although—"

"I suppose," he mused, glancing at his mirror, "they saw me
make that big haul—and followed us . . ."

She said something. He murmured, "I beg your par-
don?"

"I just swore, that was all. Don't you realize *why* we're being
followed? The envelopes—the ones I gave you!"

He touched a pocket. "Those letters?"

"Letters! Ye gods, Professor! *Letters!* The police staged the raid an hour early. Surprised us. They were after the operating capital of the Club Egret . . ."

The car lurched a little. "You mean to say—in those envelopes—?"

"—are two unopened packets of thousands, and one partly gone. Something like two hundred and sixty or seventy thousand dollars. Look out! You'll ram a tree!"

His voice squeaked. "You mean to say I've got a quarter of a million dollars right here in my pockets?"

"I mean you have."

"Then who . . . ?" he glanced at the mirror again—and now he was afraid. Chillingly afraid.

The girl said, "If you turn in, the firemen will call the cops—and they'll get it, after all."

"Corrupt police," he murmured bitterly.

"Corrupt police, nothing! They were just carrying out orders. It's somebody bigger than cops, who would get that money—or a piece of it."

For a moment, he merely drove. He had started at a careful thirty. He had notched it up to thirty-five, from nervousness. He dropped back, as self-discipline.

"The car behind us," she went on, after a pause, "*could* be a lot of people. But it is most likely somebody who knew the police were going to spring their raid early in order to snatch Double-O's money. And that, most likely, would mean the Maroon Gang. Have you ever heard of them?"

"Yes, I have," he said jerkily. "There's an excellent monograph by Longreve and Bilchard on the Maroon Gang. Organized in the prohibition era by a man named—"

"Never mind the lecture! If that's who it is—and if they think we have the money—which they must—we'll be lucky if we're alive tomorrow morning."

He turned into Dade Boulevard—the tranquil canal on one side, the empty, night-hung golf course on the other. He cast a reluctant glance at the fire station.

Thought, he kept assuring himself, was imperative. The men

in the following car were—by his own definition—virtually incapable of thought. He found, however, that thinking was difficult, under these circumstances.

For one thing, he could not drive up to the nearest police station, like any ordinary citizen in distress. That would mean some sort of infamous "confiscation" of the funds now in their care. Illegal funds, to be sure, but Professor Burke disliked to surrender a quarter of a million dollars either to hostile gangsters or corrupt politicians.

He drove out onto the first of the many bridges which connect the Venetian Islands with Miami and Miami Beach.

"What are you going to do?" she asked.

"Think," he said.

"It's too late! My house isn't far ahead. If we go there, they'll get us there. If we go on, they'll stop us—probably in the dark stretch where the street divides."

Up ahead, at the side of the road, a red eye gleamed. A siren growled.

Instinctively, he slowed. There were signals to show that one of the two drawbridges on the causeway was about to be raised. With the tail of his eye, he caught sight of a moonlight excursion boat moving toward the span.

The girl said, "Step on it!"

He did so—as he saw what she meant.

The bridge siren growled loudly. He perceived that they would get under the first gate. He heard a bellow from the bridge tender. Their wheels hummed on the steel lattice of the lift-spans. The far gate ticked the top of the car. The headlights of the pursuing sedan wobbled as brakes stopped it. The bridge tender blew a whistle. But they were going fast. Across Rivo Alto Island— across more bridges—and onto Di Lido. The car behind them was held up.

He stopped—under a street light.

The girl moaned. "Keep *going!* We might duck them in Miami! We've got a couple of minutes, anyhow!"

The professor spoke tersely. "In the glove compartment!

Postage stamps! When I put them in my pockets, they stick together in this steamy climate. When I put them in the compartment, I forget them." He had taken out his fountain pen. He
also took out his wallet. He transferred its contents into the least
bulky envelope. "This Mr. Double-O Sanders' address?"

She had opened the compartment. "He lives at the Bombay
Royale Hotel on Collins Avenue." At their side, she saw the green,
metal mailbox. It was for this—not light—that he had stopped.
He was already scribbling.

He handed one to her and she licked it. She pressed firmly,
with a shaky hand. "It's pretty heavy . . ."

"Stick a lot of stamps on it! You'll find fifty threes, there."

She tore, and stuck on, a lot. The next was ready. Then the
third. She ran with them to the box and hurried back to the car.
He let in the clutch.

"Turn right at the next corner. *What* an idea!"

He drove two blocks. They could hear the siren purr as the
bridge opened. She pointed out a large house, looming whitely
among still larger trees. A wall surrounded it—a white wall with
an iron gate.

He swung the car around and parked on the grass, under the
thick limbs of a sea grape. He left his lights on, purposely. "Do
they know you live here?"

"If it's anybody from the Maroon Gang, probably."

"Then, listen," he said. "They don't know me. We've driven
very slowly—and rather erratically—all the way. If they know
you live at this address, they will probably drive by here. We will
have had very little time to dispose of a large sum of money. For
all they can be sure of, we may never have had the money. Our drive
together may have had a—romantic—rather than a commercial—
reason. If we were now to give that possibility some verisimili-
tude . . ."

In the dashboard light, her handsome eyes flickered a little.
Her hands went to her hair and did something. It tumbled around
her shoulders like suddenly sickled wheat. She wiped her lips on

a small handkerchief and dropped it. "Might as well look as if we'd prepared for it," she said.

Then she kissed him.

It was necessary to get the right amount of lipstick—not too much, but enough—in the right places, she thought.

Cars began moving on the Venetian Way, two blocks below. One slowed, and turned. It was the large, dark sedan. It picked up speed—evidently as their lights were observed.

"You better have your arms around me," she said.

"Do you always—kiss people that way?"

The sedan crossed to the wrong side of the road, and stopped, bumper touching bumper. Five men got out, fast. They had handkerchiefs tied under their eyes. All of them held guns. One—the fattest—said, "Out, Miss Maxson, please. Out, whoever you are, if you please. Be quick!"

The professor spoke indignantly. "Really, I haven't a dime. Well—a dime, perhaps. Some change. My bills—frittered away at the club. The young lady—"

"Out!" said the fat man.

Professor Burke got out. He was swiftly searched.

"You will stand between our car and the wall. If a car comes on this street, kneel. If you yell—zut!"

The accent was French. But what kind of French? Belgian? The Professor waited for more words, as he and the girl moved between the wall and the big, black car.

"Now, Miss Maxson. Where is the money?"

"What money?"

The fat man with the accent slapped her face.

Professor Burke had never before seen such a thing. He walked up to the Frenchman. "See here, my good man. More brutality of that sort and I shall either compel you to shoot me or make mincemeat of you. Violence is intolerable. Violence to a lady is beyond countenancing."

There was a long silence. Finally the fat leader said, "Just who are you?"

"Professor Burke, the socio-psychologist."

There was more thought. "Who is La Cavour, then?"

The "ou" sound was Germanic. *Alsatian,* the Professor suddenly felt sure. "Phillippe La Cavour is a second-rate French criminal psychologist, born in Lyon, and guilty of some atrociously superficial hypothesizing—"

"What, precisely, are you doing here?"

"Isn't it rather painfully obvious?"

The fat man turned. "Miss Maxson, you were the only one in Double-O's club not on the list to be taken to Headquarters. I assumed you would have the club's valuables."

"You assumed a lot."

The masked face turned farther. "The car—boys! Upholstery and all. A couple of you make sure they didn't toss it over the wall."

Time passed.

Professor Burke tried to back up far enough to see the license number. A wobble of the gun and a soft, "Ah, no!" stopped him. He looked the car over, trying to fix the details in his mind. He was not very good at the years of cars. The wheels showed traces of a white mark which makes sticky ruts on certain minor roads in South Florida. Some vegetation was caught in one of the door hinges. By leaning against the car and clinging to that hinge, he was able to remove a sample of the vegetation. Hedge or driveway shrubbery, he thought. He shifted his position and put it in his pocket.

The sound of upholstery being rent by a knife came from the coupé. Rustlings were heard as two of the men inspected the ground under the shrubbery behind the wall. A car approached. They knelt. The men ripping up the coupé put out their flashlights and sat down. The car swept on.

Eventually, the fat man sighed. "I could, of course, have made an incorrect guess."

"Several," the professor said emphatically.

The Frenchman ignored that. "Naturally, I regret the damage

to your car. You seem, however, to be a man fond of unusual risk."
He looked thoughtfully at the girl. "So you will not mind this
comparatively trifling misfortune. Good night, Professor."

"*Bon soir,*" the professor said. "*Mauvais rêves.*"

The four men had given up. Their leader beckoned with his
gun. They climbed into the sedan. Their car could be heard on the
now-silent causeway as it gathered speed.

"Come in," the girl said, after they stopped listening. "I'll
make you some coffee."

"Thanks, but I think not. Bedelia will be worried."

"Bedelia? The little woman?"

"My landlady," he said in an injured tone.

She kissed him suddenly. "Thanks. See you." The gate banged
behind her.

It was uncomfortable, driving on the hacked upholstery, with
bare springs protruding here and there.

VI

Men who receive their early, ethical training from a woman
and who, as a result, respond automatically to feminine suggestion,
are inclined to resent the fact and to feel dominated. Professor
Burke could not repress a sensation of almost childish glee as he
drove up to Bedelia's home.

The night was still, the stars were wan but numerous, and the
air was sweet with the various flowers that had accumulated around
Bedelia's house from years of trading among garden club members. A light glowed in her living room—like the light that burns
in windows for sailors. When his wheels touched the drive, a light
came on in the car porte. Bedelia appeared, enormous, anxious,
and swathed in decorous kimono.

"Good heavens, Martin, it's nearly two o'clock!"

He stepped out of the car. She saw the lipstick and followed it here and there on his composed features. Then she saw the ripped upholstery.

"Mercy!" she gasped. "What was she—a tigress?"

Over a pot of coffee, he told her the story. He omitted, however, his first reactions to Miss Maxson and his later sensations when she had kissed him. These were, beyond doubt, the most important elements.

"So—as you can see—" he summed up, "the whole fantastic affair demonstrated that mere intelligence is sufficient to deal even with criminals of the stature of that fat Alsatian."

"Plus a lucky break in the matter of a drawbridge . . ."

"I include that. The causeway drawbridges are constantly being raised for passing boats. Quite frequently, even at night. But here—also—it was a matter of intelligence. Miss Maxson's. She simply capitalized on an opportunity."

"And if the bridge hadn't gone up?"

"We would doubtless have contrived other measures."

She poured more coffee and stared at him. "Martin, do you realize that you carried your life in your hands? For such a sum— for a fraction of it—a gang like that would have murdered you both without a scruple!"

"Possibly." He glimmered his eyes at her. "But 'all's well that ends well.' I shall be able to make the experience into a separate lecture. I have here materials to demonstrate the essential stupidity of the criminal, the superiority of the resourceful mind, and the futility of such imbecile pastimes as gambling."

"But it wasn't! You won eight hundred dollars!"

"Not 'won,' Bedelia. Dishonorably accumulated. And it's gone."

"You mean—you don't expect to get it back?"

"Certainly not! Double-O Sanders is, after all, a gambler. I enclosed my winnings—and the balance of the money I had from you—simply because I hated it to fall into the hands of whoever operated the following car."

"And you aren't going back to the Club Egret?"

"Whatever for?"

She slowly shook her head. There were times when what he regarded as clear thinking, or proper behavior, seemed obtuse to her—and more than obtuse: downright dumb.

The morning was clear and rather cool: towards dawn, a very slight high pressure front moved in from the northwest. People had wood fires going on their hearths and in iron stoves. These sent over the inhabited rim of the peninsula a drift of pine smoke which carried far out to sea. Inland, the pungent aroma drifted over the campus of the University, about which there was a definite vacation motif.

Professor Burke conducted his last two recitation classes with unusual vivacity. His students, being themselves in good spirit, attributed it to the same cause: imminence of the holidays. Had they known that on the previous night he had defied and successfully outsmarted five members of the Maroon Gang, with the aid of a blonde who looked not unlike a movie star, they would have been flabbergasted beyond precedent.

They had, of course, no such knowledge. He intended to divulge it months later—when he was thoroughly detached from it. A professor could mention gambling "last year" with decorum. "Last night" was far too recent.

At noon, he finished his seminar on freshman socio-psychology and started across the footpath through the Bermuda grass to the College Inn Tearoom. Here, he encountered Miss Marigold Macey—because she had been waiting for him.

"Hello," she said. "I wanted to ask you a couple of questions." This was a mild deceit for he was meant to presume the questions referred to his science.

He said, "I was just about to have lunch. Perhaps . . . ?"

"That would be divine!"

Professor Burke did not, as a rule, dine with students. Their "gay banter" seemed, to him, insufferable twaddle. Miss Macey, being somewhat older, might be looked upon as an exception.

The tearoom smelled like the hot raisins in its infinitudes of muffins—a large chamber with oak pillars where the waitresses were semicostumed in starched, colored aprons. They found, luckily, a table for two.

Miss Macey had seen to it that her curly-casual hair-do was in proper condition, her lipstick was on straight, and her white sandals were immaculate. As she had said to Wally Stratton, she was not an extraverted Southern belle. Thus she was not able to sit on his desk casually—pat his hand, hold his arm, call him "honey" in a becloyed manner, bat her eyes at him, or switch herself about. The circumstances did not leave her without certain resources.

After they had ordered lunch, she looked up at him with a polka tempo in her large, brown eyes. "I'm getting a great deal out of your course, Professor Burke."

"I'm delighted!"

"I really wanted to apologize for being so impertinent, yesterday. I wish I hadn't been."

If she only knew! he thought. He beamed at her. "Argument is the staircase on which knowledge climbs." It sounded fuddy-duddyish. He wondered what fuddy-duddy had said it—and realized he had coined the maxim himself! "You know," he said, in a less sententious tone, "it's very dull when there isn't any—criticism or resistance. You get the feeling that you're not really teaching anybody anything. Just setting up echoes from sources that won't retain the sound at all."

"I never thought of that. It must be discouraging." She returned to her "impertinence." "What I did yesterday was very unfair. Nobody in his right mind expects a professor to do the sorts of things he presents in theory."

He found himself trembling, slightly. Miss Macey possessed the power to affect him. And what she had just said supplied a perfect opening for an exchange of such affects. He ate a forkful of creamed chipped beef. "As a matter of fact," he finally said, "and in the strictest confidence, I—understated the case yesterday. I wouldn't want it to get beyond you—"

Her lips were parted. The expression in her eyes now was entirely uncontrived. "Of course not!"

"—but I've had a good deal more—ah—vivid experience with the world of crime—with gangsters, gambling, and so on—than most people."

"No! You—Professor?"

He raised one shoulder and let it fall. "I've won—and lost—" he added hurriedly, "at roulette. Not—recently, of course. I've seen gunplay—"

"Gunplay! Where?"

He was unsure that the use of firearms merely for hold-up constituted "gunplay" in the technical sense. He hastened away from the subject. "One or two of the nation's foremost criminals know me. At least one is somewhat beholden to me."

"Why—that's the most wonderful ever!"

He frowned. "Wonderful?" He was beginning to feel that he had overstepped. But the effect on Miss Macey was a pleasing radiance. The brevity of his sleep on the previous night had, no doubt, made him slightly toxic—and the toxins had perhaps produced a lightheadedness.

"Wonderful—of course," she said. "But you know"—her eyes were disturbingly bright—"I think I sort of suspected it. I had a hunch that inside—underneath—you were entirely different."

"No man," he replied, "keeps all the cards of his personality face up." He felt the figure was particularly apt. "No man—and especially, no professor."

"Couldn't you come over to my house, sometime? Dad and Mother would love to meet you. I've often talked to them about you. Or—wouldn't it be fair for me to get an extracurricular education from you?"

Extracurricular education. It was an interesting phrase. "I'm afraid—from what I've heard—that I'd have to fight my way through a swarm of male undergraduates."

Miss Macey laughed—and stopped laughing. She said gently, "You wouldn't have to fight at all, Professor."

That did it.

Women seldom acknowledge the fact; more often, they repress it vigorously; but the fact remains, as all men know: there is a certain contagion in romance, at least among males. The man who breaks down and kisses Girl A is more liable to kiss Girl B than the man who held himself aloof from A.

What was happening to the Professor was a variant of that phenomenon. He was looking at Miss Macey—thinking about Miss Maxson. He recalled, with the utmost clearness of detail, his sensations at the time of her kiss. Or kisses. He perceived that the same sensation—or possibly a different and even more powerful one—could be produced by, or elicited from, another: Marigold Macey. It is a shattering experience. He stared at the girl in a way which, he reasoned afterward, must have been appalling. She merely blushed a little and looked away. He decided to ask her when he might see her at home.

A hand pounded his back. "Wellll—Burke!"

The trancelike mood collapsed. He turned. Feebly, he said, "Ah. MacFalkland."

"What are you doing—flirting with my golf partner?" He saw surprise. "Yeah! She and young Stratton and Mrs. Ames and I have a foursome this afternoon, old boy. Hi, Marigold!"

"Oh, I see. Very pleasant."

"You ought to get out more, Burke," MacFalkland said. "Rode by your lecture hall yesterday. Heard you droning away. Well— see you by and by, Marigold!"

He strode away, waving heartily at people here and there in the room. Professor Burke sagged. MacFalkland was, after all, a natural leader—the sort of man who should head up a department.

"He's a friend of Daddy's," Miss Macey said uncomfortably. "Daddy's a judge, you know."

"I didn't."

"Yes. Mac—Professor MacFalkland—works with Daddy on several things. Slum clearance projects."

The luncheon regressed into a rather ordinary professor-student meal.

VII

His schedule wound up, that day, at four. He walked home, reflecting on the range of moods which accompanied any regular route, such as his. Item one, Miss Macey. He could see her happily married to such a chap as that ex-pilot, Stratton. Item two. Mac-Falkland. When the University could afford a full-scale Socio-Psychology Department, MacFalkland would be the director. He, Burke, would live in the imminence of that boisterous voice and sudden back-slap. The third item was more difficult to define: a vague, almost sad sense that a bright light had winked in his life—and gone out.

Bedelia called from the side porch. "Want tea?"

He came around the house.

"Your car's been hauled to the garage. The man estimated it would cost around a hundred dollars."

"Gosh." He munched a bit of orange cake.

"I sponged your dinner clothes. With alcohol—for the lip-stick. And sent them to the cleaner this morning."

"Thank you, Bedelia."

"There were pieces of fern in the pocket."

"Fern? In the pocket?"

"I didn't know what it was, either. I took it to Alice Beardsley. She's secretary of the garden club."

"However—oh!" He smiled faintly. "Last night. I really was dramatizing myself, Bedelia. Looking for clues. Observing closely.

All sorts of idiocy. That wad of plant stuff came from the hinge of the sedan that held us up."

"It did?" she leaned forward interestedly.

"What of it? Hedge somewhere."

"It only grows on certain Keys. A subspecies. The fronds are much wilder on one side than the other."

"You don't say!"

"Which means, of course, that car last night had very recently made a trip to the Keys."

"Marl."

"What?"

"I said 'marl.' There was whitish marl on the tires and wheels. The kind you see in ruts on those little side roads in the Keys."

"That proves it! Alice gave me a list of the Keys where the fern is known to grow. Only four or five. We could drive down Sunday . . ."

"Drive down? What on earth for?"

"Aren't you curious? Wouldn't you like to know just *what* a carload of gangsters were doing in the Keys? And *where* they did it?"

"Heavens, no! Why should I? Fishing trip, perhaps. Maybe they own a juke joint down there. What of it?"

"I would be mighty curious." She settled back. "Do you remember the tires?"

"Diamonds and dots," he said. "Alternating. But I'm not going on any wild-goose chase in the Keys. I'm going to finish up the marks for the month, and eat dinner, and read Conover's *Hidden Social Culprits*—and get a good night's sleep. I'm tired out."

He was not too tired to hurry down the stairs when, at six, she called him to the phone. There was something in Bedelia's voice.

"Hello?"

"Hello, darling!"

His reaction was like near-electrocution—short of fatal, but violent. "Miss—Maxson!"

Bedelia put the lid on the veal curry, quietly.

"I wheedled your number out of the University operator. What you doing this evening?"

"Well—I was—that is—"

"I'll pick you up around eight-thirty—after supper . . ."

This time, he made it more effectual. "I really couldn't, Miss Maxson. I've got work to do. And—my dinner things—"

"The hell with your dinner things! Wear shorts, if you feel like it. A certain person wants to meet you."

He opened his mouth to say it was utterly out of the question. But the light had winked on again. And it was not his doing. He gave her the address.

Bedelia was elated. "You know, Martin, girls aren't any different now, from my time. They simply go out and act the way we merely used to feel."

"I have no business letting her do it."

"You have no business missing such an opportunity! Even if only for my sake—so I can get a look at her. I'll be at the window curtain, sure as shooting!"

VIII

Miss Constance Maxson drove up quietly, walked through the lush front yard, and knocked on the door. Bedelia answered, and called up the stairs for the professor. He came—rather nervously. "You've met?"

Connie nodded and Bedelia boomed, "Prettiest girl this house has seen in ages!"

The car at the curb was a convertible, long and grey and brand new. Connie drove toward Miami. She seemed to be serenely pleased with the world—and not inclined to talk.

"What happened?" he finally asked, breaking through their occasional amiable platitudes.

"Double-O will tell you. How do you like this car?"

"It's a beauty."

"It's yours."

He gasped. "Mine!"

"From Double-O. In repayment for your coupé!"

"I couldn't accept it! It's—fabulously magnanimous. But I couldn't think of such a thing!"

Connie smiled. "I told him you'd refuse it. You know, Professor, you're something of a sweetheart." After a while she said, "I suspect that Double-O may be a shock to you. You better get set."

"I'm quite prepared to meet him on his own terms."

Connie turned over the new grey convertible to the doorman of the Bombay Royale, whisked the professor through the lobby so fast he only glimpsed the photomurals of Hindu temples, and took him to the roof in a private elevator. On the roof he could taste the sea and hear a rumba band playing in the patio far below. The girl knocked at the door of a small penthouse; it was opened by a butler.

"Come in, Miss Maxson. Professor Burke, good evening," the butler said.

The professor experienced a series of stupefactions. The room behind the butler was furnished with modern pieces and a few Eighteenth Century French chairs. A fire was burning on a marble hearth. There was a white cat curled under the piano. On the walls were etchings of cats by Peggy Bacon and a magnificent print of a Cézanne.

A man rose from a chair which was set in front of corner bookcases, beside a lamp and a small table. He turned a book face down. This he did slowly, unhinging his long frame—and smiling. The book was Professor Burke's own *Ruminations of a Socio-Psychologist.*

"Very kind of you to come over," Double-O said. "I should really have called on you. I've been reading your collected lectures. Most interesting. Before the evening's over, perhaps I could add a few bits to your theory of crime. It was theoretical interest that brought you to the Egret last night, my niece says."

His eyes were twinkling. He held out his hand.

Professor Burke looked at Connie in a sort of frenzy. "Niece?"

The tall, lanky gambler said, "Oh-oh!" He cocked an eyebrow at the girl and then at the professor. "Who did she say she was?"

"I told him," Connie answered, giggling, "that I was a hostess. It's true enough. I think he assumed I was your moll, Bill. So I let him think so—for punishment."

The professor was scarlet. "I honestly—as a matter of fact— the truth is—I made no estimate."

Double-O walked to the grate to hide his grin. He poked the fire. "Women," he said, "are cads, Professor. Born bounders. Connie's mother is my half sister, and hardly proud of the fact. I'm the family black sheep. Connie herself, however, has a drop of the restless Sanders blood. This year—since no polite institution for young ladies could hold her—I hired her to keep people happy at the Egret."

"I supervise the kitchen," Connie said proudly. "And I helped re-do the gambling room. Isn't it gorgeous?"

"Very," said the professor—that being as much as he could say for the moment. Fortunately for him, the butler wheeled in a tea wagon and Double-O mixed a Tom Collins for Connie and a Scotch and water for the professor. For himself he made nothing, and explained that he did not drink.

"Now," he said, taking the chair in which he had been sitting, "I would enjoy hearing the story from you, Professor Burke."

"First," the professor said, "I'd like to know—how things turned out?"

Double-O laughed. "They kept all of us at Headquarters till morning. They searched the place—ripped it up a bit. Let us go finally. I called Connie—"

The girl had taken a seat on the floor by the fire and the cat was in her lap. "I asked him to look at his mail."

The gambler went to a desk and took an envelope from the drawer. "Your money, Professor. Connie says part of it represents winnings at my tables. I'm delighted!"

"In other words—the—funds—reached you?"

"Yes, Professor. They did. Thanks to you. Now—let's have the story."

Professor Burke told it, in bare outline and with several deletions. Double-O listened—his face reflecting understanding, excitement, appreciation. "I suppose," he said when the professor finished, "that you knew French Paul would just as soon use a gun as not?"

"He slapped Miss Maxson—with no need. She hadn't even refused to answer his query. He simply slapped her. Brutally. There was no alternative for me but to tell the swine—"

"No alternative, eh?" Double-O's grey eyes seemed amused. "I also suppose you realize you quite possibly saved a very large sum of my money from confiscation? Not to mention my niece's life—perhaps—if she'd been alone."

"He wouldn't accept the car—" Connie said.

Double-O nodded. "I was afraid of that." He stretched his legs and looked at his shoes for a moment. "Professor," he said, "I'm possibly a curious man—from your viewpoint. My ideas of ethics may differ from your ideas. But I think our concept of gratitude must be about the same. I never owed any one so much as I owe you. It was foolish to offer the car and hope you'd accept. I realize I haven't anything you would accept. One trifle, perhaps— the hospitality of the Club Egret. If you will be our regular guest for dinner this winter—with your friends—I'll be happy. I'll be disappointed if you won't. The Club is yours. And if I could think of anything else . . ."

To his astonishment, Professor Burke found himself very much moved. He momentarily felt that tears might come in his eyes, which would have been a hideous embarrassment. He had looked forward to meeting the notorious Double-O as a source of firsthand—and scornful—lecture material. But the man in front of him—obviously cultured, plainly sincere—was very upsetting.

The professor's eyes moved away—and fastened on the Cézanne. It was not, he realized, a print. It was real.

"I told you," Connie said softly to her uncle, "the guy was nice."

Double-O nodded very slightly at her. His grey eyes followed the professor's. "Like it? I do. One of my—clients—lost quite a large sum of money. He happened to be pressed for cash at the moment and offered the painting." The cat walked over and the gambler stroked it absently.

Professor Burke's mind finally churned through his emotions and the surprises which had given rise to them. Somehow, he felt, he had been guilty of an indecency. Intuition led him to say what he did. "Mr. Sanders, I'll be glad to be your guest some evening. I'd like Bedelia—my landlady, and a unique character—to see the Club Egret. But there *is* one thing you can do for me."

The barest trace of surprise showed in the gambler's face. It was followed by a smile. "Name it!"

"For years," the professor said quietly, "I've postured as an authority on—on—"

"—the way the other half lives?"

"Exactly. But the fact is, I'm an ignoramus. My information is thirdhand—fourthhand—theoretical . . ."

The gambler looked at the face-down book and hid the ghostly beginning of a smile. "On the contrary. I thought—"

"No college professor has had an opportunity for a—a briefing, by anyone who really knows the story. If you could understand the difficulty of discussing a subject without firsthand knowledge . . ."

Double-O nodded. He walked over and again poked up the fire. "We'll start, Professor, with the gents you met last night. French Paul—who's the present chief of the Maroon Gang—"

"An Alsatian."

The gambler turned his head and smiled. "You're quick. Yes. Born in Strasbourg, actually. The Maroon Gang began moving in

on Greater Miami several years ago. I once ran their gambling—
in three cities. We had a disagreement about—ethics. I'll tell you
their political setup here. It's as good an example as any. Their
interests in Miami, at first, were bookmaking, a few protection
rackets, and the usual other enterprises. I gather from word that
gets around that lately they've branched into the business of
bringing in aliens who shouldn't be here. Former Nazis who got
out with loot. Possibly a few well-heeled people working for Russia.
After all, Florida is full of tricky back doors to the U.S.—the
rivers that run into the Everglades—the Ten Thousand Islands—
the Keys . . ."

Professor Burke concealed a sudden, internal start. *Marl and
fern,* he thought. He hadn't mentioned these matters, in his account
of the pursuit and holdup: his sleuthing impulse had seemed
childish.

Double-O went on. "Whatever makes money, interests the
Maroon Gang. I'll tell you how they muscled in here—and how
they got set. I didn't believe, until last night, that they were going
to work me over. What happened makes it plain they have a better
setup than mine. They know the whole score. They intended to
beat the cops at a snatch of my working capital. I've banked it
now, incidentally. Even my own club isn't safe any longer. However. When I sketch the background on the Maroons—who they are
—how they operate—where they come from—how they got that
way—you'll know as much as I do about all of the gangs. I'm a
gambler, Professor. Never had another angle. If I get pushed out
of business, I'll go. My connections are sound, so it will take a
lot of pushing. After I tell you about the Maroon Gang, I'll tell
you the long and not always dull story of my own life. How I
grew up. Why I quit college. Where I learned—my profession.
Is that what you want?"

"I'd like to hear it myself," Connie said.

Double-O lighted a cigar, and smoked for a minute. "What
you are going to learn, Professor, you never heard. I never told
you. If you use it as background for lectures—or books—or any-

thing—it'll just be your surmises and bald assertions. Every big shot in the rackets and every involved politician will deny it. Will that suit your purposes?"

"Yes," the professor said. "And more than repay any debt you may feel in my direction."

It was after one o'clock when Connie accompanied him to the lobby.

He said, bemusedly, "I'll get a cab . . ."

"I'll drive you over."

"Not at this hour—with the long ride back. I refuse!"

"Will we—I—see you again, Professor?"

"Absolutely."

The doorman brought her car. They stood on the broad hotel steps. Already, the northwest high was diminishing. The warm winds of the Gulf Stream were pushing back over the immense, flat peninsula. Connie turned from her car—the one intended for him. She kissed him. "So long, Martin."

He was scarcely conscious of the ride in the cab. The amount of the meter shocked him. Then he remembered his winnings, paid, and tipped liberally. The driver thanked him and the red taillight of his cab whisked away on West Cortez Circle.

Bedelia was waiting up—naturally. The glass coffee-maker was full, and hot.

"You've got lipstick again," she said. "But not so much. She was a very nice girl. So much more refined than I'd expected. What *else* do you know?"

"Ask me what I don't know—it would be the shorter part." He sighed then, and sat down tiredly at the kitchen table. "One thing, to start with. We're going to go down in the Keys and try to locate that fern subspecies, next Sunday. Bedelia!"—he shook his head—"you have no idea—no *idea*—of the way this world runs! And there are one or two things I mean to stop right now— or perish in the attempt! You're game, aren't you?"

For a few seconds, she had an odd, almost premonitory feeling. A feeling of violence, horror and sudden death. The kitchen seemed unfamiliar and she found herself thinking of the Keys— not in the brilliant light of day, but at night, with the sea quiet and ominously listening. She had launched the professor's little escapade. It was turning into—*what?* The feeling passed.

"You bet!" Bedelia replied.

IX

Few pastimes are more innocent than amateur botany. Few persons, as a class, are more innocent than professors and the elderly widows of Naval officers. A less innocent pair of plant hunters than Professor Burke and Bedelia Ogilvy in all probability never existed. What they undertook to do, on a warm and sunny Sunday, was to verify the idea that certain members of the Maroon Gang had been smuggling aliens into the United States, by way of the Florida Keys.

The T-Men knew that an organization of some sort had been bringing notorious aliens into the country, by way of Canada, Mexico, or the seacoast. Two T-Men had been shot to death in a widespread attempt to add to this information—information which, such as it was, had been shared with F.B.I. and the Coast Guard.

Bedelia and Professor Burke had no notion of such facts. If they had been less ardent and more sophisticated—and particularly if he had not clung to his theory of the essential stupidity of criminals—they would have reported their suspicions to the police and let it go at that.

"What we know," he said chattily, as he drove his reupholstered coupé onto the first of the Keys-connecting bridges, "is, basically, that a car belonging to the Maroon Gang had marl on its wheels—"

"—and had some ferns caught in its hinges that Alice Beardsley says grows only on DeWitt Key, Little Tango, Key Dent, and

Lower Beacon Key." Bedelia was fully prepared for the adventure. She was wearing riding breeches and boots, and carrying a bee-hat, in case the insects became unbearable. She went on enthusiastically, "We have Mr. Sanders' hint that these Maroon people are engaged in the—business—"

"—and I will be able to recognize the tire-marks of that big sedan, if we find them. In marl of that sort, with no rains since, they should be very plain."

It was little enough to go on, in a sense. Little enough, but the multitudes of officials searching for the smugglers would have given much to know that little. It was for such small facts that they searched coast and border.

They drove to Lower Beacon Key, as a starting place. It was farthest from Miami, and the smallest of the four. They reached it before noon—an islet of twenty or thirty acres, without a tree. The ferns with the lopsided fronds covered about half of it. There was not a byroad on it—nothing but the main highway with its crescendo-diminuendo of Sunday traffic.

"We can rule this out immediately," Bedelia said with assurance. "No cover. No lane. No wharf. Nothing. A swimmer wouldn't try to smuggle pearls ashore here."

Key Dent was bigger, and wooded. After lunch, they explored. There were three side roads on Key Dent. Two led to fishing camps, over dry coral. One led to a lobsterman's cabin, through a certain amount of damp, whitish marl. But there were no tire tracks of any sort in the marl.

They returned to their car. With no diminution of enthusiasm, they drove back to Little Tango which was the largest of the suspect four, in spite of its name. It boasted of a half-dozen homes, another fishing camp, and a combination filling station and marine curio store. There were many side roads and they spent the best part of the afternoon exploring them—without success. Some were a few hundred feet in length and some were several hundred yards. None even passed through the lopsided ferns, although many were rutted deeply in marl.

Before they continued on to DeWitt Key, the professor decided to fill up his gasoline tank. He drove in at the single pump of the filling station and curio shop. He blew his horn. An old man with a limp, a quid of tobacco, faded trousers and no shoes finally appeared and began to crank the gasoline by hand.

Bedelia liked shells and corals. She got out to inspect the collection in the shop. She returned disdainfully.

"Just junk," she said, "and most of it broken up. Poorly collected. But"—and she lowered her voice—"there's a road on the other side of the building that goes to a ramshackle garage—and also beyond it, toward the sea."

Professor Burke paid. "Do you mind," he enquired mildly, "if we go down your road? We're fern collectors—"

"Private property," the old man said.

"I realize that. I'd be glad to pay a dollar or two, however. We are hunting for a particular fern. It has been reported on four keys, only. This is one."

"It is lopsided," Bedelia said brightly. "I hope you won't object to our just looking."

"Sure do! Anyhow—place is full of mosquitoes."

"We're accustomed to that!" Bedelia popped the bee-hat over her head.

The old man was startled. He spat.

"Come, Martin," she said, "I'm certain he won't mind if we just take a peep. It would be a pity to leave Little Tango without finding the fern."

"Lady, I said this was private property."

Bedelia's head loomed from the open car door—bee-hat and all. It was quite a sight. "You sound," she said reprovingly, "as if you had something to hide back there. Have you, my good man? An alcohol still, or some such nuisance? I shall report that you have a still. I'm convinced you do have! Martin! We will stop at the office of the Peace Justice. Better still—when we get to Miami—"

"Lady," said the old man resignedly, "there is no still back there. No nothing. There is a dock where my son keeps his fish-boat. He's outside fishing now. For Lord's sake, go back and see the danged ferns!"

The professor drove past the dilapidated garage and proceeded beneath the locked branches of trees toward a spot of water shining at the end of the long, green tunnel. Inside her bee-hat, Bedelia was chuckling.

Presently she said, "There are the danged ferns."

"And the marl!"

They got out. The ruts in the road were deep. They showed signs of frequent use. He bent over. The alternating diamonds and dots of automobile tires were plainly embossed here in the earth. "This is it," he murmured.

They walked toward the water, mosquitoes rising about them. The trees thinned and the ferns began. They were perhaps four feet in height, and the fronds of dozens had been broken off by whatever had passed on the road.

The water off the end of the wharf beyond was disappointingly shallow. Two feet, perhaps—weed beds and sand shoals. Sun-blanched tree limbs marked what was not so much a channel as the least shallow approach from the light blue sea over the distant reef and the far, purple line of the Gulf Stream. A lazy chop splashed on the low, white claylike shore. The lighthouse was a distant, dim finger. No boats were in view—nothing save the flat prospect of the ocean and the cloud-patterned sky. The dock foundation had been in place for a long time. But its jerry-made decking was nailed on two-by-eights and could be hauled inland at the prospect of rough weather.

The old man limped out on the wharf behind them. Professor Burke noticed the sag of his right suspender and the bulge in his pants pocket. "Find the still?" he chuckled.

"We found the ferns," Bedelia answered. "And small thanks to you!"

"Don't like snoopy people."

"No more do I like tobacco-chewing old gaffers!"

There was a clearing where a vehicle could be turned. Pro-

fessor Burke spun his wheels in the deepest, slipperiest hole. Then
they were on the road—the insects left behind.

Bedelia removed the bee-hat. "Now what?"

"Honestly, I don't know. I don't believe I really expected we'd
find anything. However, we have found quite a bit. The car did
go to that wharf—and that wharf is on the sea side of a Key.
Boats could be rowed up to it. At high tide, one of the commercial fishermen's boats might get in. A light down there at night
would be visible for several miles. But it does seem a devilishly
unlikely and inconvenient place to bring anybody ashore. And if
it was at all rough, it wouldn't be possible."

"Which may be the reason they use it. So unlikely."

"Quite." He drove frowningly. "What I must do, is reconnoiter."

"Reconnoiter? 'Way down here?"

"My vacation," he reminded her. "And it need be only on
calm nights—as you point out. I'll watch."

"Shouldn't you go to the police?"

"They would laugh at me. We need definite information."

She shook her head. "You can't watch, Martin. Don't you
realize the insects would eat you alive? Especially on the kind
of nights when they could land there. Still nights. That's probably
one more reason they use such a spot."

"Insects!" he said. "Mosquitoes and sand flies! One would
hardly be rendered *hors de combat* by a few pests."

X

It does not require a profound philosophy to expose the ironies
of life. And one of the ironies is this: the good deed of a good
man may be observed by thousands and will be forgotten in a day,
but any appearance of scandalous behavior in a decent citizen
will get itself bruited about indefinitely. The good repute of Pro-

fessor Burke was caught in this process, by an almost expectable chance. On the evening of his visit with Double-O Sanders, two undergraduates had been dancing in the patio of the Bombay Royale Hotel. As they came through the lobby to summon their car and start home, they saw two persons emerge from an elevator.

The girl undergraduate said, "Why—there's Professor Burke —and a babe! Who would have imagined such a thing?" Naturally, they hung back a little and thus observed the good-night kiss tendered to the professor by the young lady.

By evening of the day following, the story had progressed through a considerable portion of the student body.

Because of it, Miss Marigold Macey was listless the next morning at breakfast. Her mother noticed it as she quietly engineered the juice squeezer, the toaster, the percolator and the waffle griddle. Her brother noticed it vaguely as he studied the brief of a law case. And her father finally became aware of it as he perused the paper. It annoyed him.

"What in hell," he enquired, "is the matter with you?"

"Matter?" Marigold temporized.

"Nibbling at your waffle! Rolling toast crumbs!"

"Jizzling," her brother added, without looking up.

"Well," Marigold said, "I'm in love."

Both men now looked at her. Both said, "Again!"

"This time," the girl said morosely, "it's different."

"It's different every time," her mother murmured.

The judge glanced sharply at his wife—was caught doing it— and winked. His wife winked back.

"How different?" asked her brother, skeptically.

"He's older, Steve. I feel maternalish about him—and scary. And then . . ." she rolled crumbs.

"Then what?" her father asked.

Marigold spoke petulantly. "Don't cross-question me! Ye gods! When your father's a judge and your brother's a lawyer, a girl lives practically in the witness box!"

"You brought the matter up," Steve said.

"I did not!"

"Rolling crumbs and jizzling. Perjorative behavior."

"He goes around with Other Women," Marigold said slowly. "He was seen a few nights ago—necking one."

Judge Macey folded the paper neatly. "Marigold," he said, "did you ever hear of *quid pro quo?* I mean to say—what in the devil were you doing with that Stratton boy on the porch the other night? And the long list of his predecessors? Studying the nocturnal habits of the glowworm?"

Her mother saved her from answering. "Who is he?"

"Martin Burke."

The two men looked blankly at each other. Mrs. Macey explained. "He's one of her professors. Now, Simon! Contain yourself! I met him last year at a drainage meeting." She saw she had to explain that, too. "Everglades-draining problems. He's quite young—for a full professor. He's extremely attractive, too—although he doesn't seem to realize it. His manners are simply dazzling. And he comes from New England."

The judge said, "Really?" He looked at his daughter with interest.

"Bring him around," said Stephen. "Both ways."

Her father nodded. "This is the first time I ever heard you worrying about what you somewhat hypocritically call 'other women.' It *must* be serious, by gad!"

Mrs. Macey smiled at a waffle. "With Professor Burke, I would imagine that pretty much everything is serious."

"It is not!" Marigold spoke with heat. "Do you call publicly necking a Miami Beach blonde, serious? And that's just one thing! Professor Burke only acts stuffy and superpolite. Actually—he's an authority on crime. He's been right in the midst of gang wars. He knows personally half the big shots in the underworld. He's two distinct personalities—and it's terribly fascinating."

"Nonsense," said her father. "A professor?"

"Drag him over here," Steve repeated.

"I've tried," she said.

Her brother snorted. "Lookie, cookie. If you try—he'll come. I don't know what it is. The big brown eyes, the well-made if slightly undersized chassis, or that wobble in your vocal cords. But they work, if you work them. Now, be a good kid and drag your prof over here."

She looked mournfully out of the French windows and down the arched patio, over the sun-polished Macey lawn to the garden hedge. "I'll try again," she said miserably.

Just exactly how he found himself walking home that afternoon with Marigold Macey, the professor could not be sure. He was preparing his work for the next term—a morass of pressing details. The strong easterly which had risen on Sunday evening might die down soon; if so, he would have to be absent from Coral Gables for a time. He was trying to get ready when Marigold appeared in his office.

She asked some trivial question about the work in the following term. She sat on his desk, patted his arm, batted her eyes, switched herself about, and urged him to accompany her home for tea. She did not call him, "honey-chile"; a girl has to draw the line somewhere.

Her home was several blocks away, in the opposite direction from Bedelia's—and he found himself walking with the girl at his side. She seemed very happy. And he was not displeased. He recalled the unmistakable leer he had given her in the College Inn Tearoom, the notion that had prompted the grimace, and his subsequent conclusion that it had doubtless forever alienated Miss Macey. It seemed not to have done so. On the contrary.

As they walked, she talked of this and that. "You detest Miss Orme, don't you?" she said.

"There's something about her. The snood. Always reminds me of a beaver's tail."

Marigold chuckled. "Your star student—*but* . . . *!*"

"Intellectually overenergetic, if such a thing is possible." He smiled. "Going to be a social worker, she says. I have no doubt of it. I can imagine her thrusting principle and theory on the under-

privileged—with all the whelming purposefulness of a bulldozer.
I shouldn't make such a statement about a student. But Miss
Orme . . . !"

"Not liking her, shows good taste in women."

"Really?" He had never viewed it from that angle.

"Of course! Don't be naïve!"

They reached her residence. "We'll go in the side and around
to the garden," she said. "Tea won't be ready for a while—not
till Dad's home."

The garden was hedge-enclosed and contained, besides a round
pool where fishes swam and water lilies floated, some aluminum
furniture and a barbecue fireplace. Marigold chose a languorous
double chair and patted the place at her side. He sat. The sun was
very low and the air was suffused with orange light.

She took his hand. "Nice of you to come over."

"I'm very glad I did it."

"I thought you sort of—disliked me."

"Nothing could be farther from the truth."

These, and some further platitudinous remarks, along with
the warm feel of the girl's hand in his own, led to a recrudescence
of a recent sentiment. It became so acute that he let go of her
hand and rose with the thought of sauntering over to the pool.
Marigold, however, interposed herself between him and the pool.
Why not? his brain suggested. She was looking up at him
with an extravagant brilliance in her eyes—which at least
suggested she might consent to the experiment. He stepped forward, put his arms around her, and kissed her firmly, unprofes-
sorially.

"Great gad, man!" the judge bellowed, coming through the
hedge.

Professor Burke's mind rocketed back to what constituted
reality for him. He loosened his hold of the girl. He thought of
his situation in the terms in which he had been reared to think.
The man with the grey temples, flushed face and irate voice was
plainly her father. At that moment the professor felt passionately

enamored of Miss Macey. So he said, rather croakingly, "My intentions are perfectly—"

"To hell with your intentions! You're trampling my pineapple!"

Professor Burke jumped.

Marigold, who was both pleased and astonished by the past twenty or thirty seconds of her existence, burst into laughter. "Father," she said, when she could, "is trying to sprout a pineapple." She pointed to its top—in a small, mulched bed. "Daddy, this is Martin Burke."

The judge said, "Delighted," fell to his knees, and began replacing the tilted plant. "Tea is ready," he continued. "The next time you decide to kiss anybody, Marigold, for heaven's sake keep out of the flower beds. I told your mother it would root—and by gad, it's rooting!"

A short week ago, Professor Burke would have regarded even the idea of amorously kissing a young lady as something to be pushed into the nebulous future. A short week ago, he would have regarded being caught doing just that, by the girl's father, as a shocking catastrophe. He was, however, changing.

"I got lipstick on you," Marigold said. "Hold still."

Even this did not utterly dishevel him. He intended to kiss her again, at the earliest opportunity. He had tried to say that his intentions were honorable—idiotic phrase!—and he now saw that they were merely to kiss her.

Judge Macey satisfied himself that the pineapple was not ruined. He rose—and shook hands. "Don't be embarrassed," he said. "My daughter's impulses are familiar to the whole family. She's really quite a nice girl—though headstrong. Come in and meet my wife and my son, Steve."

This, in the professor's opinion, was both the civil and the mature way of looking at the matter.

"I hear," the judge went on, "that you're a New Englander. So are we. Expatriates." No topic could have been more fortunate.

Throughout the tea which followed, they indulged in a kind

of nostalgia—a fest of place names, of recipes, and of worrying
over the spread of the Dutch elm disease on New England's com-
mons. They found mutual friends—and, as was inevitable, Es-
perance Perthnot, who came to America just after the *Mayflower*
and who was a remote ancestor of the Maceys as well as of the
Burkes. Naturally, they invited the professor to stay for dinner;
being a New Englander, he refused politely. Naturally, both he
and his hosts realized that he would accept a later invitation.

When the professor had gone, stepping lightly into the bland
dark, the judge said, "Marigold, I really believe you're growing
up. That's a very intelligent young man."

She regarded her father demurely, "He can neck like hell,
too!" It was a boast rather than a fact.

The judge was a New Englander, but aware of modern trends.
Hence he took no umbrage. He looked his daughter steadily in
the eye. "Of course he can neck like hell. Comes from good stock!"

"What were you and he talking about, when you spent so long
showing him your den?"

The judge smiled. "He was asking my advice. Talking about
what you called the—other side of his personality."

"Was he? What'd he say?"

"Just put a hypothetical question. Asked me what I would do
if I had inside facts which led me to suspect that a certain group
of men were engaged in a particularly nefarious and antisocial
activity. Would I report my suspicions to the authorities? Or
would I continue my observations until I confirmed them beyond
doubt?"

"And what did you advise?"

The judge picked up the evening paper and walked to his easy
chair. "It was a pretty nebulous question. I told him that I thought
the 'authorities' would tend to regard the suspicions of a person
like himself with a good deal of doubt—unless he had some very
convincing evidence. After all, a professor running around to the
police station talking about 'antisocial activities' . . . ! These
Miami cops probably wouldn't know what he meant."

"Isn't he exciting!"

"I'm reading," her father answered rather plaintively. "Exciting? Burke? Sound as a rock! Nothing exciting about the man. Good chap!"

XI

Professor Burke sat down in the sea. It was nearly midnight. It was Christmas Eve. It was no time for a man to be wading—and now sitting—in the pitch-black ocean off the Florida Keys. The water was lukewarm over the flats, and there was no wind. The stars were glowing balefully. Near at hand loomed the underbrush on shore. Far away, in the opposite direction, a lighthouse swept its pale, impalpable arms round and round forever, encircling nothing, revealing only the endless flicker of salt sea. Insane, he thought. He should be up at Bedelia's, opening their reciprocal gifts beneath her small, electric-lighted tree.

But the easterly had dropped that morning. The wharf would be usable. The fact was scant indication it would be used; it was, however, the only indication he had to go on. Christmas Eve might suit them.

Behind him, up the coast of Little Tango Key, his coupé stood on one of the roads they had explored. He had parked it there with the coming of darkness. He had eaten his sandwiches and cake and drunk coffee from his thermos in solitude. Every half hour he had walked down to the waterfront and looked. It was well past eleven when the lame man—presumably—had set a gasoline lantern on the little dock.

No one, as Bedelia had pointed out, could stand the torment of exposure in the underbrush or on the near-by water. The professor had worked out a protective device, based upon the bee-hat. He donned it—a helmet of fine screen which sat on his shoulders.

It was painted a dull black. Fixed to it were numbers of wires covered with green paper, which Bedelia used for securing vines. Twisted in these wires were many small branches which the professor had picked before dark. He put on gloves.

In this regalia he was able to wade down the coast line. When he was satisfied that his wading sounds might soon be distinguished from the occasional splash of a fish, he moved out to sea. The bottom—now sandy, now oozy—slippery and then weedy—forced him to go very slowly. He found, finally, a spot with sandy bottom some fifty yards or so beyond the yellow-green, faintly hissing, gasoline lantern. He eased himself down.

There, his plans completed themselves. From anything but direct inspection, he was safe: above water, he looked like any clump of mangrove branches which floats in the currents around the Keys.

The lame man had left the dock. The night was quiet. He thought of sting rays and barracudas and morays. He reminded himself not to budge if some creature bumped against him. And not to cry out under any circumstances.

He forced his thoughts along rational channels: sting rays and morays did not attack unless disturbed—and barracuda struck seldom, under any conditions. It was much too shallow for large sharks.

He conquered his nerves and then thought about the Coral Gables Choir, which would still be caroling wherever a candle showed in a window. No snow—nothing here to suggest Christmas. No loose tire-chains clanking against fenders in the crystalline dark. No icicles hanging like glass stalactites around the eaves. Just people standing around amongst rosebushes, jasmine, hibiscus—to sing "Silent Night" and "Little Town of Bethlehem."

Small waves lapped around his portable greenery. Insects hummed indignantly outside his screen. He switched his thoughts to Marigold. Connie Maxson intruded. So he turned back to the matter of carols. Mentally, he hummed, "The First Nowell." He heard a washing, gurgling sound, out toward the open sea. Cautiously, he turned around.

For a long time, he saw nothing. Sea—stars—the remote lighthouse. Then he heard a car on the land. Its motor whined a little. He knew its wheels were sluicing in the soft, white marl. Feet sounded on the dock. He glanced back. Men were there now—two of them. The light had been dimmed. He turned his attention toward the sluicing sound.

And suddenly it took form—a dark, huge shape, and a white combing at the water level. He heard the muffled voices of men, grunting. The thing came steadily nearer. He began to fear it would run him down. As he considered a retreat from the path of the great, black blob, he made it out. It had wings.

It passed him, slowly, splashingly, at a distance of a few rods. When it came between himself and the gasoline light, he could see it perfectly. A two-motored seaplane. Or amphibian. It bobbed and eddied as it was pushed toward the flimsy wharf by two men in the water. The propellers, he saw, were many bladed—and the blades were wide. They looked like the vanes of a windmill.

Somewhere he had read about just such propellers. They were said to be very quiet. Certainly, although the plane must have landed within a half mile of where he was concealed, he had not heard it. And naturally enough, it had showed no light. Instrument landing? Perhaps. Perhaps an accurate knowledge of the area— and a glint from the lighthouse, enough to show the pilot the sea surface. A plane with quiet propellers and, doubtless, engine-mufflers.

A windless night for a gentle landing—and this method of hand-taxiing across the shoals. The coastal authorities, he reflected, would not think of the possibility of pushing a plane, by wading, across a mile of flats. It was, all in all, exceedingly ingenious.

The plane was swung around at the pier. A door opened.

"Howdy, Chuck."

"Hi, Solo. Six customers."

"Well—get 'em out. These bugs . . . !"

The professor watched the six passengers of the plane step out. They required help. He could soon see why: their hands were linked together behind their backs and they were bent forward, as if pulling against their hands.

Handcuffs, evidently. Then the professor could make out not only the glitter of the steel, but the sash weights which were wired onto the handcuffs. The cargo was disposable. Dropped overboard —from aloft, or in the deeper water—these passengers would vanish. No incriminating evidence.

They were rubbing their arms and hands, now. One of them sobbed, suddenly. "Shut up, sister!"

Another "passenger" asked something in a low tone.

"Naw, you damned hun! Not here. You got a long ride in a trunk compartment. Then you'll be in good old U.S.A. to celebrate Christmas. Only—you probably won't feel like it. Come on, guys. I'm being eaten alive!"

It was then that something struck the professor. Forcibly. It might have been a turtle. A ray. A bonefish hurrying in the night. It might have been any of a hundred creatures. He did not cry out. But he lost his balance. He made a swimming motion with his hand to regain it. And the motion set up a sharp splash.

The men on the dock fell silent. A strong beam from a flashlight shot over the water and began sweeping in circles. The beam found the miniature greenery and held on it.

"Weeds," a voice said. "What's the matter? Spooky?"

"Fish," said another voice.

"Lemme look." The professor recognized it as the old man's. The light once more blinded him.

"People been pokin' around here lately," the old man said. "Maybe it is weeds. Looks kind of funny. Floats high. I'll send a bullet into it."

"Cut it out, you fool! Chuck! Johnny! Walk back in and take a squint at that bunch of weeds."

They came close. One carried a boat hook. The professor

heard the other murmur, "Something in it, anyhow! Look in the water—underneath!"

"Shall I take a slam at it?"

With an emotion like cosmic self-censure rather than fear, the professor rose to his feet. "Never mind, gentlemen. I surrender."

The spectacle of the greenery lifting itself from the sea startled the two men. The professor thought of running. But he knew he could not run fast in water that deep. The light would be at his back. And the range would be easy. He started wading toward the little wharf.

When he got there, the six airplane passengers were gone. The old man and a husky-looking, well-dressed fellow with sleek, black hair were alone on the dock. Each covered him with a gun. The younger man was slapping at his face with his free hand. "Take that thing off!"

The professor removed it. Light struck his eyes.

"That," said the old man, "is the same jerk came poking around here a few days back."

The professor's clothes dribbled. The two men from the plane, also dripping, came up beside him. The round, white stare of the flashlight was very close. "Who are you?" The voice was the younger one—cold, furious, afraid.

"Martin L. Burke—University of Miami. An amateur—interested in gang methods. I—"

Professor Burke heard a sound. The light danced. A hot feeling came in his cheek. His ear rang. He realized he had been hit —hit hard.

"Who? A Fed? Treasury? Customs? Talk fast!"

Professor Burke was panting, now. "I told you—"

They hit him again.

"Look in his pockets!"

"He wouldn't be carrying anything, Solo."

"Look anyhow."

They looked. The professor got his breath and his grip on himself.

"Put cuffs on him, Chuck. And drop him over—about halfway back. Whoever the hell he is!"

XII

The handcuffs held his arms together behind his back. The weights—twenty-five or thirty pounds of them—pulled achingly. He was left standing on the wharf while Chuck and the other pilot —Johnny, the professor thought—went up on the bank and talked with Solo for a minute. Then he was pushed up the board and into the cabin of the plane. He heard the car leave.

They used the flashlight briefly, in order to tie him into a seat. Then they went out the door and onto the nose of the plane. He heard their splashes. Slowly, the plane turned.

He had a glimpse through the door of the lame old man, carrying the gasoline lantern away. Then it was dark. The door shut quietly.

For a long while, the plane moved in slow surges out across the flats. Then it rocked as the two men clambered back on board. They threw a light on him and checked the knots they had made.

One of them then thrust his head through the hatch and turned in a complete circle, slowly. "Coast's clear."

Forward in the plane, a very faint light now glowed. The man put down a heavy pair of binoculars. Presently, there was a tick and a cough and one engine started. It was astoundingly quiet. The professor did not hear the other motor fire and take hold. He simply felt the plane start along the smooth sea, gather speed, and, at last lift itself.

They flew for what the professor had estimated as twenty minutes and then one of them turned on a meagre light in the cabin. He stripped off his wet clothes, toweled himself, and brought dry garments from some point in the rear of the ship. He put them on.

"Okay, Chuck!"

The other pilot now changed his clothes.

When he was dressed, he sat down across from the professor. It was so dim that only his square profile, the gleam of his eyes, and his crew-cut hair could be discerned.

His voice was flat. "All right. Who are you?"

"I told you. A college professor interested in criminology. I've made a hobby of gangs. I have nothing whatever to do with the police, the F.B.I., or any other such agency."

The man called Chuck sat quietly for a moment and then moved a little. Something glittered in his hands. "I know a guy," he said, "who has a jackknife, like this one. When he wants people to talk to him—he uses it. Just the tip. That's the name of the guy: The Tip. He just uses the tip—under fingernails, to start with. After the tip of his knife has loosened up ten fingernails, a person has ten toenails. Doesn't kill a person. Just seems to make them talk. If nails don't work, a person has eyeballs . . ."

"I told you the truth."

"Maybe you did. It's just that I don't believe it. Talk some more." He leaned over and seized one of the professor's hands. The professor felt the knife point slide under his nail and into the quick. For a moment, it was a mere shock. Then the pain came.

"I've been studying the Maroon Gang a long time," he said, when he felt he could talk evenly again. "I'll tell you some of the things I know about it. I'm a scientist—not a cop. I'll tell you things that the cops don't know. When I do, you'll see that I am what I say."

Chuck said, "So shoot."

Professor Burke had been thinking feverishly. He had dismissed from his mind the near-certainty that the plane would be throttled down, the door would be opened, and he would be pitched out, to fall an unimportant number of thousands of feet, to land with a violence that would surely knock him senseless and probably kill him, and thereafter to be pulled down by the weights through two or three more thousand feet of Gulf Stream. No trace. No body to be recovered.

But Bedelia would know what to do.

It followed, therefore, that they would need to discover who he was and what his connections were—how much of his information was already known to others. They would be stupid to pitch him over without questioning. The questioning methods would be drastic. What, then, to tell them? What would be most effective? He had settled on the truth—with limitations.

He began, now, to talk to Chuck about the Maroon Gang. He had a grim abundance of information on the theme, supplied by Double-O. He had selected certain high spots. As he talked, his manner became discursive. Soon, he was lecturing. His right index finger throbbed, but no more fingers were adding to the pain —yet.

For perhaps a half hour, Chuck merely listened. But he listened with gathering awe. No man lacks interest in the hidden lore of his own occupation or in the low-down on his betters. The professor was capitalizing on that fact. Finally, Chuck began to comment.

"So they bought the Police Commissioner?"

"And six months later sank him in cement, in a river."

Chuck whistled at another point. "They shot Lorrie?"

"—but he didn't die. He's living in Mexico."

"The girl did that?" he asked, again.

The professor nodded. "Yes. Sarah Brown—nobody ever knew her real name—did precisely that."

It was the other pilot who finally stopped the eerie talk. He looked back and called, "Hey! We're halfway over! And then some!"

Chuck said a doubtful, "Yeah." He peered at the professor. "How come you never gave that to the coppers?"

"I told you. I'm a scientist—not a stool pigeon."

"Be damned!" The man chuckled. "Some of the things you told me—it is going to be mighty handy for me to know. I can use 'em if I ever need to."

"I was sure you could," the professor said. "I told you because I don't want to get dumped in the sea."

That surprised the man with the crew haircut. "Yeah? I thought you were just—keeping clear of the tip of the knife. Mister, you get dumped. That's all there is to that!"

The professor, like every man, had speculated many times on what he would think, feel, do, when his hour came. Here it was. And he found himself analytical. He was relieved that his death —although dramatic—would not be overly painful or long-drawn. One finger would hurt as he somersaulted down the thousands of feet. He wondered how long Bedelia would wait for him before going into action. He could think of nothing else to help himself. His back and arms were beginning to ache so much that his finger —given time—would have been the lesser pain. He knew now— very completely—why the six smuggled aliens had stretched and rubbed themselves and hardly seemed to notice the mosquitoes, when they had come ashore.

Now the man named Johnny said, "Hey, Chuck! Get set!"

The motors were cut down. The professor could feel the air push against the plane like a brake. Chuck went to the door. Something squeaked. He was prying it open against the streaming air, with a crowbar. Cold wind rushed in. The professor shivered in his sodden clothes. *Somebody*, he thought, *everybody, in fact, should be made to understand the ferocity of the criminal.*

His own efforts—his lectures, his book—had been pitiably inadequate. In the presence of the fact, all theory was inane. He deserved, in a sense, the pitch into blackness which was coming. Chuck began to untie the knots that held him in the seat.

XIII

As the seconds trickled, Professor Burke found in himself a sudden, tremendous anger. They might have thrown many people out of their plane and down to the sea when they had a signal that landing was inadvisable. And those people might have died submissively. They had come a long way through risks and hardships; the last leg of their illicit journeys might have brought death; and they might have half-expected it. But Professor Burke knew he was not going to jump willingly through the door where the wind howled. They had guns. But he might take a lot of killing. It was murky in the plane. He would move as fast as he could.

"Okay," Chuck said.

The professor stood. "Could I have—a last cigarette?"

"Hell, no. Get up."

He gathered his feet under him.

And Johnny turned from the controls. "Hey!" He took off earphones. "Hold everything."

"What's the matter?" Chuck asked sharply.

"Call coming in!"

"Put it on the speaker."

Static crackled. Chuck kept his eyes on the professor and listened.

"Miami Marine Operator," a metallic, female voice said harshly. "Calling the yacht *Mary Fifth*."

There was a wait. Then a man's voice, fainter. "Yacht *Mary Fifth*. Go ahead please!"

"Here's your party!" the Operator said.

Professor Burke realized that the plane was equipped with a radio which enabled it to pick up ship-to-shore phone conversations. Any boat with ship-to-shore apparatus could listen to all others; whoever telephoned from land to a fishing boat at sea, for example, made a call public to all other fishing boats. And public also to this plane.

"How's fishing, Hank? This is Paul."

The professor's skin prickled. It was *French Paul.*

The faint voice answered heartily, "Pretty Good! We're trolling off Virginia Key, now. Doing okay. Some tarpon around here."

"You got one?"

There was a pause. "What say? Over!"

"I said—you got one?"

"Sure."

"Got him in the live well?"

"Yeah. We got one in the live well. Over."

"See if you can bring him back, will you? To put in the pond at my place. Over."

"Okay. We'll try it."

"Coming in after an hour or so?"

"Yeah. Hour or so."

"Well—we'll have something to eat up here for you. Stop by our dock. And bring us a tarpon if he'll stay alive in the well."

"Okay. Will do."

"Well—good fishing!"

"Roger! *Mary Fifth.* Signing off."

Chuck talked inaudibly with Johnny for a minute. Then he strode past the professor and removed the block with which he had jammed open the door. He came back.

"Want those weights off, professor?"

"I—don't get it."

Chuck took a key from his pocket. A lock clicked. The professor's arms were free. He was able—barely—to move them into his lap. He began chafing them.

"Pretty cute?" Chuck asked, then.

"I'm not quite sure I understand—"

Chuck laughed. "You know so damn much! You should be wise to this! On the nights we fly, maybe the *Mary Fifth*—that's

a Miami boat—goes out fishing. Or maybe just out for a moonlight trip with some guys and gals. She keeps tuned to the Marine
Operator. And we keep tuned, too. If anybody wants to send us
a message—you know who—they just raise the *Mary Fifth* on
the ship-to-shore phone. Then they do a little double-talk about
fishing or late supper or a charter for the next day or something.
What they talk about, means different things to us. See?"

"Yes."

"Like—suppose there were Feds nosing around Little Tango
Key . . ."

"I get it."

Chuck was pleased with the system. "Tonight they want a
live tarpon brought in—just in case we have a live tarpon on
board. That Ely sure caught on fast to what he was supposed to
say. Anyhow, the boss wants a live tarpon in his pond. And you're
it."

The man in wet clothes with stiff arms smiled barrenly. "I see
how it works, now."

Chuck laughed again. "They could listen for secret radios till
doomsday. We communicate right over the regular public telephone system!"

"Very ingenious. And very timely."

"What? Brother! Was it! Old Paul's tarpon darn near fell
overboard!" He slapped the professor's shoulder.

The plane flew. By and by Chuck took the controls and
Johnny stood—or sat—watch on the professor. Johnny had light
hair and he was thin. A silent silhouette. The professor did
not feel like talking anyway. He continued to rub his wrists and
arms.

He was conscious of the descent. The landing was expert.
This time, a rope was thrown to the plane and a rowboat toiled in
the darkness until the bottom grated. Chuck opened the door.
"*Señores,*" he called softly. "*Com esta?*"

"*Muy buen.*"

The professor was taken to the door, between the two pilots.

He was turned around; he felt with his foot for a step. Then he was on shore.

It was as dark in Cuba as it had been in the Keys. Cuba, he felt certain. Double-O had mentioned Cuba. The men in the boat spoke Spanish. The flying time was probably right for it—long, perhaps. There were men about, talking softly in the dark. Two of them gripped his arms.

"See you, Professor!" Chuck called softly.

They went for a distance on a dirt road. Then they were among houses with an occasional light. One of the men who held him said in his ear, "You are drunk, if anybody appear. You stagger. We will laugh—your *amigos*—taking you home."

They walked from the dark street into a less dark one. Down a side street, he heard laughter, and a rumba band. Over a radio, in a building that seemed dead of its age, he also heard a snatch of Christmas music.

It was not a large town. Some little Cuban seaport. They took him around another corner and through a narrow arch. It led to the inner court of a big building. Tall trees grew there. A fountain dribbled. The place smelled of mold and human generations. A door was opened and he was hurried up a turning flight of stone steps. Another door, unlocked with an immense, old-fashioned key.

He was pushed through this door and it closed.

He expected to find himself in a prison—probably a windowless chamber, possibly without a light, and certainly alone.

There were four people in the room, sitting around a kerosene lamp on a table. One was a woman—brunette, young, very pretty. One was an extremely old man, with a white beard. The other two were in their thirties or forties. The windows were high and boarded up. Open luggage lay about.

The woman said, *"Bien venu, ami—et joyeux noel!"*

The professor thought, *the next load.*

"You are wet." The old man said it calmly. "Franz. We could lend him dry clothing."

"*Ja wohl.*"

The third man stared blankly at the professor. "Who are you?" he finally said.

The woman laughed. "The old one"—her English was heavily accented—"is called Herr Wasser. So Franz is also Wasser. This other has no name. I am Lorraine Dumond." Franz was rummaging in a suitcase. "I will turn my back," the girl continued.

The professor demurred. "Really—my clothes will dry. It is a warm evening. My name is Burke, incidentally."

The man called Franz Wasser smiled a little. "Go ahead. We are to leave the baggage in any case. These are good garments. English. Use the small bath."

Reluctantly, embarrassedly, the professor changed.

The old man watched for his return. "The finger bleeds," he said.

They all looked at his finger. "A splinter," he said. "I had to climb—then to swim."

"I have some . . ." the girl did not know the name. But she went to her own suitcase and brought a bottle of peroxide with a French label.

"Iodine," said the third man, "is better."

He offered iodine.

Professor Burke nodded. The bottle produced by the third man had no label. The man put cotton on a match stick. He dipped it and probed the wound with needless force. The professor turned grey, but his finger did not shake.

The man said, "That will be sufficient." He had quite dark skin, but light hair.

The man with the beard began to read a book printed in German. His son Franz walked over to a rickety cot and lay down, closing his eyes. The man who had no name sat at the table again and became immersed in his thoughts. They had accepted the professor, taken him for granted. He chose a chair in the corner. There were several in the room.

Presently the girl walked over to him. "Be cheerful," she said. "Six went this very evening."

"Splendid!"

"You have been in—America?"

He looked at her steadily. "I lived there for some years. It seems a long time ago."

"*Moi—jamais.* I am excited."

"It is an extraordinary country—"

"It is," said the nameless man, "a hell!"

The old man spoke, "Shall we sleep, friends?"

They took places—a chair—another rag-covered cot—and the nameless man on the floor. The bearded man blew out the kerosene light.

XIV

Professor Burke thought about them for a while. Who were they? Spies? Perhaps. People escaping the shambles of their world. *Nazis who had got away the loot.* That might fit Herr Wasser and his thin son. Who was the nameless man? The bleak, grey eyes, the overzealous application of iodine, the chilly confidence in himself. He could be anybody.

In the dark, the professor woke and wondered where he was. He remembered slowly, and slept again. The next time he woke, he remembered instantly. There were footsteps outside the door.

It was a man with a gun—a Cuban—and a fat woman with a heavy tray. She said, *"Buenos dies, señores y señora!"* She put down the tray. Fried fish and boiled rice, a long loaf of bread, butter, and coffee.

The professor took his turn in what a better class of hostelry would have called the "adjoining bath." It had no windows. The

plumbing was a European import of the nineteenth century. The
only light was a candle, which each one lit and each blew out. He
washed his face. His finger was sore, but not throbbing.

After breakfast, as if they had done it many times, the nameless man walked under the windows and lifted Franz until he could
put his ear against the crack in the boards. It was a feat of considerable strength.

Franz listened. "I hear nothing," he said.

The girl explained to the professor needlessly. "We fly—as you
must know. But only in the still weather."

"Once," said the old man, "so we were told, there were fifty
people here. The wind blew many weeks without stopping. They
showed us how to listen."

The nameless man sat silently all morning with his nameless
thoughts. Herr Wasser and his son played chess, under the lamp.
The girl began a low conversation. "When the Nazis came to
my town," she said, "I married an officer. I collaborated, they
say, though I did nothing but marry the enemy. When France was
liberated, I had become a Displaced Person in Germany. My husband had left some money in the Argentine. It took two years for
me to get there. But coming to America openly is hopeless. So . . ."
she shrugged. "My jewels paid this passage."

During the morning, the Wassers told a somewhat simi-
lar story to him, told it mechanically, in detail so that he realized
it was not the truth. They claimed to have been anti-Hitler Ger-
mans.

The nameless man said nothing.

About noon, the door opened. Two Cubans beckoned. The
professor was escorted to a room down the dark, tiled hallway.
It was a smaller room, well furnished and electrically lighted. More
men sat in it—men he had never seen. Americans. One of these was
bald and bug-eyed. He did the talking.

"My name is Wilser. Sit down, Professor."

He looked pasty, the professor thought. Like a big-eyed larva.

"Paul," said Wilser, "was unable to cover over this morning.

I have talked with Chuck and Johnny." He hesitated. "Your knowledge of our—organization—surprised me. How did you come by it?"

Professor Burke smiled a little. If he had thought that his removal from the room of the aliens was a hopeful sign, he did not think so now. Not after looking at Wilser. "The way I found out all I know. Watching. You hardly need a diagram of my methods. Your men uncovered them."

"How did you know about The Foot's dock?"

"Haven't you figured that out?"

"We know you and that horse-faced landlady of yours were down there looking for ferns. Now. Tell us how you got onto it. We want to keep it from happening again."

The professor smiled once more, slightly. "In that case, Mr. Wilser, before you drive your cars north from the Keys you should wash the white marl off their wheels. And you better cut back the ferns along the road to the dock. They are a special kind of fern— a sort of sport of a Glades genus—which is peculiar only to a few, small Keys."

"Where'd you see a car—with marl and these ferns?"

"You might ask French Paul."

Wilser thought that over. "Oh." His eyes lighted unpleasantly—as if there were little hot places in them. "Naturally," he then said, "we went right after that landlady of yours."

Professor Burke's heart turned to stone.

"Is there anybody else?" Wilser asked.

"Nobody."

"We want to be quite sure of that, Professor. Quite sure. We intend to be—before . . . ! There's another matter. Chuck has told me some details of your knowledge of the Maroon Gang. Paul thought that under the existent circumstances you might be willing to write it out for us. Make everything less—painful—for you, in the end."

"I'll write it out."

"Every angle you know. There are several that Paul would

find very interesting, I think. Singular information. Who gave it to you? Double-O Sanders?"

"I told you, I've spent years in—research."

"It doesn't matter. You can work in the room with our waiting clients. It's—secure. How long will it take?"

The professor said, "A couple of days."

"*Days!*"

"I know a lot about the Maroon Gang."

Wilser thought that over. He turned to one of the men. "Okay. Give him the stuff to write with and a table of his own. Another lamp. Pick up his copy from time to time. I'll see you again, Professor."

He spent the afternoon writing.

The other people in the room did not question or interfere. They were accustomed to holding back questions and to avoiding interference. The members of the Maroon Gang would have many reasons for wanting to know all they could of their predecessors, associates and contacts. Blackmail was only one.

As he wrote, the professor paused frequently—apparently to recall details of his subject. Actually, he was thinking. They had Bedelia. They had no intention of letting him go alive. Bedelia might already be—gone.

Before dinner, Franz and the man without a name listened for the wind. It had not risen. This fact put three of the foreigners in a state of eagerness; the nameless man did not show any emotion. The professor went on writing into the evening. His ink-covered pages had been collected several times.

It might have been eight o'clock.

He needed three things. One of them could stay where it was; he could get it if he had the right opportunity.

He quit writing and went over to the nameless man. "Tovarich!" he said sharply.

The man looked up instantly. It was the only undeliberate move the professor had seen him make. Not proof of anything, except that the man knew Russian.

"Could I borrow your iodine again? My finger—I am afraid it may be getting infected."

The man did not speak at all. He rose, went over to his suitcase, and came back with the bottle.

"I will soak it," the professor said, "in a little iodine and water."

He took the bottle to the antediluvian bathroom. He poured about half of it in one of the two dirty glasses of the washbowl and hid the glass behind the battered bathtub. He diluted the iodine in the bottle with water, and—after delaying—returned it with thanks.

The man accepted it inexpressively.

The professor sat down beside the French girl.

She was nervous. They were all nervous. For, if their illicit conveyers found themselves watched, or if they became suspicious in any fashion, the aliens would not be smuggled into the United States. They would die. They knew it—or feared it.

The girl welcomed his talk. She asked questions about life in America. Was hailing a taxi the same as in France? Eating in a restaurant?

He explained the various restaurant check systems. He told her about cafeterias.

Her compact and lipstick were in the chair at her side. He made a half dozen furtive stabs at stealing the former before he got it. He put it in the pocket of the borrowed slacks he was still wearing. By and by he grimaced. "My finger. I will soak it again."

He transferred half of her powder to a folded sheet of writing paper which he had prepared. Then he came back. She hadn't missed the compact and she did not see him replace it. He went back to his work.

Time crawled. It was growing more and more difficult to keep his mind on the history of the Maroon Gang. He thought of Bedelia and the thought stiffened his will. Shortly after midnight, the door was opened. There were several men in the murky hall—among them, Chuck. They carried two lanterns.

"Everybody get set! Five minutes!"

Frantically, they rummaged for the last time through their treasures. The old man stuffed photographs into a pocket. The girl went into the adjoining room and the nameless man followed next. It was a better chance than the professor had hoped for; he slipped in the room.

The man struck a match and walked toward the candle.

The professor bent down and slid his hand along the floor. He found the rusty wrench that he had decided was the best available weapon. He did not know how hard to hit.

The candle was lighting. The professor struck. The man made no sound, but he shook from head to foot and kept standing.

He struck again. The man's scalp began to bleed. He sagged. The professor caught him.

He moved swiftly now. He shut the door. He picked up the hidden tumbler of diluted iodine and poured some of it over his face. He dried it with a filthy towel and peered into the mirror. His skin was dark, now—Indian dark. He washed his hands in the rest of the solution and wiped them. They were dark, also. He took the paper of powder from his pocket and sprinkled it in his hair. He rubbed his hair furiously and combed it with his fingers. It looked grey rather than hemp-colored, like that of the man on the floor.

He bent over the man. There was nothing in his trousers pockets. The professor stripped off his coat, donned it, and dragged the man to a dark corner. He was breathing; the professor took time to listen for that.

Now he strode to the candle and blew it out.

He opened the door a crack. They were talking—even laughing—laughing with a creepy, hysterical sound.

The outer door was unlocked once more.

"All right, you! Come ahead!"

The professor walked boldly into the room and across it. The girl had gone first—the old man and Franz were right behind her. He joined them.

"Where's the other one?" Franz asked. "Weren't you both . . . ?"

The professor gathered himself. This was the first of an unknowable number of crises. "He said—he was not to come with us." He had made his voice low like the voice of the unconscious man.

Chuck spoke. "The professor's staying," he agreed. He slammed the door and turned the big key.

They went down the turning staircase and through the patio with the huge trees. Into the street—walking together—with men ahead and men behind.

Light hair, dark skin, the same height, though the Russian —if he was one—was broader. Smelling of a woman's face powder and iodine. Unfortunate, but inevitable. He would see. They crossed streets, turned corners, passed the old buildings, the shops closed for the holidays, the radio behind the ancient walls. They left the small town for the soft road. A warm night—very warm for Christmas, even in Cuba. Still and starlit.

Trees closed above the road. A dull flashlight prodded the jungle, up ahead. Presently, it touched the open door of the plane. When the French-speaking girl realized what the weighted handcuffs meant, she screamed. Someone put a hand over her mouth. One by one, they went aboard, clanking a little.

The professor recognized Johnny's silhouette in the murky cabin. *Better than Chuck,* he thought.

He need not have worried. Johnny used his flashlight only to tie them to their seats. He sat down in their rear. "Any fuss, and you are tossed out. Okay, Chuck!"

The quiet engines started. The plane taxied and lifted. All the long way, nothing was said.

The professor listened—listened for the crackle of static and the flat voice of the Miami Marine Operator. Listened for some amiable discussion with a fishing boat which might convey to the men in the plane that one of their passengers was an impostor. It did not come.

The plane descended. The professor expected the two men to jump overboard and begin pushing. But Chuck taxied the plane for some distance. Then there came a feeling of coasting and a gentle arrestation. Hands had gripped the wings. Johnny opened the door.

The next crisis was at hand.

They were herded ashore. The handcuffs were unlocked and the weights removed. The girl wept quietly.

It was, as far as the professor could make out, a lake, of some size, with a grassy shore and trees behind the grass. A small dock. Lanterns. The same man who had driven down to the Keys on the night before—husky, with patent-leather hair. Solo, they had called him.

They were walked along the dock, to the trees. A car stood there, a car different from the black sedan. In the lantern light he saw it was greenish. Big.

"The old bird and the girl can sit in back with Cliff," Solo said. "You two—in the trunk."

The rear compartment lid yawned. Franz climbed in. The professor followed. Solo said, "Duck." They ducked—and the lid came down.

The road was atrocious. They banged into each other. The floor came up and struck them. They slid about. A better road came, finally. They lay still, panting. The tires whirred. The car was going fast.

Another eternity passed.

The car stopped, waited, and started. Traffic began to stir and horns to blow around them. They were getting into Miami.

Finally, the smooth pavement gave way to another rough ride—very short. Once more, the car stopped.

This time, the rear compartment was opened.

There was no light. Stars overhead—treetops—underbrush. "All right, you guys. Get up!"

Franz and the professor painfully climbed over the bumper. The girl and the old man were gone.

Solo did not bother to use his flashlight.

"Listen. You both understand English."

"Very well," Franz said. The professor grunted.

"Oke. Now, get this. You're on a street that leads to a main highway. When we leave—start moving. Separate before you get to the highway. If the cops ever pick you up—you don't know anything about who got you here—or how. See? Not that you know much. But one of you tell anything, and we've got an organization that can make you regret it, wherever you are." He turned, "Let's go, Cliff."

The big green car drove away. The delivery was completed. "Comfortable trip!" Franz murmured. "Shall we go?" He laughed a little. "I am a free American citizen! Living with my retired father, I knew you were one of the Soviet lice, the day you came in there."

"It is a poor time for that argument," the professor said. The highway appeared ahead of them. Occasional cars, busses, street lights. He was home again. And alive.

XV

Franz went out on the highway first. He had dusted off his clothing and made himself presentable. He walked to a painted lamp post and waited. The professor watched him board a bus.

He had recognized his surroundings: Brickell Avenue—about a mile from the business district.

He did not have bus fare. He had no plans. He began walking. Nobody seemed to be following. Nobody much seemed to be on the street. *Christmas Night,* he thought.

A police cruise car passed.

He had an impulse to yell at it.

Then what? The Station. Questioning. Delay. Doubts. More

waiting for higher authority, perhaps. Christmas Night—and higher authority unwilling to leave festivities. He was without any proof of his story. They might even think he was crazy—iodine on his face—powder in his hair. And there was Bedelia.

He stepped into the gutter and thumbed. The cars swished past —on their way home from late evenings in the night clubs, from parties in homes, from pleasure and safety and an innocence of the world. Then a car stopped. A dark face leaned out and a soft voice said, "Ride, friend?"

They were colored people on their way to Coconut Grove. "Drop you anywhere, mister," the driver offered.

The women in the back seat said nothing.

He picked the closest point on their route and walked from there. Coral Gables was mostly asleep. It was late for the Gables, even on that day. He left the sidewalks of West Cortez Circle at the distance of several houses and went through back yards. They might, by now, be expecting him.

There was a light in Bedelia's home.

He stood in the shadows of their neighbor's garage and looked —not daring to hope that Bedelia was there, fearing to investigate. His feelings overcame his judgment. He was about halfway through her leafy yard when a man stepped in front of him. A man with a gun. "What do you want, bud?"

"I—I live here." The professor hated himself.

"Yeah? You Burke?"

"I'm Burke."

"Come along." The man followed the professor to the porch. He knocked. After a while Bedelia called, "Yes? What is it?"

"Guy here says he's this Burke. I got him covered."

He heard the downstairs couch creak. He heard her big, boney feet cantering in the hall. The porch light switched on. "Martin! Thank heaven!" They embraced.

She addressed the man with the gun. "Thank you, Dusty. Keep a sharp eye out for anybody else."

"Okay, Miss Ogilvy." The night ate him.

She hurried the professor into the kitchen.

"What on earth have you done to yourself?"

"It's a long story," he said, grinning at her fondly. "Who's your guard?"

"That's a story, too."

He sat down at the familiar enamel-topped table. "They told me, in Cuba, that they'd caught you. Well—not exactly. That they'd gone after you."

She was staring. *"Cuba!"*

"I've been over the whole route," he answered. "Is the coffee hot?"

"It's been hot—pretty steadily, since early Christmas morning, Martin." Her spectacles misted up and she polished them on the hem of her kimono.

"I'm not sure we're safe—even with that guard."

"We've got three of them," she answered.

"Three! What are they? Private detectives?"

"My story will keep."

"And mine will take a long time. I need to know about the guards."

She looked at him—at his powdered hair, his face and hands, yellow-brown from the diluted iodine, and at his unfamiliar garments. She sighed.

"Just to reassure you, Martin. And I hope I did right." She poured coffee in her two largest cups. "I didn't expect you till some time in the morning. By ten o'clock, when no word came, I began to worry. You'd had time to drive back—after sunrise. It was possible, of course, that you were on to something that prevented your return or even making a phone call. But it was also possible that they'd caught you at it."

His eyes were grim—and the odd color of his face emphasized the fact. "They did."

"Oh, Martin . . . !"

"Take it easy, Bedelia. I'm right here, now."

"Well. I reasoned that if they had caught you, they might be after me. Correct, wasn't it? I closed up the house. But first I put hairs across several doors, with Scotch tape. My mother did it to jam closets. Then I went to the Duffys for Christmas dinner. I came back with them—the whole family—to show them our Tree. I felt nobody would bother two carloads of people and nobody did. But the hairs on the doors were broken, so I knew they had been here. When the Duffys left, I also went.

"I couldn't think what to do. I wanted to be at home—in case you arrived—and I was afraid to be there alone. I couldn't call the police—"

"You should have!"

Bedelia looked at him. "Then—why aren't you?"

"Go on."

"I felt I couldn't because you might return and it might be premature. Finally, in the late afternoon, I got hold of Mr. Sanders. I told him that you had gone looking into something and weren't back. I told him my house had been searched and I was worried about staying there. I asked if he could possibly send me a man or two to stand watch. He was delighted to help out."

"Good heavens!"

"He did ask me what you were doing—and I said I had no idea. I think he finally concluded that I was an overnervous woman. But he sent three dandy men. They arrived—at Laura's, where I was then—around five. I came over here with them and that's all. Now you talk!"

At the conclusion of a story that left Bedelia numb, he looked at the telephone. "I suppose I must call the police, or the F.B.I., or both of them—now. And yet I hate to. What I have found out will cause the arrest of a lot of underlings. French Paul and that detestable Wilser and a hundred more will probably get out of it. The whole, hideous thing should be untangled quietly for a while. And I'm absolutely exhausted. I don't know how I can even go to police headquarters—or any place—and answer hours of questions."

"I wouldn't, then. I'd go right upstairs and get a good night's

sleep. Morning's sleep. Then you can go to the head of the F.B.I.
Right now, there wouldn't be anybody on duty but a clerk of
some sort. A minor person. And the police—from what Double-O
says—aren't to be relied on entirely. You might be giving information to one of them who would pass it straight to the
Maroon people."

He thought about it. "I believe you're right, Bedelia."

"I'm sure of it! Anyone who tried to come in here after us
tonight would get hurt!"

He lowered himself into his tub. He was bruised, scratched,
strained—sore from head to foot. He scrubbed at his hands and
face without much success. He nearly fell asleep.

The trousers of Franz Wasser and the jacket of the nameless
man lay on a chair in his bedroom. He picked them up, sat
tiredly on his bed, and examined them. No labels. The customers
of the Maroon Gang were careful about labels. The jacket was
rather thick. He squeezed it—and went to his bureau for scissors.
He ripped the lining. Inside was a second, double lining of black
cloth. Stitched in sections were ten one thousand dollar bills and
many hundred dollar bills. The professor was becoming accustomed to such sums. He started to the stairway door to call Bedelia.
He decided the fact would wait till they had slept. He tossed the
jacket with the stitched-in money onto a chair. His bed creaked
just once.

In a little-patronized, old-fashioned hotel in the coastal town
of Vellehomez, in Cuba, the owner of the coat—the nameless man
—came into a numb consciousness about an hour after a plane
had quietly taken off.

The man's head hurt. He reached out and felt walls. One
wall was cold and smooth. He remembered the antique tub. He
remembered everything, then.

His coat was gone. That fact filled him with fury. The plane
for America would be gone too. He got to his feet and found the
door.

The kerosene lamps were still burning in the big room. No one was there. Abandoned luggage lay about.

He walked over to the larger table and took matches back to the bathroom. He lighted the candle. He looked at himself in the mirror. His hair was sticky. He started to wash. Then he noticed the diluted iodine spilled on the dirty, cracked sink—and the face powder on the floor.

He peered at his own face for a moment, and thought about the last one to arrive: Burke—the man who had spent most of the day scribbling something which their guards had taken away, every few hours. Burke—whoever he was—had dark hair and a light skin. Iodine and powder would reverse those characteristics. They were the same height and build.

The nameless man knew what had happened—although not why. The other, whom he had estimated to be something of a fool, had gone in his place. His rage increased.

Without the money, without the coat and its lining, his arrival in America would be a mistake. He would have to return, now, to Havana—and explain to Borston. Borston would be enraged. Moscow would be bitter.

To live his life—to put behind his career—and then to be slugged by a mild-looking capitalist imbecile!

He combed his hair without a grimace. He went into the big room and sat. He waited; he could wait.

The guards who came were unfamiliar. Two of them. Slight men and tipsy. It was Christmas Night, the nameless man reflected. *Bourgeois sentimentalists.*

He asked, in Spanish, for their chief.

"He has gone home to his wife—his children—long since, Professor."

"Well, I must leave. My plans are changed. I will not wait for the next trip."

"Leave, Professor?" They laughed.

He decided that it would be futile to try to explain the substitution to them. And he understood why Burke had impersonated him. They picked up the last few sheets that Burke had written. The nameless man wished he had read them.

He watched for an opportunity—and lunged.

He had overestimated his own condition and the drunkenness of the guards. One shouted and the other stepped aside. A knife flashed. The man without a name sank slowly to his knees and fell suddenly on his face.

"Idiot!" said one of the Latins.

"He would have killed me!"

"We must get word to Julio. He will be like a whip!"

At two o'clock in the morning, a phone rang in the Havana hotel room of Wilser. He answered and listened.

"If they had to," he finally said, "they had to. You know the procedure." He hung up and turned on the light. *More work to do.*

Long before daybreak, a handcart rumbled through the silent back streets of Vellehomez. It ceased rumbling when its wheels touched the dirt road. At the water front where, not very long before, the plane had taxied quietly into the harbor, a body was lifted from the cart into a skiff. Handcuffs with weights were fastened to the body. The skiff rowed slowly across the harbor. Its oarlocks did not squeak. The sea beyond was calm—and very deep. The body sent up a long chain of sound, the muttering of bubbles.

An amateur radio operator in the suburbs of Havana got in touch with a brother "ham" in America. They chatted cheerfully and familiarly of various matters, for a long time.

In the Bayfront residence of French Paul, two men played gin rummy. They had been playing, off and on, all night. They always did. A telephone buzzed. One of them answered and asked questions. Finally he switched the call to an upstairs bedroom.

French Paul woke, as Wilser had wakened less than an hour before. French Paul listened.

One of the men had come up from downstairs.

The fat Alsatian hung up and thought for a long time. Finally, he smiled. He threw back the covers of his bed.

"Our professor," he said, "has met with a mishap. He was a clever man. A little too—enterprising." He walked over to a desk, yawned, and sat down. "A friend," he said, "must send condolences—and a warning—to his landlady. The police in Vellehomez can announce the rest."

French Paul chuckled.

XVI

Bedelia had dressed, served breakfast to Double-O's men, and was dusting when the mail truck drove up. Her guards did not interfere with the arrival of the special delivery letter. It contained one sheet, of single-spaced typewriting with neither salutation nor signature:

Professor Burke committed suicide last night near the town of Vallehomez, Cuba, after writing a confession of his jewel-smuggling. He was seen to leap from a skiff. His body was not found. Portions of a full confession—in his own hand—were recovered. So this letter may be regarded as an amicable warning. He had led you to believe he was hunting for certain persons—rather than acting as a member of a criminal organization. It would not be wise to take erroneous information to the police! The facts will be made clear to you soon. Wait. Do not act!

She read it and sat down heavily. "Well!"

Presently she rapped on the windowpane with her ring. One of the guards appeared at the kitchen door. "Professor Burke came home last night, as you know," she said. "But I want you three men to keep that fact quiet."

"Sure. You need somebody around all day? The other two boys are getting kind of sleepy."

"I'll let you know. But you might take turns napping on the side porch." She emphasized the need for secrecy concerning the professor.

Just who, she wondered, would have sufficient prestige—and know-how—to accomplish her object? Worriedly she dismissed one after another. She thought of the name of a man she did not know, who would be right. She looked in the book and dialed.

When the professor came down for breakfast, a car was leaving the driveway. He had a glimpse of a face.

"Morning, Bedelia! That looked like Marigold Macey."

"It was." Bedelia's large eyes were brilliant. "Sit down, Martin. And start your breakfast. I have news for you."

"News?"

"You're dead!" She showed him the letter.

He read rapidly. "Who sent it? How did it get here? Are the Sanders men still around?"

"The men are. Getting tired, too."

"They—Bedelia! I killed that man!"

"Maybe you did—and a good thing, too!"

He was horrified. "Not for anything on earth—no matter how low—even a foreign agent—would I have—!"

"Martin! Collect yourself! Isn't it much more likely that he came to, tried to escape when he found he had been left behind, and they killed him?"

"But how could they confuse him with me? His hair was light—his skin very dark . . ."

"It's obvious from the letter that they *did* confuse him! Perhaps the men who killed him were unfamiliar with him—you—whoever. Disposed of the body hurriedly—in the sea—as the letter says. It looks like that to me."

He shuddered. "The unlucky devil . . . !"

"Good gracious, Martin, where is your sense of proportion? Don't you see what an opportunity this is?"

His mind worked jerkily. "Confession," he said slowly. "Yes —I can understand that. They could select a page here and there —and it would certainly look like a confession. In my own hand-writing!"

"Please, Martin. Go on with your breakfast! Look at it from their point of view. They think they have murdered you. They know there will be an investigation, in any case. All the police— the Vellehomez police—will need is a few pages from that account you wrote of the Maroon Gang—select pages, as you say—and a couple of witnesses to your 'suicide.' The Maroon Gang down there can supply the witnesses easily enough and handwriting experts will attest to the confession, so-called."

He stared at her.

"I phoned Marigold Macey an hour ago," she went on.

"What for?"

"Because I knew she'd come right over. I knew, further-more, that she'd believe what I told her. Few would. Martin, there are—sometimes—really formidable disadvantages in a perfect reputation. And I knew she could get straight to her father—even if he had to be called out of court."

"Judge Macey? But—"

"He could determine, properly, who should be informed. That's important. The police? The F.B.I.? And not only that. He can persuade the top man to see you—so there won't be any mistakes."

He waved his oatmeal spoon. "All right. What do we do meantime?"

"You just lie low. Don't show yourself. If anybody comes by —go upstairs and keep quiet."

Noon. One o'clock. Two.

Marigold neither returned nor reported back. No carload of police rushed to the verdure-clad gate of the house on West Cortez Circle. Calls to the Macey residence were not answered. The professor became alarmed.

Shortly after two o'clock, there was a brief, hard shower. The sun came out again. A scissors-grinder began to work his way down the street, calling his profession in a doleful voice and walking to each door in search of business.

"I won't wait any longer," the professor said, at last. "Something must have happened to Marigold!"

Bedelia was equally as worried. She heard footsteps at that moment, however, and peered through the window. "It's that scissor-grinder! You better duck." She went to the door.

The man was tall and dirty faced. He wore a leather apron. He held out some sample knives and scissors. "Sharpen anything, lady," he said. "Expert job. Low rates—"

"I don't want—"

He held the knives and scissors under her nose. Amidst them was a badge. Bedelia saw the letters, F.B.I. "Come in," she said. "I'll get together a few things, at that."

He entered the hall. His voice was low and quick. "There are at least two men skulking around outside."

Bedelia rapped on the window. "All right, Dusty. You can leave now. And thanks just infinitely. Remember. Tell nobody about any arrival here last night."

Dusty was weary but game. "Yes, Miss Ogilvy."

"Who was that?" the G-man asked.

"Just—friends. Watching. Now, I want better proof that you are who you say you are."

He glanced around the living room. "Phone?"

"In the kitchen."

"My name is Harmon. I'm the head of the local office. From what the Judge said, I decided to come, myself. From what his daughter said, I used that scissor-grinder gag. I haven't done anything like it for a long time. But we thought the Maroon Gang might be covering the place. I've got men up and down the street. You call the office—and then we'll both talk." He grinned at her.

She smiled back, but she called. *Anybody*, she thought, *could have a G-man's badge.* Her call satisfied her. She faced him with relief. "I'm so glad it's over!"

274 THREE TO BE READ

He had, she thought, really handsome dark-blue eyes. His lips twitched. "Over? I suspect, Miss Ogilvy, you've just started. Where is the professor?"

She looked at him and he could see tension return around her eyes, determination in her jaw. *Quite a dame,* he thought.

"Martin!" she called up the stairway.

He ran down the stairs. He was carrying the coat of the nameless man. She introduced them.

The G-man's eyes took in the coat, the lining-inside-the-lining, and the bills in their stitched compartments. They moved to the professor and his copper-stained face. "Suppose," he said, "you begin at the beginning—wherever that is. The Judge and his daughter were pretty lurid, but not too coherent. If it had been anybody else, I would have sent a psychiatrist out here."

The professor nodded. "I was lecturing about civic corruption and crime—my last lecture class before vacation—" He broke off. "Good lord! It was only a little over a week ago! Seems years! Anyhow—"

The G-Man interrupted him an hour later to drive the scissor-grinding truck out of sight and to make a contact with his men. He came back and talked until it was dark.

"Professor Burke," he said as he was leaving, "it's up to you. We have no right to ask it. You already know the risk . . ." His amiable mouth straightened.

"I'll do it, naturally."

"See you, then. And thanks."

Professor Burke picked up the evening paper and went indoors. There was a smell of dinner in the air. He yelped.

"Something the matter, Martin?"

He rushed into the kitchen.

There were headlines on the front page:

MIAMI PROFESSOR SUICIDE AFTER CONFESSING UNDERWORLD LINK

Noted Psychologist Was Gem Smuggler

Bedelia gave the black type only a glance. But she looked at the professor keenly. "Read it, Martin. I've got something on the stove I can't leave."

His voice shook slightly. "It's a special dispatch to this paper," he said. " 'Vellehomez, Cuba, December 26. Martin Luther Burke, professor of socio-psychology at the University of Miami committed suicide here early today after writing a dramatic confession of his connections with the underworld. The professor, a leading authority in his field and the author of *Ruminations of a Socio-Psychologist*, was seen by local fishermen to row out at dawn into the deep water off the harbor at Vellehomez, where he had been staying for the past twenty-four hours at a local inn. He seemed to meditate for a time, according to the witnesses, and then plunged overboard, leaving in his skiff the numbered, handwritten pages of his confession, many of which were blown into the sea and lost before the skiff was recovered. What was saved, leaves no doubt of his affiliations with the infamous Maroon Gang, a fact extremely shocking to his University associates. The body was not found.

" 'In the professor's room at the run-down hotel jewels valued at many thousands of dollars were found and these, together with references to "smuggling" in his extraordinary confession, have led the police to assume that the reason for his presence in Cuba was to bring the gems illegally into the U.S. His wallet—"

He said vehemently, "I didn't have a wallet!"

"They provided you with one!"

" '—contained cards to some of the more notorious gambling resorts in South Florida and Cuba, a souvenir blue chip, and a considerable sum of money. Handwriting experts, examining pages of the confession which were immediately flown to Miami by Cuban police officials say it is unquestionably the work of the late Professor Burke. Samples of his writing were supplied by the University.

" 'The professor's masquerade completely deceived his associates. When told of it on the phone by a Miami *Times* reporter,

President Tolver of the University flatly refused to believe it and took it as some form of practical joke. "Burke," he insisted, "is a man above reproach." Professor Lothar MacFalkland, Burke's colleague in socio-psychology, a science in which the University hopes to develop a major department, took a different view of the matter, however.' "

Bedelia said, "M'm'm'm. I bet he did!"

The professor swore. It was the first time she had ever heard him use a real, ringing oath.

"Listen to this!" The newspaper shook in his hands. " 'According to MacFalkland, the late Professor Burke "suffered from a condition of overrepression and developed a dual personality from inner psychic pressures. Burke," said Dr. MacFalkland, who is a specialist in the field of personality, "is a typical bi-cerebral. This means he has two natures—one of which seems to be in control, while the other is actually in control. I have long perceived that the overperfection of his work at the University has pointed to a blowup. I used constantly to urge him to get out more among people—to live a more normal life. I have been anticipating some news of this sort for a long time." ' "

"That fathead! That oaf! That overstuffed shirt!"

Bedelia made a sound like a giggle.

He read on: " 'Further developments in the fabulous case are expected momentarily. Cuban police are now searching for a handsome brunette who vanished from the hotel at Vellehomez. She is suspected of having brought the jewels into Cuba from South America and it is believed that her arrest may lead to the unmasking of the smuggling "ring" mentioned in the random pages of the professor's confession. These are now being studied by police of both countries.

" 'Professor Burke was thirty-three years old, a bachelor, and a New Englander by birth. He is survived by no close relatives. He was educated in the public schools of Massachusetts, Israel Putnam Teacher's College, where he graduated with honors, and Harvard. He taught for some time in the University of New Jersey.

During the war he served as a foreign language expert attached to the 118th Training Service Corps. He has been a full professor at the University of Miami for the past three years. Pictures on page 4.' "

He turned to page four and looked at a photograph of himself—enlarged from a panoramic picture of the faculty—a photograph of President Tolver, and one of MacFalkland. He hurled the paper on the table. "The imbecile!"

He stalked around the kitchen. "Wilser—or one of them—must have picked out pages of my account that didn't mention the Maroon Gang very definitely—pages that made it sound as if . . . !" He shrugged. "I did use phrases like, 'According to my knowledge—' and, 'the inside truth is'—and I suppose it would seem like a confession—if you only had a few pages carefully chosen—"

"Dinner," she said, "is just about ready."

"I am going to punch that MacFalkland square on the nose! Bi-cerebral, my eye! There is no such term! A cheap play for newspaper publicity! Tampering with science!" He sat down then, with a sort of groan. "Bedelia, do you realize this thing will follow me all my life? Do you realize I'll be marked! Academically ruined!"

"I wouldn't worry about that now, Martin. You have problems that are much more immediate."

XVII

The ensuing days were busy ones for the professor.

He spent them with the F.B.I.

His name—for this purpose—was Mr. Skeat. It proved that Professor Burke, in his school years, had been called "Skeet"—for "Skeeter"—a name which referred to his then markedly small size.

It also proved that he still responded, even from the most absent-minded reverie, to "Skeet." This became "Mr. Skeat."

The professor was now adorned with horn-rimmed glasses which had tinted lenses. His hair had been cut very short and bleached to a light hue. As the iodine faded from his skin, it was replaced by a scientific colorant. Flamboyant sports clothes were purchased for him—clothes typical of those worn by Florida tourists. The synthetic Mr. Skeat registered then at a downtown hotel in Miami: the Palm Plaza.

Bedelia and her premises were kept under constant, covert surveillance. She objected; but Harmon did not agree that she was "old enough to take care of herself."

"Mr. Skeat"—Mr. Ralph Skeat, of Newark, New Jersey— was a very plausible hotel guest and tourist. He went to the races. He attended the Orange Bowl Game. He visited the night clubs nearly every evening. Sometimes he was accompanied by a gentleman—sometimes by a lady.

He was engaged in a comparatively simple enterprise. He had given a veritable encyclopaedia of fresh information to the F.B.I. But the personnel of the Maroon Gang—especially in its comparatively new smuggling activities—was not all known to the government agents. The connections between French Paul and the other leading figures in the Gang were plain—as the professor's investigations had shown—but that fact did not constitute legal evidence. "Mr. Skeat" was therefore visiting those places where gang members known to him might appear.

In the course of this research, the professor saw his first prize fights, wrestling matches and the interiors of dozens of night clubs, cabarets, bistros and dives. His work was not without result. He identified "Chuck" in one of the late night spots and he pointed out the man known as The Foot at the race track.

Chuck and The Foot, thereafter had the F.B.I. on their heels by day and by night, though they did not know it.

The professor was also taken on several daylight flights over the lakes and lagoons of the flat, marshy wilderness that is South

Florida. He and his pilot searched for a lake that would have the necessary qualifications: water enough for a plane, a grassy shore line, a background of trees—probably cypresses—a rough connecting road, and possibly, although not necessarily, a small dock. It turned out that there were dozens of sites which more or less satisfied these requirements. Professor Burke did not succeed in locating the one where he and the three aliens had been landed.

From scraps of information gleaned cautiously in Cuba, the F.B.I. learned fairly clearly how the nameless man had been mistaken for the professor, how he had tried to escape, how he had been killed and disposed of. This knowledge was very comforting to the professor, who feared his two blows with the rusty monkey wrench had killed the man.

It was thus certain that the Maroon Gang and even the police of Miami and of Cuba were convinced the professor was dead. Bedelia's apparent obedience to the terms of the anonymous letter substantiated the conviction. She joined those who discussed the professor's sinister *alter ego*. And such is the mixed nature of South Florida society that, quite probably, word went back to the Maroon Gang that Bedelia Ogilvy was no longer a peril to their activities—that she, too, believed in the professor's sins and his suicide.

New Year's Eve was calm. That night, the *Mary Fifth* put out to sea with a gay party aboard. But there were no ship-to-shore messages. Nothing untoward happened in Vellehomez. The radar of a Coast Guard vessel did, it is true, pick up an unidentified plane flying north from Cuba—a plane that was inaudible at a range in which it should have been heard. But neither the place of take-off nor of landing was ascertained.

An important fact was established, however: the Maroon Gang had begun smuggling again. French Paul evidently felt that his rapid calculations and activities had ended all suspicions and inquiries concerning the professor. Even the newspapers—excepting for one nationally circulated Sunday supplement—had ex-

hausted the saga of the social scientist who "turned against society." The Sunday magazine, however, began publication of a
series of articles by MacFalkland, called, "The Psychology of
America's Slickest Criminal—as told by One Who Knew Him."

XVIII

Two nights after New Year's, Professor Burke was recognized. His duties had taken him back to the Club Egret. As "Mr.
Skeat," he had been there on several occasions. He had caught
glimpses of Miss Maxson and yearned to speak with her. It had
been out of the question.

This evening, he went out to dinner alone. Harmon said that
one of his men—Cleves, from Tacoma, Washington, whom the
professor now knew—would join him later. "Mr. Skeat" saw
nobody save the night club habitués. He had finished his dinner
and was smoking a cigarette—another addition to his disguise
and one he, as a pipe-and-cigar-smoker, did not enjoy—when the
lights went down and the same comedian appeared, with a joke
that dated back to a situation in a comedy by Terence.

The professor was listening rather idly when a girl's voice said,
"Your slip's showing, darling."

Connie Maxson was standing in the luminous gloom.

He pretended not to know she had spoken to him.

"May I sit? After all—I'm a sort of hostess."

He beckoned with his cigarette. He did not rise. He glanced
at the nearer tables. Nobody was interested.

She laughed softly. "What magnificent publicity you've been
getting!"

"How did you—?"

She leaned forward and spoke quietly. "You dope! I've been
watching for you for over a week!"

"Watching for me! I'm—dead."

Connie chuckled. "You don't look it. You look pretty sporty."

"What gave me away?"

"Remember the night your dear old Bedelia asked for protection—and Bill sent it? Well—naturally Dusty and the boys told Bill that you'd made it back. Nobody else. And naturally Bill told me. And nobody else. So we knew you were somewhere, and we expected you'd be doing—what you evidently are. Acting as eyes for—people. And looking quite different. When you came in and took this table by the wall, tonight, I began to think it was you. And when you didn't laugh at Benny's joke, just now, I took a better look. The spotlight shows up your profile. And a girl gets to know the profiles of the men she's kissed."

"I've wanted to see your uncle. To thank him. To ask him to forgive me for spreading around so much of the confidential information he gave me. I was careful—always—to shield him."

Connie nodded her high-piled, wheat-colored hair. "He noticed it. And appreciates it. How's it going?"

"So-so."

"I better not stay long."

"No," he said wistfully.

"I suppose you know how Bill will feel if you pull off what you must be trying?"

"Sore at me, I guess. I spilled a lot of beans."

"Sore at you!" Her voice dropped still farther and she leaned closer to him. He could smell the perfume. He was used to such perfumes, now. "Bill's having a tough time. It's a big season. But those people are muscling in. They have some sort of an inside track Bill can't figure. He's afraid he's going to have to close up. He won't cut them in—and that's all there is to that." She rose, patting his hand. "It was nice seeing you. And don't worry. I doubt if anybody else on earth—including your own best friend —would realize."

She left and he felt lonely. He found his imagination introducing her: "This is Mrs. Burke." She would be a sensational professor's wife. But he would be a sensational professor—too sensational. Even granted that this interminable impersonation ended, that everything ended well, his career would be a wreck. Who would want, on a dignified faculty, such a character as he had become—not just by newspaper allegation, but in fact?

He smoked a cigarette and watched the tango act.

Her penetration of his disguise made him vaguely uneasy. It was true that she had known he was alive. True that she had been expecting him to appear in a disguise of some sort. But he had come to think of his changed appearance as impenetrable. Chuck, for example, had looked straight at him and shown no sign whatever of recognition.

He put out his cigarette, paid his check, and strolled into the gambling room. He bought a few two-dollar chips and took a stance at a roulette table which gave him a view of the dice tables, too. Harmon had told him that men of the sort for whom he was searching would be more likely to shoot dice than to play roulette.

He began winning. He had been uncommonly lucky in the occasional gambling he had done during his undercover travels through the nighttime world of Greater Miami and of Broward County, to the north. Harmon had wanted to pay all his expenses —with government funds. The professor had insisted on using his own money—the eight hundred dollars from his first night's try at roulette. There was, in this process, an irony that amused him: the world of gambling, corruption and vice, the world about which he had once so innocently lectured, was paying for an investigation of itself.

It was about ten when the man entered the gambling room. He knew a lot of people, waved at them, stopped to chat. He congratulated one or two winners over their heaps of chips and frowned with pleasant sympathy at those who complained of bad luck. His hair was as slick and shiny as the fender of a new black car. The comparison came to mind because the man made the professor think of cars.

It was Solo. The man who, twice, had picked up loads of "passengers" from the silent plane.

The professor went on playing. Among the people to whom Solo had spoken was a middle-aged woman in a scarlet evening dress who was recklessly distributing chips on the numbered geometry of the table. He moved, presently, to her side. She had looked, several times, at the stalwart back of Solo, who was now watching one of the dice games. An overweight female, flushed from too many cocktails, and talkative—a type with which the professor had become familiar.

When he approached, she said, "Welcome, partner!"

He waited until she stole another look at Solo. The croupier was calling the spin.

"Handsome egg."

The woman turned. Her eyes glittered over her puffy cheeks. "You said something!"

"Who is he?"

"The Tip? He's the assistant manager of this joint." She leaned to place a chip and turned to watch the little ivory ball dance in its hypnotic vortex.

The professor felt coldness enter his veins. *The Tip.* "I know a man," Chuck had said, while the plane winged toward Cuba, "who only uses the tip of his knife." And Chuck had demonstrated.

The woman had just said, furthermore, "He's the assistant manager of this joint." That meant—if it were true—that Double-O had an associate who also belonged to the Maroon Gang. He thought of Connie's words: "They have some kind of an inside track that Bill can't figure."

They did have—unless . . .

The woman nudged him. "What's the matter? Can't you dream up a number?" He started and put a chip on six.

Unless Mr. Sanders and his niece were subtler than he thought. Subtler and—something else. Unless Mr. Sanders was *still* associated with the Maroon Gang. He had once worked for them. Could it be that he belonged? That, knowing an intense, secret investigation of the Maroon Gang was being made, he hoped the field would soon be cleared of them, and open to himself?

It was possible.

That was the trouble. It was possible. And it was not only possible, but it sounded very much like any of fifty schemes, stratagems and double crosses with which Mr. Sanders himself had filled in the sickening history of the Maroon Gang. He and French Paul could be feigned antagonists, but actual associates. Yet Double-O could be planning not to warn French Paul and his immediate associates but to let the law take them. In order to clean up afterward.

Gangsters—gamblers—criminals, the professor thought bitterly.

The Tip—Solo—whatever his name was—may have felt the stare that was boring into his back. He may have tired of watching the dice roll. He turned quickly. His eyes met those of "Mr. Skeat."

And, in the new dubiety about his incognito, the professor's eyes did the wrong things. They tried to look back casually; but they faltered and showed self-consciousness.

The Tip inspected the professor for a moment—in the way of a man who remembers a face and cannot place it. Then he shrugged a little and turned to make a laughing comment to one of the men at the table. Soon afterward, he sauntered from the room. The professor went on playing, automatically. His mind seethed.

It was his duty to go quickly, unobtrusively, to a phone and call a certain number. Not Headquarters, but a private house. It was his duty to invite the woman who would answer to join him later—at another place. He would also tell her where he was. She would decline and he would hang up. An F.B.I. agent would appear shortly—and thenceforward the third man to be identified by "Mr. Skeat" would be relentlessly pursued, checked, shadowed and investigated.

That was his duty.

If Double-O did not know his assistant manager was a member of the Maroon Gang, Connie's words about the "inside track" were now clear—and Double-O had a very treacherous employee. He should be told.

That, in such a case, was also an obligation: Professor Burke felt his debt to the gambler intensely.

But if Double-O *knew who The Tip was* . . . ?

The dangers of that situation were too numerous and varied for quick reckoning. Not the least of them would be his own danger at this moment. At every moment from now on.

XIX

The Tip left the room with a sense of frustration. He had a memory for faces and he had seen that face. He had seen that face and, he vaguely felt, hated or feared it. Light had been reflected up into it from the green baize and the light had filtered down upon it from overhead. He had seen that face before—in a funny light.

He stood in the foyer. The dance band was playing. Dinner was over for most of them, but not drinking. The bar was crowded. Big night for Double-O. The Tip moved up beside one of the men in tuxedos who seemed to live in that foyer, close to the curtained entrance of the gambling room.

"Guy in there at the cheap table, Al. Tinted specs. Light hair—crew-cut—dark complexion—medium size. Who is he?"

Al went through the curtain and came back back shortly. "Fellow named Ralph Skeat. Been around here a little."

"For how long?"

"Last ten days or so."

"Where from?"

"Don't know. Tourist. Never saw him, other years. There's millions like him, Tip."

"I know. Please be careful." She sighed unevenly. "All my life, Martin, I'll remember you. *You're something!*"

He drove back toward the low, white building where the people danced and the little white ball danced, too.

The Tip had returned—his face so pale that the doorman had said he surely must be off his feed. He had looked for "Mr. Skeat" and learned of his departure with Connie.

He put in a very private phone call.

When he came from the booth, he saw Connie vanishing through the rear door of the barroom.

He rushed to the front entry.

"Mr. Skeat" was just driving away. He got the number of the license. Then he ran to the parking yard for his own car.

In a drugstore, many blocks down Collins Avenue, the professor dialed a number and anxiously watched the street outside. His car was parked where he could see it.

"Harmon," he said into the phone. He added a little more.

"I was just leaving," Harmon said hurriedly. "They're working tonight; we think."

"Look! I'm on Collins—phone booth—first drug store below the Egret. Double-O's general factotum—The Tip—"

"I know him."

"—is also Solo, the driver of—"

An explosive, "No!" came over the wire.

"Right! I've told Miss Maxson. She has told Double-O. I think The Tip recognized me—"

"*Recognized you!*"

The professor's voice changed, but was still quite steady. "Harmon! *He recognized me, all right. He just drove by and gave my car the once-over!*"

"Listen, Professor! This is the sort of thing I was afraid of! I can't get to you or send a man to you! Can he see you from the street?"

"When I come out—sure."

"He'll shoot."

"But there might be a back door, too."

The G-man talked fast. "Okay. Use it. Or stay inside there. Do the best you can. If you try moving, Burke—hide. Don't go near Bedelia's. Don't go back to the hotel. Go—I've got it! Go to Judge Macey's place—"

"Macey's?"

"I'll send them word. I can't hang on any longer, Burke. Thanks. Thanks for everything. Good luck!"

Professor Burke opened the phone booth door. He peered again. The Tip had double-parked and was waiting.

"Is there a back way out of this place?"

The drug clerk looked at him. "What for?"

"There's a man out there I don't want to meet."

The druggist stared a moment longer—at direct, steady eyes. "Okay, bud. Turn left."

He passed shelves of bottles, entered a room stacked with cartons, and he saw the door. It led to a narrow walk.

He peered around the corner of the building.

The Tip was leaving his car. He moved toward the store— his right hand inside his jacket.

The professor waited an instant. He heard the automatic door-closer hiss. He ran across the walk. As he had expected, The Tip's motor was running.

He did not drive slowly—this time.

XX

The car went like a leaf in a wind tunnel. Even so, before the professor came to the first turn in Collins Avenue, he saw head-lights twist from the curb. His car. The Tip would be frantic. A dead man had come back from the grave—a man who knew him in both identities. The Tip's reaction was simple: *get that man as soon as possible.*

Collins Avenue curved. There was a red light. The professor

howled his brakes and went through the light. He made an S-turn. Ahead was a wide, straight stretch. He pressed on the horn-rim and followed its blast. When he had another opportunity, he looked in his mirror. The Tip was gaining.

Collins Avenue turned left at the end of that stretch, but the professor went straight ahead on Indian Creek Drive. He got around a truck and in front of a convertible, came out again on Collins, and looked back. The pursuing car was still closer. Down the avenue, beside the Roney-Plaza Hotel—pink and tremendous in the brilliance of Twenty-third Street—traffic waited in a solid huddle for the light to change. He stopped and jumped out, abandoning the car in the midst of many others. He ducked through them and ran across a parking yard. He heard The Tip's brakes scream.

In front of him was the blind pocket of water called Lake Surprise, a salt pond connected with Indian Creek and the canals. Sightseeing boats were tied up there. A high, curved bridge spanned the backwater. A man with a megaphone was still barking a late ride. Small private craft lay at numerous little docks; around one were several water bicycles. People were pedaling them about on the lake. The professor snatched bills from his pocket, pressed five dollars into the hand of the water-bike attendant, jumped onto one, and churned furiously toward the canal—and comparative dark.

A car on the shore behind him backfired. A fast bee buzzed past the professor. A tiny wind fanned his cheek.

The Tip was shooting.

Ahead, the waters were contained between cement banks over which bushes hung. He pedaled with all his might. There was another report. The bullet ripped his jacket. He went around the first of the overhanging shrubs.

On the street behind him came the faint sounds of people yelling. He drove the pontooned craft down the dark canal and saw another bridge ahead. He scrambled ashore, setting the water-cycle adrift. He ran across Dade Boulevard and into the golf course, behind the fire house. He caught his breath.

A large, white hotel stood on the other side of the golf course. He reconnoitered it from behind a clump of oleanders. People on the street. Cars coming and going. A cab driver reading a comic book.

The Tip had probably eluded any chase that might have started and was doubtless hunting again. Possibly he had called the mansion on the Bayfront and reported to French Paul. Perhaps the Maroon Gang was getting the word even now—and starting from houses, night clubs, gambling places, bookie joints and other regions to hunt in the city for a man with light hair, crew-cut, and a dark complexion.

The professor walked up to the cab. "Want to go over to the Gables," he said. "In kind of a hurry."

He got out near the center of Coral Gables. They might expect him to head for Bedelia's. And he wanted to walk, wanted to be certain, before he approached the Macey house, that no one was following.

He came up to it from the rear. Lights were burning. He entered the hedged garden and sat for minutes in the chair where Marigold had once sat beside him. He breathed and listened. There had been no one—all the way. He knocked on the back door.

The kitchen light went on. Marigold was wearing her hair down. She had on a housecoat—white and gold. She peered through the glass and unlocked the door. "I've been practically out of my mind! Mr. Harmon called over an hour ago and I expected you right away!"

He came in. "Better pull the blinds."

She stared. "Good heavens! Look at you!"

"Where's your father?"

"Out. He and mother went to Fort Myers to visit friends this afternoon. And Steve's out, too—with his girl. That usually means four A.M. So I've got you in my clutches."

He said, "Thank the lord!"

She was shaking. "What happened? Bedelia has given us an idea of what you were working on. Come in the den and tell me. It's

got Venetian blinds and draperies you can pull. Mr. Harmon told
me to keep you out of sight—and above everything else, to keep
you. What tore your coat?"

He followed her through a hallway and into the judge's den.
She repeated her last question.

"Bullet," he said.

He was not prepared to have her throw her arms around him
and kiss him. "Oh, Martin! You're—all right?"

It made, he thought, two girls and two major kisses for the
evening. A double life—with two women in it. He gathered her
long, curly hair in his right hand, pulled her head back so that her
face was turned up, and kissed her again.

"I'm all right. The guy missed."

"Who was it?"

He sat down in the judge's leather easy chair. "Look, Marigold.
For Heaven's sake stop asking me things! I *think* I've done everything I could. I let Harmon know. I told Connie."

"Connie who? Martin—is that the blonde you were necking
a few days ago at the Bombay Royale? Jim Ellis and Nancy Beatty
saw you. It was all over the campus the next morning."

His eyes twinkled. "A small matter—in view of subsequent
findings! I am a criminal, a gangster, a jewel smuggler—not to
mention dead by my own hand!"

"I was jealous," she said simply. "Martin. Would you like
coffee?"

XXI

He lighted one of the judge's cigars and watched blue smoke
spiral toward the ceiling. Harmon would have gone to wherever he
was going. The place, he silently hoped, where the plane would land.
Sanders would have made whatever provision he felt necessary con-

cerning The Tip. But it was not likely The Tip would return to the Club Egret. Not ever.

He was out of it. After tonight, his incognito would be worthless. He could emerge from it. Resign from the University, he thought somberly. Make a last call on MacFalkland. Find another position, if he could.

Marigold came with a tray. Light brown hair lying softly on her gold and white shoulders. She poured coffee. He watched her achingly. In a few days, he'd be on his way. Never see her again. Never see Connie again. There was a French folk song:

> *Oh, les fraise et les framboises,*
> *Les vins que nous avons bu,*
> *Et les belles villageoise,*
> *Nous ne les verrons plus.*

And the pretty village girls, we'll never see them again. It was supposed to be a gay song.

She poured coffee and put the cup on a table beside him. "Can I sit in your lap?"

"No!"

"Why not, Martin? The other day—when you stepped on Dad's pineapples—I thought—"

"That, Marigold, was because you are beautiful and I used to be a professor in good standing—with a lot of admiration for you and a certain amount of curiosity."

"Was it the limit of your curiosity?"

He shook his head. "I'm somebody else, now, Marigold. I don't even know who."

"That—*Connie!*"

"Connie's a wonderful girl, too. But I'm—psychologically a little dated for you modern girls. I was brought up to be old-fashioned."

"Don't you know that a great many modern girls act modern just to get a chance to become old-fashioned?"

"Do they?" He smoked and smiled and finally shook his head.

"You sit down over there, Marigold, and let me be. I want to think. Harmon—out in the Glades—down in the Keys. A plane flying—a grim business that's got to stop."

"Bedelia told me. It's—"

"Inhuman!" He flicked ashes into his saucer. "Such a profound amount of imagination and skill in the thing! Right now —out somewhere on the Gulf Stream—there's a boat called the *Mary Fifth*—" he broke off.

"Doing what?"

He did not hear her. His mind had gone back to the plane cabin—to the feel of sash weights wired on his handcuffs—to Chuck's voice: "On the nights we fly, maybe the *Mary Fifth*—that's a Miami boat—goes out fishing."

He had told the F.B.I. that it *was* the *Mary Fifth*—that the *Mary Fifth* always went out, when they flew. Suppose Chuck had meant that maybe, at times, it was *some other boat?*

"Where's the phone?"

"Mr. Harmon said you were just to sit here!"

It was one thirty but he dialed the Fishing Pier. The phone rang, rang, rang on and on. Finally a disgruntled voice said, "Yeah?"

"Is the *Mary Fifth* there?"

"This is a hell of a time to call about a charter! I'm the mate on the *Binney*—and you woke me up—"

"Is she there?"

"Yeah—she's here and locked up tight and the crew gone home hours ago. Gimme your name—and I'll leave a note for them to call in the morning."

He dialed another number.

"Federal Bureau of Investigation."

"This is Mr. Skeat."

"Wilson speaking."

"Is it possible to reach Harmon?"

"No, Professor. What's up?"

"The *Mary Fifth* didn't go out tonight."

"We know that. They're probably operating without her."
Wilson's voice was amiable. "Make it that much easier for Harmon
and the rest."

"They might have used another boat."

"Yeah? Did you mention it?"

"I just thought of it."

Wilson swore. "Harmon overlooked it."

"He didn't overlook it, man! I told him there was just one
boat. The rest of my information was right so we took that statement for granted, too."

"I don't know how we—at this point—"

"Can you find out from the Miami Marine Operator what
boats, if any, are outside tonight? Getting calls?"

"Sure!"

"Ring me here. You know where I am?"

"Macey's house. Oke."

He waited tensely. The phone rang within three minutes.

"Wilson, here. Look. Marine calls have been pretty slow tonight. One to Cat Cay. A houseboat named the *Spanish Galleon* is
out with a party up around the Haulover some place. They had a
long talk, half an hour ago. A lot of stuff about hanging a shark
and fighting it and planning to beach it."

"Beach it?"

"That's what the operator said. *Good lord!*"

"You'll need men all along there, then!" The professor spoke
fast. "There's that empty stretch between the Haulover and Golden
Beach."

"Professor—we haven't got one man left."

"Police."

"We've got fifteen names on the list. How long will it take
one wrong guy to find out—if the cops start getting up a posse
now?"

"Certainly you could pick your men . . ."

"I can try. Harmon will probably shoot himself if the whole
gang's working on a bum lead!"

The professor hung up. "You got a car, Marigold?"

Her eyes were vivid. "In two seconds, I'll change!"

"We haven't two seconds—and I'm going alone."

"Unless I can go with you, I won't be able to find the key."

He looked at her for a long, thoughtful moment.

"Get your clothes. Change in the car."

She ran upstairs and ran back in seconds. She led the way to the garage.

Coral Gables unwound behind them. They cut from the Tamiami Trail to Twenty-seventh Avenue. It was wide, empty, and fast. He ran clear to Seventy-ninth—a causeway street—and within twenty minutes he was moving north in Miami Beach. At the bridge over the waters which make an island of Miami Beach, gasoline lights burned and a score of diligent net-casters stared concentratedly into the swift, slick tide below.

He drove smoothly up the road. The sea was a dozen feet below them and not many yards away. Here and there, a beach fire glowed. A few cars were parked on the land side; it was a favorite rendezvous for people who weren't ready to go home yet. For young people, especially.

The professor turned off the road and switched out his lights. "If that houseboat is operating off the Haulover, it should be somewhere yonder." He pointed to the sea, a murmuring darkness that extended to a final nothing, above which stars shone.

"What do we do now?"

He looked at her in the beam of a slowly approaching car. She had changed to a dark dress—and pinned up her hair—somehow, in the rocking, bumping seat. The car passed and went on. "Just watch," he said. "If they intend to beach a shark, they'd do it here."

"Why?"

"Too many hotels and people—too much doing—below here. Above here, there's another long stretch where people live." He opened the door. "We'll go out on the road and patrol a bit."

They crossed the highway. Small waves spilled and hissed on the sand. Far to the north, city lights glowed. To the south were the gas lanterns of the bridge-anglers. In between was a mile and a half, or perhaps two miles, of beach, dunes, underbrush, and road. Not a house or a building.

"Wouldn't it be better," she asked, after they had walked for several minutes, "if we split up? If I patrolled in one direction and you in the other?"

"Do you think it's a good idea for a girl to be walking around in this place alone?"

"It would just double our chances of seeing anything. What happens, if we do see anything?"

"We run for the car, and wait, and follow them."

She looked at him a moment. "Okay. You go north. I'll go toward the bridge and come back. Meet here."

XXII

He walked at the edge of the road. Every few rods he stopped and strained his eyes out toward the sea. In the remote distance, Fowey Rock periodically displayed a wan, white flare and channel markers winked in the oblivion between. He had long since lost sight of Marigold—a dwindling figure, visible for a while in the sudden illumination of the cars that passed her. There were not many.

They passed him, too. In one of them, he thought he saw uniformed police, but he was not sure. He went to the end of his beat where habitation began again. He walked back more swiftly, looking less often at the sea and worrying about the girl. She was waiting for him opposite the car.

"See anything?" They said the same thing at the same time —and laughed.

"It's probably foolish . . ." he said. "The information from the Marine Operator was suggestive—that's all."

"Let's go again."

She had walked about halfway back from the Haulover bridge when she heard the launch. She moved from the road down to the beach, and found a sea lavender behind which she could hide. The motor was not running fast—idling, rather. It came toward the shore very slowly. She could not see it. But she thought she had better get the professor. She expected that she would have to go the full length of the uninhabited beach. But she did not.

He had decided it was too great a risk for her to be there, alone, and turned back before reaching the end of his route. They met a few hundred yards north of her car. Panting, she told him.

He led her back to the car. He started the motor but he did not turn on his lights. He drove up over the shoulder and headed south, going slowly. No one approached from either direction.

"It was about here," she said.

He turned from the pavement and parked.

Together, they went down to the beach. They squatted behind the sea lavender.

The motor was plainly audible. He thought he could hear voices out on the dark water.

"It's much nearer!" she whispered.

"I think I can see it. Not quite straight out. A little to the left. A white blur—"

"It is!"

"Coming in gradually."

Behind them, on the road, a large sedan approached—so slowly that he pulled her around to the ocean side of the bush to keep from being noticed. The car went beyond them for perhaps a city block and stopped. It backed into one of the parking places and its lights died out.

"More people necking," she whispered. "Lucky them!"

He murmured, "Maybe."

The white blur became boat-shaped. Voices above its engine sounded cheerful and urgent. *Was it possible . . . ?*

It was not a large boat. But he made out many heads silhouetted against the less dark water. A considerable splashing accompanied the slow progress toward shore.

One voice, louder than the rest, came to their ears: "Stay with it, Doc! You only got a few more feet to go!"

More babble. More splashes. The launch was such a craft as a good-sized, well-appointed houseboat might carry in her davits —for fishing, or for emergencies. And now the professor could see a rod bent in her stern.

The conversation reported by the Miami Marine Operator had not been bogus. Somebody on the *Spanish Galleon*, off Baker's Haulover, had actually hooked a big shark, a couple of hours before and, lacking the equipment for gaffing such a fish, was beaching it. The big sedan behind them was as innocent as the rest of the random traffic.

The professor jeered at himself.

He had entertained a slight suspicion. On the strength of it, he had roused the F.B.I. He had severely worried Wilson. He had, perhaps, sent others out on a false errand.

He should have left the affairs of that night to men who knew their business.

"What did you say?" she whispered.

"I was swearing."

"That's what I thought." She reached for his hand. "Never mind! It was quite a buzz—while it lasted! Look! They're getting out in the water. The boat's aground. Let's stay and see what they caught. Nothing, I bet, but an old hammerhead. Maybe even just a big nurse shark."

"Wait a minute!" His whisper was sharp.

He had seen something that no fisherman would do: the man with the bent rod had tossed it into the sea. And the people were not encouraging an "angler" any longer. They were getting out of the launch swiftly, silently, and wading toward the beach. Half a dozen men—and two women. One of the men was very fat.

"They *weren't* fishing!" Her voice was low and tense.

He shook his head.

"Then they *are* . . . !"

He nodded and pulled her down behind the bush on the cool sand.

The fat man waited until the last person had stepped out of the water. "Rudolph!" he called loudly. The lights of the big sedan turned on.

The people on the beach were not directly in the rays, but they were near enough to be visible, now. The professor bit hard on his lower lip. French Paul—Wilser—and some strangers. Strangers who had doubtless just arrived, by a very quiet plane, from Cuba. French Paul either knew or had guessed that every agent in South Florida was concentrated on the Keys and in the Everglades. So he had boldly brought the travelers ashore almost on Miami Beach itself, superintending the maneuver personally—as he had on one other occasion the professor knew of.

The eight people started to scramble up on the road.

"Stand right where you are everybody! Hands up!"

The hard voice had not finished when a pistol cracked in the hand of the fat Alsatian. Wilser knelt and began firing. The others scattered, running back along the beach. From the road came the blast of automatic guns. A woman screamed. Bullets burned above the heads of the two people lying behind the bush. Feet pounded on the road. Car lights blazed up and down the beach.

"Stand still! Everybody!"

The shots ceased. The whole beach above was well illuminated. The sand below was shaded by dunes.

Police were rounding up the men and the two women. "This way! Bring 'em up this way," a voice commanded.

Weeds whispered close beside the girl and the man. The professor rolled over on his back. He wanted to see—but he did not want to stand up suddenly and be shot at.

French Paul was creeping through the brush, in the shadow of the steep slope beside the road. He was out of sight and he would soon be far enough out of range to run. Or to wade into the calm sea and swim. A man like French Paul could probably swim a long distance.

"Drop your gun, Paul," the professor said sharply.

Paul turned toward the tangle—staring. The professor kicked up at the man's arm with all his might.

The gun flew. Paul lunged. Marigold yelled.

Police rushed toward them . . .

The morning paper displayed a banner headline:

FBI SMASHES MAROON GANG

Prof. Burke, Thought Dead, Credited for Coup
Leaders Jailed
Alien-Smuggling Ring Bared

EXTRA!

There were similar headlines throughout the day in the nation's press.

The radio networks talked breathlessly about it.

Harmon read the headlines in his office. He had not slept and his eyes revealed the fact. But he did not seem interested in going to bed. It was the day of his life.

At Bog Key, the night before, he and his men had intercepted a second plane—and its crew of two: Chuck and Johnny. G-men, in a dozen cities, had arrested more than a hundred members of the Maroon Gang and people associated with them. Thirty-eight persons had been arrested in Cuba.

When Harmon had rushed anxiously back to Miami, he had found French Paul, as well as the others on board the *Spanish Galleon* and her launch, in the custody of the police. Professor Burke and Marigold Macey were waiting for him—the professor with a suggestion which led to the predawn capture of The Tip. It was a clean sweep.

Reporters crowded around the desk of the G-man. "How good," they asked, "is your case?"

Harmon laughed. "While Burke was going around as 'Mr. Skeat' we had time to make it watertight. And listen, fellows. You haven't even started to give Burke the credit he deserves." The G-man tapped the newspaper on his desk . . .

Mrs. MacFalkland nervously woke her husband. "There's some rather disquieting news in the paper, dear . . ."

He muttered and opened his eyes. "Those Russians!"

"Nothing like that." In spite of her anxiety, she concealed a sudden grimace. It might have been a smile. Perhaps she enjoyed the prospect of seeing—just once—the complete discomfiture of her too-positive husband. "It turns out that Professor Burke isn't dead."

"*Isn't dead!*" He grabbed the paper. Horror filled his eyes . . .

Connie heard it on the radio while she was eating breakfast. She drove to the Bombay Royale. Double-O was wearing a red dressing gown with a monogram of two linked zeroes on its pocket. He grinned at her and sent his butler for another coffee cup.

"What happened?" the girl asked feverishly.

"Most of it's in the papers. This edition came out too early to mention The Tip."

"They got him?"

"Burke suggested last night to Harmon that I could tell them where The Tip might hide. I did. I went down to headquarters about four o'clock and stayed a while. Identifying a couple of miscellaneous clucks the G-men didn't know."

"The professor and that girl could have been killed!"

Double-O walked to the window. "Yeah."

"The police—and French Paul's people—were shooting right over them!"

"Nobody got killed," Double-O replied dryly. "Only one guy hit. And the State Department must be very glad he isn't dead. He might tell them what other spies came in."

"Did you see the girl when you were at headquarters?"

"Yes," he said.

"Is she . . . ?"

"Nice? Yeah. Pretty? And then some! Look, chick. Are you in love with the guy?" Double-O put his worry on the table, like a card it hurt to play.

When she didn't answer, he shook his head sadly and turned to repeat his question. She was laughing!

"Love Martin Burke?" she said. "Me? I'm fond of him. I think he's marvelous. But I'm the restless type, Bill. I couldn't fall for some one like that. It would have to be somebody who loved bright lights all the time, somebody who could tango like dreaming, somebody who could keep a girl on her toes—not settle down with her."

Double-O blew a long, relaxed cloud of cigar smoke. "Don't know what gave me the impression—"

"Of course, you do! I enjoyed necking with him—he seemed so surprised! He can be one of my favorite men friends as long as he likes."

"The lucky guy who finally does get you," the gambler said, "is going to need his luck. How else will he figure you out?"

Connie dismissed the problem with a gesture. "I asked about Marigold Macey because I hoped she would be nice—and pretty —and I knew he had some romantic ideas about me. I was kind of—embarrassed by it."

"She's the undergraduate's dream of what a gal ought to be, I'd imagine. If the professor is interested, he'll have competition . . ."

Connie thought about that—anxiously, it seemed.

He dropped into a chair, his long arms and legs sprawling. "It's going to seem funny, now—without the Maroon boys pushing on me."

"That," she said, "is the main reason I busted in on your morning reveries, Bill. You owe that guy a lot."

"I owe the professor *plenty!* It's funny! That's what my family wanted me to be. A professional man. A doctor or a lawyer or a teacher. Only—I learned the wrong things too young, where I started college." He considered that for a moment. "I owe the guy everything. And I've cooked up an idea about that. See what you think."

As she listened, her eyes grew bright . . .

XXIII

It was late afternoon. The professor had slept almost around the clock—with Bedelia's aid and protection. Protection from reporters, news photographers, numerous other visitors, telegrams, phone calls—an excited, impatient and to him, unfamiliar, world. When he appeared, she hurried him through his breakfast and sent him to the grocery store for a "few items" she said she had forgotten. He decided to walk.

The air smelled of pine smoke as he started home; another high had come in from the northwest—and time for it, too, he thought. He came to the vacant lot and what seemed to be the same ballgame was in progress. He stopped to watch for a moment, smiling rather forlornly, as a man might who was trying to imprint on his mind a pleasant spectacle he would soon see no more. One of the youngsters shouted, "It's *the professor!*"

The game stopped in mid-inning. They ran up to him.

"Is it true," one boy asked in excitement, "that you captured French Paul without even a gun?"

The awe was such as the professor had never before experienced. "Some day soon," he said, "if I'm around, I'll tell you all about it."

"Just us kids? *Promise?*"

He smiled at a freckled face. "It's a promise."

There were cars in front of Bedelia's house. One was a grey convertible and a girl sat in it.

"Hello, Martin!"

"Connie! What in the world . . . ?"

"Bill's inside—Double-O. And President Tolver."

"President Tolver!"

"They're having a conference. They threw me out. Also"— she smiled—"Bedelia said you'd be coming along—and I wanted to see you a second. Hop in!"

He put the paper sack on the ground, against the trunk of a poinciana tree, and sat beside the girl. Anxiety and amazement confusingly filled his mind. Why had Tolver come to Bedelia's house? What would Tolver think when he found the gambler there? And why had the gambler and his niece called, anyway? Probably to offer unwarranted thanks.

"I had lunch with Marigold Macey," Connie said.

He started. "I didn't realize you knew her!"

"I didn't. But I called her up. Nice girl."

Somewhere, in the log jam of his thoughts and emotions, the professor felt a lifting of painful stress. "You aren't—upset—about . . . ?"

Connie understood him. "Martin, I'm very fond of you. But what I'm in love with, I guess, is glamour. I know it doesn't exist —in my mind. I suppose I have to learn it doesn't, in my feelings —before I can care about just one guy."

He said, in a low voice, "Oh."

"Remember the first night I kissed you?"

He would never forget. He nodded.

"Martin, I think you need some advice."

"I need barrels."

"The man—not the girl—is supposed to do the kissing. To begin, anyhow. With a gal like Marigold—"

He flushed. "I know. Once—I—I—"

"Once isn't enough! That's my barrel of advice. And you better go in. They're waiting for you."

President Tolver was a man with reddish hair and light blue eyes. A very large man, but graceful—and gracious. A former science professor with an intuition for diplomacy and a talent for administration. He rose when the professor came out on the porch. Double-O occupied the settee with Bedelia. Between them, they strained its capacity.

"Burke!" the president said. "I tried to phone all morning! But Bedelia fenced you in. I wanted to be first to congratulate you—instead of last."

The professor swallowed. "I appreciate it, Doctor Tolver."

"Magnificent feat! Has the eyes of the whole country on the University! I suppose you're getting—offers—from everywhere—"

"He is," Bedelia said. "But he doesn't know it yet. I've kept him busy."

The president went on hurriedly. "—but I'd like to have mine among them, Burke. Your friend"—he nodded toward Double-O—"has made the University a most generous gift. Insists it be anonymous. It will enable us to establish at once a tip-top department in your subject. Naturally, we'll offer you the Head. Your salary, as a Department Head, would be doubled."

The professor looked at the gambler. He swallowed harder. "That—that is—damned fine of you . . ."

Double-O's adzelike eyes moved out toward the variegated foliage—a stagey green in the last, level bars of sunlight. "Mighty little, considering."

The professor struggled for composure and said to the president. "I'd expected that—my notoriety—would make me undesirable as a faculty member. Quixotic folly!"

"Notoriety! Great heavens! Fame is the word for it! Not Quixotic, man! Homeric!"

"I'm grateful for the offer. And also for the confidence you showed in me, Doctor, when MacFalkland and the others were 'explaining' me in the Sunday magazine sections."

"I never believed that rubbish," the president said.

"I deeply appreciate the fact. But I can't teach."

"Can't teach!"

All three people were astounded.

He went to a chair and sat down. He stared at the floor for a moment. "Don't you understand? I have lost my faith in my own scientific position." He had to clear his throat. "I was a believer in intellect. In pure reason. My career was postulated on that. I held crime to be, in essence, a symptom of inferiority. It was an axiom of my lectures. But—in the past three weeks—" he sighed unevenly.

"You found it different," Double-O said mildly.

"I found it different. Ingenious. Imaginative. Resourceful. Highly organized. Skillfully employing the most modern techniques. Anything in the world but stupid!"

"Nevertheless," President Tolver put in shrewdly, "you succeeded in trapping them. A man with a higher education, but no experience whatever in their environment. Doesn't that clinch your hypothesis?"

The professor leaned back in his chair. His body seemed lifeless. He shut his eyes. Only his voice had a spark. "On the contrary. I used very little intelligence. Cunning, yes. But what motivated me? What forced stratagems into my consciousness? *Emotion.* Pure *emotion!*"

Bedelia said, "Rats, Martin! Harmon himself thinks you're headier than any of his own men!"

"Consider the facts, not Harmon's flattery," the professor answered. "Why did I think—at the start of this whole business—of mailing the money back to Double-O here? Because I was infuriated at the idea of being robbed! Why did I note the marl on the tires of the sedan and seize a handful of frond ends? Because I was determined to revenge myself on that fat Alsatian, if I could!"

He leaned forward, now, and scowled at them. "Why didn't I give the evidence to the police, or the F.B.I.? Vanity! Egotism! Why did I spellbind Chuck with the data Double-O gave me? Because I was afraid to die—and stalling off the moment! Why did I think of the stratagem which got me out of that pesthole in Cuba? Because I was crazed with rage over what I thought was murder of Bedelia. Why—even at the end—did I risk Marigold Macey's life to find that launch? Because I had grown to detest the Maroon Gang with all my soul! Nothing of the abstract mind about it! Pure instinct produced such ideas as I had! And that is contrary to everything I have taught!"

There was a moment of silence on the porch. The last bar of orange sunlight faded and the evening was grey.

"Still," the president said, "when you've thought these things over, won't you feel that the social psychologist has a function?"

"Function?" Professor Burke hesitated. "Yes. He has the function of showing that the potentiality of what we call 'crime' exists in every human being. His function is to prove that crime is intellectual *disease*—not inferiority. That apathy toward evil is criminal! A college graduate needs to know more than merely to refrain from crime; he needs to be a lifelong crusader against crime! His emotions—his *instincts*—should be permanently aroused. And that, Doctor Tolver, is as much an inspirational function as a function of teaching. I am afraid such classes would scandalize many faculty members!"

The president, like the gambler, was looking into distances. "Has it occurred to you, Professor, that you're in an ideal situation to launch precisely such a course? A position that would—truly—inspire?"

"It will," Bedelia said, "when he reads his telegrams."

The professor looked incredulously at the president. "You mean, you'd stand for that sort of teaching?"

"We shall welcome it!"

The doorbell rang.

Bedelia looked at the watch on her fleur-de-lys pin. "That's the reporters. I told them to come at five thirty." She left the porch before the professor could reply. President Tolver announced the new appointment.

MacFalkland, accompanied by another man, called soon after the others had left. There was no boom in MacFalkland's voice. His hands trembled. He immediately—and nervously—introduced the stranger. "This is George Drufton, publisher of the *Inter-World Press*. The Sunday supplement that—appears in so many papers."

Professor Burke said, "Come in."

"My firm," said Mr. Drufton, "owes you amends."

The professor was feeling in a less somber mood. "I should say so!"

"I'm—hideously sorry—" MacFalkland began.

"So I suffer from overrepression!" The professor said, his eyes gleaming. "As a result, I am a bi-cerebral! What in hell is that, MacFalkland?" His colleague had turned scarlet; the publisher was fidgeting. "I am the schizoid type of renegade! My early childhood 'inclined me, by the law of controposite-neurotic-reflex' —to take up crime! *Gibberish!*"

"We realize," Mr. Drufton put in urgently, "that you have grounds for a damage suit, although we have stopped the series. Such suits, of course, are expensive."

Professor Burke now stared at the publisher. "I was 'dead' —so you weren't worried! Not even relatives to fight for my reputation! And MacFalkland here—dreaming up that half-baked psychological explanation of how I came to be a smuggler! I should say I have a suit! However, I won't sue. Rest your minds about that."

"Won't sue?" the publisher repeated, unbelievingly.

"No. All I ask is that Mac here attend my lectures for the next few months. As my subordinate, he has a lot to learn."

"I must say," the publisher murmured, "that's generous!"

MacFalkland seemed to choke.

Professor Burke walked over to him and slapped his back. Slapped it mightily. "Buck up, old boy! All you need is to get out in the world more!"

"There was another matter—"

The professor turned to the publisher. "Yes?"

"No doubt you are getting offers for your life story. I mean— the real story . . . ?"

"Bedelia says so. I haven't looked into it yet."

The publisher seemed cheered. "I see. Well, in view of the fact that my supplement has such immense circulation, and was the medium which made so many misstatements about you—"

"*Misstatements!*"

Mr. Drufton glanced at MacFalkland in a pained way. "Whatever you wish to call them, Professor. I deeply regret it. And I am eager to buy your story. Appearing in my supplement, it would undo the harm that's been done. I will pay twenty-five thousand dollars."

The professor's voice was high. "Twenty-five thousand dollars!"

"Don't accept," Bedelia called, marching unabashedly into the room. "You already have an offer for thirty."

"Thirty-five!" Drufton said instantly.

She smirked at him. "We'll let you know. Now, gentlemen, it's far past dinnertime—and the professor has an engagement at eight thirty."

The professor sat at the dining-room table. "Thirty-five thousand dollars . . . !" he muttered wildly.

Bedelia served soup. "Figure out the income tax, before you get too elated."

"What engagement have I at eight thirty?" he asked, after tasting the soup.

"I told Marigold you'd be over to see her."

He drove the shadowy blocks swiftly.

"She's in the garden," Marigold's mother said.

"Isn't it kind of chilly?"

"The barbecue fire is burning. And the house is full of people who want to meet you. So she went out there, when she heard your car."

The fire made some light and a considerable warmth. She was standing beside it. "Hello."

The professor did not stop to reflect that he was following

instinct rather than reason. He gathered up the girl and proceeded along the lines suggested by Connie Maxson.

"I trust," he finally said, "you won't mind being a professor's wife."

Her curls shook—horizontally. "Nope."

"Because if you did mind, you'd just have to bear it, somehow."

"Martin."

"Yes?"

"Will you promise not to hunt criminals again?"

He considered. "It seems unlikely I ever will. But promise? No. I won't promise."

Martin Burke had found himself. Intuitively, he knew it. He always would know—now. It satisfied her and she put the satisfaction in simple words. "I guess you're boss—"

"You're darn right I'm boss!"

Their silhouettes became a unit which threw a complex shadow on the grass.

Impatiently, the judge strode to the hedge and leaned through the opening. They had stepped off the lawn and his pineapple was menaced again. He started to protest, grinned instead, and turned back to the house. His guests could wait. And the hell with the pineapple.

Professor Burke's first class of the new year was held, at the request of President Tolver, in Memorial Hall and attended by the faculty, by reporters, and by certain guests, among whom was a tall man with level grey eyes and his beautiful niece—a couple pointed out by hundreds. There were no absences among the regular students. All other undergraduates who could crowd into the hall were present. Bedelia sat on the platform.

"The topic of my last lecture," Professor Burke began, "was crime, vice and civic corruption. I am going to repeat that lecture because, since giving it, I have obtained new material on the subject."

The distinguished guests laughed. The undergraduates whistled and stomped.

Only Miss Orme—the student with ensnooded hair that resembled a beaver's tail and the firm life purpose of becoming a social worker—disliked the new course. It was too realistic, she felt: too harrowing—and not intellectual enough. Professor Burke had deteriorated, in her opinion. One day she entered his office to tell him so. She found him with Miss Macey in his arms.

"Come on in," he grinned at the shocked student. "Another branch of socio-psychology. Courtship. Fascinating study!"

Miss Orme fled, and in the next semester, changed over to economics.